IN YOUR CORNER

SARAH CASTILLE

sourcebooks
casablanca

Published by Sourcebooks Casablanca, an imprint of Sourcebooks, Inc.
P.O. Box 4410, Naperville, Illinois 60567-4410
(630) 961-3900
Fax: (630) 961-2168
www.sourcebooks.com

Library of Congress Cataloging-in-Publication Data

Castille, Sarah.
  In your corner / Sarah Castille.
      pages cm
  (trade paper : alk. paper) 1. Mixed martial arts–Fiction. I. Title.
  PR9199.4.C38596I5 2014
  813'.6–dc23

                          2014011625

        Printed and bound in the United States of America.
              VP 10 9 8 7 6 5 4 3 2 1

To Kaia, Sapphira, and Alysha and your forever love of stories.

And to John…because you gave everything and expected nothing.

Chapter 1
RAH, RAH! GO, TEAM, GO!

HELL.

In the five seconds it takes James P. Farnsworth III, managing partner of Farnsworth & Tillman, LLP, to step into my office, my life goes from happy to hell in a heartbeat.

"Good afternoon, sir. Is that a new suit? I'm guessing Armani, new label. And your tie, Italian silk, maybe Salvatore Ferragamo?"

I can do obsequious with the best of them.

Unfortunately, Farnsworth isn't in a mood to be fawned over today. With a frown, he tosses a file folder on my desk and folds his arms, his biceps straining against the fine wool of his black suit jacket.

Farnsworth isn't like most other law firm managing partners I know. No jowls or reddened cheeks from excess drinking at client functions. Not an ounce of fat around his tall, toned frame. His silvery-gray hair is impeccably styled, his skin overly tanned, and his jaw impossibly square. On the outside, he is undeniably handsome in a George Clooney kind of way.

"I hope you don't have any plans for the next few months, Amanda." His dark eyes gleam with the power of being able to ruin a junior associate's life with a mere seven words. "I have a new case for you."

"I live to serve, sir." The firm motto slides off my tongue like a corked Merlot.

His thin lips twitch. "That's what I like to hear."

I'm guessing what he doesn't want to hear is that I already have twenty-six cases on the go, as well as ten secret pro bono files for the community legal aid clinic I just can't give up. If not for the twenty-four-hour cafeteria and coffin-like sleeping pods Farnsworth & Tillman graciously provides for its associates, I wouldn't be able to manage.

Farnsworth rakes his eyes over my body, and it isn't difficult to tell what he's thinking. From the day I started at the firm almost three years ago, he has made no effort to hide his interest. I suspect if he weren't my father's best friend, I might have suffered more of his attentions. Rumor has it he has a fondness for young, blond, blue-eyed associates.

"Tight suit."

"Yes, sir." What else can I say? It isn't so much tight as it is tailored. Not that I would ever dream of contradicting Farnsworth. Cold, hard, ruthless, and fiercely intelligent, Farnsworth suffers no fools, and associates have been dismissed for less than asking a question. Clients love him. Opposing counsel hate him. In the California Bay Area courts, he's known as the Barracuda. Relentless. Merciless. The ultimate predator. Feared by all. Defeated by none.

"The client is a privately held real estate development company based here in San Francisco," he says to my breasts. "They have a new, very young and inexperienced chairman, the son of the founder, and they've just been hit with a multimillion-dollar lawsuit from a company called Duel Properties. You will have an opportunity to showcase your skills under my guidance. Your performance on this case will help us decide whether you are partnership material."

Folding my arms over the objects of Farnsworth's interest, I flash my most sycophantic smile. "Wonderful, sir. I relish the opportunity for a new challenge. And you won't be disappointed."

He studies me for a long moment. "We'll see."

We'll see? If ever two words struck fear into the heart of a desperate and ambitious junior associate, those would be the words. *We'll see* means he isn't confident I'll make it through to partnership. *We'll see* means he knows something I don't know. *We'll see* means I might not receive the sleeping-pod sized, Farnsworth & Tillman duck-down duvet my department head presents to every associate who becomes partner.

We'll see means I'd better kick ass on this new case, or my father will disown me.

"The client will be here in fifteen minutes, and I'm double-booked with a pressing engagement, so I'm letting you handle the initial interview. Make an appointment with my secretary to debrief this evening." He pauses and then his forehead creases. "And, Amanda…"

"Sir?"

"Although our new client isn't a big company, their opponent, Duel Properties, is a target client of the firm. We want to hit Duel Properties hard. We want them to hate us, so the next time they need a law firm, we're the ones they call because they know we'll make their opponent suffer the way we made them suffer. I'm taking a chance by giving you the file instead of handing it over to a senior associate. Don't fuck it up."

"Of course not, sir."

He turns and breezes out my door as if he hadn't just given me the warning to end all warnings and dropped a bombshell that could mean the end of my career at Farnsworth & Tillman.

We'll see.

"Penny!" I race out of my office and call for my secretary slash personal assistant slash willing slave. "New client. Fifteen minutes."

"I'll meet you in the restroom." Her slick, brown ponytail swings violently as she leaps from her chair, her perfect English-rose complexion paling when she stumbles over her spare pair of kitten heels.

Penny is from England. Although she's only in her mid-twenties like me, she dresses the way I always imagined English women dressed when they had tea in the garden in the 1950s, all floaty florals, pearls, and pastels. She has the most delicious accent, an offbeat sense of humor, and, except when she is bossing me around, a gentle manner. She once told me the English described her as a Scouser. Sounded dirty to me. I suggested it wasn't information she needed to share in America.

Three minutes later, Penny bursts into the restroom and hefts my makeup case on the counter. With the efficiency that made the firm offer her a permanent position one week into her exchange program, she pulls out a handful of brushes and orders me to sit.

Obediently, I drop onto the padded stool beside the vanity table etched with the Farnsworth & Tillman logo, a crest with an F resembling a fox and a T resembling a tiger battling over the scales of justice. Classy.

"Male client?"

"Yup."

"Age?"

"Founder just passed the mantle to his son, and Farnsworth described him as young and inexperienced, so I'm guessing early thirties."

She discards a few selections and sorts through the bottom of the kit for my "younger face," then spends the next ten minutes fixing me up.

After a quick glance in the mirror, I sigh and lean back in my chair. "You did your best, but it's no use. We'd need an entire crate of concealer to get rid of the circles under my eyes. Hopefully, the new client will think an exhausted attorney is a good attorney because it means she's working hard. What do you think? How do I look?"

"Haggard." Penny gently wipes away some of the excess makeup and touches up my cheeks with her blush brush.

"I'm hoping that's a British word for *lovely*."

Penny snorts. "It means you're pushing yourself too hard and it shows. It's those pro bono cases you're running on the side. They're eating into the time people normally reserve for sleeping and basic body maintenance."

My eyebrow lifts at Penny's gentle rebuke. "I'm meeting a new client in a few minutes and this could be the case that cements my path to partnership. My father, my grandfather, my great-grandfather, and probably all my relatives back to the beginning of time were law firm partners before they were thirty-two. I can't break the family tradition. I need to be cheerful and happy. I need to be motivated. I need the 'Rah, rah! Go, team, go!' speech we are forced to endure in our morning meetings."

Penny studies me for a long moment. "Is that really what you want? Partnership at the age of thirty-two with all the burdens and responsibilities of running a law firm?"

"Of course that's what I want." I follow her out of the restroom. "It's the next logical step. It's what I've been working toward since I got my kindergarten report card. Nothing will make my parents happier or more proud than to have me carry on the family tradition."

"Rah, rah. Go, team, go." Penny adorns her monotone with a bland expression.

I go. But, for once, I'm not feeling the rah.

———~~~———

Ten minutes later, after a wave to Penny, I grab my cell phone and notebook, and head to the elevator bank through a labyrinth of gray felt partitions. As I step into the shiny steel and glass elevator, my phone buzzes. A smile curls my lips when I check the caller ID.

Drake. Or, to be more formal, Dr. Donald Drake. My long-term friend with benefits, and one of Oakland's preeminent heart surgeons, has kept me going through the worst of times. Tall and muscular with natural blond hair and brilliant blue eyes, I thought he was an Adonis when I first laid eyes on him. Still do.

"Well hello, stranger," I breathe into the phone. "How long has it been? Two...three months?" The doors close, and almost immediately, I am catapulted toward the client reception area at light speed. Time is money at Farnsworth & Tillman.

Drake chuckles. "Long time no sex."

"I was thinking that myself. Unfortunately, I've been hit with a new case, and it's going to eat into my sex time."

Drake makes a disapproving noise into the phone. "Sex is a basic human need, like food or sleep. As a medical professional, I can't in good conscience allow you to risk your health by depriving yourself. How about I pick you up tonight for a quick fix? I'm ring doctor at Redemption until about ten p.m., and then I can come straight to your office."

My chest tightens when he mentions Redemption. My best friend, Makayla, met the love of her life, Max, aka Torment, at what is now one of Oakland's up-and-coming MMA fight training gyms.

And I lost mine...Jake.

I try to wipe out the memories of Jake that are intimately associated with the fight club as the elevator hurtles me toward my destination, but once he's in my mind, he refuses to leave. I can't decide which memory is worse. The devastation on his face when he walked into my apartment after our breakup and saw Drake in my living room wearing only a towel, or the hurt and anger in his voice at Torment's near-fatal fight when he told me exactly what I'd thrown away.

"I would love to use you for sex, Drake. It's been far too long. But I'm not getting out of the office any month soon." My voice catches and I hesitate before bringing up the topic I have successfully avoided for the last few months. "Actually, I've been meaning to talk to you about our arrangement..."

The elevator jerks to a stop and I end the call, promising to meet Drake for coffee after he's done at Redemption as I step out into the gaping maw of the client reception area. Designed with the sole purpose of intimidation, the vast foyer with its twenty-foot ceilings and almost three-hundred-sixty-degree views gives a whole new meaning to the word *fishbowl*.

With a nod to the team of receptionists, all wearing their matching navy blue and teal Farnsworth & Tillman uniforms, I check the TV monitor for the room number and then turn in to the maze of marble corridors, stilettos clacking as I head toward unlucky room thirteen.

The murmur of voices drifts up the hallway, and two men round the corner walking toward me. As they get closer, my heart lifts and then sinks.

Ray, my favorite private investigator contracted by the firm, is wearing his usual commando attire: dark khaki cargo pants and a tight gray T-shirt that highlights every plane and angle of his muscular torso. His dark hair is military short and he walks with an easy grace that belies his height. *Powerful* was the first word that came to mind when we met. *Dangerous* was the second. He catches my gaze and gives me a wink.

Beside him, in startling contrast, is Farnsworth's protégée and my least favorite senior associate in the firm, Evil Reid, aka Reid Cravath. Evil Reid and I crossed swords the day I joined the litigation department. Unfortunately, I didn't realize he was in charge of the weeklong induction for new associates or that I was supposed to drool over his shoes and smile when he pinched my ass. After I slapped his hand away, we fought over the last croissant at the new associate breakfast, and things quickly went downhill from there. After I turned down his offer for a quick drunken hookup in the firm sleeping pods during a firm party, I thought that was the end of it.

Unfortunately, like his mentor, Evil Reid never gives up.

Even now, as I approach, his gaze slimes over my body and his thick pink tongue darts out to lick his full lips. Evil Reid is tall, rich, handsome, suave, and…well, evil. His dark hair is thick and neatly cut. His eyes are two black holes in a broad, smooth face. Not a day goes by that someone doesn't suffer from the bite of his sharp tongue or the seemingly inadvertent brush of his roving octopus tentacles.

Ray nods as I draw near. "Had a great time at that Giants game, Amanda. Thanks for the tickets."

"My pleasure. Just wanted to thank you for all the great work you do for me."

Evil Reid huffs his annoyance and stalks past without so much as a shoulder brush or ass pinch. Although I'm years away from partnership and no threat to him, he doesn't like to be shown up. I guess *he* didn't buy Ray any Giants tickets.

Moments later, I reach room thirteen. Taking a moment to compose myself, I push open the ten-foot-high door—yet another example of the ridiculous ostentation that is Farnsworth & Tillman—and step into the room, ready to meet the man who could make or break my career with his damned multimillion-dollar lawsuit.

Light floods across the plush, royal blue carpet through floor-to-ceiling glass windows. Dust motes dance in the sunbeam. A large mahogany table surrounded by eight black leather chairs dominates the center space. I inhale the scents of leather and furniture polish and a whiff of something else, sharp and clean like an ocean breeze.

Familiar.

Across the room, the client is pouring himself a glass of water from the tray on the credenza. From the back, he takes my breath away. Sleek black suit pants hug the curves of his tight ass. His crisp white shirt is tucked into a narrow waist and stretched tight across a broad, strong back. His shirtsleeves are rolled up, and I catch a glimpse of a strong, muscled forearm as he lifts the water glass.

But it's the thick, blond, wavy hair just brushing the top of his collar that makes my pulse race. Soft. Silky. Hair that is meant to be touched.

Have touched?

The latch clicks as I close the door and he turns to face me.

"Christ! Amanda!" His hand jerks and water sloshes onto the carpet.

My heart stutters in my chest and the legal pad falls from my fingers to the floor, the world falling away as if everything until now had been an illusion.

"Jake."

Eyes wide, jaw tight, he stares at me, dismay and disbelief etched on his handsome face. I can't believe over two years have passed since the night we broke up. Whether a result of maturity or the passing of time, he is even more gorgeous than I remember. Strong cheekbones and a firm chin give his face an angular look, made more rugged by the small scars on his forehead and cheeks, a testament to his success in the fight ring. His eyes are a startling, brilliant blue and when he smiles, dimples appear in the corners of his cheeks. But he isn't smiling now.

He shakes himself and looks away, then gestures toward the legal pad on the floor. "You dropped it."

"You startled me."

He gives me a half smile. "Yeah, I know the feeling. I forgot you worked here."

Two years of longing and regret. Two years of fantasies and dreams. And yet our first words after two years are so mundane I want to cry.

His gaze skims down my body, taking in my fitted black suit, white silk blouse, and black stilettos. Black or blue only for associates at Farnsworth & Tillman. Like a bruise. The very fact that he is checking me out sends little flutters through my stomach. When he looks up, his eyes warm and spark with interest.

"You look good…professional." The low, husky rumble of his voice makes my toes curl. So different from his harsh tone and cold words the last time we met.

By force of will alone, I manage a smile. "Firm uniform. They put the policy in place after we…broke…" I choke on my words and then swallow past the lump in my throat. "If I had a choice, I would liven things up. Maybe add a splash of color."

His lips curl up and the dimples appear. "You always were one for color."

My throat tightens at the oblique reference to his shocked expression the first time he walked into my apartment in San Francisco's Marina District. He said he had expected clean, bold, modern lines, blacks and reds. Instead, he got country chic and a riot of pastels, sex toys hidden in a refurbished pie cupboard, and naughty costumes hanging in a pink-stenciled wardrobe.

"I haven't changed."

But he has. The once rough-and-tumble fighter and carpenter is now chairman of a midsize company. New furrows mark his once-smooth brow, and crinkles adorn the corners of his eyes. His shoulders are tight, his back stiff and straight. There is no hint of the easy, carefree attitude that attracted me to a cheeky kickboxing instructor at a local gym so long ago—an attraction so strong we wound up making out in the fitness studio only seconds after the last student had walked out the door. He seems older both in appearance and at heart. But the same restlessness simmers beneath his skin. Power. Barely contained.

His mouth thins, and I wish I could take the words back. Amanda-now isn't the same as Amanda-then. Now, I could never hurt him.

"If I'd remembered you worked here, I would have picked another firm," he says, his voice tight. "One of the division presidents recommended the partner I was supposed to meet."

Swallowing hard, I shrug, playing it nonchalant while inside the part of me that had always dreamed we would get back together again shrivels. "We never really talked that much about work. I don't think you ever came by my office." I give a tentative smile. "You'll probably get to know me better during this case than…"

His choked grunt cuts me off, and I catch a flicker of pain in his eyes. "I don't think…"

Oh God. He doesn't want me on the case. And why would he? How difficult would that be? It could be years until trial.

My stomach clenches and I force my words out through a tightened throat. "Of course. I wasn't thinking. I probably shouldn't be involved in the case because we were…had…" I take a deep breath and steady my wavering voice. "It could be considered a personal conflict, because if you were unhappy with our service at the end of the case, you might allege I wasn't able to properly represent you because we…we…"

"Broke up," he says gently and, from the softening of his brow, clearly relieved.

"Yes."

Tension eases from his body, loosening his shoulders. "I think that's for the best."

My heart sinks to the floor and then falls through the fifteen stories that is Farnsworth & Tillman, shattering into a million pieces in the concrete parking garage. Rejected. All over again.

Years of training enable me to remain professional, while inside I crumble. "I'll have to ask the managing partner to take me off the case and find a replacement associate. It means you'll have to come back another day. Is that a problem? I feel bad inconveniencing you."

Jake shakes his head and his beautiful hair brushes over his neck. "No, that's okay. I got the papers a week or two ago, so I think I have some time. I don't understand the legal stuff."

Falling back into my comfort zone, my heart rate slows. "I'll take a look at the documents for you, just so you don't miss any deadlines."

He opens the backpack resting in a chair beside his leather jacket and hands me a file folder. His finger inadvertently brushes over mine during the exchange, sending zings of electricity straight to my core. Nothing has changed. He is the only man who has ever had that effect on me. One touch and I'm gone. Just like the night we first met in his class. He put his hands on my hips to steady me while I was practicing kicks with a classmate and I almost melted into a puddle on the floor.

I jerk my hand away and smooth the papers on the boardroom table. Jake perches on the table beside me, his tight ass so close to the document I have to grit my teeth to stop my finger from wandering too far in the wrong direction. The richly masculine scent of his cologne makes my pulse race. And his heat…

My cheeks burn and a shiver of desire winds its way up my spine.

"Cold?" His voice cracks on the word, and I lift my gaze to his.

"No." I try to cover up my body's response by lightening the mood. "Badly drafted complaints give me the shivers."

His gaze skims over my cheeks and then fixes on my eyes again, studying me intently as if he can see into my soul. His jaw tightens almost imperceptibly and he slides off the table and walks over to his backpack. "So, what's the damage?"

"Uh…" Shaken by yet another rejection, I force my eyes to focus on the document. "You have thirty days to respond, so you have just over two weeks left. I'll ask Mr. Farnsworth to arrange a meeting with the new associate as soon as possible and he or she can apply for an extension. You don't want to miss the deadline, or Duel Properties will file for a default."

Jake picks up his jacket and shrugs it over his shoulders, transforming himself in an instant from impossibly handsome to badass breathtaking. I return the documents to him, and he tucks them into his pack and grabs his helmet.

"You brought your motorcycle." The inane comment falls off my lips before I can catch it. "Are you still riding the Kawasaki?"

"Nah. Changed a lot of things in the last few years. Replaced it with a Blackbird when I took over my dad's company. Stopped training at Redemption, too. It's a whole new me."

Stopped training at Redemption? I have to bite my tongue to stop from asking why. When we were together, Jake lived and breathed Redemption, at that time an underground MMA club but now strictly legit. After he got off work every day, he taught classes, trained, fought, and ran the underground promotions for Torment. And when he was there, I was there, helping out where I could, sneaking into Torment's office with him for a little lovin' between classes and getting down and dirty in the gym after it closed.

"You seem the same." But the words are true only in the sense that he still takes my breath away.

His mouth tightens in a thin line, and for the briefest second I see the hurt beneath his steely gaze.

"Maybe on the outside." He pulls open the door, and I grab my legal pad and follow behind him.

Looking back over his shoulder, he gives me the briefest of smiles. "I can see myself out."

"It was nice to see you again." My soft, wavering voice makes me cringe. But not as much as when he turns and walks away.

I guess it wasn't nice to see me too.

Chapter 2
GO. TO. HELL.

WHAT A DISASTER.

After I return to my office, I sit and stare at my computer. The Farnsworth & Tillman logo bounces slowly across my screen. Associates are allowed a choice of two screensavers. The first, the initials "F & T," looked too much like "FAT" for my taste, and I turned it down. Not good for the self-esteem. Who wants to see an accusatory FAT FAT FAT upon returning from the firm cafeteria or a client lunch? So I chose door number two. A full scale "Farnsworth & Tillman." Big, bold, and bouncy.

The logo blurs before my tired eyes. I bill nothing for two hours. At Farnsworth & Tillman, we are required to account for every six minutes of our time. Two hours of nothingness is going to earn me a visit to HR and possibly the firm shrink. Lost in memories of the short time Jake and I spent together, I can't bring myself to care.

Two months. For some people, two months is nothing. For me, it was the longest relationship I'd ever had. My parents were bitterly disappointed when I told them I was dating yet another "unsavory character" and hanging around a fight club, but there was no resisting Jake. He was warm, affectionate, and kind—everything my parents were not—and fun and adventurous in the bedroom, more than willing to try anything I asked.

But the more time we spent together, the more demanding he became of me. He didn't want just fun and games. He wanted something more, something I couldn't give. And when I realized I was falling in too deep and he was getting too close, I took the first chance I could to push him away. Trusting people—opening up to them—in my experience, invariably led to disappointment and heartbreak. I've learned the hard way the only person I can trust is me.

Clearly disconcerted by my inactivity, Penny breezes in and out of my office on all manner of false pretenses. "Just doing the weekly check on the computer cables." She tugs on the cords at the back of my computer and smiles. "Nice and tight."

Ten minutes after the cables, she waters my plastic plants. Then she sharpens my already sharp pencils and dusts my clean desk. Finally, she slams the door closed and folds her arms. "This is the first time you've missed your session at the community legal aid clinic, something I only thought would happen in times of war, plague, or natural disaster. I called to tell them you couldn't make it and they thought you were seriously injured or dead. What's wrong?"

Other than Makayla, no one knows as much about Jake as Penny, so I reveal the horror of my meeting in a barely audible monotone. She comforts me British-style by bringing me a cup of tea. Then she tries to talk me out of my plan to get back into Farnsworth's good graces by suggesting he put his lap dog, Evil Reid, on the case instead of me.

"If you do that, you'll never convince Evil Reid you actually hate him. He'll think you were doing him a favor. You'll spend the rest of your career fighting off his advances."

"I've been fighting him off since I joined the firm," I say with a shrug. "Not a big deal." Two months after I turned down Evil Reid's post-party nookie offer, he tried again. This time by trapping me in a meeting room after a firm seminar and sticking his tongue down my throat. My response was a swift and firm smash of the knee into the family jewels and a report to HR. He didn't take it well. Nor, surprisingly, did he give up. His methods just became more circumspect—a brush against my arm when passing me in the hallway, the occasional knee fondle when we had to share a cab. He is the admirer I never wanted to have.

Farnsworth's evening secretary calls to tell me the lord and master is ready to see me. After a final check in the mirror, I take the elevator up to the top floor and traverse another mazelike set of corridors. Despite the late hour, the office is buzzing with activity. Farnsworth & Tillman attorneys live to serve their clients' needs twenty-four hours a day, three hundred and sixty-five days a year. Fire, flood, earthquake, or tornado, in sickness or in health, war or peace, a Farnsworth & Tillman attorney will be available to meet every client need.

Till death do they part.

Unless, of course, the client doesn't want the associate in the first place.

———

Farnsworth is seated at his massive glass desk when I arrive.

"Come in, Amanda. Close the door."

Close the door? Farnsworth & Tillman has an open-door policy. The partners like visibility and transparency. They do not like associates wasting billable hours surfing the net. Computer screens face the door. Walls are made of glass. Cameras are visible in the hallways. Associates quickly discover that the sleeping pods and washrooms are the only places for a little privacy or to get down and dirty with their colleagues.

Farnsworth motions me forward, and I close the glass door behind me, jumping at the unexpected click of the latch. For a moment I am disoriented. And then I realize my claustrophobia is a result of Farnsworth's totally frosted walls. Privacy. For real.

As managing partner, Farnsworth scored the best office in the firm. Extending across the entire length of the building, it is larger than most family homes. Why he needs a wet bar, two lounges, three worktables, and a media center to manage a law firm, I don't know.

Someday, maybe, I'll find out.

He smiles. At least I think it's a smile. With his lips peeled back and his teeth bared, he could be a predator about to spring.

"How did it go with the new client?"

"Um." I twist my silver chain-link bracelet around my wrist, a present from my late grandmother, and suck in my lips.

Farnsworth raises a combed and manicured eyebrow. "Lost for words? I hope this doesn't happen in court." Although he laughs as he speaks, there is no humor in his voice. Everything at Farnsworth & Tillman is a test. A missing comma on a document. A misspelled word in a pleading. A miscalculation of damages. A missed lunch. There are myriad ways for an associate to lose her job, clearing the way for the more competent lemmings to throw themselves off the cliff.

Taking a deep breath, I spit it out, "Mr. Donovan requested a different attorney on the case."

Incredibly, he shows no signs of shock or surprise. Instead, he leans back in his chair and folds his hands behind his head. "Did he now?"

"Yes, sir."

"Why?"

The question I hoped to avoid is the first question any good litigator worth his salt would ask. And Farnsworth isn't just a good litigator. He's one of the best in the state, the other bests being my parents, both partners at Sawyers, Saunders, and Solomon LLP, and good friends of Farnsworth and his wife.

"I have a…personal conflict. I assured him you would find someone to take my place."

Farnsworth's lips curl into a sinister smile—the type of smile usually seen on television and accompanied by the twirling of a black mustache. With no mustache to twirl, Farnsworth flips his pen across his fingers instead. "What kind of personal conflict?"

My cheeks heat and my knees wobble. Although it's against protocol to sit in front of the managing partner unless specifically invited to do so, I choose the protocol breach over an undignified collapse on the floor. With an apologetic smile, I slip into one of the comfy leather chairs across from his desk.

"We were in a relationship a few years ago. And it ended. Badly."

"Hmmm." Farnsworth drums his fingers on his desk. "Well, I can't say I'm surprised. I was expecting this type of conflict to arise much earlier…given your reputation."

My breath leaves my lungs in a whoosh. *Given my reputation?* What the hell is he talking about? I have conducted myself with absolute propriety at Farnsworth & Tillman. I'm one of the few associates who hasn't had sex with any of my colleagues or clients. I've used the sleeping pods solely for sleeping. I haven't even overbilled. "What reputation would that be, sir?"

Farnsworth snorts a laugh. "You don't need to put on the act with me, Amanda. And you're far from stupid. You know exactly what I'm talking about."

Not exactly, but I can guess. Sure, I've dated a lot of guys. Slept with a fair number too. I had to do something as a teenager, home alone night after lonely night. And in those sweaty kisses and fumbles in the dark, I found a sort of happiness. For a few hours, someone cared for me, touched me…loved me. I've been chasing that feeling ever since.

"I'm afraid you'll have to spell it out for me." I return his cool, calculating stare as bile rises in my throat.

Farnsworth shoves a thick, blue file folder across the desk.

Paper. How quaint.

"Here it is in black and white," he says evenly. "I'm surprised you didn't realize it would come out in the morality check we do on all associates we are considering for partnership. We've had a private investigator following you for the better part of a year. I have to say your file has made for the most entertaining reading. You go through men faster than my wife goes through money, and that's saying something."

Breathing slow and deep, I fight the instinctive urge to flee. Blood pounds through my veins, the rush so loud in my ears it drowns out the rest of Farnsworth's words. My stomach clenches and roils. I'm going to be sick.

"Take a look." Farnsworth stands and rounds the desk, perching his ass on the lip in front of me as he holds out the file.

My mouth waters with horrified fascination as I stare at the blue folder in his hand. But if I let Farnsworth know I care about what's in that file, I give away what little power I have, and right now I don't even know what he wants.

Although I've had enough experience with men that I can guess.

With a shrug, I wave the file away. "If there's something you want me to know, you'll tell me."

Damn I'm cool. No one would ever know I am a total wreck inside.

The look he gives me is speculative, thoughtful, and sends a chill down my spine. He turns and places the file on the desk beside him.

"There is something I want you to know. I think you're one hell of an attorney. Probably one of the best damn junior associates in the firm. There is no doubt in my mind you are partnership material. But the morality check is a problem. I've always been quite relaxed about these things. Not so much the other partners. If any of them saw the file, it would be a deal killer."

Threat heard and noted.

"That's crazy." I feign nonchalance, dropping my shoulders and resting my hands lightly on the armrests. "There's nothing in my personal life that should raise any professional or moral concerns about my ability to fulfill my duties as an attorney in this firm. I've never let my personal life impact on my work."

He leans over and squeezes my shoulder and I have to fight back the urge to flinch.

"I know becoming a partner means everything to you, and especially to your father. It's all he's talked about for years. He's so pleased you followed in the family footsteps. You'll make him so proud." He pauses and affects the sad smile of a poor method actor. "Or…you would have."

Clearly Farnsworth isn't satisfied with stabbing me in the heart with his file of Amanda's sordid activities. He wants to twist the knife. Twist and twist and twist. What does he hope to achieve? Does he think I'm going to break into tears? Does he think I'll beg for mercy? Does he really think I'm going to give him what he wants?

"Is that all, sir?" I make the mistake of standing. Unfortunately, I am now face to face with Farnsworth, our bodies only inches apart. He smells of cheap Bordeaux, Greek cigars, and the $9.95 Shrimp Special the cafeteria offered for dinner. My nose wrinkles. I hate shrimp.

"No, Amanda. That isn't all." His voice lowers to a seductive purr and he twirls a strand of my hair around his fingers. "It would be a shame for all that talent to go to waste." He strokes a thick finger along my cheek and a violent shudder wracks my body.

"Hands off." I slap his hand away and his eyes narrow.

"You're a clever girl, Amanda. I don't think I need to spell it out for you. I have something you want, and you have something I want. We can both achieve our goals and enjoy ourselves while we do."

"Not a chance."

His jaw tightens almost imperceptibly. "I may be twice your age, but I know how to please a woman. And I know for a fact you know how to please a man. We could have something special together. Something..."

Taking a deep breath, I sidestep around the chair. "I'm not playing this game."

His cold smile chills my blood. "I have an entire file that says you do play this game. You play this game with strangers. You play this game with doctors. And right now, you're going to play this game with me. Can you imagine what your father would say if he saw that file? His abject and bitter disappointment? I don't know what would be worse for him—finding out his daughter is the biggest slut in San Francisco or knowing she'll never make partner in any law firm in the state."

In response to my quizzical look, he laughs. "You're forgetting who I am. I know every judge in every court in California. I know every partner in every major firm. I can blackball you with one phone call. If you turn down my offer, you'll never work in another Big Law firm in California again. It'll be back alleys and legal aid clinics for you."

As if that is such a bad thing.

My hands clench into fists and my lip curls. "Bastard. I'm going to drag you through the courts in the biggest sexual harassment lawsuit the state has ever seen."

Farnsworth's eyes glitter and he laughs. "I'm a bastard and you're a slut. So what? No one's going to believe you. If you file a lawsuit, I'll argue that you propositioned me because you were so desperate for partnership you would do anything to get it."

I stare at him aghast. "Why would anyone think I was that desperate? I'm one of the best associates in the firm. You said so yourself. Why would people think I would throw it all way?"

Farnsworth shrugs. "Who knows? Lack of self-confidence? Self-destructive tendencies? It doesn't matter. I've already laid the groundwork in the event you refuse. You should know by now every case is won before it even begins."

My lungs tighten. Outfoxed and outmaneuvered. He's clearly been planning this for a long time, waiting for the perfect opportunity. And I just gave it to him.

A whiff of Bordeaux breath assails my nostrils, and I fight the nausea roiling in my gut. I am NOT going to puke on the navy blue, Farnsworth & Tillman embossed carpet.

"And even if you were foolish enough to pursue a lawsuit," he continues, "how will you fund it without a job? I have an entire law firm at my disposal. I can have hundreds of associates working twenty-four hours a day to destroy you before you can file your complaint."

"Go. To. Hell." I take a step back and then another. Seemingly unperturbed, Farnsworth slides off his desk and drops his hand to his belt.

"I'm sure I will one day. But I plan to make the most of my time before I do. And so should you. Look what you have to gain. I can brush that file under the carpet. I can make sure your father and none of the other partners ever see it. And I can talk to the right people and ensure you make it through the partnership selection process. All I want is a taste of that honey you've been spreading around."

My nose crinkles in disgust and I back right up to the door. I might have lost everything, but I haven't lost my self-esteem. His choice is no choice at all.

"I don't do blackmail," I snap. "You want to send that file around, then send it and I'll deal with the fallout. But there is no way on this earth you're getting anything from me."

Greed and lust flicker in his eyes. And anger. A lot of anger. Just like Evil Reid, Farnsworth won't take no for an answer.

"There are women in this firm who were grateful for the opportunity I offered them." His lips curl in a snarl. "You walk out that door and you'll lose the partnership, your career, your father's love and pride, and the regard of your friends and colleagues. You'll have nothing left when I'm done with you."

"I'll have my self-respect."

Farnsworth gives a bitter laugh. "Really? What self-respecting woman takes a new lover every month…or is it every week? The file is so thick, I can't remember. Wake up, Amanda. Self-respect does not mean running the gauntlet through every dick in the city."

His words are aimed to cut, and although this is not a part of myself I ever share, I am not ashamed of the choices I've made. I pull on the frosted glass door and throw a derisory glance over my shoulder. "Consider this my notice. I'm done with the firm."

Farnsworth tightens his belt and narrows his eyes. "You may be done with the firm, but the firm is not done with you."

<center>~~~</center>

A week goes by.

At least I think it's been a week. Time has no meaning in the pit of despair or at the bottom of a vodka bottle. At least it's finally dark outside, more fitting with my mood, and I don't have to pull the covers over my head to evade the evil reach of the sun through the cracks in my curtains.

I tried to be good. I really did. After the shock of losing Jake, for a while I dated only parent-approved doctors, lawyers, and accountants. I stayed away from all but the most conservative clubs and bars. I tried to be who my parents wanted me to be. Uptight. Monogamous.

But it didn't work. I couldn't resist my attraction to the "unsavory" characters they had so despised when I was in high school—gritty, rough, and dangerous. The opposite of me. Apparently, however, even the scaled-down version of my reprobate behavior was enough to fill a blue file and give Farnsworth all the wrong ideas.

With a defeated sigh, I throw the covers off the bed, grab my cell, and flip to Drake's number. Since I no longer have any hope of garnering my parents' approval, I might as well embrace my chosen lifestyle. Go big or go home.

"Long time no sex." I don't even give Drake a chance to say hello.

Drake's sharp inhale is clearly audible when I use his favorite line on him.

"Amanda. Where have you been? What happened last Friday night? You weren't at work. You haven't returned my calls all week…"

Talk. Talk. Talk. I don't want talking. I want oblivion, kinky style, and Drake is the man to deliver. Swallowing past the lump in my throat, I interrupt his monologue of worry by giving him the basic facts: Jake,

Farnsworth, quitting. No need to tell him about the blue file or the harassment. Some things are better kept under wraps, especially from busybodies like Drake.

"So, you want to come over?" I try for a light, breezy tone that belies my desperate need for mindless fucking.

Clearly, it isn't enough because Drake's voice drops to a horrified whisper. "You quit your job?"

Tongue loosened after drinking too much vodka, the words that have been bottled up inside me all week spill out. "Unfortunately, in the heat of the moment, I made a rash decision and threw my career away, ironically, for what I believed to be self-respect. However, upon further reflection, I have determined that I do not, in fact, have any self-respect and so I called you."

"I feel honored," he says dryly.

"So do you have some time free tonight? I believe I left you hanging last Friday and I want to make it up to you."

Drake chokes. "Do you really…?"

"I do really. Desperately. I need it hard and I need it fast and I need it without any emotional strings. I'm embracing who I am and I want to get started right away."

"Tsk. Tsk." Drake chastises me with the tone one would use on a wayward child. "Sex isn't always the solution. And you're not thinking clearly. This is an opportunity and not a reason to run away. You have a chance to remake your life, choose a new path. We can talk…"

My head falls back on the pillow and I groan, cutting him off. "Are you coming over or not?"

Drake sighs. "Actually, I've just been paged and I'm en route to the hospital. How about I come to your place after I'm done? We'll talk."

There's that word again. *Talk*. Drake and I don't talk. We have sex. That's what friends with benefits do. And I don't want to talk. I don't want to think. I just want to lose myself in the void of mindless physical pleasure.

I make my disapproval audible with a soft grunt. Drake snorts a laugh.

"You've been drinking. All the more reason to stay home and let the doctor take care of you. I'll be there as soon as I can. Might not be until the early hours of the morning though. Just don't go out and do anything stupid. You don't sound like yourself, and this is the kind of situation that often leads people to self-destructive behavior."

"Sure."

After he hangs up, I stare at the clock and the half-empty bottle of vodka. Then I call a cab.

"So, where are we going tonight?"

The cab driver pulls away from the curb and into the endless traffic of the Marina District as he glances at me through the rearview mirror. With his soft, round face, brown hair fading to gray, and twinkly blue eyes, he looks like a family movie dad.

"Hellhole. It's a bar in Ghost Town, you know, in West Oakland." I want to get drunk since my earlier buzz has worn off, and I want to get laid, and I plan to take home the first decent guy who wants nothing more than to show me a good time, no strings attached. And there is no better collection of commitment-phobes than in Hellhole. Rough, gritty, but not particularly dangerous since I know the staff well, Hellhole is only a few blocks away from Redemption but suits my mood to a tee.

"A nice girl like you shouldn't be going to a place like that."

Ha ha. Little does he know the girl in his cab is anything but nice and not-nice girls belong in not-nice places. "It's not *that* bad. When I lived in Oakland, I used to go there for drinks with my friends. They spin the best metal and thrash." And right now I'm in the mood for some down and dirty.

"You sure? It's changed over the last coupla years. Gone downhill. And it's a half hour drive over the bridge on a good day. Ten o'clock on a Saturday night means you're looking at at least forty-five minutes through traffic."

I fall back in my seat with a groan. "I'm sure it's fine."

We drive through the city for no more than five minutes before he starts again. "I have a daughter around your age. If I found out she was going to Hellhole, I'd be down there in two seconds to drag her home. And then I'd have something to say."

"If someone told my dad I had gone to Hellhole, he would sit at his desk and start typing a new version of his 'I'm bitterly disappointed in you' speech."

Lights flicker around us, blurring as we whizz through the streets. I close my eyes to block out the sight of irritatingly happy people. Finally, I begin to relax. Maybe I should have called Makayla, but she would talk me out of indulging my sorrows in meaningless sex, or worse, offer to come along. And the last time that happened, she almost lost Max. I couldn't do that to her again.

By the time I open my eyes, the Foster Hoover Historic District aka Ghost Town is in sight. Broken lights. Rundown buildings. Youth gangs lurking in the alleys. We pass Redemption and my chest tightens at the sight of the unassuming metal warehouse with the new Team Redemption logo painted on its side.

"That's one of the top MMA fight gyms in the Bay Area." The cab driver slows the taxi to a crawl. "My son trains there and teaches some of the classes. He's with the Oakland police. My wife and I are so damn proud of him. Neither of us finished high school."

My mood takes an even deeper nosedive. I hate proud parents.

"What's his name?" Not that I care because I will never step foot in Redemption again, but curiosity is an insatiable beast. "I used to…hang out there. My best friend is going out with the owner."

He glances at me through the rearview mirror. "My boy's name is Theodore, but we always called him Tag. His ring name is Fuzzy."

"Don't know any Fuzzys. He must have joined after I…stopped going. They're good guys, though. Like a family."

The cab driver pulls the cab over to the curb and turns around. "Why don't I drop you at Redemption? You can hang with your friends and I can introduce you to my boy. Not that I'm trying to set you up or anything, but…you know…it would be safer than Hellhole."

"If I wanted that kind of safety, I would have stayed at home."

His look of consternation makes my stomach clench, and for a brief second I'm afraid he won't take me to the club. But after a few moments, he sucks in his lips, pulls away from the curb, and we leave Redemption behind.

"Something happen to you?" He throws the question out almost casually, but I can hear his concern in the tightening of his voice. And since I'm slightly inebriated and don't give a damn who knows how badly I fucked up my life, I give him the same story I gave Drake, leaving out the bit about the blue file.

He commiserates with me until we reach Hellhole, and then he turns around, worry lines creasing his forehead. "How about I wait outside? I'm almost done with my shift and I'll be here in case you change your mind. It's not easy to get a cab out here at this time of night…"

My heart squeezes in my chest. I'm a stranger and he's more worried about my safety than my parents ever were. "It's okay. Really. I know the staff. They'll help me out."

After the warm glow of the cab's taillights fade into the distance, I knock on the familiar metal door inset in the crumbling brick wall of the building at the corner. Two of the streetlights are burnt out, and with no other businesses visible in the area, the street is dark and deathly still.

I wait and wait. A cool breeze rustles my coat, sending a chill down my spine and bringing with it a faint whiff of piss and stale beer. Just as I'm second-guessing my decision to come to Hellhole, a viewing slot slides open.

"You got a membership card?" The rough, leering voice makes the hair on the back of my neck stand on end but not enough to scare me away, despite the fact that I have left my membership card at home.

"Look at me." I wave my hand over my white sheath dress—chosen simply because it makes me stand out—the lamb offering herself up for slaughter. "Do I really need a membership?"

The door creaks open and a bald, burly bouncer steps to the side to let me pass. His face is pierced everywhere a face can be pierced and then in places I wouldn't have considered piercing.

"Cover is forty bucks." He holds out a hand. Also pierced. I slap a few bills in his palm and he points me down a long, dark, narrow flight of stairs.

"Welcome to Hell."

Chapter 3
The Devil's Name is Bob

Hell doesn't disappoint.

Decorated in peeling shades of black and red, the dank underground club boasts a cluster of scratched wooden tables, a tiny dance floor, and the delightful aroma of pot, sweat, and stale beer. Keeping my gaze firmly fixed on the bar, I weave my way through the assorted punkers, bikers, and Goths, slapping away the occasional stray hand and ignoring the lascivious winks.

The violent ear-smashing riffs of the thrash metal band Evile scream through the cheap speakers, and the tables vibrate against the black painted concrete floor as I cross the empty dance floor. A few greasy metalheads pound their fists in time to the beat. Even rougher than I remember. The cab driver was right. The place has gone downhill.

"We don't do girly drinks," the bartender snarls before I even open my mouth. Big, burly, and bald, he looks like the bouncer's twin brother but with an overabundance of facial hair and an extra few rolls around the gut.

"Good thing I don't drink girly drinks." I place my white beaded clutch on the bar. "Vodka straight up."

He pours. I pay. He pours again. I pay again.

"Is Dave working tonight? Or Stella?" I don't recognize any of the staff, readily identifiable as denizens of the underground in their black T-shirts with a red devil logo emblazoned across the front.

"Don't know Dave or Stella. The bar has been under new management for the last year. They mighta got booted out when the place changed hands."

A scuffle breaks out in the corner, and a tall Goth crashes

backward into a table only to be manhandled out the door by one of the bouncers. Maybe this wasn't such a good idea. "The atmosphere has certainly changed."

He lifts an eyebrow. "So, you a good girl lookin' for a bad boy? Rebelling against your parents? Wanting to walk on the wild side?"

"None of the above."

"So what's the story?"

"Story is…she's with me." A leather-clad arm slides around my waist, and I look over my shoulder to find myself pressed tight against the Devil himself.

Tall and slim, his black hair slicked against his head, my new friend has the unnaturally pale skin and sharp, cruel features of a comic book villain. His eyes are dark, rimmed in red, and his mouth a thin slash between hollow cheeks. Despite his slender frame, he is surprisingly strong and I cannot pull away.

He presses his lips to my ear and nibbles the shell.

Clearly, there is no wasting time in the new Hellhole. No coy looks, brushed fingers, winks, or bad lines. No flirting over drinks or surreptitious feel-ups on the dance floor. See a girl you want to fuck—grab her. Nibble her ear. I can hardly wait to see what's next. Is he going to bend me over the stool and have his way with me right here? Will he do for the night's tickle and tease?

"Name's Bob," he murmurs.

Dear Lord. The Devil's name is Bob. Well, better the Devil you know than the Devil you don't.

"Hi, Bob."

"You've attracted a lot of attention, Angel. We don't often get your type in here."

More nibbles. Maybe I should give him some cheese. Unfortunately, I don't need nibbles. I need dark and dangerous. I need rough, meaningless sex with a man who doesn't give a fuck about me and will walk away in the morning without so much as a good-bye. I want to hurt on the outside as much as I hurt on the inside.

"Good attention or bad attention…Bob?" I manage to say this in a sultry, non-laughing voice.

"Doesn't matter. I'm the only attention you're gonna get tonight." He trails his lips down my neck and bites the sensitive area near my shoulder.

Ah, Bob has bite. Nice. A little bite is just what I need.

But nice quickly transitions into uncomfortable when Bob doesn't stop at a love bite. His teeth dig in harder until pleasure gives way to pain and a frisson of fear shoots through my body.

"Let go." I try to pull away but Bob tightens his grip.

"This a game for you, Angel? You picked the wrong place to play. We don't like cock teases here."

Suddenly I don't want to be in Hell. The lights are too dim, the air too smoky, the music too loud. And Bob is a little too extreme, even for me.

I twist in Bob's grasp, but before I can escape, he yanks my hair, tugging my head sideways to expose the unmarked side of my neck. My pulse takes off down the speedway. God, what a mistake. I should be home in bed, waiting for my kinky friend with benefits to show up with his medical bag full of sanitized sex toys, not offering myself up for feeding time at the zoo.

"Stop." I stomp my stiletto on his instep and Bob releases me with a howl.

"Fucking bitch."

My breath leaves me in a rush. Ice floods my veins. Bob's mouth is still moving but I can't hear him for the pounding of blood in my ears.

Grabbing my purse off the bar, I edge back toward the rear exit door and give the bartender a beseeching look. He snorts a laugh and walks away muttering, "Good girl just found herself a bad boy."

Taking another step back, I hold up my hands, palms forward. "Look, Bob...I think we've had a misunderstanding."

"You paid your entrance fee, Angel. It's my job to make sure you have a good time, unless you got something extra in that fancy purse to buy yourself some time alone."

I swallow past the lump in my throat. "You're the owner?"

He lifts a thin, black eyebrow and smiles.

Is that a yes or a no? I can't tell and at this moment, I don't care.

Pulse racing, mouth dry, legs trembling, I glance quickly at the sea of tables, chairs, metalheads, and Goths in front of me. A few of them are looking at us. Surely, they aren't just going to sit around and watch me get robbed or assaulted. Or maybe that's what they do for entertainment in Hellhole.

"I made a mistake coming here." I force my voice to stay calm and even despite the violent trembles wracking my body. "You keep the entrance fee and we'll pretend I had a good time." Then I whirl around and hit the back door running.

Heart pounding, I take the stairs two at a time, no easy feat in heels. A few moments later, I burst into the alley and race toward the street. But before I make it to safety, the bouncer rounds the corner, blocking my way. Rough hands grab me from behind and pull me, kicking and screaming, behind a Dumpster.

"Her purse is behind you." The bouncer jerks his chin toward the exit door as Bob pins me against the wall. He covers my mouth with one hand and brackets my wrists over my head with the other, holding them against the rough brick surface.

Maybe his real name is Beelzebub and they call him Bob for short.

"We could have had such a good time." Bob strokes my cheek. "Sure you won't change your mind?"

The bouncer joins us and frowns. "I thought you just wanted her purse."

Unable to imagine a "good time" that involves Bob in any way, shape, or form, I renew my writhing, kicking, and screaming efforts. My foot makes contact and Bob groans. He releases my hands, but before I can run, he grabs my hair. Twisting to get away, I lose my footing at the same time Bob releases his grip. Before I can catch myself, I go flying into the Dumpster.

Something cracks.

My head.

Someone screams.

Me.

But the echo of my scream isn't the only sound I hear as I slide to the ground.

Tires screech. Doors slam. Feet thud on concrete.

Voices. Shouts. Roars.

"There in the alley. That's her. The girl who was in my cab. Damn. I think we're too late."

Shadows race toward me. Dazed, confused, flitting in and out of consciousness, I watch them as if I'm far away.

"Fuzzy, better turn away. There's gonna be some illegal activity going on in about ten seconds." The deep voice is familiar. I last heard that voice at Redemption and it was attached to someone wearing a yellow happy face vest. My gaze focuses on a huge barrel chest. Rampage! What's Rampage doing here?

"Fuck that," someone answers. "Nothing illegal about taking down two criminals who I'm pretty sure are going to resist arrest. I won't even mind doing the paperwork at the station tonight."

A cop. Rampage called him Fuzzy. Oh my God. The cab driver's son. Tears prickle my eyes and I wish I had a run-to-the-rescue kind of dad too.

The shadows converge, and as they come into the dim light, I recognize them from Redemption: Rampage, Blade Saw, Homicide Hank, and Obsidian. When I was with Jake, we partied with the Redemption crew every weekend. Best bunch of guys I ever knew—big hearts, big muscles, and a bond so tight they were almost like brothers.

And right now the brothers are on a tear with fury in their eyes.

Rampage grabs the bouncer and tosses him through the air like a discarded tissue. I catch a glimpse of red hair and a thin, wiry body as Homicide Hank screams and drives his fist into Bob's gut. But Bob is fast. He spins around and an inattentive Blade Saw gets a punch to the jaw. Blade Saw's face curdles with rage and I look away. A former semi-pro heavyweight bodybuilder with fists of steel, Blade Saw is not a man to be trifled with.

A crack. A scream. Bob drops to his knees. "My arm!"

The bouncer lumbers to his feet and races over to help Bob. A shadow darker than night bellows with a voice so low my toes curl, intercepting him midstride. The bouncer flies through the air and crashes against the wall. Throws and takedowns are Obsidian's specialty.

"Hey, leave one for me. I can't write up a report saying I just stood around doing nothing." A tall man with broad shoulders and a shaved head wades into the fray of thudding fists, cracking heads, groans, and screams. This must be Fuzzy, the cab driver's son.

Although I try to push myself up, pain knifes through my shoulder and arm, driving me back down to the ground. The cab driver kneels beside me and strokes my head. I wait for him to tell me how disappointed he is in me, one of my father's favorite phrases. Instead, his face crumples. "I shouldn't have left you. I should have dropped you at Redemption and driven away."

My mouth opens and closes but no sound comes out. Speaking is too much of an effort. All my energy is focused on not succumbing to the blackness creeping into my vision.

"Amanda."

Nonononononononono. Squeezing my eyes shut, I turn away from that voice. The voice I hear in my dreams every night. The voice I heard in the boardroom last week. I must have hit my head harder than I thought. I must be delirious. Jake is not here. He said he didn't fight anymore at Redemption.

"Look at me."

Unable to resist the opportunity to torture myself further, I turn and look into a deep blue sea of concern.

Jake. So handsome. I can't look away.

"Jesus Christ." His face contorts into a mask of anger. "What did they do to you?"

I would answer if I knew, but the world is a jumble of sounds and memories...and pain.

The cab driver puts a hand on Jake's shoulder. "We need to get her to a hospital."

"NO." I find my voice as darkness creeps across my vision. "No hospitals." Hospitals mean my parents will find out where I was and what happened. Hospitals mean confrontation and anger and a father's disappointment.

"What were you doing here?" Jake gently brushes my hair off my face. "I mean...this isn't your kind of place."

"She told me she lost her job," the cab driver interjects.

Hmmm. Maybe he's not so great after all. Kinda meddlesome. And violating my right to privacy. Doesn't he know what's said in the cab is supposed to stay in the cab?

"I got the feeling she was going off the rails," he says, clearly unable to read my thoughts. "I tried to talk her out of it."

Jake's face tightens. "What do you mean she lost her job? I saw her at her office last week." The blood drains from his face. "When?"

"She said it happened last Friday."

"Friday?" Jake's strangled tone has me shaking my head. "Fuck. It's because of me. It's my fault."

My heart squeezes at the pain in his voice. I want to tell him it isn't his fault. I want to tell him it would have happened anyway.

But the words don't come. Instead I close my eyes and succumb to the darkness.

Jake's anguished face is the last thing I see.

"I have never been so disappointed in my life."

My father brushes off his gray Hugo Boss suit and glares at me across the hospital room. Although he's almost fifty-five, women still think he's quite a catch with his piercing blue eyes, trim body, and square jaw. But I think my mom was the catch. Five years younger than my father, her soft blond hair curls gently around a perfect oval of a face, and her eyes are a soft blue, like a summer sky.

"Your mother called Farnsworth to tell him you wouldn't be in to work and he told her..." He draws in a ragged breath and turns to my mother. "Tell her, Viv. Tell her what we had to hear from one of our dearest friends."

Head fuzzy from painkillers and still dazed after being rudely awakened by my father's bark of anger, I tilt my head to the side and frown. Well, at least they aren't going to bother asking how I am.

My mother shakes her head and sighs. "He said you were worried you weren't on the partnership track so you propositioned him. He was mortified, especially since you're his best friend's daughter. He said if it had been anyone else, he would have reported you to the State Bar, but as a favor to our family, he just asked you to leave."

I draw in a sharp breath, inhaling the scent of antiseptic and the faint floral fragrance of my mother's perfume. Farnsworth's story is already in play, but he took a risk that my parents would believe his story over mine. Or maybe it was no risk at all.

"He's lying." My voice is a soft rasp, barely audible over the beeping of the machines beside me. "He propositioned me."

My father gives a bitter laugh. "As if I would believe you. Do you think we didn't know what went on in the house when we were working hard to put a roof over your head? Even now, every time we see you, you have a different boyfriend in tow. A person who is incapable of sustaining a stable relationship wouldn't think twice about offering herself up to get ahead."

Mom puts a hand on his arm. "Stan. I think you've made your point. She's been hurt. We should let her rest. Why don't you wait in the hall?"

Shocked, my father and I both stare. Mom never took sides between my father and me when I lived at home. She listened, kept her own counsel, and then sent me to my room. Except this time, I'm already in my room. Maybe that's the reason for her first ever attempt to diffuse the hostility that permeates my relationship with my father—the hostility that began the day I dared to be born a girl. Disappointment number one.

Unfortunately, my father doesn't heed Mom's warning. He's on his high horse and clearly determined to ride it to the end.

"Rest? She had all morning to rest and she was well enough to give a statement to the police. She needs to understand the extent of my frustration. Imagine. I was pulled out of bed on a trial prep weekend because our daughter, a Westwood, was found at a sleazy bar in Ghost Town." He scowls in my direction. "You certainly got what you deserved. You should have known better than to go to a place like that."

"You're being a bit harsh." My mother taps my father lightly on the elbow. "She's obviously learned her lesson. Look at her. She's…injured."

Mom's voice cracks. I am disconcerted by her unexpected show of emotion. I must look pretty bad.

"Harsh? She'll never be a partner at any law firm in California. After propositioning Farnsworth, she'll never get a reference, and if people find out what she did, they won't touch her with a ten-foot pole."

"He tried to blackmail me," I croak. But before I can explain, my father cuts me off with a cruel laugh.

"As if I would believe that. A girl like you? You're a goddamn sl—"

"Stan." My mother interrupts. "She's our daughter and I'm sure she knows she's let us down." She takes a step toward the door, urging my father forward, only to stop short when a tall figure dressed in black brushes past her.

Jake.

My foggy brain, already struggling to keep up with the family nightmare, freezes at the breathtaking sight of his hard, muscular body clad in a leather biker jacket and low-slung jeans.

"Am I interrupting something?" He casually interposes himself between my father and my bed.

My father pulls himself up to his full six-foot height, but he still has to look up to meet Jake's gaze. "Who the hell are you?"

"Jake Donovan." He tosses his helmet on the bedside chair and folds his arms, treating me to an up close and personal view of his broad back and tight ass.

My father harrumphs. "Mr. Donovan, we're in the middle of a private family discussion. I suggest you visit another time."

Jake's shoulders stiffen. "Private? Everyone in the hallway could hear you. Not only that, but she's hurt. Is this really the best time for a verbal assault?"

Emotion wells up in my chest at his unexpected support at the only time in my life I haven't had the will or energy to defend myself.

"Jake…it's okay. I'm used to it."

"It's not okay to me." He looks back over his shoulder and catches me with his breathtaking gaze, at once furious and concerned.

The pulse in my father's jaw throbs double-time and the blood drains from his face. Instinctively, my hands curl into the sheets. I know that look. And I know what comes next. I am suddenly so profoundly grateful for Jake's intervention, my eyes prickle with tears.

"She's my daughter and I'll speak to her when, where, and how I choose," my father barks.

"She's my friend." Jake closes the distance between them in two quick strides, his body quivering as if he wants to punch someone. "And I suggest you consider another time and place."

Two inches taller than my father, heavily muscled, and many years younger, Jake in a rage is intimidating even to me. But my father didn't get to be a partner at one of the top law firms in the city by backing down. Ever.

"Are you threatening me?"

"Do I need to threaten you?" Jake takes a step closer to my father and his voice drops to a low, warning growl.

"You're out of line, young man." My father's lips curl in a snarl.

He's right. Jake is out of line. But then, Jake doesn't care about lines or rules or convention. His cavalier attitude was one of the things I liked best about him. A total disregard for the things that defined my life.

"Stan." My mother wraps an arm around my father's bicep and tugs. "It's time to go. We can have a family discussion later. Let her visit with her friend."

But my father doesn't move. Instead, he and Jake face off. Eyes locked, chests heaving, fists clenched.

"She's no family of mine," my father mutters after a few tense moments. "There's only so much disappointment a father can take. As of this moment, I never had a daughter." With a final harrumph, my father breaks the stalemate and storms out the door. Mom takes a step after him, pauses, and then pats my foot under the covers.

"I talked to the doctor and he says it was just a minor concussion and a lot of bruising and you should be out of here tomorrow. If you need to come home…" Her gaze flicks to my father's departing back and then to me. "I suppose we could hire someone…we're both in trial…"

"I'm good, Mom." I force the words out. "I'll be fine."

She gives an absent nod and looks up at a glowering Jake. "You almost had a lawsuit on your hands. You should be more careful. If he finds out who you are, he may press charges for threats."

"Jake Donovan, Chairman of Donovan & Sons." Jake pulls a card from his pocket and hands it to her. "Tell him to do his worst."

I stifle a laugh. In his jeans and leathers, his hair just brushing his collar, and the faintest five o'clock shadow on his jaw, he looks like a badass biker and not a corporate chairman. Still, he has courage to throw himself on the mercy of one of the city's top litigators.

Mom likes brass. Her mouth twitches slightly. "Well then, Mr. Donovan, maybe I'll see you again, although I hope it's under better circumstances." She walks toward the door, her Louboutin heels clicking across the tiles.

"Aren't you going to kiss your daughter good-bye?" Jake settles himself in the chair beside my bed, as if he's here for a long stay.

Mom looks over her shoulder and gives him a tight smile. "Not that it's any of your business, Mr. Donovan, but we aren't a kissing kind of family."

"Nice parents," Jake says after she leaves the room. "No wonder you never introduced us."

I tense at his words. "Mom's okay. She's just always been preoccupied with her work, and my dad…well, he always wanted a son to follow in his footsteps. They're both high achievers with very high standards, and they expected the same from me. Unfortunately, I often disappointed them, especially with my choice of boyfriends."

"I thought I had a rough time growing up." Jakes shakes his head. "I was a bit of a wild kid and my parents blamed me for everything that went wrong in the family. But they weren't cold people."

Touché.

He tilts his head to the side and studies me so intently I wonder for a moment if I said the word out loud.

"Being a disappointment is hard enough." His face softens and he tucks an errant curl behind my ear. "But without the affection to balance it out…it must have been really hard."

Disconcerted by his sympathy, I lean back against the pillow and shrug. "I survived. I learned how to be independent and self-reliant.

That way no one can let me down. Not so sure how I'll get back in their good graces after this fiasco."

Jake gives a bitter laugh. "Sometimes no matter how hard you try, it isn't enough."

A smile ghosts my lips. "I know that feeling well."

Jake's eyes meet mine and something changes in the air between us. Whether it's the realization that we actually have something in common or a mutual sympathy at being unable to meet parental expectations, for a brief moment we are bonded by a force other than the attraction of opposites.

Tearing my gaze away, I reach for the water glass on the tray beside my bed, only to wince as the IV tugs at my wrist.

"Here, let me." Jake holds the straw to my lips and I take a sip. The cool water soothes my parched throat, but Jake's tender gesture makes my stomach flutter.

When I'm done, he sits back in his chair. "Makayla is on her way. I called her last night to let her know what happened. If she hadn't been on a double shift with the ambulance crew, she would have been here when you woke."

Tears sting my eyes and my throat tightens. "Thanks. I lost my purse last night, and I was just about to call her from the hospital phone when my parents walked in. I reported my stolen purse to the police when they came this morning to take a statement…"

Jake pulls my purse from his pack and places it on the nightstand. "Fuzzy brought it to the station after he arrested those two goons. They were charged with assault and attempted theft." He clasps my hand and runs his thumb back and forth over my knuckles. His seemingly absent caress electrifies my skin. But I can't deal with the rush of remembered emotions that come from his gentle touch and I jerk my hand away.

"Hey," he says softly. "Are you okay? Something hurt? Do you want me to call the nurse?"

"No. I'm just…I can manage."

A pained expression crosses his face. "I wish we'd gotten there sooner. We wasted time sorting out who got to go and who had to stay."

Relieved to switch to a neutral topic, I relax back on the bed.

"I was surprised to see you. I thought you said you didn't go to Redemption anymore."

"I wouldn't have been there if I hadn't bumped into you. But after I saw you at the law firm, I started thinking about how big a part of my life it had been when we were together, and how much I'd enjoyed training and fighting and teaching classes. I decided to give it another try and see if I could fit it into my schedule after all."

"I'm glad you did."

Jake shifts uncomfortably in his seat and then reaches for his helmet. "I should really get going. I'm sure Makayla will be here soon and I've got a meeting in an hour. I just wanted to make sure you were okay. After all, it was because of me you lost your job and wound up where you did."

Whoa, Nelly.

"It isn't your fault, Jake. It would have happened anyway. And I didn't lose my job. I quit. Over a totally different issue."

But he isn't listening. He scrubs his hands over his face and shakes his head. "Fucking things up is what I do best. My parents got that right about me."

A screech startles us both. I glance up to see Makayla and Max in the doorway. Makayla's thick auburn hair is tied up in a ponytail and her hazel eyes are dark with concern. Tall, dark, and chiseled, Max has an arm around her curvy body. They are the perfect picture of an overprotective alpha male and a daredevil woman hell-bent on keeping him on his toes.

Jake pushes himself out of his chair and gives Max and Makayla a nod as he heads out the door. "Take care of yourself, Amanda."

My heart sinks. If that wasn't a "good-bye forever," I don't know what is.

"So." Makayla takes a seat beside me as Max follows Jake into the hall. "Jake called me last night and told me what happened. Why didn't you phone me?" She gives me her best Makayla glare, which just makes me laugh. Anger isn't Makayla's style.

"Look what happened last time I asked you to accompany me on an ill-fated adventure to a dangerous place."

Makayla pales. She doesn't like to be reminded of the night we were kidnapped and she thought she'd lost Max forever.

"I was on the graveyard shift and couldn't get off work, so I called Drake and ordered him to get down here pronto. Did he make it?"

"Don't worry," I say. "I was in good hands. After the police left, he was here for an hour checking me over like he knows all about head injuries, scolding me for not waiting for him to come to my place last night…"

She frowns. "I thought you were done with him months ago. Are you guys still—?"

"Not for a long time." I lower my voice to a hushed whisper. "I kept meaning to tell him, but I never got the chance. The friends with benefits thing was fun for a bit, but it left me kinda empty inside."

Makayla glances out the door where Max and Jake are engaged in a heated discussion in the hallway and leans toward me. "What about Jake? I thought you said he didn't want to have anything to do with you after he saw you at the office last week. And yet, he was the one who called, and here he is now."

My heart squeezes in my chest. "I guess he feels responsible for what happened, although it's totally ridiculous. He's here because he's just…you know…a nice guy." Too nice for someone like me.

"And you're a nice girl." Makayla pats my arm. "Otherwise, you wouldn't be my best friend. Nice girls and nice guys belong together. Maybe he's forgiven you and wants to try again. People have a great capacity for forgiveness. Look at me and Max. After everything that happened, we worked things out."

Tears well up in my eyes. "You guys were meant to be together. I knew that when I saw you—the girl who can't stomach violence—sitting on the bleachers in Redemption, watching him fight the first day you met. It's not the same with me and Jake. I hurt him, and in the worst possible way. He'll never forgive me for that."

Makayla's eyes flick to the doorway and then back to me. She jerks her chin ever so slightly in the direction of the hallway. Max is gone, but Jake is leaning against the doorjamb. He studies me for the longest time, his blue eyes boring deep into my soul, and then he turns and walks away.

Chapter 4
'Manda, 'manda, 'manda

Tap. Tap. Tap.

The incessant knocking at my front door wakes me from a deep sleep. For a moment, I consider ignoring the irritating tapper and returning to oblivion, but only Makayla and Drake know I've moved into my grandmother's Tudor-style house in Oakland's sleepy Montclair Village, and if I don't answer the door, whichever of the two it is will have no qualms about breaking it down.

With a sleepy sigh, I brush the matted hair off my face, pad through the house, and pull open the heavy front door.

My blurred vision makes out a non-Makayla, non-Drake-shaped figure. Tall, broad shoulders, muscular chest. Distinctly male. Holding a backpack.

Blinking several times, I focus on startling blue eyes and soft, golden hair.

Jake.

Shock mercilessly slaps me into acute awareness. "What are you doing here?"

He frowns and peers over my shoulder. "What are *you* doing here? Makayla said you'd moved out of your apartment, but I didn't think you would move into a house especially after…" He grimaces and cuts himself off.

After I lost my job. Great. Just what I need. Another reminder.

"Sorry."

I shrug and make a mental note never to speak to my busybody friend again. Why is she talking to people about me when she knows I just want to drop off the face of the Earth?

"This is my grandmother's house. She died last year and left it to me in her will. I used to come here and stay with her when I was really lonely at home. It's too much for one person, but I haven't decided what to do with it yet." He doesn't need to know I had to give up my apartment because I could no longer afford the rent.

Without so much as a by-your-leave, Jake pushes his way past me and marches into the house, dropping his backpack on the table.

"Um…can I help you?"

"Interesting place. Not a lot of houses left in Oakland with this much character. I'll just take a look around."

For the next ten minutes, I trail after him as he thumps walls, taps windows, jumps on floorboards, and opens and closes cupboards and doors.

"Good house." He takes a look around the kitchen and then leans against the counter. "Clean lines, strong foundation, impeccably framed. Tons of character with all the period details and the wood floors, and I see you still like the country chic decor. But if you're serious about selling, the inside needs updating and it could use a new roof and windows."

Irritated by the intrusion and missing the warmth of my bed, I snap, "Well, seeing as I have no job, that won't be happening any time soon."

He flinches and I immediately apologize. But seriously, why is he here? Why won't he just go and leave me in peace? Desperate to get away from the sudden onslaught of emotion and back to the numb stupor of the last few weeks, I put my hands on my hips. "Anything else I can help you with?"

Jake's gaze drops to my chest and he sucks in a sharp breath. Then his eyes travel down my body. And up. And down. And part way up. And stop.

My cheeks heat. I am suddenly and uncomfortably aware I am wearing a pajama tank top and shorts and nothing else. Like a bra or panties. My attire for the last few weeks is not really appropriate for visitors. Especially male visitors. Not that it seems to bother Drake when he stops by every few days to feed me coffee and donuts and harass me about getting out of the house. But with Jake…

"Maybe I'll go put on some clothes." My voice barely rises above a whisper.

His jaw tightens. "S'okay. I'm not staying. I just came to deliver the backpack for Makayla. I was up at Grizzly Peak chilling with Max when she came back from shopping. She said you weren't looking after yourself, so she'd bought a load of food and other stuff she thought you might need. But she got paged for the ambulance crew just as she was walking out the door so she asked me to bring it."

"Thanks." I try to sound thankful when all I really want is to get my hands around the throat of my interfering best friend. My grandmother's house is only fifteen minutes from Max's place and Makayla virtually has to drive right past if she takes the Warren Freeway into work, which she almost always does.

"Not a problem. I was heading to Redemption and you were only a couple minutes out of my way."

"Are you teaching tonight?"

"No. Just going a few rounds in the practice ring, but if I ever get the company back in the black or convince my family to sell, I might start training seriously again and try to work my way through the amateurs."

"Why did you agree to run the company if it's not what you want to do?"

His jaw tightens. "Peter was killed in a car crash eighteen months ago and my dad fell apart. He was going to lose everything he had worked for. I couldn't let that happen. In the end, they are my family."

"I'm so sorry about Peter." My throat tightens with sympathy. "Makayla told me about the accident. I called but I got your voice mail, so I left a message…" Jake hardly talked about his family when we were together, but I knew he and his brother, Peter, were close.

"Yeah, I got it. Thanks. I just wasn't up to speaking to anyone at the time." He opens my squeaky cutlery drawer and closes it. Open. *Squeak.* Close. Open. *Squeak.* Close. Then he opens it and frowns. Suddenly all my cutlery is on the counter and my drawer is upside down on the table. He grabs a bread knife and viciously attacks one of the screws on the rail.

"Dad was so happy when I took over the company. Said it was the first useful thing I'd done with my life. But I prefer to be outdoors, working with my hands, rather than stuck in an office all day. And I'd rather live in a place like this...lotsa space with a big backyard so I could get a dog like I had when I was a kid, but I had to get a condo in the city so I could be close to work." He replaces the drawer and gives it a test.

Open. Close. Open. Close. No squeaks.

"All fixed."

"Thanks." I fiddle with my bracelet in the awkward silence that follows. Why is he sticking around? As if the depths of my despair aren't deep enough without having to watch him strut his perfectly toned body around my house.

His gaze rakes over me in an entirely assessing and nonsexual way and then he frowns. "Makayla was right. You've lost weight. I'll fix you something to eat before I go."

Ummm...hello? But then, this is Jake, and once he makes up his mind about something, he doesn't let trivial things like manners or what other people want or not knowing how to use a stove get in the way.

"You're going to cook?"

"Yes." He points to the stool at the kitchen counter. "Now sit while I whip up a gourmet feast."

"You?" I don't sit because first, I have no food; and second, I never once saw Jake in front of a stove the entire time we were going out. He lived on protein shakes, protein bars, and meat lover's pizza, hold the crust.

Jake pulls open the fridge door and frowns over his shoulder. "There's nothing in here. When did you last eat?"

"I can't remember."

"How can you not remember when you last ate?" His incredulous look is almost comical.

I give a theatrical valley girl sigh to hide the emotion welling up inside me. On top of everything else, seeing Jake making himself at home in my kitchen is just too much. I just want to retreat back to the warm, cozy darkness of my bedroom. "Eating isn't important. Nothing is important. Now, if you'll excuse me, I'm not really hungry so I'm going back to bed."

Before I even make it halfway across the kitchen, Jake grabs my arm and pulls me back. "Makayla said you haven't left the house since you got discharged from the hospital. She said if she hadn't done your shopping, you would've starved to death. She thinks you're depressed."

"You know Makayla." I sigh and wrench my arm out of his grip. "She's prone to exaggeration."

"I know you've been through a lot, but don't you think two weeks is enough? Don't you think it's time to rejoin the world?"

My hands ball into fists and I press my lips together. Who is he to waltz in here and tell me how to run or not run my life?

"Jake?"

He raises an eyebrow.

"Thank you for bringing the backpack and fixing the drawer and offering to make me dinner. It was lovely to see you, but I have sleeping to get back to. Good-bye." I may be depressed, but at least *I* have manners.

With a firm click, I flick off the kitchen lights and stomp up the stairs to my bedroom. My home away from home when I was growing up. Grandma and I decorated it together over the years—first, the bed with its wrought iron frame, then the antique night table and a chest of drawers. Over the years we added a desk, repainted the walls a soft lilac, and sewed soft furnishings in country-chic pastel colors. It is the one place I feel I belong. Safe. Loved.

As I throw back the covers, a floorboard creaks behind me.

"Now what?" I spin around and glare.

Jake leans against the doorjamb, arms crossed, biceps bulging under his tight, white T-shirt.

Tease.

"I'm giving you a choice." His voice drops from conciliatory to commanding. "Option one. You shower. Get dressed. Do girly things. We stay here and I cook up whatever is in that backpack. Option two. You shower. Get dressed. Do girly things. We grab some burgers. You come to Redemption. Say hi to the guys. Watch me fight. We go for more burgers. I take you home."

My brow wrinkles with a frown. "How about option three? Amanda stays in her pajamas, climbs back into bed, and goes to sleep. I haven't fully recovered. Maybe in a few more weeks."

"Makayla says the doctor gave you the all clear."

And that's one less person on my Christmas list. The backpack was definitely a setup. "Makayla talks too much."

"She loves you," Jake says quietly. "She's worried about you. She says she's never seen you like this. She thinks you've given up."

With a groan, I puff my pillows and slide under my fluffy down comforter. "I haven't given up. I'm taking a break from life. I'm catching up on all the sleep I lost while I fruitlessly banged my head against the partnership wall at Farnsworth & Tillman. I'm healing my battered body and soul. Eventually, I'll find a job at another big firm and redeem myself in my parents' eyes. But not right now."

Jake crosses the room in two long strides and whips the comforter off the bed. "Yes now. You need to face the world or life's gonna get tired of waiting for you."

In my fury, I think nothing about snatching the cover out of the hands of a glaring six-foot-two tattooed fighter with a bee in his bonnet. I rearrange the blankets over myself and sink into the pillows. "You can see yourself out. I'm taking option three. I'm exhausted from all this talking."

His eyes narrow. "There is no option three. Right now, you're going to take a shower and eat. Tomorrow, you're going to look for a job—"

"Says who?"

"Me."

Torn between being extremely irritated and highly amused, I fold my arms and revert back to the taunting voice of my childhood. "You and what army?"

"Shower," he barks like a drill sergeant.

"Go to hell," I respond like a clueless new recruit.

Wrong thing to say. Down goes the comforter. Up goes Amanda. I screech as he secures me over his strong shoulder, my ass in the air, my legs pinned tight against his broad chest.

"Beast. Let me go." My fists thud uselessly against his tight ass.

Jake rumbles a laugh. "Oh, I will."

He dumps me unceremoniously in the shower, and before I can

escape, he turns on the freezing cold water. With a wicked grin, he bolts and closes the door behind him, laughing when I yell obscenities at his departing back. "You are going to be so damn sorry."

Half an hour later, showered and dressed for the first time in I don't know how long, my "girly stuff," aka makeup and hair, done, I descend the stairs. Jake is tapping a wall with a small hammer and muttering to himself about plaster.

"Ahem."

He spins around and I pose for him in the only clean pair of jeans I own, a sparkly tank top, and kitten heels.

A grin splits his face. "Wow. You do clean up well."

"Now it's your turn." I give him an evil smile before I drench him with the pitcher of freezing water I had been holding behind my back.

His shocked expression is worth the risk. His subtly raised eyebrow and menacing growl are not. Laughing, I race through the house, but my heels slide on the hardwood floor and Jake catches me around the waist before I can make it to the patio doors.

"You know better than that." His fingers dig under my ribs, tickling me until I can barely breathe. My heart squeezes in my chest. This is how it used to be between us. Fun. Playful. Hot.

"Let me go." I mock a growl. "You know I hate being tickled."

His arms tighten around me and his lips brush over the sensitive skin of my neck sending a shiver down my spine. I try to wriggle away from his sodden clothes. I wiggle and wriggle.

"Amanda...stop." His words are barely more than a pained whisper, but I freeze instantly and for the longest moment he holds me against him. His face buried in my hair. His heaving chest pressed against my back. His erection nestled into the crack of my ass.

Oh God.

"Sorry." Pulse racing, I wrench myself away and half turn toward the stairs. "I'll get you a towel."

Before my brain has even processed that he has moved, I'm in his arms, my breasts pressed tight against his rock-solid body.

"I have a towel," he rasps, deep and low. "And she's not running away."

So hot. So hard. So utterly masculine. One slide of my body against his and my nipples tighten into hard peaks. My blood turns molten, burning its way through my veins. No one has ever aroused me the way Jake does, and even after all this time, it is clear nothing has changed.

A shudder runs through me, but when I try to step away from the tormenting rub of his body against mine, he tightens his arm around my waist and threads his fingers through my hair, gently easing my head back until I am forced to look up into eyes as dark and stormy as the ocean.

"Fuck." He growls the word, holding me so tight I can barely breathe.

My body trembles at the unexpected firmness of his touch. Jake in the bedroom was always gentle and fun. We traded pleasures equally, teased each other mercilessly, but never once did he push past my boundaries. We were partners in every sense of the word. But this Jake, dominant Jake—forceful, aggressive, and unpredictable—sends my desire to a whole new level.

"Jake." His name emerges from my lips in a squeak of whisper as I press my hands against his chest. No longer am I the woman who just wants a good time and winds up in Hell, in its infinite variety of forms. For the first time, I want something more, and I won't get that with the man I hurt. I couldn't give myself to him before, why would anything be different now?

Shoving him back until he loosens his grip, I wiggle free. "I'll get you that towel."

"Amanda…"

Without looking back, I bolt up the stairs. I can't be the fun, crazy girl he remembers. That girl would probably be having sex right now on the living room floor. She would be adding another page to Farnsworth's blue file. She would know he was only teasing and in the morning, she would be alone.

"'Manda!"

Rampage throws his arms around me and gives me an enormous bear hug at the entrance to Redemption. "'Manda, 'manda, 'manda," he chants, lifting me so high my feet leave the ground. "You're okay!"

"It's *A*manda," I say dryly. "And I'm okay thanks to you and the other guys."

"Everybodddeeeee. 'Manda's here!"

Damn.

"Actually, I was hoping to fly under the radar tonight and just…"

A stampede of fighters swarms me, cutting me off from any possible escape. I am squeezed, hugged, kissed on the cheek, and petted like a kitten while Jake watches from the corner, bemused. But when someone cops a feel of my ass, he dives into the fray and pulls me out.

One big happy family. Another pang of longing and regret washes over me. When I gave up Jake, I gave up these guys too.

Still, it's good to see nothing has changed in the two years I've been away. Well, except for the fact that the club is no longer illegal. A shiny new license takes up space by the door. The chalkboards covering the walls in the spacious main foyer now list upcoming sanctioned fights in addition to all the new training classes. Rules are posted on the bulletin board, and a huge Team Redemption MMA logo flashes on a screen in the corner.

Jake tours me through the renovated facility, a whopping 24,000 feet of the best MMA gear money can buy. The strength and cardio area now boasts three long rows of shiny new cardio equipment and a sea of weight machines, benches, and free weights. The walls have been painted bright shades of blue, red, and green, and wall-length mirrors brighten the space. We turn a corner and a blue sea of mat space stretches out before me. Grapple dummies line the walls like an army of soldiers, and across from them hang a small corps of punching bags. Three practice rings dominate the corners, and the gym is heaving with sweaty bodies.

"Wow. Makayla said Max—"

He cuts me off. "Don't forget you have to use ring names in the gym."

Rolling my eyes, I continue, but with ring names. "Doc said Torment had invested heavily in renovations, but I never imagined anything like this."

"I was blown away too." Jake nods back toward the entrance. "On that side, he has a CrossFit training room, fitness studios, snack bar, speed and agility facility, video room, equipment shop, lounge, and Doc's first aid room. There's also a whole wing that's still undeveloped.

And there isn't a class he isn't offering: wrestling, boxing, Muay Thai, Brazilian jiu-jitsu, grappling, general fitness. You name it. He's got it."

"It looks more like a secret Special Forces base than just a place to train."

Jake laughs and throws an arm around my shoulders. "Come see the main attraction."

Although his gesture is casual at best, I like his arm around my shoulders. His warmth seeps into me, and for a moment, I pretend the last two years never happened and I gave Jake everything he wanted. I gave him me.

We drop our shoes at the door and cross the mats into the center of the warehouse. Where once there was a roughly constructed, elevated ring surrounded by folding chairs and wooden bleachers, there are now two high-tech, solid fight rings with mats and flags emblazoned with the new Team Redemption logo. An octagon-shaped cage sits on a platform a few feet off the floor.

A shiver runs down my spine. Something about that cage makes my toes curl. In a good way.

"Cage fighting too?"

"He can't run a serious MMA gym without a cage."

"Do you…cage fight now?"

Jake's eyes flash. "Yeah. Been practicing for a couple weeks. Always thought I was a ring man, but one taste of the cage and I was hooked. Homicide Hank has been taking me through some basic strategies. The cage can be used as a tool or as a weapon, so it requires a different set of techniques."

Catching the slightest hitch in his breath, I look up and frown. "Is that why you're stressed? Because you're cage fighting tonight?"

His eyes widen as if I just caught him out. "Everyone's gonna watch me in the cage and decide on my new ring name tonight. My old ring name, 'Giant Killer,' was taken by someone else when I was away, and because I've got a few fights under my belt now, the guys decided I need a new name. I'm just worried they're gonna stick me with something humiliating, like Fuzzy."

"I like the name Fuzzy. It's cute."

Jake gives me a look of mock disgust. "The guys gave it to him 'cause he's such a hard-ass in class and they thought he needed to be taken down a peg. But seriously, in a fight between guys named Torment or Homicide or Blade Saw or even Hammer Fist and a guy named Fuzzy, who do you think will win?"

"The guy who's so fierce his teammates gave him a cute name to keep his ferocity at bay?"

"Wrong."

His anxiety is almost palpable, and I try to reassure him as best I can. "I'm sure you won't have to worry. Once they see the vicious termination machine you are, they'll be afraid to give you anything but the most fearsome of names."

Jake laughs and brushes my hair behind my shoulder. "I forgot about your dry sense of humor. But really, I am a vicious termination machine."

Someone shouts his name and he excuses himself to say hello. I spot Sandy, the once ex of both Jake and Max, climbing into a practice ring and wander over to investigate. Sandy's platinum hair is piled on her head in a messy haystack and her curvy body is poured into a tight pink sports bra and pink bike shorts. She glares and then whispers to her opponent, Shayla, aka Shilla the Killa, a lean, muscular woman with a short, dark ponytail. They both turn to look at me and giggle. Suddenly I am in middle school all over again.

As they take their places at the corners of the ring, Jake comes up behind me and taps me on the shoulder. "You running away from me again?"

Mortified at the reminder of our break up, I turn to apologize only to catch his lopsided grin.

"I'm still wet." He points to his hair and a relieved breath whooshes out of me.

The ref blows a whistle, and Shayla throws a right hook at Sandy's face. I pray she knocks out a few of Sandy's perfect, white teeth. Aside from scooping up Jake on the rebound after our break-up, a jealous Sandy tweeted a picture of Makayla's ass when she found out Makayla and Max had hooked up. As Makayla's best friend, I am duty-bound to hate her vicariously. And I do.

"You ever see Shilla fight?" Jake casually shoves a spectator out of my way, glaring the innocent six-foot leviathan into submission when he dares open his mouth to protest. "She's got real talent. I'm pretty sure she has a good shot at the state championship."

He twists a strand of my hair around his finger, but I don't have time for him. I've never watched female MMA fighters before. And although Sandy was a ring girl when I last saw her, she is now holding her own against Shayla.

A crowd gathers as they circle the ring. Although physically not as strong as most of the male fighters I've seen, they are no less violent, no less skilled, and no less fierce. They kick and punch and spin and tackle. Sandy is clearly on the back foot. Blood drips from her nose but she doesn't back down.

"Earth to Amanda." Jake waves his hand in front of my face, breaking my concentration.

"Shhh. I'm watching the fight." I swat his hand away and focus on the ring. Shayla pulls off some impressive moves, rolling with Sandy trapped between her thighs and then locking Sandy's head between her legs and pinning her to the ground in an impressive submission.

Damn, that Shayla can fight. Probably better than some of the guys I've seen at the club. I can't imagine anyone throwing her against a Dumpster. She would have had Bob and his bouncer groaning on the pavement in thirty seconds flat.

"I have to go and get ready for the cage," Jake murmurs in my ear.

"Sure." I give him an absent wave.

"Amanda." His sharp rebuke yanks me out of the fight, and I look up at his furrowed brow.

"I want you to be there."

"I'll be there, Jake."

"Don't be late."

"It's only fifty feet away. I'm sure I'll make it in time."

Still, he doesn't move. Instead he shuffles his feet and sighs. Finally, I turn and give him my full attention. "Anything else?"

"The ring name." His voice drops to a low whisper. "It's important. If I ever did get free of the company and go pro, I would need a good ring name. Something tough. Something that will make people afraid. You can hold your own in an argument, and you're damn good at convincing people to do what they don't want to do. Maybe you could convince the guys. I just…"

The little hint of vulnerability warms me, as does his faith in my legal skills. "I'll do my best, Jake. I promise."

Chapter 5
RAGE IN THE CAGE

"CAGE FIGHT."

The words whisper through the gym and people drift toward the octagon like kids to an ice cream truck. Although it isn't a sanctioned match, a cage fight, even when the fighters are just sparring, is always good entertainment, and a nameless fighter in the cage, apparently even more so.

After a quick glance around the gym, I spot the experienced fighters huddled near the weight equipment, no doubt discussing possible ring names for Jake.

Showtime.

Stiffening my spine, I saunter over to the huddle and they break for a moment and let me join the circle. The gang is all here: Homicide Hank, Blade Saw, Obsidian, Hammer Fist, Rampage, Torment, Drake, aka Doctor Death at Redemption, and Fuzzy. Only Makayla is missing and she had better stay missing. If she dares show her face, I'll let her know exactly what I think of the backpack setup.

Drake gives me a wink and waggles his finger, motioning for me to stand beside him, but with Jake over by the cage, I deem it not worth the risk. I don't know if they've sorted their issues or whether Jake still wants to rip out Drake's throat.

I glance quickly over my shoulder. Jake is stretching on the mats while his opponent, Master Mayhem, a bald bulldog of a fighter, is joking with a few ring girls. Jake has changed into a pair of fight shorts, navy blue with teal Chinese characters down the sides, and what looks to be bike shorts underneath. The color combination reminds me of Farnsworth & Tillman, and I shudder.

"Don't like that name?" Blade Saw lifts an eyebrow.

"What name?"

"The Wolf."

My nose wrinkles. "Not really him. If you want to name him after an animal, I would go with the cat family. I mean, look at his hair; it looks like a mane."

"I fucking hate animal names," Hammer Fist grumbles. "The lists are full of grizzlies, wolves, bears, lions, and tigers."

"Cougar?" I give a little shrug.

"That would be you." Rampage gives me a grin.

My hands find my hips. "I am not that old. I just turned twenty-seven. I have a good twenty years before I become a cougar. And by then, that totally sexist and offensive term will no longer be in use."

"And here I thought you were thirty-five." Rampage shakes his head as if in disbelief.

"Thirty-five? Do I look thirty-five?" My voice rises in pitch and then drops when I hear snickers around me. My eyes narrow, and I give Rampage my best monotone. "Ha ha. Very funny. You're a funny guy, Rampage. My sides are splitting. I can barely contain myself."

"She sounds forty-five now." A suicidal Drake steps into the fray.

"One day, I'm going to learn how to fight," I mutter. "And I won't forget this conversation. You'll be a sorry bunch of guys when I'm done with you."

Glances all round. Smiles. Chuckles. "Now that's something I'd like to see." Rampage brushes his thumb over his bottom lip in mock contemplation. "'Manda in the ring. I have a feeling she'd really kick some ass."

"Yeah. Starting with yours."

"And she means it." Makayla slides an arm around my waist and joins the group.

"Traitor." I glare and mutter under my breath. "I knew there was no emergency call."

"Best friend watching your back," she whispers. "And I did have an emergency. You needed someone to shake some sense into you and I wasn't able to do it. Looks like my plan worked better than expected."

"You can expect to have no best friend tomorrow." I push her hand away and follow the crowd to the octagon, but Makayla only laughs and falls into step beside me.

"How many times have you unfriended me only to refriend me twenty minutes later? Why not save yourself the stress and just realize I only have your best interests at heart?"

"Because you need to learn that my feelings are not to be trifled with—especially where they concern Jake. However, I'll forgive you this time because I'm turning over a new, conservative, chaste leaf, and that means finding someone new, conservative, and…"

"Chaste?"

My lips quiver with a repressed smile. "Could be challenging."

"Could be over fast." Makayla giggles and a second later we're both in tears.

"For a second there, I was worried about you," she says between breaths. "I thought maybe you'd lost yourself after all."

My smile quickly fades, and I bite my tongue before I tell her that she's right and if not for Jake, I would still be in bed wondering where to find me.

Fuzzy joins us in the spectator's area, and we chat about his dad and sister until Jake and Master Mayhem enter the cage. I shudder when the doors to the two entry-exit gates in the metal chain-link fence slam shut.

"Is it a real UFC cage?"

Fuzzy nods. "Now that the club is sanctioned, everything has to be regulation. The cage is thirty-two feet in diameter."

"Torment also got the taller fence to accommodate our taller fighters." Makayla gives me a wicked grin. "Like Jake."

Jake spins around and I am treated to a perfect view of the strong, muscular planes of his broad back and…I take a step closer and frown. "When did he get those tattoos? He only had two when we were going out."

Fuzzy shrugs and gives me a curious look. "I joined the club about a year and a half ago. Met Jake. He was going through a rough patch. His brother had just died and he was trying to sort out some other…personal stuff. One night we went out, got really hammered. He decided to get tatted up. And that wasn't all he did."

Makayla has the good sense to give an apologetic shrug when I turn and give her a "why didn't you tell me" glare.

"I didn't think you'd want to know," she says.

Shayla, now sporting a black and white referee shirt, checks Jake's gloves, and I take the opportunity to check out his ink. His new tattoos are breathtakingly gorgeous. A tribal design spans his upper back, covering the tops of his shoulders and his shoulder blades like wings. The two sides mirror each other with two curved lines gracing either side of his spine. I imagine running my fingers over his muscular back, tracing along the lines and ridges…

"I love tats too," an all-too-observant Makayla whispers over the crowd's chants of "rage in the cage." "Sometimes I just want to lick Torment's tats all over, but the minute I get my tongue anywhere near him, it all goes to hell and I find myself in yet another new position. His creativity boggles my mind."

For a moment, I indulge myself in my own lick-the-tattoos fantasy but with Jake as the star, only to be rudely interrupted by the shrill blast of Shayla's whistle.

Moments later, the fight begins. Master Mayhem rushes Jake and slams him up against the cage. Shayla blows a warning whistle and Master Mayhem backs away. Although he's around the same height as Jake, Master Mayhem is twice as wide, with the physique of a professional bodybuilder and the powerful moves of a bull.

Jake circles on the outside as they feel each other out. Master Mayhem steps between Jake and the cage and throws a left, hitting Jake in the jaw before driving him into the fence. Jake pushes him off and staggers to his feet. Master Mayhem trips him. My heart skips a beat as he falls to his knees, but in seconds he is back on his feet.

"Maybe he should be sparring with someone less…experienced." I shoot a worried glance in Fuzzy's direction as if he would be able to stop the fight.

Fuzzy barks a laugh. "Jake's playing him. He doesn't fight the way people expect him to fight. He'll fake weakness or an injury, stagger around the ring. Sometimes he just outright breaks the rules."

"Most times he doesn't follow the rules." Makayla glances over at a frowning Torment and sighs. "Torment said Jake's had warnings at every practice fight over the last few weeks. Not good for the reputation, especially if he wants to fight on the amateur circuit."

A few seconds later, Jake pulls an illegal move, a downward elbow strike. He gets a warning. When the fight resumes, he pounces on Master Mayhem and digs his fingers into his opponent's clavicle. Master Mayhem's face contorts in pain. Shayla blows her whistle and stops the fight again.

"Two warnings now." Fuzzy shakes his head. "If this was an actual event, he would risk disqualification. Damned renegade fighter. If he keeps up that kind of behavior, Torment will throw him off the team."

Shayla gives Jake a final warning, and the two fighters move back to the center of the octagon. The fight increases in intensity with Jake and Master Mayhem trading kicks and punches. All that raw power unleashed in a primitive steel cage sets my blood to a boil. Jake's pecs ripple with each punch, his tight abs strain, and his tantalizing ass teases me as he circles the mat. He is constantly in motion, moving in for the punch and then backing away. In and out. Back and forth. Almost like dancing. Or sex.

The crowd, now three people deep around the cage, cheers as Master Mayhem grabs Jake's legs and takes him down to the mat. But Jake is quick. He wraps his arm around Master Mayhem's leg and twists himself into a pretzel shape, holding on for dear life.

"I don't think Master Mayhem will be able to shake his leg free from Jake's half guard," Fuzzy says, as if that means something to me.

In a blur of sudden motion, Jake twists Master Mayhem's leg backward in a way legs are not supposed to go. The crowd roars in approval. Master Mayhem taps out.

Fuzzy gives Jake a begrudging thumbs up. "He's a good fighter. Despite all the rule breaking, he won."

"Renegade fighter."

Fuzzy glances over at me, a frown creasing his brow. "What did you say?"

"He's a renegade. Might make for a good ring name."

"Amanda."

My head jerks up and I catch sight of Jake leaning against the cage, arms crossed, his perfect body glistening with sweat. He meets my gaze and my cheeks heat. All the awkwardness of high school returns in a flash. I shift from foot to foot. My hands clench and unclench. My eyelashes drift down over my cheeks and I turn away.

At least I think I do. But my feet are still stuck to the mat. And I am lost in a sea of blue.

———

"Renegade."

Rampage dumps a beer on Jake's head and Jake officially becomes Jake "Renegade" Donovan.

A grin splits his face and he gives me a wink before he is swarmed by well-wishing fighters who all want to celebrate his new ring name by thumping him on the back or punching him in the gut.

"Do you like your name?" I hand him a towel when he finally breaks free and joins me at the side of the cage. He's still pumped from his fight and his "christening," eyes shining, muscles quivering, adrenaline still pulsing under his skin.

"Fuck, yeah." He grabs me around the waist and crushes his lips against mine, then releases me so quickly, for a moment I wonder if it even happened. "Thanks to you. I heard you came up with the name."

Stunned, with the sweet burn of his kiss still lingering on my lips, I breathe slow and deep, trying to quell the sudden rush of arousal that has turned my mouth dry and sent my pulse into overdrive.

"You're…welcome." My voice is a throaty rasp, made even more painful when I lick my lips and taste his salty sweetness on my tongue.

"You ready to grab some burgers?" He throws a casual arm around my shoulders, which I take as a signal his kiss was just a friendly kiss, a thank-you kiss, and not meant to be a kiss that rocked my world in a way I'm not sure I want anyway.

"Sure. You can't get too much fat, carbs, and grease into your system, I always say."

He chuckles and gives me a squeeze. God, I wish he would stop doing that. Despite my brain's warning that these are friendly gestures, my body is entirely misinterpreting his signals. My panties dampen. My nipples tighten. And I am so hot, I am tempted to strip down to my undies on the pretense of doing some fighting of my own in the cage.

"I'd have to give up the burgers if I wanted to train seriously," Jake murmurs half to himself. "Don't think I can swing it though. I need to put more time into the company if I'm going to turn things around."

We walk in comfortable silence down the corridor and then Jake turns into the changing room. "Just going to grab a shower. Back in a few."

Desperate for a distraction, I wander around the foyer. The chalkboards are filled with schedules of the daily training regime. No yoga, tai chi, step, or low-impact classes at this gym. Instead, there is "Ground and Pound," "Grunt 'n' Grapple," and "Mission: Submission."

"You interested in training?" Fuzzy stops on his way to the changing room and gives me a wicked grin. His number two buzz cut does look delightfully fuzzy under the bright, overhead lights, but I restrain myself from running my hands through his hair.

"Just looking."

"Well, if you are interested, you should start with my boot camp class, Get Fit or Die." He taps the chalkboard beside his name. "It's best to get conditioned first, so you don't injure yourself."

"What do you do in Get Fit or Die?"

His eyebrow twitches. "I kick your ass until you beg me to stop and then I kick it some more."

"How can I say no to a good ass kicking?"

Fuzzy's smile broadens. "You can't. Next session starts on Monday. I'll be expecting you."

"I'll think about it."

After he heads into the changing room, I chat with the few remaining fighters in the hallway, catching up with old friends and making a few new ones. Makayla, tucked tight under Torment's arm, gives me a meaningful wink as they saunter out the door.

Finally I am alone. The screen in the corner flashes the new Team Redemption MMA logo. Showers whoosh in the changing rooms. The gentle murmur of voices and Sandy's sharp laugh drift from the workout area.

The door behind me opens and closes, letting in a rush of cold air. Footsteps thud softly across the concrete floor. Only when a large shadow swallows my little one does the hair on the back of my neck prickle. I turn quickly to see who is behind me.

"Well, look who we have here." Bob's lips press into a thin line and he glances over at the hulking form of his bouncer and then back to me. "Come on, Angel, don't keep us waiting. Say hello."

Violent tremors shake my body, and my heart pounds so hard I fear it might crack a rib. It is all I can do not to turn and run, but I *will not* give them the satisfaction. Brave in the knowledge that I am in a gym full of testosterone-fueled fighters who would destroy Bob and his side-kick no questions asked if I so much as scream, I grit my teeth together.

"Thought you two would still be in jail after your arraignment."

"We got friends in high places." Bob takes a step toward me. "Got out on bail. And you know what we did first? We met with our lawyer 'cause someone has to pay for these." He holds up his arms covered in thick, white casts that extend from his wrists to his elbows. The bouncer does the same.

"Seriously?" Nervous laughter erupts from my chest. "You and your bouncer broke both your arms in the exact same place during the fight? And you both got the exact same casting?"

"You think that's funny, girlie?" The bouncer reaches over and grabs my ponytail with the dexterity of someone not in need of a cast. "We can't work no more. You see us laughing?"

Jake and Fuzzy choose this moment to emerge from the shower room with Obsidian, Rampage, Blade Saw, and Homicide behind them.

Their chatter fades and the world stills. Save for the thunder of blood pumping through my veins, I hear no sound. Although the bouncer is still holding my ponytail, I feel perversely safe. Like I'm all rolled up in my comforter in my cozy bed. And safe makes me brave.

Jake's steely gaze flicks from me to the bouncer and then back to me. "What's going on?"

"Something from Hellhole is attached to my ponytail." I shake my head and the bouncer stupidly tightens his grip.

Jake stiffens and his lips curl, baring his teeth. "Let her go."

The five fighters move forward as one. The bouncer takes a step back, one hand on my ponytail, the other on my shoulder, holding me like a protective shield. Fighters forward. Bouncer back. Fighters forward. Bouncer back. Fighters growl. Bouncer whimpers.

"Maybe we should ask them what they're doing here first." I hold up my hands, palms forward as if I could stop the tidal wave of testosterone bearing down on us.

Jake grunts. "Fight first. Ask questions later."

The bouncer releases me with a barely audible whimper and my ponytail swings free.

"You got something to say?" I look over at Bob. "Better say it fast or I guarantee you won't get another chance. Renegade doesn't give a damn about the law."

Brave now that his hand is within inches of the door, Bob snarls, "We're gonna fucking sue their asses. We got a doctor who says we'll never work again. We got a lawyer who got their names from the police report and said we got a ten-million-dollar claim. Told us to bring these docs and hand 'em out."

Fighters fall back with a collective whimper. Apparently nothing is more terrifying than a lawsuit.

"Unbelievable." My hands find my hips. "Are you kidding me?"

Emboldened by the fighters' collective terror, Bob takes a step forward and waves some documents in the air, but at waist height and awkwardly because of the cast. The fighters cringe and shrink back as if they were made of Kryptonite.

Oh for...

"Give me those." I stalk over to Bob, stopping only a foot away and acutely aware that Jake is now hovering by my side.

"Easy, baby." He rests a hand on my shoulder when I snatch the documents away. Only then do I take note of my heaving chest and my tight jaw. Hell hath no fury like a woman whose friends are being threatened with a totally bogus lawsuit by gold diggers with no conscience, even less sense, and a terrible attorney. After giving the documents a cursory glance, I roll my eyes.

"First," I spit out, "since you are involved in the proceedings, you can't serve legal documents. So...bad legal advice right there. Second, in case you didn't notice, you were engaged in *criminal activity* when you broke your arms, if they are really even broken, which I totally doubt. Third, this"—I wave one of the documents at Bob—"is not a proper lawsuit. Again, bad legal advice, or maybe you thought you'd just come over here with a pretend lawsuit and try and shake my friends down. Not gonna happen. Finally, I just may decide to file a civil lawsuit against you for smacking me around like a rag doll, so you may actually want to find yourself a good attorney for that and your criminal trial."

Bob narrows his eyes. "You sound like a fucking attorney. Are you an attorney?"

My mouth opens and closes. Am I an attorney? I don't have a job and no chance of finding one, at least not in California.

"She's an attorney and a damn good one." Although Jake's voice is cool and calm, I can hear the telltale tremor of a man on the edge of losing control. "She worked at one of the biggest law firms in the state and she was one of their best and brightest. She's damn smart, a crackerjack litigator, and she knows every trick in the book. She's gonna destroy you."

"Yeah." The fighters punch their fists in the air and cheer as one.

"Uh…Jake." Aside from the fact I have no law firm and no insurance, I haven't even agreed to take on the fighters as clients. But Jake is on a roll.

"She'll put you on the stand and carve out every last detail of your sordid lives until you're a quivering mess on the floor."

"Yeah," chant the fighters.

"She'll rack up your legal bill so high you'll wish you'd run screaming the night she walked into your bar. She'll run that case into the ground until you crawl in here begging for mercy."

"Yeah." The fighters whoop and cheer like we've already won the case.

"Jake…"

"'Manda, 'manda, 'manda." Rampage starts up his humiliating chant and then glares at Bob and the bouncer. "We got 'manda. You got nothin'. Now GIT."

They "git."

Jake watches them for all of two seconds and then turns to Fuzzy.

"Man sees his girl being roughed up in his place of relaxation, sees someone dragging her around by her hair…that considered provocation?"

His girl? "Don't answer that," I bark at Fuzzy. He and Jake share a look and then Jake snorts.

"Thought so."

The door opens. Slams. Jake is gone. Rampage with him. And Obsidian.

I collapse onto the couch and slap my hand to my forehead. "They're going to get hit with a real lawsuit if they actually break any arms. I'm pretty sure those two were faking their injuries."

"But even if they weren't, you'll get us out of it, won't you?" Homicide takes a seat beside me. "I mean, me and the wife got a baby on the way. I can't afford a big shot attorney and I sure as heck can't afford ten million dollars. None of us can."

"Don't worry." I try to calm the agitated fighters around me. "It's a totally bogus lawsuit."

"But what if it isn't? What if they do find a good attorney? You gotta do something, Amanda." Blade Saw's voice rises as he flips through the documents. "You have to take our case…"

The front door slams behind us and a brush of cold air sends a shiver down my spine. I cut Blade Saw off mid-rant. "I quit my job. And I've been blacklisted. No firm will hire me."

"So start your own firm. You always talked about it." Jake walks toward us, all cool and calm as if he didn't just chase after two lunatics and probably beat them to death.

My own firm? How many billable hours did I waste daydreaming about my own firm while at Farnsworth & Tillman? A firm where we would have time for pro bono cases. A firm where the staff wouldn't wear flight-attendant style uniforms. My employees wouldn't live to serve. No shrimp at the firm cafeteria. No cameras in the hallways. No glass walls. No sleeping pods. No logos shouting FAT FAT FAT.

No money.

All my savings have gone toward my student loans. My only asset of value is my grandmother's house. Not something I would ever sell.

The dream will have to stay a dream. Revenge will definitely be a dish served cold.

"Did you break any bones in the thirty seconds you've been gone?" My facetious tone gains me a couple of raised eyebrows.

"He hurt you."

My hand flies to my mouth, and I shoot out of my seat. "Please tell me you're kidding. The bouncer just tugged my ponytail. It was no big deal."

Jake cups my jaw and brushes his thumb over my cheek. "It was a big deal to me."

My fingers hover over his bicep, bulging from beneath the sleeve of his shirt and a thrill of fear races through me. "Did you…really? That fast?"

He catches my hand, pressing his lips to my knuckles, and my body throbs in response to his touch.

"One of them got away. The other got so scared he pissed himself five feet out the door, then passed out. No point breaking bones if he can't feel the pain."

I lift an eyebrow in mock reproach. "Of course."

Jake laughs and releases my hand. "So, your own firm…you'll need capital. You can ask Max…er Torment. I'm sure he'll be happy to help you, and if not, Doc and I can twist his arm."

"He's a venture capitalist, not a bank," I say softly. "This is the kind of thing banks do."

Jake shrugs. "So he'll invest in your firm and take a return when you earn money. Same as investing in any business. I'll talk to Doc and get the best time to set something up."

"Whoa!" I hold up my hands. "First of all, she's my best friend. If anyone talks to her, it will be me. And second, I haven't said I would do it."

"Look at their pathetic faces." Jake gestures to the assembled fighters. On cue they all affect sad expressions, mouths turned down, brows furrowed.

My lips quiver with a repressed smile. "They couldn't look pathetic if they tried."

"They can't afford big law firm fees," Jake continues. "They stuck out their necks for you. Don't you want to get back to doing what you do best but the way you want to do it?"

"I never said…" But I cut myself off. My life has been one goalpost after another. I've never stopped to think about what I really wanted. Maybe it's time I did. I don't have to follow the family tradition and become a partner at a big law firm at the age of thirty-two. I could run my own firm. I could help people with their problems instead of helping companies shuffle their money around. I could start a lawsuit against Farnsworth, put him in his place, and repair my reputation. How could my father not be proud?

"I saw you watching Shilla the Killa fight," Jake says. "I'm sure Torment will waive your club fees if you want to do some training, maybe get into the ring one day, and the guys will be happy to help you out if you take on their case. Then you'll never have to worry about Hellhole scumbags."

My body stills. "Me fight?"

He moves his hand to my jaw, a lingering brush of his thumb over my cheek. "You've always had a fighting spirit."

Learn to fight. Not because it's a client networking opportunity or because it would look good on a CV, but because I want to. I could walk with confidence knowing I can defend myself. I could be part of a world that has nothing to do with law and everything to do with friendship and camaraderie and being the best you can be.

"Okay. I'll give it a shot."

A slow, warm smile spreads across Jake's face. He leans down and his lips hover over mine. I hold my breath, waiting, hoping for the kiss I don't want, the kiss I do, the kiss that never comes.

His lips brush over my forehead and he ruffles my hair.

Then we go for burgers.

All of us.

Chapter 6
You're a dangerous man

THE HAIGHT-ASHBURY DISTRICT, ONCE the center of San Francisco's hippie movement and now an eclectic neighborhood filled with exclusive boutiques, vintage clothing stores, and hip restaurants, is not the first place I would have chosen to set up my new law firm. The just-rolled-out-of-bed vibe is about as far from the corporate rat race I have lived and breathed in the city center for the last few years.

The contrast is put into stark relief when Max's driver pulls over to the side of the road and Max steps out of the vehicle. Resplendent in a chic Armani suit, he is immediately verbally assaulted by a motley group of panhandlers congregated around the steps of one of the crumbling Victorian buildings across the road. Of course, all it takes is one look from über alpha Max to send them scurrying down the street.

Makayla sighs as she reaches for the door handle. "He's always doing that. Sometimes he doesn't realize just how intimidating a look can be."

I glance through the window at Max, now leaning against the vehicle, his arms folded across his massive chest. "Oh, I think he knows. And he enjoys it. Maybe a little too much."

Max's driver opens the passenger door and Makayla and I step out onto the sidewalk. A group of neo-punks walks past us and snickers at the sleek, black Mercedes wedged between two rusted out Volkswagen Beetles.

"Maybe this isn't such a good idea," I say as Makayla and I follow Max across the street. "I mean…Hippie Land? This is where Max thinks I should open a law office?"

Max doesn't even turn around. "Yes. And there it is."

My heart sinks as I follow Max's gaze to the crumbling, three-story

Victorian building across the street. Decorated with peeling gingerbread scrollwork and painted a brilliant robin's egg blue, it fits in well with the other buildings on the street. Unfortunately, it is not quite the glass and steel tribute to modernity I had imagined for my first law firm.

"Good location. Safe. Accessible. Lots of parking." Max motions us across the street. "And I guarantee you'll get a good deal from the landlord if you ask nicely."

Makayla snickers and my skin prickles. Oh God. She's up to something. Again. As if it wasn't hard enough to go to Max's office with my business plan and ask him to invest in my law firm, she now wants me to beg for cheap rent too. My already-bruised pride cringes at the thought. If Makayla hadn't threatened to disown me as a friend, I wouldn't have called Max in the first place.

"I don't need a whole building." My steps slow. "Just an office. Preferably something small and cheap, but modern and professional. And without vagrants decorating the steps." I gesture toward a scruffy man hunched on the stairs. "He looks like he needs a bed and a hot meal."

Max's face tightens. "He does."

Puzzled, I near the object of Max's derision and my breath catches in my throat.

Jake.

But not like I've ever seen him before. He's wearing a black baseball cap backward and pulled low over his forehead, hiding his blond curls. His AC/DC T-shirt is worn and frayed and his jeans show more thigh than my tiniest dress.

He glances up and his gaze fixes on me. Dull eyes, bleary. A perfect match to his unshaven jaw. How can a man change so drastically in only a few days?

"What happened?"

Max sighs. "He's running himself down trying to balance fight training with the company. You can only run on adrenaline for so long."

Jake straightens as we approach. His gaze flickers from Max to me and then back to Max. "I thought you said you had someone interested in renting the property. I don't have time for socializing."

Max folds his arms. "Here she is."

Jake turns away and his voice drops to a low grumble as he confronts Max. "I told you before this wasn't a good idea."

AWKWARD. I glare at Makayla and she gives me a sympathetic cringe.

"It's okay." I raise my voice loud enough for them to hear me. "The office space I proposed in my business plan will do fine. I was looking for corporate and professional, not quirky and full of character. I had already spoken to the landlord…"

"But it won't be fine for Jake or for the district." Max frowns and shakes his head. "He needs a tenant or the building and most of this block will be torn down by developers."

In response to my questioning look, Jake shrugs. "Peter entered into a verbal agreement with Duel Properties to level this block and turn it into a shopping center. Goddamn travesty. But if the buildings are occupied, it will slow the process long enough for the city to consider the residents' application to have the street marked as a historic district. The minute I took over, I started dragging my feet over the agreement to give the residents a chance to get their application together. In response, Duel Properties started the lawsuit I brought to you."

My law brain kicks into gear. "Is the company legally obligated to…?"

"I know what I'm doing," he snaps.

Taken aback, I stare. Jake stares back. His eyes are bloodshot, jaw tight. Exhaustion has drawn creases in his impossibly handsome face. Without thinking, I smooth my thumb over his furrowed brow and along his jaw, scratchy with a five o'clock shadow.

"You're not looking so good."

He captures my hand, twining his fingers with my mine and rests it against his cheek. His eyes close for the briefest moment and then he lets me go.

"I just need sleep. It's been a coupla days." His voice is still gruff, but his tone softens. "Maybe a vacation, too."

"And a few burgers?"

A smile tugs at his lips, transforming his face from haggard into handsomely haggard, and my insides melt.

"Burgers are always good." He pulls open the door. "Come in and take a look."

Makayla pushes past me and steps inside. Max follows behind her. But I hesitate.

"You don't have to do this, Jake. I totally understand. I don't want things to be uncomfortable between us…"

"Amanda."

"…and having me for a tenant would mean we would have to see each other, which I know you don't want because of how things ended between us, and how you just dropped me off the other night…"

"Amanda."

"…and that's probably for the best. I'm sure you've moved on, and I need to move on…have moved on. We aren't the same people…"

"Amanda."

"…and it's not the kind of place…"

He cuts me off with a kiss. Soft and sweet, his lips press against mine, awakening old memories. Our first kiss in the storage room in the fitness studio, and then our second stretched out together on the mats after everyone left and we were alone. Two months of gentle kisses, tender kisses, warming my body but never breaching the walls around my heart.

My hands tremble by my sides. Do I push him away or pull him close? Do I want sweet kisses wrapped in guilty memories, or do I want something new and someone who doesn't want what I cannot give?

And then Jake decides for me.

With a groan, he threads his fingers through my hair, holding me still as his tongue plunges into my mouth. Sweet becomes demanding, soft becomes hard. He kisses me thoroughly, remorselessly, leaving no part of my mouth untouched. My blood turns to lava and races molten through my veins.

"You're right." His lips burn a trail across my cheek. "I'm not the same person. Peter's death changed me. Now I see how short life can be. There's no time to dwell on the past. There's no time for regret. We have to move forward." He steps back and holds out his hand. "Might as well go inside and you can see why I didn't think this was a good idea."

Still reeling from his kiss, I just stare. "You kissed me."

"Yeah." His face softens and he gives an apologetic shrug. "I've been wanting to do that since you first walked into the meeting room at your old law firm. Guess I needed to get it out of my system."

Ah. Regret and not reconciliation. An end. Not a beginning. For a moment, I am almost overwhelmed with the need to cry. But years of forced stoicism come to my rescue, and I just nod and grit my teeth, counting the seconds before I can convince Makayla to leave. "Sure."

Jake pulls open the door, and I step into an elaborately tiled hallway. Red velvet wallpaper hangs off the walls in long strips. An ornate chandelier clings precariously to the ceiling, threatening to crash onto the worn brocade carpet covering the hardwood floor. I inhale the musty aroma of mildew and stifle a sneeze.

"It needs a lot of work." Jake crosses the hallway and pushes aside a rotted wooden door. "Check out this room. It's even worse."

A soft "oh" escapes my lips as the tired majesty of what must have been a living room is revealed in all its glory. High ceilings, sweeping sash windows, and a magnificent tiled fireplace crowned with a heavy oak mantel are the focal points of the room. Dark wood paneling and the rich jewel tones of the dusty, soft furnishings lend to the ambiance of an old-world gentleman's club, as do the scents of mothballs and wood smoke.

Max and Makayla disengage from an intimate clinch in the corner, and I stifle a groan. Seriously? Even after two years they can't seem to get enough of each other. Usually I don't even notice, but today my heart squeezes in longing and I breathe out an exasperated sigh. "Get a room."

"We did." Makayla grins, and then her smile fades. "What's wrong?"

"Nothing." After over twenty years of friendship, Makayla can read almost every nuance of my expression. Unfortunately, tact isn't one of her defining traits.

"It's pretty bad, isn't it," Max says, oblivious to my emotional disquiet. "Everything is falling apart. The study behind us is even worse."

Grateful for the opportunity to have a moment alone, I skirt around the sheet-draped furniture and enter the adjoining study. Floor-to-ceiling bookshelves line one wall and a huge bay window overlooks a jungle of a back garden. The orange fingers of dusk settle on a ridiculous, massive Victorian-style couch covered in a busy pattern of birds, leaves, flowers, and grapes.

I'm in love.

Jake steps into the room and pokes at a wall. Plaster crumbles onto the floor. "This is why I can't rent it out and why I never even thought of offering it to you." He scrubs his hands over his face and then turns to me. "It needs serious renovation and I don't have the time to put in the work. No one else…"

He cuts himself off and frowns, studying me as if I were a curiosity in the zoo. His gaze flicks around the room, then back to me and his frown deepens. "You like it."

Caught off guard, my breath catches in my throat. Am I that transparent? "I…uh…yeah, it's an awesome place, but not for an office. I mean, you've been in Farnsworth & Tillman. This doesn't really scream 'serious professional.'"

Jake's face softens. "But it screams 'Amanda.' It reminds me of your old apartment and, to some extent, your grandmother's house. You must have inherited your quirky sense of style from her."

I'm sure he can't imagine how much his words mean to me. Just the thought that I am somehow still connected to her makes my throat tighten with emotion. I twist my bracelet around and around my wrist. "Yeah, we had the same taste."

"Then it's perfect."

"Jake…" I hesitate. I love it. I want it. But it's all wrong. Just like Jake and me. "I would love to, but I just can't. I need to project a certain image and crumbling Victorian with a hint of country chic isn't it."

He gives me a considered look. "What if I hauled the Redemption crew in here to fix it up? I got lots of favors I can call in. Get enough guys and they can do all the hard work…stripping the walls, refinishing the floors, rewiring, putting up the drywall… Not much we can do about the structure and moldings, but you could do it up modern inside, make it just like Farnsworth & Tillman if you want." He twists his lips to the side. "Still…it's a lot of work…"

Oh God. Suddenly I want it so bad I can barely breathe, even though it's totally wrong for a law firm. Now I'm worried he'll change his mind. *Pleasepleasepleasepleaseplease.* "I would help," I say into the silence. "And Makayla… Probably Max too, if we told him it was dangerous and Makayla might get hurt."

Damn. Now I sound desperate. Not good. I rest a hand on the worn oak desk and try to look casual, like I get kissed, brushed off, and teased with the house of my most-secret-inner-desires-that-is-so-wrong-for-a-business every day. Hmmm. Maybe too casual if I'm trying to convey a mild interest. I drop my hand to the side. Now I look like a soldier. How about behind my back? Oh God. Now I look like one of my professors. In front? Nope. He'll think I'm penitent. I resort to the tried and true, brushing of the hair over the shoulder.

Jake's eyes sparkle, amused. He leans back against the floor-to-ceiling bookshelf and folds his arms. Even in his worn, ripped clothes, he makes my mouth water: jeans hanging low on narrow hips, T-shirt torn just enough to reveal a ripple of muscle on his chest, and biceps bulging from tight sleeves. I am almost launched into a torrid fantasy where I shred his clothes in a frenzy of lust.

"If the guys come over and fix it up…will you rent it?"

A shiver races down my spine, but I play it cool and twirl a lock of hair around my finger. "Are you sure you want me? I mean, it's a lot of work and I have another office lined up so don't think I'm desperate or…"

"Yes. I want you."

Every bit of warmth rushes to my center, but I hesitate. Do I want the place bad enough to endure the torture of having Jake for a landlord? Sure, he's been kind and helpful, but he clearly still hasn't forgiven me. And maybe I shouldn't be so quick to forgive him. How many times did I try to talk to him about what happened? How many times was I rebuffed?

Simply out of curiosity, I ask, "What's the rent?"

"Whatever you want to pay."

My eyebrow lifts and I fiddle with my hair, twisting it in a knot. "If I was interested, I would want to pay whatever you were asking of the other people who came to see the place."

Jake names a figure I am sure is nothing near what he could get from someone else. I tell him so. He shrugs and says it isn't negotiable. I offer what I was going to pay for the other office. His eyes harden and he lowers his initial offer. I begrudgingly capitulate and dance a secret inner dance of joy.

"You're a dangerous man," I say after we haggle through a few details. "First you convince me to leave my house and venture back out into the world. Then you convince me to start a business. And now, I'm renting the least likely place I ever expected to see myself running a law firm. What's next?"

A slow, sensual smile curves his lips. "If I told you what I had planned, you'd run for the hills." He closes the distance between us and runs his fingers through my hair, working out the tangle my fiddling has created as if he couldn't bear to see it anymore. His touch is gentle, his breath sweet on my cheek. Maybe he doesn't like tangles. Or maybe he needed to get that out of his system too.

~~~

"Move that ass, Westwood."

Fuzzy bellows the order like a pumped-up drill sergeant and I join the class in yet another soul-destroying sprint across Redemption's overly long warehouse.

Good as his word, Jake arranged with Max for the cost of my classes to be covered in exchange for my new role as Redemption's unofficial attorney. Although Max already has a stable of attorneys at his beck and call to deal with his business matters, he spread the word in the gym that if anyone needs general advice, they can come to me.

And I already have one new client. Except now, instead of shuffling his feet and mumbling about needing an attorney because the bank is foreclosing on his parent's house, Fuzzy is screaming abuse like he's trying to get us ready for the front line instead of just getting us fit.

"Come on, ya buncha losers," he screams. "Whaddya thinking? That we're having an afternoon stroll with Grandpa? MOVE."

My legs wobble as we turn and race across the mats. Foolishly, I slow my pace to catch my breath.

"Westwood. You've already had a warning. You need a kick in the ass too?"

"Gimme a break, Fuzz." I whine a breath. "I've spent the last few years in a…"

"What did you call me?" His usually cheerful face turns an unusual shade of purple.

"Um…Fuzz?" A warning prickle creeps over my skin, and I look around for someone to tell me what I've done wrong. Curiously, the entire class is huddled down at the other end of the warehouse and looking in the other direction. A few fighters sparring on the mats smirk. Over by the free weights, a betraying Jake is talking to Obsidian when he's supposed to be protecting me from Fuzzy's wrath.

"In this class, you address me as Sir," Fuzzy shouts.

Swallowing hard, I give him a mock salute. "Yes, sir."

Fuzzy scowls. "Not funny. On the floor, gimme twenty-five push-ups. NOW."

"Someone is suffering from delusions of grandeur."

"FIFTY."

With a loud sigh, I drop to my knees, lean forward, and place my hands on the mat. Fuzzy kneels beside me and hangs his head upside down in my line of vision.

"What the fuck are you doing?"

"It's a woman's push-up." I grunt my annoyance. "We have a different center of gravity. It's just as hard for me to do the push-up from my knees as it is for you to do a push-up with your toes on the mat."

"Jesus fucking Christ." Fuzzy clambers to his feet and hollers for Shilla the Killa. A few moments later she joins us, a grin plastered across her face.

"Amanda here thinks women need to do push-ups on their knees." His derisory tone sends a shiver down my spine. "Gimme twenty…man style."

Shayla snorts a laugh and drops her cut, muscular body down to the mat. Her thick, brown ponytail swings violently over her shoulder as she does twenty perfect, man-style push-ups without breaking a sweat.

"You want another set with me clapping my hands between

each push-up?" She looks over at Fuzzy and grins. "Or maybe with one hand?"

"Nope. We're good. Dismissed." Fuzzy gives her a high five. Shayla's cheeks glow pink and she bounds back to the fight ring. Fuzzy glares at me sitting back on my heels and points down.

"You gonna keep scowlin' at me, or are you gonna do the push-ups? The class is called Get Fit or Die for a reason."

I glare at Fuzzy. I don't like him anymore. He's mean, mean, mean. It's like he had a personality transplant when he stepped into the gym. I wish I had never signed up for Get Fit or Die. I wish I had never set foot in Redemption. I wish I hadn't had burritos for lunch. They're weighing me down.

With a sigh, I drop to my knees. "I can do maybe five…*sir*."

He folds his arms and then gestures to someone behind me. "Gotta girl here with a lotta attitude. Needs to do fifty push-ups before she rejoins the class. Can you watch her for me?"

"I dunno." Jake joins Fuzzy, a smile curling his lips. "That scowl on her face is kind of scary. What if she attacks me?"

Fuzzy laughs. "Don't think you have to worry about that any more than you'd worry about getting scratched by a declawed kitten."

As I open my mouth to protest, Fuzzy holds up one finger. "One more word outta you, and you'll be doing the push-ups with Renegade on your back."

Mmmm. I picture Jake lying on top of me—naked—as I struggle and strain to push myself off the mat, my body slick with sweat, my ass rubbing up against…

"So…fifty push-ups?" Jake stands in front of me arms folded, legs spread. My kneeling position puts my eyes directly in line with the bulge beneath his fight shorts.

Oh God. So big. Look away. Look away.

My cheeks burn and I stare at the mat. But maybe it's not all him. Fighters usually wear a cup. He must be wearing a cup. Of course, he's wearing a cup. I look up just as he squats down beside me. Now I am treated to a close-up view of his lean, ripped body glistening with sweat and tight thigh muscles bunched under red fight shorts and…

Nope. He's not wearing a cup. That's all him. How could I have forgotten an important detail like that?

"Buncha deadbeats," Fuzzy yells at the cowering class across the gym. "Did I tell you to stop running? MOVE."

"Sir, yes, sir," they chant.

Ah. That's why Fuzzy was still pissed off after I said "sir." I only said it once. Nice of no one to tell me.

"Amanda. Push-ups." Jake's voice drops low with warning and I immediately drop into position.

After five man-style push-ups, I collapse on the mat and moan. "Kill me now."

Jake laughs. "I'll let you take a break because I'm such a nice guy."

"Gee, thanks." I rest my chin in my hands and look up at him. "You'll be here all night if you have to wait for me to do fifty push-ups. I thought you had classes to teach."

He brushes a finger over his bottom lip, considering. "True. I only have half an hour. Maybe it's your form." He leaves the weight bench and stands over me. "Here, I'll help you."

"I don't need help…"

But before I can finish my sentence, his feet are on either side of me and his hands are firm around my hips. "Yes you do. Up we go."

I push myself into the torturous push-up position and Jake holds me in place, his fingers pressed tight against my hips. My body goes from hot to boiling in a heartbeat.

Jake gives me pointers about hand and foot placement, weight distribution, and elbow angle. He is thorough and patient. A good teacher. I go down. I go up. He takes most of my weight, his hands tightening when I wobble. The most erotic form of torture I have ever experienced is so delicious I don't want it to end. But my body has other ideas.

"Keep going. You're up to twenty," he murmurs when I begin to shake.

Oh God. That voice. Deep and warm, his voice wraps around me like a blanket, reminding me of dark sultry nights, twisted sheets, and…oh. My chest tightens and a rush of emotion sucks away the last of my strength. But before I can collapse on the mat, Jake slides his hands around me and pulls me up off the floor and against his bare chest.

For a long moment we don't move. Fuzzy glances over, raises an eyebrow, and then crooks his finger gesturing me back to the class. But I can't tear myself away. Longing suffuses every pore of my body bringing with it the deep ache of desire.

Curiously, Jake doesn't seem to be in a hurry to let me go. His hands tighten around my rib cage, his thumbs only an inch below my breasts. I tilt my head back and look up at him. His sensuous lips are only a whisper away. What would it be like if I had a little lick?

As if he can read my mind, his eyes darken to an azure blue and his body stiffens. So warm. So hard. I feel so safe in his arms.

"Amanda…" His voice is low, husky, and so damn sexy. Heart pounding, I lick my lips and strain up the tiniest bit.

"Is this a new kind of push-up?" I murmur, unable to resist teasing him. "I'm not sure where to push."

He growls deep in this throat. "You started pushing when you walked into the gym dressed to leave little to the imagination."

Sweat trickles down my spine. Whether from his hard, hot body pressed up against me or the exertion of the push-ups, I don't know. "Sports bra and gym shorts? I'm dressed like all the other women."

Jake leans down and presses a kiss to my neck that sends all sorts of wrong messages to the right parts of my body. "You don't look like the other women. You're all soft and sexy and fucking cute when you're frowning at Fuzz behind his back. And none of the other women needed my hands." He caresses my bare midriff while his thumbs move higher to trace the underside of my sports-bra-squashed breasts.

"Your hands were very…helpful." Moisture pools between my thighs and I swallow hard and look over my shoulder, unable to stop myself from pushing him. "Now…not so much, unless you're planning on getting me down on the mat for something other than push-ups."

Jake groans. "God, don't tempt me. When I saw you on your knees in front of Fuzz, and then doing your push-ups all wrong with your sexy little ass in the air…" He draws in a ragged breath. "I promised myself I wouldn't touch you, but when I saw you needed help…"

"I still need help." I lean up and press a soft kiss to his cheek.

His breath catches and he freezes, his fingers digging into my waist as a pained expression crosses his face.

"You're off the hook for the last thirty. I'll tell Fuzzy you gave it your best shot." He lets me go so abruptly I stagger back.

And suddenly I'm alone on the mat, heart pounding, mouth dry, masochistic streak glowing like a beacon in the night. I only have myself to blame.

Fuzzy says nothing when I rejoin the class. For the next half hour, he tortures us with circuit training, weight lifting, and yet more running. I throw myself into every exercise as I try to exorcise the memory of Jake's arms around me. By the time Fuzzy calls it quits, the entire class is groaning on the floor. Sex is the furthest thing from my mind.

Shayla and Sandy laugh as they stop beside me to refill their water bottles from the cooler.

"He went easy on you today." Shayla's gaze darts over to Fuzzy and then back to me. "But he'll get you in shape. I thought I was fit until I took one of his advanced classes. The next day I couldn't get out of bed. But now look at me." She flexes both arms and her biceps bulge.

"He's a sadist," I mutter. "I think he enjoys seeing us suffer in class."

Shayla holds out a hand to help me up off the mat. "Maybe, but he's a hot sadist."

"I'll tell you who's hot," Sandy sighs. "Renegade. He's so sexy when he's teaching. Patient but demanding." She glances at me out of the corner of her eye and smirks. "Too bad he has a new girlfriend, some cute little brunette, or so I heard."

My already bruised heart sinks into my stomach. Oh God. No wonder he pushed me away. He has a girlfriend. Of course he has a girlfriend. He's the hottest guy in Redemption. He must have women falling at his feet.

"Hey, Amanda!" Fuzzy jogs up to us, a smile on his evil face. "Good class today. I know it was your first time and you put in a great effort. You'll be in that fight ring in no time."

Totally disconcerted by his encouragement and warm smile, I mock a puzzled frown. "Sorry, do I know you? You look just like the evil drill sergeant from my Get Fit or Die class. Or maybe you are you but you have a split personality."

Fuzzy snorts a laugh and then slaps Shayla on the back. "Shill. Thanks for helping out today."

"No problem." Her face brightens.

"Later, girls. Got another class to teach."

Shayla's face falls as he walks away. "He thinks I'm one of the guys," she says morosely. "He treats me the same as he treats Blade Saw or Hammer Fist. A punch in the arm. A slap on the back. The occasional thumbs-up. Sandy suggested I wear this pink sports bra today, but it obviously didn't work. I'll bet if I showed up naked, he wouldn't even notice."

Pushing my own troubles aside, I give her a sympathetic smile. "Maybe he doesn't know you're interested. Guys can be shy about making a move if they don't get any signals from you. No one wants to be shot down."

She gives me a look of pure dejection. "It goes both ways."

"Yeah. But sometimes if you want something bad enough, you have to take a risk."

Chapter 7
I LIKE HOLES IN SWEATS

"BEER ME, BABE."

Fuzzy holds up his hand and I toss a cold beer through the air. Instantly, a dozen hands go up.

"You're supposed to be renovating," I yell over the deafening sounds of AC/DC as the sea of hopeful Redemption fighters, spread out over the main floor of Jake's Haight house, waggle their hands for a beer. "The party starts after."

"Chill, 'manda. This is the party." Rampage grabs the last beer from the cooler and downs it without taking a breath. I take a step back, awaiting the inevitable. Rampage courteously delivers the inevitable in Hammer Fist's face. Hammer Fist slaps him on the head. Rampage grabs the paintbrush from Hammer Fist's hand and paints a line across the floor. Blade Saw shouts encouragement as Hammer Fist makes a big show of stepping over the line and screaming abuse at Rampage. He delivers his signature blows to Rampage's stomach. Rampage belches again, louder this time and in Hammer Fist's ear. Fists fly. Paint cans spill. Fighters cheer.

Max steps into the room and lifts an eyebrow. Almost immediately, everything is back to normal. As Max's second-in-command, Fuzzy keeps everyone on a tight leash, but he doesn't wield even a fraction of Max's power. The only fighter who comes close is Jake. Not for the first time do I envy my best friend.

But hey, this is definitely a party. Beers all around.

"Your new office is going to look great." Makayla gives my shoulders a squeeze. "I can't believe how much they've done in twelve hours or that thirty guys showed up. I wish Max and I weren't going away tomorrow. I would have loved to help you shop for furniture and decorate."

"Don't remind me." I swallow past the lump in my throat. "Who does Max think he is, dragging you on a month-long holiday across the world? Maybe you have better things to do than hang out on exotic beaches or in fancy hotels. What if there is a major accident and the city needs every paramedic to help out? Or what if Drake can't cover your shifts at Redemption? He should be thinking about the people who need you instead of taking you away when they need you the most."

"Awww, honey." She hugs me so hard tears leak from my eyes. "It's not like I won't have my phone. We can still text, and you know you can call me anytime. I'm always here for you. I've helped you avoid Jake all day…"

"By agreeing with him that I should work alone in the kitchen?"

Makayla takes one end of the empty cooler and motions for me to take the other. "By keeping him away from the kitchen when he wanted to check up on you. You don't even appreciate all I do for you." We lug the cooler into the kitchen for a refill.

"I do appreciate you, which is why it'll be so hard when you're gone."

Someone turns up the music and the house vibrates to the nu metal version of "Ice, Ice, Baby" as we load up the cooler and spend a few minutes chatting about her upcoming holiday.

Over the pounding bass of Disturbed, I hear the slam of the front door, greetings and cheers, and then Jake's voice rises above the buzz of power tools. "Quitting time. Everyone out back for the barbecue." Damn. He's back from his supply run way too soon.

The door bursts open and fighters stampede through the kitchen, pausing long enough to pick up the refilled cooler and empty the fridge of barbecue fixings.

"You coming?" Makayla grabs a box of hamburger buns and heads for the door. "It's supposed to be our bon voyage barbecue. I won't be able to enjoy myself if I know you're still working."

"I think I'll just finish up here and then go home."

Her eyebrow lifts. "This is really about Jake, isn't it? You've been avoiding him all day. Max said he hadn't heard about a girlfriend, so why don't you talk to him? Or are you planning to sabotage this relationship like you did last time, except you haven't even given this one a chance?"

Frowning, I grab a can of paint and a stir stick. "We don't have a relationship, and I almost ruined whatever fledgling friendship we'd started to build by pushing too hard and forcing him to make it clear he's not interested. And no wonder. I haven't changed. I couldn't give myself to him before, and I won't be able to give myself now."

Makayla shakes her head and then pushes herself to her feet. "You're dressed in torn sweats, covered in dirt, and painting cupboards in a dilapidated Victorian house that is soon to be your own law firm. We've been friends since kindergarten. I didn't even know you owned sweats or would even contemplate working anywhere other than a big law firm. So don't tell me you haven't changed."

"He's brushed me off. Twice."

"I know," Makayla says softly. "But did it occur to you he might just want to be cautious? You can't blame him for trying to protect himself. I can tell you from my experience with Max: he may be a tough fighter on the outside, but inside he's just as vulnerable as we are."

She grabs the box and pushes open the door. The faint sound of someone yelling "Hey, Makayla, lemme grab your buns" is cut off by Max's low growl, the thud of a fist hitting flesh, and Makayla's high-pitched shriek telling Max that Homicide was just joking around.

Fifteen minutes pass and then the door squeaks open.

"Don't move."

Totally immersed in painting the cupboard, I freeze mid–paint stroke as Jake's deep voice rings out behind me.

"What? Am I doing something wrong?"

He closes the distance between us and runs his finger along the waistband of my gym pants, sending delicious tingles up my spine. Then he slides his hands around my waist, bared by the rise of my T-shirt as I stretch to reach the top of the cupboard with my paintbrush.

"Yes. You look too damn sexy. Do you know what it does to a man when he catches a glimpse of something he isn't meant to see?"

"I hope it makes him tell the woman she can call off the panic attack and drop her arm." I boldly do just that. "I also hope it makes him decide his hands might be of better use somewhere other than around her waist."

Jake slides his fingers over my hips, resting them just above my mound and his voice drops to a low growl. "I could make use of them here."

"So says the man who turned down a good offer just the other night at Redemption." I remove his hands and turn to face him, putting on a brave face while inside I seethe. Who does he think he is coming on to me after brushing me off?

"No games, Jake. You made your position clear. I got that. I'm not interested in being screwed around."

He presses his hands against the cupboards on either side of my head, caging me with his body. "What are you interested in?"

"Moving on," I say honestly.

His pulse throbs in his neck and his eyes harden. "With whom?"

"No one right now."

He gives a satisfied grunt as if I had just cleared up a question in his mind. "Everyone is out back having a good time. You should be there too."

"There's a lot of work to do. I want to get it done. The faster I open shop, the faster I can start my lawsuit against Farnsworth." I slip under his arm and edge along the counter.

"You've been working since six o'clock this morning."

Grabbing a clean cloth from the counter, I make an effort to wipe the dirt off my face. "I'm used to working long hours. I'm not afraid of hard work." But I am afraid of mercurial fighters who run hot one minute and cold the next.

His face softens, and he takes the cloth from my hand and holds it under the tap. The pipes gurgle when he turns the rusty faucet and water gushes out, skimming over the cloth and trickling into the sink below. Without warning, he lifts me and settles me on the counter.

"You don't have to work like that anymore." His voice is calm, soothing. I am momentarily lulled out of work mode and into heat mode as he eases his hips between my legs and reaches to turn off the faucet. "It's Saturday night. Time to relax and have fun." With a firm hand, he cups my jaw and then wipes the cloth gently over my nose, forehead, and cheeks.

His gentle touch, the warmth of his hand, his breath, minty and sweet, and his hard body nestled between my thighs all converge in an unbearable rush of sensation. I grab his wrist, forcing his hand away.

"Jake…I'm good. Really. There's so much to do. I'll come out when I'm done and I've cleaned myself up."

"I like you this way," he murmurs. "You look…cute. Real."

"Real?"

He brushes his thumb over my cheek. "Amanda without the armor. Your clothes, hair, makeup…nothing is perfect. It's just the real you. I never got to see the real you before."

Torn between being mortified and pleased, I reach for another cloth. "Real Amanda is covered in dirt and has holes in her sweats."

He traces a finger down my neck to rest in the hollow at the base of my throat. The room heats to one hundred degrees, and if I'm not mistaken, I hear the sound of my blood boiling.

"I like holes in sweats." His voice drops, husky and low, and his finger continues its downward journey into the vee of my shirt.

"Jake…"

He traces lightly over the crescent of my breast. "I like dirty girls," he whispers, his voice thick with desire. "I can't stay away."

Oh God. Every bit of warmth rushes to my center as his deep, sensual voice ignites one of my dark fantasies. Jake, straddling my bound body, growling commands, telling me what he's going to do to me in the filthiest language I know. A soft moan escapes my lips and we're back on the roller coaster again.

"This game you're playing confuses me," I say. His heart beats strong against my palm when I lay my hand over his chest.

"Me too."

"Then what are you doing?"

His eyes take on a feral gleam and my breasts tingle.

"Playing dirty." Tangling his hand in my hair, he tugs my head back, exposing my throat to the heated slide of his lips. "Sometimes you have to stop thinking too much and just go with it."

My breath comes in short pants as he sucks gently on the pulse at the base of my throat. Barely able to form a coherent thought for the pounding of blood in my temples, I scramble for sanity. "There's too much between us to just go with it. We need to talk…"

His hand closes in my hair, twisting roughly. "Lawyers talk. You don't look like a lawyer now. You look fucking sexy, and your mouth is all lush and pink and needing to be kissed. You want to talk, Amanda, or you want that kiss?" He nips the sensitive spot between my neck and shoulder blade.

Pleasure and pain meld together and I whimper as a heated rush of sensation floods my veins. "Kiss."

Jake smiles. "My dirty girl wants a dirty kiss." Holding my face, he slants his mouth over mine and kisses me.

Soft kiss. Sweet kiss. Warm, firm lips tasting faintly of coffee. His five o'clock shadow brushes my chin as his tongue eases my lips open to stroke against mine. My body melts against him as he explores my mouth, leaving nothing untouched. Tongues wind and tangle. Two years of fantasies coalesce in a single rasping breath.

"'S not so dirty," I mumble against his lips.

"Oh, you don't know how dirty I can be." Jake grips my hair and tugs my head back with a firm, hard yank, sending little bolts of lightning straight to my core. Then he kisses me hard and fast. Rough. His teeth scrape my bottom lip as his tongue dives deep, filling me, taking what I have to give and demanding more. The pounding of my heart shifts from lust to fear as he consumes me, and for a moment I worry he has forgotten I need to breathe.

When he breaks the kiss, I draw in a long, ragged breath. "You never kissed me like that before."

"You were never like this before." His fingers ease up my shirt, his thumb tracing over the crescent of my breasts. "Raw and open, vulnerable, needing my help. So fucking real."

My breath catches in my throat as he explores, cupping and squeezing my breasts and then teasing my nipples through my lace bra until they are tight, aching peaks.

"My clothes. Take them off."

Jake's sensual growl is the only warning I get before his hands slide around my rib cage to unhook my bra. Moments later, I am bared to him, my clothing a soft puddle on the counter, my skin on fire despite the cool night air whispering through the cracks in the window.

"Beautiful," he whispers as he palms my breasts. Then he bends down to tease my nipples with his clever mouth, nipping and sucking until I am panting and grinding against his erection, pressing against my throbbing sex.

"Fuck, baby. Tighten your legs around me and give me what you've got. You get off before I get into your pants, I'll give you a special treat."

"I hope that special treat is big and hard and lickable." I tighten my legs until he is nestled exactly where I need him to be and rock my hips against the bulge in his jeans. He loved my mouth on him before. I only had to lick my lips to find myself on my knees, his hand fisting my hair, his cock hot and heavy in my mouth.

Jake's nostrils flare and darken and he reaches for his belt. "Change of plans."

Before we can indulge in the change of plans, a door slams. My heart kicks into overdrive at the sound of heels clicking across the floor in the main reception room. Jake helps me tug on my clothes just before the door swings open.

"Jake, honey? Are you coming back out? Everyone is wondering what happened to you." The slender brunette who joins us in the kitchen is exactly who I pictured as Jake's perfect woman when I tortured myself night after night imagining who he was with. She has a tiny pixie face, porcelain skin, and high cheekbones. Gazing up at Jake with liquid brown eyes, she parts her ruby lips and leans up to kiss his cheek.

My blood turns to ice and my stomach clenches so tight I can barely breathe.

All cool and calm, Jake gives her a warm smile. "We'll be out in a sec. This is Amanda. She's my new tenant."

New tenant. Not friend or lover or even ex. I'm the new tenant. And she's…

"I'm Sia." She slides an arm around his bicep and leans in to give him a squeeze.

For a long, uncomfortable moment I simply can't speak. This must be the girlfriend Sandy told me about. So what is he doing in the kitchen with me?

A choked "Hi, Sia" is all I can manage before I slide off the counter. "I think I'll go check out that barbecue after all."

"Amanda." Jake's words fade away as I push open the back door and step out into the night.

First stop: Makayla. I spot her laughing it up with Rampage and Blade Saw beside an overgrown clump of weeds. I plaster a smile on my face and drag her away.

"You told me he didn't have a girlfriend."

Makayla frowns. "He doesn't. At least not that Max knows about."

"Her name is Sia."

"Oh." Her face pales and my stomach sinks. "Actually she is a girl and a friend but not a girlfriend in the traditional sense of the word. At least not that I've heard. He's more like a stand-in big brother for when Fuzzy's not around. Something bad happened to her a few years ago and Fuzzy never lets her go out alone."

I give a begrudging sniff. "They seem pretty close."

Makayla twists her lips to the side. "Well…they spend a lot of time together, but I've never seen them kiss or hold hands or be intimate in any way."

Jake and Sia choose this moment to join the party. When she clasps his hand and leads him over to the picnic table, my heart squeezes in my chest. "I can't stay here. We almost…in the kitchen…and now… It's too humiliating."

"No." Makayla grips my arm and rearranges her features into her cute scowl. "Talk to him. That was your problem before. Too much sex. Not enough talking."

Shaking her free, I take a step toward the exit. "If I talk to him, I'll hear things I don't want to hear. Better to leave now and imagine them than to stay and find out they're real."

Chapter 8
DO NOT OPEN

A WEEK GOES BY. The Redemption Renovation Extravaganza is a resounding success, as is my furniture and decorating shopping spree. My newly renovated office is clean and fresh and ready for clients.

Despite the Victorian fittings, I have decorated with corporate style. Navy and gray striped curtains hang from the windows in the massive reception room. Two navy couches and a wingback chair boast matching gray cushions and arm protectors. Glass tables, modern lighting, an abstract sculpture, and an abstract painting of navy and gray lines round out the look.

After two weeks of hard work and hours of financial analysis since agreeing to open the firm, I have started an eight-million-dollar civil lawsuit against Farnsworth for sexual harassment and effectively forcing me out of the firm. Max wrangled one of his litigation attorneys to help me with the finer details of preparing the complaint and to be on call to help when needed to compensate for my lack of experience. A security blanket. Max style.

The rich aroma of freshly brewed coffee reminds me that I'm wasting my third cup of the morning, and I take a sip and stare at the blank piece of paper on my desk that was supposed to be a completed and actionable marketing plan three hours ago.

"Excuse me. I'm here about the ad for an office assistant."

My head jerks up and my eyes widen when I catch sight of Penny in the doorway, neatly dressed in a peach pencil skirt, cream blouse, and a strand of pearls.

"Penny! What ad?"

Penny settles herself in the leather chair across from my desk. "I sensed you were about to advertise in the paper for a personal assistant. Here's my CV." She shoves a bundle of papers across the desk and smiles a cheeky Penny smile.

"What?" My brain is so busy playing catch up, it's forgotten to tell me what to say.

"Am I too late?" She looks over her shoulder and then leans forward and peers under my desk. "Did you already hire someone? Is she or he hiding somewhere?"

"What's going on?"

"If you're planning on dazzling clients with your wit, charm, and eloquence, you may wish to expand your vocabulary." Penny laughs and leans back in her chair. "Now, I can work eight until eight. Half an hour for lunch. On call weekends and evenings. I've taken a tour of the waiting room. A bit disappointing. It looks like a miniature Farnsworth & Tillman but with gray instead of teal. I also see you have mono-grammed everything. Again, very Farnsworth & Tillman. I thought you would have taken the opportunity to do something unique…something you. But we can work on that. The room to the side will serve nicely as my office, but until you have a receptionist, I'll sit out front."

My jaw drops to the desk. "But…but…what about Farnsworth & Tillman? You have a great job there. I can't pay you anywhere near what you are making with them. I can't give you the same benefits. I don't have big, exciting clients. And it's just me. No gossip. It's a lose-lose proposition all round."

"You'll need to work on your delivery for future interviews with office staff," she says lightly. "You're hiring people, not chasing them away."

"I don't understand."

Penny smiles. "You don't have to understand. I'm here and ready to work. Although you probably already know this, my favorite color is yellow. My favorite footie team is Man U. I love creamy desserts, shepherd's pie, and, of course, I drink tea. I'm a closet death metal fan. Single. No dependents. Family lives in England. I'm still switched into the Farnsworth & Tillman gossip network. And I've just had a lovely breakfast with a hard-bodied private investigator named Ray who is looking to take on some extra work. He'll be here later this afternoon."

"Ray?" My mouth drops open. "Ray is going to work for me too? I'm just starting out. I can't even pay myself, much less you and Ray. I have a handful of pro bono files I brought with me from the community legal aid clinic and only two cases: my lawsuit against Farnsworth and a case for one of the guys at Redemption. There's also a bogus lawsuit against some of the Redemption fighters that I'll handle if it becomes real, but that's it."

Her lips curl into a grin. "Good for you, suing Farnsworth. After you called and told me what happened, I wondered if you would. Someone needs to take that puffed up jackass down a peg." Then her smile fades. "But you do realize he'll pull out all the stops. A sexual harassment lawsuit could destroy his reputation and dent his humongous ego. He'll come at you with both guns firing."

"I know. I thought about it for a long time, but in the end, I couldn't just walk away. What if he does it to someone else? How could I live with myself? Men like him get away with harassment all the time, and the more they do, the cockier they become. I couldn't let it happen. I want him to pay for what he did to me. I'll run it until I can't run it anymore, and I'll make his life damned uncomfortable while I do."

She drops her jacket on the chair. "Then you'll definitely need me."

"But how will you live? Your rent, your car…"

"Secret." Penny retrieves her CV and tucks it into her bag.

"Secret?"

"That's right. Secret. Everyone has a secret. My secret enables me to pick and choose my jobs regardless of salary. Except for the boring, stuffy, corporate decor, I like it here. Now, where should I hang my coat?"

Three hours later, Penny has the office rearranged, organized, and dusted. I have lunch on my desk, fresh coffee in my cup, and a long list of supplies that are apparently essential for the smooth functioning of a legal practice.

Penny sips her tea and tries to convince me to ditch my new AW logo because the AW AW AW screensaver on her computer makes her feel pathetic. When I refuse to capitulate, she suggests changing my new gray and navy embossed stationery for something funky with bold colors and fancy designs. Then she tries to get me to change the name of the firm from Amanda Westwood, Attorney at Law to Westwood and Sons, despite the fact I have no sons and, given the abysmal state of my sex life, no prospect of ever having sons in the future.

I tell her I know how to project a corporate image and this is it. She tells me I need to step out of the Farnsworth & Tillman shadow and get a life. Our stalemate lasts a whole three seconds before she sucks in a warning breath and whispers, "Courier."

Ten minutes later, we stand in front of my desk and stare at the large cardboard box with the words "Do Not Open Until Instructed" written in bold black letters across the top.

Penny runs her finger over the letters. "I think you should open it."

"It says 'Do Not Open.'"

"You don't *always* have to follow the rules." She rolls her eyes. "And I can't stand the suspense. We don't even know who it's from."

Biting my lip, I tap the box. So tempting. But I have strength. I have willpower. Amanda Westwood does not succumb to temptation. "Go get the scissors."

But before Penny reaches her desk, my cell phone buzzes and Jake's name flashes on my screen. I had forgotten we traded numbers after I'd agreed to rent the house from him.

Something in my face alerts Penny to the personal nature of the text and she gives me a wink and discretely makes her way out of the office.

Did u get my present?

If u mean big box with "Do Not Open," then yes

Did u open it?

What do u think?

Things I think shdn't be texted

Can I open it?

No

Why?

Want you to suffer

Seems to happen every time we're together

???

Now can I open box?

No. Want to hear more about suffering

Didn't know u were a sadist

Didn't know u were afraid to talk to me

Didn't know u had a girlfriend

frowns No girlfriend

Sia

Friend. Not girlfriend

Does she know that?

She wants that

What do u want?

Want u to open box.

It doesn't take me long to cut open the box. Laughter makes my hands shake and for a moment I can't text. Instead, I pull the midsize microwave out of its packaging and place it on the credenza. But when I open the microwave door, my laughter fades into something warm and fuzzy that makes my heart squeeze. The note inside reads, "Eating *is* important."

The insistent buzz of my phone tears me away.

Office warming present. You like?

Very sweet and thoughtful, but there is a kitchen here

I know u won't use it and I like my girls with curves

What girls?

U

U like my curves?

Thought about ur curves all night

I like pressie. Tx

How tx?

????

Sext tx

U want me 2 sext u 2 tx u?

winks

Respectable attorneys don't sext

Naughty Amandas do sext
How about a selfie?
Depends what part of self is in selfie
Bad Jake
You can't imagine

Cheeky. Although I'm not about to compromise my professional career with naughty sexts, I can send him something. After a fresh swipe of lipstick, I kiss a piece of paper, take a quick picture and Instagram my lips. After an interminably long silence, my phone buzzes.

More

Later that afternoon, after Penny drags me through the long supply list, I am shocked into speechlessness when Sandy breezes in looking exquisite in camel pants, a white silk blouse, and a cashmere shawl.

"She's carrying a $10,000 handbag." Penny's eyes widen.

"She's wearing $2,000 shoes."

"You want me to knock her out and steal her stuff? That might solve your financial problems."

"I'll think about it." And I do. For all of three seconds.

"I'll get a bat."

My eyes flick to Penny. "I never knew you had a bloodthirsty side. You've only been here a few hours and already I'm seeing a whole new you."

Penny's mouth opens and closes again. But her retort never comes. Instead, she sucks in a sharp breath and grips the edge of the desk. "Sweet mother of hotness. Lookit the man candy she's got with her."

My heart skips a beat. Jake.

They sweep into the office and stop in front of Penny's desk.

"I've brought you a new client," Jake says as if he doesn't know what happened two years ago between Sandy and Makayla.

My eyes flick to Sandy. She bites her lip and twists her hands around her insanely expensive handbag, then has the good grace to look away. She knows exactly what I think of representing her, which is no with a capital N.

"Would you excuse us?" I try to sound gracious, but my words come out biting instead. "I need to speak to Jake for a minute. Penny will look after you."

"What the hell?" I spit out as soon as we're in my office. "I appreciate you bringing me clients, but you need to check with me first. I can't represent her. I vicariously hate her for tweeting Makayla's ass in revenge for what she saw as stealing Max away." And because she picked Jake up on the rebound from me and still holds a torch for him. Not that I'm about to share that little tidbit of information.

He arches an eyebrow. "I admire your loyalty, but you have to get over it. You need clients, and she's desperate for a commercial litigation attorney with experience working at a big law firm. She started a company to set up summer camps for underprivileged kids, but she got into a land dispute with some developers. She's been conflicted out of the big firms because of family and business connections. It's a high-profile, five-million-dollar lawsuit, and she has the money to pay."

Summer camps for underprivileged kids? Sandy? My resolve wavers.

Sensing victory, Jake closes the distance between us and rests his forearm on the door beside my head. His body is so close I can feel his heat and a tiny, betraying shiver of need races down my spine.

"What if she showed up at your legal aid clinic?" His voice softens. "You've never turned away anyone who needed help. It was one of the things I liked about you. Even though you were insanely busy, you always made time to give something back and that's what you'd be doing by helping her. She's trying to make life better for those kids. I know she's made mistakes, but at heart, she's a good person."

I fix him with my best scowl. "You knew I wouldn't be able to say no."

"Hearts don't change." He taps my chest. "And yours is a good one."

With a heavy sigh, I text Makayla. She texts back within minutes. She's fine with me representing Sandy. In fact, she thinks it's hilarious. She reminds me she revenge tweeted Sandy's ass and it didn't trend, so she considers them even.

"Makayla's good with it too." I tilt my head and give him a begrudging smile. "Thanks. I'm sure there are lots of Big Law escapees out there you could have recommended."

Jake chuckles softly. "Is that all the thanks I get?"

"What else did you have in mind?"

He pulls me into his chest and teases my lips with his tongue. "I have a lot of things in mind," he rasps. "Most of which I suspect would be inappropriate for a law firm. But if I had to choose one, it would be bending you over your desk in that fucking hot, tight little suit…"

My body heats in an instant and I gasp, cutting him off. He's running hot and cold and I'm scrambling to catch up and deal with the sudden shock of arousal that has fired my blood.

He curls his hand around the back of my neck, holding me still as he leans in and ravages my mouth. My hands slide up his broad chest, twining around his neck to pull him down for more. With a groan, he curves one hand over my waist to grip my ass, fingers digging into soft flesh, pulling my hips so hard against him, I can almost feel every ridge of his hardened length between us.

My God. I'm sexing it up in my own law firm. All those years turning down offers to sex it up at Farnsworth & Tillman, I missed out. Big time.

"God, you're so fucking beautiful." He tugs up my skirt and traces a finger along the elastic of my panties, blazing a trail of fire across my skin. Moisture floods my sex and my knees tremble. I don't care if it's unprofessional to have sex in my office. I don't care that Penny and Sandy are just outside the door. I don't care if this is all a mistake. He says he wants me, and I want to feel him inside me so I know it's true.

"I need you." I drop one hand to his belt and work the buttons on my shirt with the other.

Jake hisses in a breath and jerks away. He takes one step back and then another, chest heaving.

Alone, on the edge, I lean against the door, my breath coming in short pants. "What's wrong? What did I do?"

His voice drops to a strained rasp. "Nothing. You didn't do anything. You're just…hard to resist."

"But…" My mouth drops open and my body aches with the sudden drop in arousal. "Is it Sia? Sandy said you were with her…"

"I tried it with her," he growls. "It didn't work out. I tried it with a lot of girls—a lot—but none of them…" He pounds his fist on the wall and the fresh plaster gives way, leaving a gaping hole. "None of them were you. None of them made me feel the way you made me feel."

"But then what's the problem?"

He scrubs his hand over his face. "Last time was too fast, too intense. Overwhelming. You pushed me away and I went. This time I want to take it slow. Do things different. Make sure it's right. I just… when I'm with you…it's so damn hard."

Humiliation hardens my heart. "Why waste your effort? I'm the same person I was. Nothing is going to change."

Before I can say anything else, he brushes a kiss over my forehead and then pulls open the door. "It already has."

Sandy and I manage to have a civilized meeting after Jake leaves. I try not to think about how he left me hanging or why I'm wasting time and energy on a man who has an agenda that involves not having sex.

As we exit my office, I catch sight of Ray, now ensconced on my new Farnsworth & Tillman–style couch, his shoes up on my new glass coffee table.

I blink. Ray nods and says, "Hey," as if he hangs out in my office every day, drinking my coffee, scuffing my table, and reading my newspapers.

Sandy's head snaps in his direction and she sucks in a breath. Ray stares at her. She stares at Ray. Penny and I exchange a glance.

"Tell me again what he's doing here." I keep my voice to a low, discreet hiss.

"You need an investigator."

"Not him. He works for Farnsworth. He has a conflict."

I clear my throat to draw Ray's attention, but he's still entranced by the fair Sandy and she by him. I have to admit, she is looking especially gorgeous today with her long, blond hair fanning over her shoulders and a jaunty tan beret perched on her head. Of course, no one could look bad carrying a $10,000 handbag or wearing $2,000 shoes.

"He says it isn't a problem," Penny whispers.

"Well, it's a problem to me." I give Ray a cold smile. "Um. Ray? Could I talk to you for a second?"

He tears his gaze away from Sandy and gives me a wink. "Sure thing. Just catching up with Pen. Nice to see you out on your own and already gettin' clients." With a nod at Sandy, Ray shifts his long, lithe body on the couch and crosses his ankles. Not the pose of a man about to get up and do my bidding, but who am I to complain? Even I am not immune to his chiseled good looks and hard-body charm. He is looking particularly commando today: buzz cut, army fatigues, black boots, grizzled chin, and a mysterious bulge on his side that looks sus-piciously like a weapon. But what would a PI be doing with a weapon?

Since he doesn't seem to have taken the hint that I want to talk to him in private, I try another tactic. "So, what can I do for you, Ray?"

"Heard you have some investigation work. Tell me what you need, and I'll get it done."

I glance at Sandy and then back to Ray. "Don't you have another… employer? Someone who can actually pay what you're worth? Someone who might be upset to find out you're doing contract work for me?"

"Nope." He smiles at Sandy. "You got a case?"

"Yes." Her tiny voice is so unlike her usual full-throated fight scream, I almost can't believe it's coming from her.

"Amanda tell you if you need a PI on it?"

Her cheeks brighten. "Yes. I told her to hire the best."

Ray gives a satisfied grunt. "Right. I'm hired. Your client wants me, Amanda. Looks like we'll be working together again."

I give an indignant sniff as Sandy waves good-bye and heads out the door. "Direct as always. I see you haven't changed. Did Penny mention I can't pay you?"

"I'm here—means I've changed," he says brusquely. "And I'm not worried about pay."

"How nice no one needs to worry about getting paid," I mutter as I head to my office. "I'm definitely in the wrong profession."

"Hey, Amanda," Ray yells as I push open my door.

Turning, I raise an eyebrow. "Check out the décor. This is a law firm, Ray. We don't yell or raise our voices here. Also, we don't put our shoes on the table. Pretend you're at Farnsworth & Tillman. Act accordingly."

Ray snorts a laugh. "You want this to be a mini Farnsworth & Tillman? Take a look around, sweetheart. This house is made for comfort and relaxation. It's a place to loosen up. Be yourself. Are you really Farnsworth & Tillman or are you something more?"

More than Farnsworth & Tillman? They are the top of the top. La crème de la crème. The firm every law student wanted to join. My father gave me a rare pat on the head when I showed him my offer letter. How can there be more?

"I want it to be professional."

"Yeah?" Ray bounces on the couch. "Nothing professional about making your clients sit on an uncomfortable couch. This couch…hard as nails. I saw a nice couch in the hallway. Flowers and birds and garden-type things all over it. Lotsa cushions, although a bit beat up. I'm thinking you should swap these out and bring it in. You want, I'll do that for you."

"Law firm. Not lounge," I snap. "I need to project a professional image."

Ray lifts an eyebrow. "You need to let go of the past."

Maybe I do. And Jake with it.

Chapter 9
THE SUBMISSION MASTER

THE NEXT DAY, THE unthinkable happens.

Rampage and the other fighters who helped me at Hellhole are served with a civil lawsuit for ten million dollars courtesy of Bob and his sidekick, now identified in the voluminous documents as Clive Custer. From the papers Rampage faxes to me, it appears they have retained some back alley attorney who has clearly taken the case on a contingency basis with the mind-set of "throw enough at them and something might stick."

I see red.

Penny and I spend the rest of the afternoon drafting retainer agreements for the fighters, all of whom, except for Jake, have agreed to have me represent them. No arm twisting needed.

"Do you want me to draft something up for Jake just in case?" Penny hands me an envelope with the completed documents as I grab my gym bag from the storage cupboard.

"Not yet. It's a bit of a tricky situation, which is why I need to speak to him in person." I shrug on my jacket and tuck the envelope in my purse. "If we were in a sexual relationship and he wanted to retain me, it wouldn't be an issue. The ethical rules allow attorneys to take a lover as a client. What they don't allow is an attorney taking a client as a lover. I'm not sure if we are in a sexual relationship. Or if our relationship from before would count. All I really know is we had sex two years ago. And now we're not having sex. Unless, of course, meaningless foreplay in the office counts as sex."

Penny frowns. "So if you have sex with him, then he can hire you as his attorney without any ethical issues?"

"Crudely put, yes. But even if I was the kind of person who would purposely have sex with someone to smooth over ethical issues for the sole purpose of getting a client, which I'm not, I don't know if I want to get involved with him again. It's just too hard. Too many emotions involved. Too much history. I'm thinking I need to start fresh, find someone new."

Penny snorts. "Sure. Whatever you say."

Now it is my turn to frown. "That sounded slightly sarcastic."

She turns off her computer and fishes around in her desk for her purse. "Only slightly? I was going for full-on sarcasm. You finally get another chance with the one guy you want more than anything else. You two almost burn up the office with the heat between you. But hey, maybe it's time to find someone new? Seriously? Just sleep with him. Get that out of the way and then deal with whatever issues are left over and sign him up for the Bob and Clive funfest. Shag 'n' bag."

"Shag 'n' bag?"

"That's right. You sleep with him. Then you bag him as a client. Problem solved."

I would laugh but Penny isn't even smiling. She is dead serious about her shag 'n' bag plan. "What if he doesn't want to sleep with me? What if he's just playing around and having a bit of fun at my expense?"

Penny rolls her eyes. "I thought you were the man whisperer. Why are you asking me for advice? I'm the one on an extended dry spell who can't get a date to save her life. But since you did, I'll give you the benefit of my experience. He's a man. He wants to sleep with you."

"Thanks for that," I say dryly.

Penny shrugs and pushes open the door. "Sometimes the simplest solutions are the best."

Almost two hours later, worn ragged by a traffic nightmare on the bridge, I make it to Redemption. With Rampage's assistance, I commandeer Torment's office for a group signing of the retainer agreements. I can only imagine what he would say if he saw fighters draped over every surface, but everyone promises to keep it hush-hush.

After the sign-up, everyone heads out, but Homicide Hank lingers by the door. He sighs loudly, then inspects Torment's bookshelves as I sort out the papers on the desk.

"Something on your mind, Homicide?"

He takes a quick look over his shoulder and then slides into the chair across from me. "Actually, the wife and I…we're thinking we should have wills for when the baby is born. But we don't have a lotta money, so I bought a DIY will kit online." He pulls out a crushed bundle of papers from his gym bag and slides them across the desk. "I just…it's kinda complicated."

Fortunately, Homicide lives in the catchment for the community legal aid clinic, and five minutes later he becomes my newest pro bono client. But the fun doesn't end with Homicide. Obsidian catches me outside Torment's office with a motor vehicle injury claim wadded into a tight ball in his fist, and Rampage hands me a bundle of insurance papers before I hit the changing room. Who needs advertising when I have Torment?

Relieved that Jake isn't around, I make it into the registration office with enough time to sign up for three grappling and fight technique classes before Get Fit or Die starts. Shayla, now working the desk part-time, walks me through the forms, but just as I hand her my credit card, Fuzzy taps me on the shoulder.

"What's going on? Why aren't you warming up for class tonight?"

"I'm signing up to learn how to fight."

Fuzzy glares as I scrawl my name on the sign-up sheets and then snatches away my pen. "You can't even manage Get Fit or Die. How are you gonna fight?"

"You can't stop me. Shayla…er Shilla the Killa says I can take any classes I want. She says I don't have to pass Get Fit or Die first. She says everything that comes out of your mouth about prerequisites is bullshit." I smile at Shayla, frozen behind the cash register with my credit card in her hand. She doesn't look pleased.

"No."

"Come on, Fuzz," I moan. "I joined Redemption because I want to fight. I want to be able to walk down dark alleys and not be afraid. You said I should take your beginners' class to get in shape and I did. Plus, I've been working out every day, not just here. I'm stronger, faster, and I can now leap small buildings in a single bound."

His face softens and his lips quirk into a smile. "I just want you to be safe. I've seen too many people hurt in the ring simply because they weren't properly conditioned. Maybe you should consider taking one of the martial arts classes. It would be a good halfway point. Girls like you don't belong in the ring."

Girls like me?

Shayla snorts a laugh. "Girls like her work out, train hard, and become girls like me. You don't think I belong in the ring?" She flexes her impressive biceps and then mocks up a few bodybuilder stances. My mouth drops open. Shayla is ripped. Everywhere. She could definitely put down most of the guys I know. I want to be like her.

"Course not." Fuzzy's smile fades. "You're a fucking machine. You didn't get your nickname for nothing. But I'm talking about Amanda. She's...different. Delicate."

Tilting her head to the side, Shayla gives him a curious look. "Did you know I was a professional ballerina before I joined Redemption? I wore tutus and pink slippers. I danced for Joffrey and toured the world. I practiced every day from the age of three until even the barest flutter of my fingers was graceful. You want delicate, you look right over here."

Eyes wide, mouth open, Fuzzy stares at Shayla like she's grown two heads. "You're fucking kidding me."

By way of answer, Shayla pulls out her phone. She flips through her photos, holding up pictures of her as a ballerina for Fuzzy to see.

He sighs over the last photo. "I don't get it."

Shayla shrugs. "We're not all born fighters. And the fact that you can't even begin to understand it is the reason you shouldn't stand in Amanda's way. She wants to learn how to fight. You should let her fight. If she gets hurt, she'll learn what not to do next time. Worked for me."

Still, he hesitates. His eyes rove over me in an assessing, entirely nonsexual way, and he strokes his bottom lip. I fight back the urge to whinny and paw the floor with a running shoe–clad hoof.

"I'll sign a legal waiver." I give a pathetic laugh.

Fuzzy shakes his head. "It's not the law I'm worried about. It's Renegade. You get hurt, he'll be all over my ass."

"Renegade? He has nothing to do with what classes I take. We're not...you know...together. And even if we were, I wouldn't let him interfere with how I want to train."

Fuzzy arches an eyebrow and then he and Shayla share a glance and a snort.

"How about we sign her up for Grunt 'n' Grapple?" Shayla suggests to Fuzzy as if I wasn't standing in front of her. "Rampage is teaching tonight. They're using dummies and just doing submission drills. Should be safe enough."

Fuzzy sucks in a breath through clenched teeth. "What if she gets a scratch—or worse, a bruise?"

Shayla's eyebrows fly up to her hairline. "I didn't think of that. How about I run interference? First sign of injury, and I'll pull her out and take her to first aid. Doctor Death can patch her up and send her home. Renegade will never know."

"Seriously?" I raise my voice in disbelief. "Is this a serious conversation? I told you he has nothing to do with how I train. And you can't possibly be that afraid of him. I mean, he's only been back in the gym a couple of months."

"Make sure you have a word with Rampage," Shayla says to Fuzzy, ignoring my outburst. "We don't want him getting hurt. He's fighting in the next event."

A few irritating minutes later, I am released into Rampage's hands with a full set of instructions about my care and handling like I'm a kid being dropped off at day care.

"This is 'manda," Rampage tells the class consisting of six guys and no other women. "She's Redemption's attorney and she's Renegade's girl, so no one messes with her. That means you don't speak to her; you don't look at her; you don't touch her; you don't breathe the same air as her. She's gonna train over there." He points to the far end of the mat. "We're gonna train over there." He points to the opposite end.

"I feel like a pariah," I mutter. "And, by the way, I'm not Renegade's girl."

Rampage chuckles. "Everyone knows you're Renegade's girl. Don't need to be shy."

"How does everyone know?" I pull away from his bulk and fold my arms. "Did he say something?"

Rampage gives my head a condescending pat. "He didn't need to say anything. A man stakes his claim, every man with a beating heart in the vicinity knows it. That was done the first day he brought you back to Redemption. Reinforced at the renovation party. The minute you walk in here, he's got eyes on you. He's got hands on you. He keeps the sharks away. You never wonder why no one bothers you? You never ask yourself why, looking the way you look and dressing the way you dress and smiling that pretty smile and with all those smarts in your head, you've never been harassed at Redemption?"

"But..."

"You're his." Rampage's face softens. "Looks like you're the only one who doesn't know it."

Stunned into silence, I go through the motions as Rampage leads us in a warm-up. Then it's over to the wall to get a grapple dummy.

"Make sure you get a submission dummy," Rampage hollers at us. "I don't want to see anyone with a practice dummy and no bags. Amanda, you take Grapple Man because he's lighter than the rest. Everyone else can take a Bubba II."

Wrapping my arms around the life-size, six-foot training dummy, I drag it across the mats. Eerily human, the fifty-five-pound mannequin has realistic and bendable arms, legs, and torso, and his skin has the feel and resiliency of human flesh. The molded hair and face give him the appearance of a giant Ken doll. When no one is looking, I check under his cotton shorts for anatomical correctness and find him lacking. Just like Ken.

"Today we're going to drill basic submissions from the bottom—arm bars, triangles, and kimuras. We'll do them one after the other, ten reps each." Rampage positions us all on our backs and ropes Drake into helping everyone position the dummy on top.

"How's my best girl?" Drake kneels down beside me and brushes the hair away from my face. "I stopped by your new office after surgery the other night and I couldn't believe the lights were out at eight p.m. Only putting in half days now, are you?"

"It's a whole new me." I grin and push myself up to my elbows. "No late nights. Getting in shape so I can learn how to fight. And I'm down to only four cups of coffee a day."

Drake frowns. "So I'll be seeing you on my operating table in fifteen years instead of ten."

"Chill. I'm feeling good."

His gaze roves over Ken tucked between my legs, his plastic face nestled between my breasts, and winks. "You're looking good. Always like to see a woman in submission."

"Shut up, Drake…er…Doctor Death. This isn't the place for sexual innuendo. I'm trying to learn serious fight techniques." I fake a scowl while Drake repositions the dummy, one plastic hand on either side of my head, one plastic pelvis where an anatomically correct pelvis might go.

"He's in full mount," Drake explains. "Dominant."

I'll bet.

"Um. Is this the right position?"

Drake sucks in a laughing breath. "It's the position I use. The ladies seem to like it." He leans closer and whispers. "You seemed to like it."

"Rampage!" Unable to move with roughly sixty pounds of dummy on top of me, I turn my head and holler. "Get Doctor Death out of here. He's harassing me and definitely enjoying himself too much to teach me properly."

More wheezing laughter and Drake helps me position my right leg around Ken's neck, my ankle tucked behind the back of my left knee. Ken's head is locked tight between my legs, his mouth tucked tight against the curve of my sex. Hoooah! I might just buy a grapple dummy for the long, lonely nights ahead.

Drake lifts Ken's head. Ken's head slides down and bumps gently between my legs. Drake tries again, but Ken has other ideas. Ken knows where a woman wants a man's mouth and if Drake keeps doing what he's doing, I'm going to need a dummy with real lips…and a tongue. I suspect Drake knows this all too well.

Finally Drake sits back and sighs. "Problem with you using Grapple Man is that he's designed for a bigger fighter. He won't stay put. And there's not enough tension in the arms. A real person will hold his head up and push against your legs. The Submission Master would be better, but he's our heaviest practice dummy and I think he'll be too much for you."

The Submission Master? My body tingles and my mouth waters. *YES, PLEASE!*

Drake removes Ken from between my legs and gives me a thoughtful look. "You want me to help you out?"

"Did you bring a body bag with you?" My voice drips with sarcasm. "Apparently, although Renegade and I are not together in any meaningful way, I'm not to be touched, looked at, or share the same air as any man in Redemption. According to Fuzzy and Shilla the Killa, you're taking your life in your hands just by helping me."

"It's just a basic submission." Drake gives me a wicked grin. "And I've always wanted to go a few rounds in the ring with Renegade, maybe wipe away the scowl that always appears on his face when he sees me."

"It's your funeral...Doctor Death." I manage to say this without laughing. So long as Drake's head doesn't fall into my now throbbing sex, I should be good.

"I'll take the dominant position." Drake kneels in front of me and motions for me to spread my legs.

My throat thickens and I part my legs to accommodate his muscular body. "Okay."

He crawls over top of me and drops his weight to his elbows. His body is warm and heavy on mine. Oh God. It's been too long since I've had a man. And Drake was my last. My body heats at his familiar touch and I focus on keeping still.

Bad body. Don't think about sex. Fires. Insurance companies. Wills. Documents.

But how can I not think about sex when Drake is throwing around words like *dominant, submission, mount, and pound*? What it would be like to have Jake show me the moves, his body mounting me, his voice driving me to submission. My cheeks flush and I turn my head so Drake doesn't see. Rampage is demonstrating a rear naked choke to one of my classmates. What I wouldn't give for a rear naked…

"You ready for the submission?" Drake is not totally unaffected by this position. His cheeks are flushed, his voice deeper. Thank God, he's wearing a cup. At least, I think he's wearing a cup.

"Ready." I swing my leg around his neck and pull his right arm between us toward my breast as I lift my other leg to his shoulder.

"What the fuck?" Jake's angry voice cracks through the whirr of machines, the grunts and thuds of sparring partners, and the low hum of training chatter.

"Now the fun begins." Although his eyes glitter, amused, Drake beats a hasty retreat off my body. Rampage helps him up, murmuring he should have known better and asking if he has a will and can he have Drake's locker because it is in a prime spot right near the shower.

My breath leaves me in a rush as Jake stalks across the mats in a fury like I've never seen before. His face is stark white, eyes cold and hard, jaw tight. But it isn't fear that makes my heart pound and my knees week—it's Jake…in his crisp, white jiu-jitsu gi, a black belt tied tight around his hips.

Oh God. How could I have forgotten how hot he looks in his gi? I mentally make a shopping list for the weekend: Submission Master, check. Gi and black belt for Submission Master, check. Vibrator, check.

Jake's gi flaps open as he walks, giving me a glimpse of the muscles rippling across his chest. The cut of the jacket emphasizes his broad shoulders and the belt is tight around his narrow hips. The stiff material swishes angrily with his every step. He looks powerful, dangerous. Predatory. I cannot tear my eyes away.

Without breaking his stride, he pushes through my puzzled classmates and hits Drake in the chest with the palm of his hand. I can imagine that hand breaking boards and smashing bricks. I can imagine it caressing my breasts, stroking my thighs…

"Whoa." Rampage steps between them. "Just a class, man. Doctor Death was just helping out. Grapple Man didn't do it for your girl, so he stepped in."

Jake's gaze slides to me on my back, legs bent and apart, cheeks flushed. Maybe this is a good time to shut down the submission position. I pull myself up and then jump to my feet.

"Don't move." Jake growls at me without taking his eyes off Drake.

"We were doing a triangle." Drake explains. "Grapple Man kept kissing her pussy, so I thought I'd step in and…"

"Oh Christ." Rampage sighs and shakes his head. "Doctor Death has a death wish tonight."

The small crowd around us stills. Even cheeky, overly confident Drake pales and steps back when Jake hisses out a breath.

Too late.

Jake strikes like a cobra. One minute he is in front of Rampage, the next he is behind Drake, an elbow around Drake's neck in an actual rear naked choke hold. *As seen on television. Don't try this at home.* Drake goes down. Drake jumps up. Now Drake is angry too. More people gather.

"Renegade. Stop." My feeble words go unheard as Jake lunges at Drake and goes for a double leg takedown. Drake hits the mat hard and rolls, taking Jake with him. Suddenly Drake is in full mount. The crowd cheers.

Jake manages to extricate himself from Drake's submission hold and jumps to his feet. He charges as Drake struggles to his knees and Drake goes flying across the mat. He lands with a loud thump and a string of curses. Without slowing, Jake lets loose with some boxing-type punches. He throws knees and Drake gets him off balance, taking him down and then following with an elbow to Jake's abdomen. Drake leaps to his feet but Jake stays on his back. I give Rampage a worried glance, but his eyes are wide with wonder.

"Didya see that? Drake grabbed a guillotine but Renegade popped out."

"Huh?"

Jake lands a big uppercut then just misses Drake with an impressive spinning turn followed by a powerful elbow strike. Drake dives down for a clinch, and the sharp blast of a whistle cuts through the cheers of the crowd.

"Fuzzy?"

Rampage sighs. "Fuzzy."

Within moments, the floor is clear. The crowd is disbursed. Rampage and the class are back on the mats under the grapple dummies. Fuzzy has the two miscreants on the bleachers and glares at them like they've committed a crime. I sit beside Jake, guilt gnawing at my stomach. I should have sent Drake away.

"We've got a rule here about fighting outside the ring," Fuzzy barks. Then he glares at Drake. "And you know better than to mess with someone's girl in the gym."

Drake's eyes flick to me and then back to Fuzzy. "Didn't know they were together. I was just helping out. Amanda and I are good friends."

Jake growls softly, then leans back on the bleachers and drapes his arm over my shoulders, jerking me into his side. Possessive. Challenging. His legs are spread, his body seemingly relaxed, but his jaw is tight, and his hands clenched into fists.

Silence.

Fuzzy sighs and dismisses Drake, promising to think up a suitable punishment by the end of the evening.

After Drake leaves, Fuzzy glares at Jake and nods toward the side door. "Fists of Fury offered to finish up your class. I have to write up a formal warning for both you and Doctor Death. You might consider paying attention to the rules because friend or no friend, you know Torment won't hesitate to boot your ass out the door if you pull this kind of stunt again."

Jake grunts his understanding but doesn't move.

"You'd better get back to your class," Fuzzy says to me. "Rampage has your Grapple Man waiting for you. I think Shilla the Killa is free. She'll be able to help you out."

Jake's hand tightens on my shoulder. "I'll help her. She's missed most of the class anyway."

Nonononononononono. My wish wasn't a real wish. More like a passing fantasy.

Fuzzy looks from me to Jake and back to me. "Maybe that's not a good idea."

"Definitely not," I say softly.

"Don't care if it's a good idea." Jake gets to his feet and pulls me up, then tucks me under his arm. "That's what's going to happen."

Jake ushers me over to the corner. He gestures me down and we sit cross-legged facing each other as he runs through the three different techniques he is going to teach me. As he talks, his face softens and his eyes light up. His explanations are clear and simple. He gives examples, asks me questions, and is infinitely patient when I struggle with the answers.

As he talks, my mind drifts back to the night we met in his kickboxing class. Even then his passion for teaching drew me in, warmed my heart. He is in his element and I wonder how he could have given it up—or how I could have given up on him.

"Amanda."

I startle when I realize he's been talking and I haven't been paying attention. My cheeks burn and I meet his stern gaze. "Sorry."

"I said I heard about what you did for Homicide tonight."

"I didn't—"

"And Rampage and Obsidian."

"I haven't—"

"And that you aren't charging the fighters to run the case against the idiots from Hellhole."

"I couldn't…"

His face softens and he reaches up to cup my jaw, stroking his thumb over my cheek. "You're really something, baby, but you can't help everyone. You won't stay afloat if you do everything for free."

With a shrug, I look away. "They helped me out. I'm just returning the favor."

"You're more than returning the favor. No one here will forget what you do for them. And neither will I."

Finally, it is time for the demonstration. Jake positions me on my back, his gi rustling as he moves. Then he kneels between my legs. For the first time, I notice he is still pumped from the fight. The vein in his neck is throbbing, his hands clench and unclench, and power simmers beneath his skin. He is all red-hot alpha male. Testosterone oozes from his pores. And in that gi, his chest slightly bared, danger clinging to him like a cloak, my body responds with a violent shudder of need. What would happen if I set him off?

"Hands out of the way. I'm going to mount. We'll try it first from the closed guard."

God, yes. Mount me. Mount me.

He leans over me, his hips between my thighs, and rests his hands on my chest. My breasts swell instantly, nipples hardening to tight peaks.

"Closed guard means your hands are around my neck, feet up on my back around my hips." He is breathing harder now, but not as hard as me.

"I feel like a baby opossum," I murmur as I take the required position. "They also like to hang upside down by their hands and feet."

Jake's lips quiver with a repressed smile and his voice softens. "*My* baby opossum. And no one touches her but me."

Except he didn't want to touch me in my office. Gah. I can't handle this hot and cold. Push and pull. Trying to figure him out is making my brain ache.

"We'll try the gogoplata first."

I wiggle my hips from side to side. "Sounds like a dance."

"Stop," he grits through clenched teeth. "It's a serious move."

"So is this." I give another wiggle and Jake hisses in a breath.

"You're not being serious. You're being tempting. And if you keep that up, it will be the Submission Master for you."

"Now who's being tempting?"

I'm pushing him but I can't help myself. Everything MMA oozes sex, and Jake in his gi is just too much. I want him. I want to drive him crazy with lust. As crazy as me. And then I'm going to walk away so he knows how it feels to be left hanging.

"Who came up with that name 'Submission Master'?" I murmur. "It turns me on just to say it."

Jake jerks back until he is on his knees between my legs. "Christ, Amanda. I'm trying to teach you something. It's hard enough just mounting you, but when you talk like that…"

Amused, I push myself to my elbows. "I'm talking fight talk. Don't I have the words right? *Submission, master, ground, pound, dominate, dominant, mount, rear naked choke hold*…can we do that one next?"

Jake's chest heaves and he studies me—focused, intent. Then his eyes narrow as if he's made a decision and it's not going to be good for me. His voice drops to a low, threatening growl, and I shiver. "Don't play a game you're not prepared to lose."

Duly warned, I capitulate. "Okay."

With quiet patience, he talks me through the rest of the move, which involves him mounting me again and resting one hand flat on my breast while I pull his other hand through and tuck his body firmly between my thighs.

Desire rushes through me like a tidal wave. Jake, hot and heavy, sexy and dangerous, lying on top of me, is more than I can take. His lips are so close it is everything I can do not to take a little taste. I want him so badly, I ache inside. I need to know if Rampage is right and he really thinks I'm his girl.

"Baby? You all right?"

His old term of endearment almost does me in. Oh God. It would be so easy to fall for him again. So gorgeous. So confident. So sexy. But I can't let myself get emotionally hung up on him. I couldn't handle it when he got close before. What would happen if he got close again? My heart thuds anxiously. Torn between fear and desire, I loosen my grip. He's right. I can't play this game because I don't want to lose.

"Why did you drop your guard?" he murmurs. "You're only halfway through the submission."

"I can't do this," I rasp. "Please…just…get off me."

His eyes darken to an azure blue and his body stiffens. He shifts his position and takes his weight on his elbows now positioned on either side of my head. But his hips are still pressed tight against mine. And… Oh God. He's not wearing a cup and he's as aroused as I am.

"Why?" His breath brushes over my cheek and my body trembles with need and the effort not to act on my most carnal desires.

Almost dizzy with the onslaught of emotion and the rush of blood through my veins, I can barely get the words out. "Jake…please…get off."

His voice drops to a low, commanding growl. "Tell me why."

I look around for someone to help me, but we are very much alone in our shadowy corner. I take several deep breaths, but my heart continues to pound. I silently beg Jake to walk away, but his steady gaze is on me.

"Please."

He caresses my cheek and presses the softest kiss to my lips. "Why, baby?"

"Because I want you." I draw in a ragged breath. "Because I want you and you don't want me and this game we're playing is too much when I have to deal with you…like this."

For a long moment, he studies me, and then he gently brushes my hair away from my face. "You think I don't want you?" His lips whisper over my forehead sending a firestorm of hope through my body. "You think I'm this hard because I don't want you?" He grinds his pelvis against mine and the press of his steel-hard erection against my throbbing sex rips a moan from my throat. "I told you before, my life is just one fuckup after another. But I thought I'd finally got my life on track when I joined Redemption, started fighting…met you. And then it all went to hell. I lost you, Peter, my fight career, and my friends."

"It wasn't your fault," I blurt out. "It was me. I couldn't commit so I used the excuse of being upset that you wouldn't reveal Torment's identity to get some distance. And then Drake…I didn't leave you with any options."

Jake shakes his head and his face softens. "Not letting you take all the blame, baby. Although after meeting your parents, I can see why it's hard for you to get close to people."

"Just people I'm afraid of disappointing."

"You walked into that meeting room, and suddenly I got a second chance," he says softly. "I'm back in Redemption, back on my game. But this time I'm doing things slow. I'm not fucking this up. Just once in my life, something is going to go right. I want you, baby, but first I need to know that you'll let me in."

He wants me. But how do I know what he's saying is true if he doesn't speak in a language my body understands?

With a groan, he leans down and kisses me. His lips are warm, firm, unyielding. His tongue breaches the seal of my lips and then he is everywhere, exploring, tasting, possessing. My body arches toward him and he slides one hand under my lower back and presses me tight against him.

Oh God. I don't want this moment to end. I concentrate on every detail, committing them to memory: his body warm and hard on top of me, his lips soft and gentle, the steady beat of his heart, the fresh scent of his soap, the taste of coffee on his tongue…and the soft chuckle of Rampage as he joins us on the mats.

Damn.

"What the hell?" Rampage scratches his head from the far corner of the mat.

Jake looks up, totally unembarrassed, and smiles. "New submission. It's called lip-lock."

"I'd like to get me some of that."

Jake curls his free hand possessively around my head. "I don't think you do."

"Not with 'manda." Rampage rolls his eyes. This I can see because I have tilted my head backward.

"Something I can do for you?" Jake shifts his weight to his elbows, caging me with his body.

Rampage rubs his hand along his shorts. "Um…Fuzzy sent me to tell you that your next class is ready. They're waiting for you on the mats."

With a heavy sigh, Jake pushes himself back to his knees and then helps me up. "Later, baby. I'll meet you after class."

"Later."

Jake teaches his class. Then he helps a new recruit with some grapple moves. Then he covers a class for a sick instructor. Then he jumps into the ring to coach some newbies.

He tells me he has a hard time saying no when people ask for help. Torment turned his life around, and he feels obligated to pay it forward. Some of his students can't afford the fees for a private coach. Always, he is solicitous and apologetic, but he never gives me the impression there is anywhere he would rather be than in the ring helping out.

After a few hours of chatting with the fighters, practicing my moves, and working on my form, I finally find my self-respect and call a cab.

First thing in the morning, my phone buzzes on my desk. Jake's name flashes on the screen. For a moment, I hesitate. Do I want to talk to him? Last night he promised me later but later never came. Maybe just as well.

My hand hovers over the phone, but finally curiosity overrides reticence, and I open the message.

☹ *about last night*

I stare at the phone. Maybe I'll forgive him. Maybe I won't. Maybe I'll make him suffer like I suffered last night since my vibrator was a poor substitute for what he promised me on the mats.

frowns
Forgive me, baby. Need your help.
What help?

My phone buzzes again. This time he has sent pictures of clothing.

Which suit?
For what?
Board meeting
Gray
Which tie?
Blue stripes
Which shoes?
Shiny black
Hate suits
I've never seen you in a full suit
You want to see me in a suit?
In and out of suit ☺
Bad girl. BEHAVE
No choice. Someone left me high and dry last night
Make it up to u. Have 4 tix to see nu metal band, Slugs.
Slugs ≠ sex. Take a friend

U

I'm not ur friend

True. I'll come by 2nite and show u how unfriendly I can be

No can do. Working 2nite. Have to interview witness

At night?

Farnsworth case. Only time she is available

Alone?

Penny is coming with me

Not pleased **frowns**

Get over it **laughs**

Will text venue address for concert. Meet u there

I haven't said yes

Say it

Bossy

Say it

Yes

One more thing…

What?

Don't wear panties

Chapter 10
I'm not liking this bossy new you

"QUESADA STREET. THERE IT IS!"

"This is so exciting." Penny bounces in her seat as I pull the car over to the side of the road. "I've never been to the bad end of town."

"There are many bad areas of town. This isn't anywhere near the worst. A lot of families live here and parts of the area have been transformed with community gardens."

Penny raises an eyebrow when I secure my vehicle with two clubs. Even though we are in the "good part" and things are slowly improving, Hunter's Point still has one of the highest crime rates in San Francisco.

After double-checking the address on my phone, I grab my briefcase. First step in collecting evidence against Farnsworth is to establish he propositioned other women at the firm and I remembered hearing rumors about Jill Jackson, an intern who left the firm abruptly last year. She's agreed to one interview and my heart thrums in anticipation. If I can establish a pattern of harassment, we won't ever get to trial. Farnsworth will be begging me to settle.

We walk past a patchwork of small plots with a sandbox and rope swing, surrounded by a barbed wire fence. Jill's house is at the edge of the garden, and a few minutes later we are settled at her kitchen table.

"She's a mini you," Penny whispers as Jill leaves to get the coffee. "Same long, blond hair. Same big blue eyes. Same creamy skin. Only difference is you have about two inches on her and bigger baps." She squeezes her breasts by way of translation.

"Thanks, Penny. Good to know you notice these things."

"How can I not? I seethe with jealousy any time you wear anything tight."

I am saved from further sarcastic retorts when Jill returns with three coffee cups and a plate of cookies. Penny records our meeting, takes notes, and eats the cookies while I ask questions.

Yes, Jill worked closely with Farnsworth. Yes, Farnsworth was overly touchy. Yes, she often found herself alone with him. He wined and dined her on the pretense of discussing cases. He took her with him on business trips. On one of these trips he came on to her, but she had a boyfriend she loved dearly. She turned Farnsworth down. He threatened to fire her and make sure she never worked in the area again. She told him to do his worst. He did. Now, she is keeping up her skills at the community legal aid clinic and still looking for a job.

After leaving Jill's house, Penny and I decide to celebrate the damning evidence against Farnsworth with a visit to a wine bar in the Marina District, but when we return to the vehicle, we have unexpected company.

"Hi," I say to the two scowling males who bear a suspicious resemblance to Jake and Ray. "How did you know we were here?"

Penny grimaces. "In my excitement, I might have mentioned our interview to Ray when he called to say he wouldn't make it back to the office this afternoon. Then he might have casually tossed out a 'No way in fucking hell are you two going to Hunter's Point.' After that, I might have said we were going anyway because we didn't need his damn consent. Then he might have tossed out a few choice swear words and muttered something about waiting for him to get back to the office so he could come with us. To which I might have replied we were two grown women and didn't need a babysitter. So who's up for a drink?"

"Jesus fucking Christ." Ray turns to Jake and growls. "And did they listen? No. They went on their own. Left the car on the street. Good thing I was in the office when Jake came by. Do you have any idea how dangerous this area is?"

With no apparent thought for her safety, Penny shrugs. "No. How dangerous is it to visit a house on the good end of the street beside a garden with swings and slides, especially when Amanda has pepper spray and takes fight classes?"

Ray clenches his jaw. "I'll take Penny home and tomorrow we're all gonna have a little discussion about taking me with you when you go to dangerous areas of town."

Penny frowns. "Does this mean the wine bar is out?"

"You don't have to look out for us, Ray." I fold my arms, matching Jake's posture, although without the rippling muscles, fierce scowl, or twitching biceps. "But I forgive your stomping and growling because I know this is your way of saying you care."

"My job is to look out for you when your man's not around." Ray reaches into the car and grabs Penny's handbag. "I'm sure he'll be lining you up soon as we're gone."

"How about we stop at the wine bar first?" Penny says. "I'm kinda thirsty."

"I thought you were a PI, not a bodyguard. And, he's not my man. He's…a friend. Like you."

Ray snorts a laugh and glances over at Jake. "A friend does not go fucking crazy when he thinks his woman is in danger. A friend does not need to be physically restrained from tackling any warm-bodied male within a one-mile radius of his woman's vehicle. A friend gets irritated, worried, and mildly annoyed. Like me."

I look up and catch Jake's gaze. He appears calm, cool, and collected if not mildly annoyed. Definitely a friend.

As soon as they're gone, Jake opens the passenger door and gestures me inside. "Get in."

"Hello to you too." I pause on the sidewalk. "But this is my car. I'll drive."

Jake clamps a hand on my shoulder. "I'm driving."

"Oh come on." I wiggle free and take a step away. "We're a long way from the eighteenth century."

"Don't push me right now."

For the first time since we arrived to find him at my vehicle, I look at him. Really look at him. Pulse pounding in his neck, body tense, mouth drawn into a thin line, eyes narrow. Maybe more than mildly annoyed. Definitely not in a mood to be pushed.

"Okay." I give an exaggerated sigh and slide into the passenger seat.

A few minutes later, we are speeding through the city streets in the wrong direction.

"Where are we going?"

"Don't talk."

A chill forms in the air between us and a sliver of resentment works its way into my chest.

"I'm not liking this bossy new you." I twist my bracelet around my wrist. "First, you crash my interview. Then, you commandeer my vehicle. Now, you're telling me to shut up."

"Please, baby…" His voice cracks, and I can see from the white knuckles gripping my steering wheel and the firm set of his jaw, he is right on the edge. Resentment shifts to wariness and I shrink back in my seat.

"Okay. I get it. You're angry. Although I think you're totally overreacting."

We drive in silence for another five minutes. Suddenly, Jake makes a sharp turn and pulls into a dark, narrow alley.

"Get out."

My heart goes into overdrive. The alley is barely wide enough to allow us to open our car doors and the only light comes from the street behind us, a dim, yellow glow that stretches the car's shadow far into the darkness. An empty Dumpster clings to the slimy brick wall and the ground is littered with debris.

"I don't want to be here."

He exits the vehicle, then stalks around the hood and tugs open my door. "Out."

"Jake…"

"Last time, baby."

His term of endearment gives me the courage to get out of the car. I tell myself he's not really angry. Maybe just concerned and, perhaps a tad worried. The sweet, sensitive part of him is still there—the part that helped me fix up the house and finish my push-ups, the part that has sacrificed everything to help his family.

After I step out of the vehicle, he slams the door closed and stalks up and down the alley. Finally he thumps his fist on the Dumpster lid, sending a boom of thunder through the dank space. As he closes the distance between us, I fight the urge to pull out my cell phone and call for help. This is Jake. He would never hurt me.

"Why didn't you wait for Ray?" He looms over me. "Or call me?"

"Families live on that street, Jake, and we weren't planning on taking a long walk through the neighborhood. We went in, interviewed the witness, and came out. And I had my pepper spray. I didn't go unprepared."

"It isn't a safe area of town. You could have been hurt."

My stomach clenches. "It's no more dangerous than Ghost Town, and I've been alone there lots of times."

"And look what happened the last time you were there…"

Tensing, I hold up my hand. "Don't go there. Not right now, when we're both annoyed and liable to say the wrong thing."

"Fuck." He pounds his fist on the brick wall. "Fuck. The thought of you in danger…it was too fucking much."

"Jake…" I touch his forearm and he jerks his hand away.

"I thought you were going to die in that alley outside Hellhole." His voice rises to a shout and he leans in toward me. "I thought I would lose you without really ever having had you at all."

"I understand you were worried, but you don't need to be so angry." I press my hands against his chest and push, but he's too big and too heavy, and if he even notices my efforts, he gives no sign. Instead, he continues to rant, and finally, I snap.

"Stop." I raise my voice loud enough for him to hear. "Back away. You're scaring me." This time when I push, I put all my effort into it. This time Jake takes a step back, and suddenly I can breathe again.

"I'm scaring you?"

"Yes. You're bigger than me, stronger than me, louder than me, and angrier than me. Not only that, you're a professional fighter and—"

"You think I'm going to hurt you?" He cuts me off and his voice rises to a disbelieving growl.

"I think you're out of control."

He takes a step forward and I flinch, turning my head away, bracing myself for the inevitable, but the inevitable never comes.

"I am always in control," he says through gritted teeth. "And I would rather cut off my arm than hurt you. But when I went to your office and Ray said you were at Hunter's Point…fuck, Amanda. I didn't know what to do."

Swallowing past my fear, I meet his furious gaze. "Shouting and pounding your fists and trapping me against the car sends me a different message. I understand you were concerned and worried, and if I didn't think it was coming from a good place, I'd walk…maybe even run away right now."

Jake bristles and opens his mouth, but I press on. He needs to hear what I have to say.

"You have to understand," I continue. "I'm used to doing things on my own. I rarely ask for help. And I've never had anyone worry about me. I'm not someone who needs to be protected and looked after. This is why I don't get close to people. If I'd known you were going to react like this…that you would care this much…I would have handled it differently."

"Would you?" His cold, bitter tone takes my breath away.

"Yes."

For a long moment, we stare at each other in a mini-standoff, chests heaving, nostrils flaring, eyes flashing. Finally, his tension eases—a slight drop of his shoulders, a loosening of his fists. "Next time, you ask me for help."

"Next time, you try to deal with the situation without using violence and anger, and you don't scare me." I smooth my hands over the heaving chest of the sweaty, pumped up alpha-male glowering in front of me and whisper, "And you accept I can handle some dangerous situations that aren't really dangerous situations on my own."

He grunts and suddenly I am hyperaware of his body so close to mine, the heat of his skin radiating through his shirt into my palms, the rapid beat of the pulse in his neck, and the full, sensuous lips only inches away from my mouth. Fueled by adrenaline and emotion, electricity sparks between us, igniting the flame of my desire.

Through half-lidded eyes, his gaze follows my fingers as they drift down over his tight abs to his belt buckle. When I tug on his belt, he grabs my hand and draws it away.

"You're heading for a dangerous situation right now."

"I like to live on the edge." I lean up and nuzzle the side of his neck, inhaling the scent of sweat and cologne and the unmistakable musk of arousal. Does he want me as much as I want him? I hope so. Fear and anger and lust make for an intoxicating cocktail, and right now I want to get drunk.

Jake groans but doesn't move. "Stop, baby. I'm barely keeping the lid on my control as it is."

"So let it go." I lean up to nibble on his earlobe. "There's no one around."

"Fuck." He grabs my wrists and brackets them behind my lower back with his hand. My back arches, pressing my breasts against his hard chest. My nipples tighten painfully. If this is his way of stopping me, it's not going to work.

"Don't you understand? If I lose control, you'll get hurt, and hurting you is the last thing I want to do."

"I'm not afraid of you."

A pained look crosses his face. "You don't really know me, Amanda. And that's my fault as much as it is yours. The more I let you in, the further you drew away, until I was afraid to be totally honest with you about what I needed."

"What do you need?" I know what I need. I need him inside me. Touching me. Stroking me. Showing me he wants me.

With a low growl, he tightens his grip on my wrists, pressing them against my lower back while his other hand tangles in my hair. He kicks my legs apart and presses his thigh against the curve of my sex. Holding me immobile, on the threshold of pleasure and pain, he kisses me so hard and rough and dirty, a moan tears out of my throat.

"This is what I need, baby. I want all of you. I won't settle for anything less, and until you can give that to me, this is as far as I'm willing to go and as close as I'm willing to get."

"Thanks for inviting me for lunch, but we could have had our meeting at the office."

I slide into the booth across from Ray and pull out my notebook.

The little Italian café in the SOMA District is packed, and the waiters have to run an obstacle course of briefcases, backpacks, chairs, and feet between the kitchen and the tables. My mouth waters at the rich, spicy scent of tomato sauce laced with the yeasty fragrance of baking bread from the brick pizza oven.

"Shhhh." Ray puts a finger to his lips and I frown. The restaurant is a cacophony of sound, from the ring of cell phones to the clang of cookware, from the shouts of the cooks in the open kitchen to the very loud buzz of the crowd.

"Why shhhh? No one will be able to hear us."

He lifts his chin toward a table in the corner. I follow his gaze and freeze. Farnsworth and Evil Reid.

Immediately, I put a hand up, shielding my face. "What are they doing here? What if they see us?"

Ray shakes his head and huffs a breath through his nose. "Our booth is situated outside their line of vision. Restroom is behind them. No chance they'll see us unless they have some reason to walk this way. Keep your menu in case they do. They're meeting someone and I want you to see him in person. I knew the meet would be here since they come to this restaurant for lunch every Thursday."

"I only just gave you the Farnsworth case. How do you know they come here every Thursday?"

Ray lifts an eyebrow. Thus chastised, I slump back in my seat. "Okay. You're amazing. Is that what you wanted to hear?"

Finally I get a smile. "Never one to turn down a compliment."

The waitress arrives to take our order, and after she leaves, Ray gives me a rundown on where he is with my cases. While he's talking, I glance over at Evil Reid and Farnsworth laughing together and a pang of regret tightens my gut. Did I really ever have a chance at partnership when Evil Reid and Farnsworth are so tight? Maybe all those years I was working hard, I should have been playing the game. Making friends. Sleeping with the enemy...or enemies.

"So who is this guy you want me to see?" I drum my fingers on the table beside the bread basket which I am NOT going to indulge in today. No bread. Bad bread. Carbs and Amanda don't mix.

Ray covers my hand with his own, forcing my fingers to still. "He's not a good guy. You ever see him, you call me ASAP. You do NOT pull shit like you did at Hunter's Point."

A smile tugs at my lips. "I sense you're a little annoyed about last night."

Ray leans across the table. "I was fucking out of my mind and that's sayin' something. I'm a pretty relaxed kinda guy. I don't interfere in people's lives. But you and Pen, all sweet and innocent, traipsing around Hunter's Point dressed the way you were dressed..."

"I'm touched by your concern," I say dryly. "However—"

"You need help, you ask for it." Ray cuts me off with a growl. "Big problem of yours, not being able to ask for help. Get over it."

"Um...thanks for the advice. You'll be pleased to know Jake agrees with you." My voice is tight with sarcasm, but if Ray even notices, he gives no sign.

"Don't mention it."

The waitress arrives with our pizzas, but before I can dig into the mouthwatering feast in front of me, Ray grabs a menu and holds it up at the edge of the table.

Instinctively, I duck down behind it. "What? What is it? Are they coming?"

He shakes his head. "Short, skinny Italian dude in the red shirt. Gold chains around his neck. Whole lotta trouble going on there."

"He looks like he's in the mafia," I whisper as I peer over the menu.

"He is."

I suck in a sharp breath. "Seriously?"

"No."

"No?"

Ray snorts a laugh. "Name's Eugene Clements. PI. Farnsworth hired him to replace me."

I press my lips together and glare. "Funny, Ray. Very funny."

"It was funny." He treats me to a rare Ray smile. "Shoulda seen your face. Sheet white."

My lips quiver with a repressed smile. "So why did I never know about your sense of humor before?"

Ray's smile fades. "Nothin' funny about Farnsworth & Tillman. Your firm, however, amusing as hell."

Evil Reid pulls a blue file folder from his briefcase with a picture attached and hands it to Eugene. Even from this distance I can recognize my firm PR shot. My heart stutters in my chest.

"Omigod, Ray. That's a picture of me." My voice rises above the din. "That file is about me!"

Ray's hand grips my wrist with what feels like an iron claw and he pulls me across the table. "Discretion. Name of the game."

"Okay."

"Silence. Also the name of the game."

"Okay."

He releases my wrist and nods to my pizza. "You can eat now."

"I've lost my appetite. It creeps me out thinking someone is watching me."

A curious expression crosses Ray's face. Regret? Distaste? Consternation? But before I can figure it out, it's gone.

Ray devours his pizza while I toy with what could have been a delightful feast, and the next five minutes pass in silence. Farnsworth and Evil Reid leave the café but Ray still doesn't speak. For some reason, this scares me more than anything, and I struggle to find a topic to divert our attention.

"Ray, can I ask you a question?"

"Nope."

"Why?"

"'Cause when a woman asks if she can ask a question, then she's wantin' to ask a question no man wants to answer. If it was just a normal question, you would have asked it. Normally."

"Okay."

We eat in silence for a few minutes and then Ray sighs.

"What was the question?"

I shrug my shoulders. "It's not important."

"Question. Now." He barks the commands like a drill sergeant. Maybe in a past life he was a drill sergeant or maybe it was a past life within this life, like before he became a PI, which would explain the commando clothes and attitude.

"Um…well…if you were a guy…"

"I am a guy."

I give Ray a nasty glance and continue. "As a guy, if a woman said to you she wanted you, meaning she wanted to have sex with you, and she said she wanted it right then, and every time you were together, she pretty much shouted it in your face, but each time you just teased her and walked away, would you expect her to keep waiting? Or would that mean you weren't really serious and you were just having fun with her? Or would it mean you were serious but you wanted to wait? And if you wanted to wait, why would you want to wait, because it's not like you hadn't had sex before?"

"Christ." He shakes his head. "I knew I shouldn't have asked."

"Well?" I hold my breath as I wait for Ray, of all people, to give me relationship advice.

"Wouldn't wait."

My breath catches in my throat. "Not for any reason?"

"Woman's in the mood, that's the time to do it. And if it was my woman, to hell with everything else. She wants it. She gets it. Done."

"You don't need some time to think about it?" My voice rises to a squeak.

Ray gives me a wry smile. "Stats say a man thinks about sex about twenty times a day. Man like me, more. When it comes available, a man does *not* turn it down. Especially if it's his woman. A real man looks after his woman. You get me?"

"Yeah." I heave a sigh. "I get you. I also get you've got some caveman blood still lurking in there somewhere."

Ray lifts an eyebrow and tightens his jaw. "That said, it's not just about sex."

"You've just told me you think about sex more than twenty times a day and you'll sleep with any woman who's in the mood. How can you tell me it's not just about sex?"

"Sex is sex. Relationships are something else."

"I've never been good at relationships." I stare at the table, toying with my fork. "Sex has always been my marker as to whether a guy likes me or not. But relationships scare me. You let people get close, and invariably they let you down. I've been hurt so many times, I just can't be that open or give myself to anyone that way."

"Fucked up."

"Yeah, I guess I am."

Ray chuckles. "Not you. I meant a man doesn't turn down a woman like you without a damn good reason."

My mouth curls into a half smile. "You make it sound so simple."

"It is simple."

"Maybe for you." I give him a full smile. "Thanks for answering the question."

"Pleasure. This mean you'll change out the couch?"

Change out the couch? Take out my stiff blue corporate boys and replace them with an old Victorian madam, torn and worn in more ways than one? Not very professional. Not very Farnsworth & Tillman. But then, neither was this lunch, or having employees work for free, one of whom lives on my couch, or running a law firm out of a partially renovated, soon-to-be historical landmark. Maybe I could be a little bit flexible.

Biting my lip, I nod. "Okay. As compensation for going out of your way to needlessly protect me last night and bringing to my attention that I am going to be followed by a man who may or may not be in the mafia, and answering my convoluted question, you can have your couch."

"And Penny's screensaver?"

"You're pushing it, Ray."

He gives me a cheeky grin. "Only pushing 'cause I know you're a pushover."

"You wish."

He flags down the waitress and his smile broadens. "I don't make wishes, sweetheart. If I want something, I go for it and to hell with the consequences. If you sit around waiting for things to happen, life will pass you by."

"Simple."

Ray gives me a curt nod. "That it is."

Chapter 11

IS MY SURPRISE UNDER HERE?

"WELCOME TO METAL HELL."

After handing our tickets to the heavyset bouncer with the ZZ-Top beard, Penny, Shayla, and I file through the narrow doorway and into the dilapidated warehouse-cum-concert venue that is the site of one of the most anticipated underground death metal events of the year. I catch a whiff of piss, pot, unwashed bodies, and stale beer all wrapped up in a nausea-inducing olfactory package. The dark, dank club is as far from heaven as one can get.

"Love death metal. Whoo. Go Slugs." Penny pumps her fist in the air and screams as we push our way through the crowd.

Shocked at her outburst, I clamp my hand around her arm. "What happened to your British reserve?"

"Reserve goes out the window when British people cut loose, and after our little warm-up party in the office, I'm looser than a hooker's…"

"We get it." Shayla cuts her off with a glare.

Penny shoots Shayla an evil look. "Have you seen the lead singer? He totally has the British rocker thing going. I know you Americans don't go for the Rolling Stones type, but to me, he is fit. That's how we say hot in England." She joins the crowd in a loud chant. "Slugs. Slugs. Slugs."

We push our way through the crowd and I scan the area for Jake. I haven't seen him since he dropped me off two nights ago except for the brief five minutes he spent at my office to hand over the tickets. A peck on the cheek, a casual "see you at seven," and a throwaway "remember, don't wear panties," and he was out the door. Penny immediately set about dousing my fire by opening a bottle of white wine. Now, I realize what a mistake that was.

Shayla tries to shush Penny again, and for a moment I worry she's going to lose her patience, but suddenly she pulls up short and grabs my arm. "There's Fuzz. Over by the speaker with Jake."

She waves her hand in the air and catches Fuzzy's attention.

"He's coming." She turns to me. "How do I look? Girly enough?"

My eyes drift over her cargo pants, kicks, and death metal shirt emblazoned with a flaming skull. "Nice. But maybe take out the ponytail."

With a sigh, Shayla pulls out her ponytail holder and shakes her head. "How's this?"

"You still look like you're a commando at a death metal concert," Penny says. "Not so good for picking up guys."

"And you look like you're clubbing on someone's yacht." Shayla gives a disdainful sniff at Penny's white skirt, matching kitten heels, and gold tank. "I don't do that kind of girly anymore. I packed it all away when I hung up my tutu and started on the 'roids. Didn't last long on those. Messed me up pretty bad."

Penny's eyes widen. "You were taking steroids? I've always wanted to try them, bulk up a bit. How did they work out for you?"

"Who's taking 'roids?" Fuzzy says as he and Jake join us. I make the introductions and Shayla shoots us a pleading glance. If anyone found out she had taken steroids, she could lose her fight license.

"Me," a quick-thinking Penny says brightly.

Fuzzy stares down at her curvy, five-foot-four-inch frame that, according to Penny, has never seen a gym, and gives her an incredulous look. "You're taking 'roids?"

"That's right." She flexes her soft, pasty arms. "Lookit these pythons. 'Roids all the way."

Shayla bursts into laughter. Not just a giggle or a chuckle or even a guffaw. Real, uncontrollable, straight-from-the-belly, tears-pouring-down-your-cheeks laughter.

Fuzzy's gaze cuts to her. His eyes linger over her soft, chestnut waves. He smiles. Then his smile fades into a frown.

"Christ," he mutters. "Almost didn't recognize you there, Shill. Did you wash your hair?" He gives her a friendly thump on the back and her laughter dries up with a choke.

Jake's arms slide around me and he pulls me back into his chest. "Your idea," he whispers in my ear, gesturing toward Shayla.

"No, she pulled out her ponytail holder all on her own."

Jake laughs. "Nice try."

"I thought you were angry with me for trying to seduce you." I look back over my shoulder and he rests his cheek against my forehead. "Except for the tickets, I haven't heard from you in two days."

"I didn't hear from you for two days either."

"This is true, but I have an excuse. I'm insanely busy at work. My witness gave me a list of women who may also have been harassed by Farnsworth, and I've already got another interview lined up. You'll be pleased to know Ray has checked the addresses and marked the interviews he wishes to attend in the guise of a guard dog."

"I'm pleased." Jake's hands slide down over my abdomen, his fingers resting in a V just over my mound. "And I'll be more pleased if you followed my instructions." His breath is hot and moist in my ear and a delicious shiver of anticipation winds its way up my spine. After only a few hours without my panties, I'm already so wet I'm afraid my arousal will trickle down my inner thigh. Not that I would tell him.

"Why would I follow your instructions when you made it clear you have…limits? Maybe I'm not up for another tickle and tease."

He tightens his arms and presses his lips against my ear. "Don't worry. I'm gonna take care of you tonight."

My body heats. "Well in that case, I have a surprise for you."

Taking a quick glance around, he slides his hand between us and surreptitiously lifts my skirt to fondle my bare ass. "Is my surprise under here?"

"Beast." I slap his hand away. "You'll have to wait."

A ripple of excitement runs through the crowd as the warm-up band hits the stage. The lead guitarist grabs his guitar and the first few notes of a death metal guitar riff fill the room.

"Eeeeeee!" shrieks Penny. "It's the warm-up band. I want to be up front." She holds her hands together like a battering ram and shoves her way forward through the thicket of long, stringy hair, faded jeans, tattoos, and piercings.

"C'mon, Shill," Fuzzy mutters. "We'd better get her. She's so tiny, she'll get crushed."

With a defeated sigh, Shayla follows Fuzzy through the crowd.

Jake nuzzles my neck. "You want a drink?"

"Sure."

A few minutes later, we're pressed up against the bar, a temporary wooden structure that looks like it could collapse at any moment. If not for Jake's strength and determination, we would never have made it through the crowd. Even now he has one hand braced against the counter and his back to the heaving mass of people to give us breathing room.

The bartender shoves two cups of beer—the only item on offer—in our direction and I wrinkle my nose.

Jake laughs. "Still not a fan?"

"Not really. Especially if it's warm, which I'm guessing it is." I dip my finger in the cup and pop it in my mouth. The beer is indeed warm and very bitter, but the heat in Jake's eyes as I slide my lips over my finger makes it easy to swallow.

"Again." His voice is husky and filled with sensual promise.

"You like that?"

"Yeah, baby, I do." His hand tangles in my hair and he yanks my head back so hard my eyes tear. With his other hand around my waist, he pulls me tight against his body. I sense a shift in the crowd around us, and then people surge toward the stage, leaving us alone at the bar.

"You drive me fucking crazy." With a nip, he parts my lips, and his tongue sweeps inside, searching, possessing, teasing, until my knees tremble and my body turns liquid.

"Remember that night we met?" he murmurs against my lips. "We fucked against one mirror and watched ourselves in the other and you told me it was how you imagined it would feel to have sex in a crowd?"

"That was a good night."

"The night I met you was the best night of my life."

Before I can respond, he deepens the kiss. Our tongues tangle, teeth clash, lips bruise. Lust, raw and ragged, tears through me, and I can only cling to his shoulders and hold on for the ride.

"We're gonna do it now." His voice deepens to a growl. "We're gonna make that fantasy come true."

"Maybe not here." But a few minutes and multiple shoves of angry fans later, we are in the shadowed alcove leading to the equipment room. Doors in back. Walls on the sides. And an entire warehouse of screaming fans in front of us. If the band could see past the glare of spotlights, they would have a front row seat to what's about to go down, and if anyone turns around and takes more than a casual glance, they would be able to see us too.

Jake presses me up against the doors, his broad back hiding me from view. He slides his hand under my T-shirt and his thumb brushes over my nipple, already peaked and aching under my bra. Lightning zings straight to my core and I gasp into his mouth.

"Been thinking about your breasts all day and how I didn't give them proper attention." His hands ease up my shirt and he shoves up my bra.

"Jake…" But my protest comes too late. My breasts tumble free into his waiting palms.

A fresh burst of energy hits the crowd as the band starts a new song. The warehouse pulses and throbs with the first roll of the drum. The venue must be over capacity, because even at the back, there is little room to move. Not that I want to move. Plastered against Jake's body so tight I can feel the beat of his heart, the rise and fall of his chest, the steel of his erection pressed against my abdomen, suddenly there is nowhere else I want to be.

He releases me with a low groan and then his hands trace my curves, over my hips, down to the edge of my skirt. Easing it up ever so gently, he traces lazy circles up my inner thigh. "I wanna hear you scream, baby."

"How about your surprise first?" I slide his hand to the front and draw it up under my skirt.

Jake sucks in a sharp breath as he strokes his finger over the fuzz-free curve of my sex. "Bare. For me."

"For you."

He gives me a devilish smile, all crinkled eyes and rakish charm, and rests one forearm on the wall beside my head while his other hand explores, his fingers spreading my folds, easing my legs apart. "Open for me."

A naughty thrill of sensation floods my body and I inch my legs apart. "When you talk like that...say things like that...it makes me so wet."

"I know." He dips his fingers between my thighs and spreads my wetness up and around my clit, tearing a moan from my throat.

"And I know you'll like this even more." He kicks my legs farther apart and glides his fingers along my wet folds, parting them, exposing my hidden depths. My brain fuzzes at the intimate touch while around us the crowd roars.

"Oh God. You're right." I slide my hands over his shoulders and thread my fingers through his soft, silky hair.

He eases one finger into my center, swollen and throbbing, and I almost come right then. My body stiffens then arches toward him, my fingers gripping his shoulders so hard I'm sure I'll leave bruises. But I can't deny the delicious thrill of his touch where the risk of being seen is so high, the danger so great, and the pleasure so intense.

"I want to hear you." He withdraws his finger then thrusts it in again, deeper this time. "I want you to come all over my hand. I want you to scream because I made you scream and you wanted me to do it."

Coiled tight, I rock my hips against his palm, seeking just the barest touch on my swollen nub to send me over the edge, but he keeps just out of reach, leaving me to grind against his fingers until I am ready to scream with frustration.

Jake gives a satisfied growl. "You like fucking my fingers, knowing any moment someone might turn and see what a dirty girl you really are."

"Yes." My head drops against the wall, my body trembling.

He rubs his fingers along my inner walls, pushing deep, deeper than I imagined fingers could go. My tension builds, but every time I near my peak, he slows his pace until I'm squirming and whimpering and begging for release. My hands are no longer gentle in his hair. Instead they are claws, dug into his shoulders so deep nothing could pry them away.

"You're tight, baby. So damn tight. I want so bad to be inside you."

His erotic words shoot me right to the edge. Stiffening, gripping him, my body burning, I whisper, "Make me come."

He presses his lips to my ear and whispers, "You'll come when I want you to come."

My brain fuzzes and my sex clenches around him. Jake kisses me softly, gently while his fingers pump hard and deep and fast inside me, an overwhelming dichotomy of sensation. I don't know whether I should cry or moan or whimper or shout or beg. All I know is my body is coiled tight, tighter than it's ever been, and the need for release is so strong it borders on pain.

"Do it now. I can't take any more." I whimper, unable to control the desperate rock of my hips as he withdraws his fingers yet again.

"Not yet."

My lust-soaked brain tries to process his words. Why am I not coming when I want to come? Why am I playing this game? But the answer comes in a heartbeat. Somewhere deep inside I wanted this. And I knew what the game was going to be the minute I took off my panties.

The next three minutes are the longest of my life. Jake brings me up and takes me down. A flick of his thumb over my throbbing clit, the stroke of his finger over my swollen inner tissue, a hand squeezing my breasts, and even a breathtaking moment when he bares one breast for his nipping pleasure. The band plays. The bass pounds. Moisture floods my sex, trickling down my thighs. Excitement and fear thunder through my veins. The fans cheer and stomp their feet. But nothing is as loud as the rush of blood through my veins or the rasp of Jake's breath in my ear, and nothing has ever consumed me so absolutely and totally as the almost painful, overwhelming need to orgasm.

"Jake…please."

"You're doing so well, baby. Breathe through it. Give it up to me." He slicks my moisture up and around my clit, so close but never close enough, bringing me down again from the peak I almost reached seconds ago. I tighten, gripping him, my body getting wetter, hotter, clenching around his fingers, and he continues to torture and tease.

The band finally segues into a new tune. My pleas become whimpers. Jake whispers encouragement in my ear. He tells me he knows it hurts, but it will be worth it in the end. He tells me to let go, to trust him to take care of me. Never have I been so completely at a man's mercy. Never have I been so out of my mind with lust I don't care.

The tempo changes. The lead singer falls to his knees. Smoke jets into the air, perfuming the venue with the chalky, sweet scent of dry ice. The music turns into one long stream of white noise. The lead singer screams and the audience screams back.

"Now, baby." Jake's voice rumbles in my ear. "Come for me." He simultaneously strokes his thumb over my clit and pulses his fingers against the sensitive tissue of my inner walls. I shoot from simmer to full boil in an instant, coiling, coiling, climbing, and then my orgasm hits like a tidal wave, crashing over me, drowning me in sensation until I can't tell the difference between pleasure and pain.

And I scream. A scream to end all screams, blending in with the screams around me. Head back, body rigid, hands locked around Jake's neck. The scream starts in my belly and radiates outward, taking my tension, my need, and my will with it. My orgasm grips me, my hips rocking violently against his hand, but he continues to stroke inside me, drawing it out until I slump, boneless, against the wall.

"Fuck. That was beautiful." He pulls me up against his chest, taking my weight in his strong arms. "I want you so bad I'm tempted to take you right here. Right now."

"Please do."

He cups my jaw with his hand and tilts my head up. His jaw is tight and tension creases the corners of his eyes. "Not yet."

"But…" I slide one hand over his erection, palming his hard steel through his jeans. "You're so hard. Let me take care of you."

"It's okay, baby. I'm good." He releases me and helps me straighten my clothes while I lean against the door, dazed, exhausted, and confused. I look out over the sea of heads and spot a flash of gold on stage. "Oh. My. God. Penny's on the stage."

Jake spins around, and for a moment we can only stare at Penny dirty dancing with the lead singer.

"Where the fuck is Fuzz?"

I scan the crowd and spot Fuzzy and Shayla frantically trying to get Penny's attention. "There. Right up at the front. They're trying to coax her down." But with the lead singer wrapped around her, and their hips humping and pumping in time to a heavy metal ballad, Penny doesn't seem interested in anything except the tribute to death metal grinding his cock into her ass.

"We'd better go give them a hand." Jake brushes his lips over my cheek. "When you said she was into death metal, you weren't kidding."

We take a few steps out of the alcove and I hesitate. "Wait. I think they're done. He's slipping something into her hand." As the last notes of the ballad fade away, the lead singer spins Penny around and plants a long, wet one on her. All tongue. No class.

The crowd goes crazy. Penny grins and curtsies. Fuzzy leaps up on stage with the agility of a pole-vaulter and helps her back down to the floor. High fives all round.

By the time we reach them, the band is halfway through their next song.

"He invited me backstage after the show," Penny whispers in my ear after I pull her aside. "His name is Vetch Retch, and boy, can he kiss."

I glance up at Vetch. He is well over six feet of skinny scrawniness. Long, unkempt hair falling to the waist; eyes ringed black with makeup; tight, black leather pants that show off his scrawny chicken-like legs. Mick Jagger eat your heart out.

"You can do better."

Penny shakes her head. "He's a British girl's dream lad. And look at that face. Stark beauty. Plus, it's been a dry year, and he's the lead singer in a famous band. Once I get a picture of us on all my social media, my mates will be seething with jealousy."

After the last of the endless encores, Shayla and I go with Penny to make sure she'll be all right on her own backstage. A huge bouncer wearing a Slugs T-shirt motions her forward with a thick finger and then he points to Shayla and me. "Ladies can join you if they want. We always like the ladies."

"*He* knows I'm a woman," Shayla whispers as we follow the bouncer along the hallway to a huge, smoky lounge. "What's Fuzzy's problem?"

The backstage lounge is heaving with people, and it takes us a few minutes to find Vetch, sprawled on a couch with a blond tucked under each arm.

"Hey, dancing girl." He waves Penny over, and Shayla and I share a glance.

"He doesn't remember her name," I say.

Shayla's eyes narrow. "From the dilation of his pupils, I'd be surprised if he remembers his own name."

"I don't like him. Something about him makes my skin crawl."

She snorts a laugh. "Could it be that he looks like he just slithered out of a swamp?"

"Hey, Vetch, you sharing?" The keyboard player, a skinny ginger-topped dude with a tiny goatee slides an arm around Shayla's waist. Her hands clench into fists and her jaw tightens. Dude is in for a whole lot of pain. I feel compelled to warn him out of the goodness of my heart.

"You might want to reconsider the position of your arm," I say to him. "Shilla the Killa is a top-ranked MMA fighter and she doesn't take kindly to uninvited affection."

"What about you?" The deep voice in my ear is accompanied by a cheeky squeeze of my ass. "You a fighter too? Because you got a mouth made for sucking and I have a special treat."

I look back over my shoulder at the greasy-haired bassist behind me. "Do you seriously think I would waste this mouth on you?"

A disturbance at the door behind us draws everyone's attention. Taking advantage of the distraction, Shayla quickly extricates herself from the unwanted arm clasp and sends the keyboard player flying across the room. She doesn't even break a sweat. In that moment, I want to be her. I want to make men fly.

She reaches up to high-five me, and the naughty hand disappears from my ass. When I turn around, the bassist is up against the wall with Jake's hand around his neck.

"That's my fucking girl you're touching."

Two burly security guards push their way through the crowd, and I spot three more coming from the other direction. I put a hand on Jake's arm. "It's okay."

"Get out of here, baby." He shakes off my arm and his eyes glitter, enraged.

Nononononono. Too many for him to handle. He's going to get hurt. "Let's just go, Jake. He just copped a feel. No big deal. I've dealt with worse."

"Amanda." He gives an exasperated shout, his body thrumming with anger. "I told you to go."

I tug on his arm and try another tactic. "I don't need your help. I have the situation under control."

And then Fuzzy is there. He puts a firm hand on Jake's shoulder and murmurs in his ear. Whatever he says has the desired effect. Jake grunts and releases the quivering bassist. He pushes me behind him, and we back out of the room while Fuzzy holds the security guards at bay with the ferocity of his gaze.

"Are you going to be okay, Penny?" I call out. "Do you want to come home with us?"

Vetch throws an arm around her shoulder and she smiles and waves. "I'm good. Vetch is going to give me a ride home in his limo."

Outside the club, we shuffle cars. Fuzzy and Shayla go home together in Fuzzy's vehicle. Jake and I climb into his Jeep. Wary of Jake's tight jaw and stiff posture, I don't even try to make small talk and we drive home in uncomfortable silence.

When he pulls up outside my house, my stomach clenches, and for once I am at a loss for words. Ever the gentleman, he walks me up the sidewalk and waits until I've unlocked the front door and flipped on the lights.

"I guess I'll see you around."

"Thanks for inviting me tonight." I give him a breezy, fake smile. "It was fun...at least until the end."

He rakes a hand through his hair and cocks his head to the side, continuing our painfully stilted conversation. "Yeah."

A moment of silence. Something in his expression falters. "I'd better get going. I've got a late-night underground fight tomorrow after the gym closes. Gotta get some sleep."

"Do you want me to come and watch?" He always wanted me at his fights before.

"Maybe not the best thing," he says, his voice tight. "We cut loose on those underground fights. No rules. No restraint. It can get pretty bloody. Some guys lose control."

My heart sinks. Something is seriously wrong, and I'm not sure what it is. I watched him at dozens of underground fights before. I was always in his corner. Doesn't he remember? Or maybe he does but he's changed his mind about us. Maybe it was a game after all. "Sure. I get it." I step inside and turn to close the door. "Good night."

"Wait."

A moment of silence. Something in his expression falters. "I just want to make sure we both know what we want before we start something."

Before we start something? The night he kissed me after the renovation party something started for me.

"What does that mean?" My voice rises in pitch. "You just want to be friends? For how long? Or do you like driving me crazy? Is that the game?"

His jaw tightens. "I don't kiss my friends."

"You kissed this one."

"I don't want you as a friend." He brushes his lips over my cheek and turns away.

What the hell? Does he want me or not? And if he wants me, why won't he sleep with me? And if not, why doesn't he want to be friends?

"I don't think you really know what you want."

He sighs and rakes his hand through his hair. "I know exactly what I want. I just don't know how I'm going to get it."

My heart sinks as he climbs into his vehicle, and for a moment I miss my old life. No relationships. No strings. No commitment. No heartache.

No Jake.

Chapter 12

SAY IT AGAIN

I DO NOTHING THE next day. No drafting documents. No checking emails. No billing time. I just sit and stare at the wall and wonder how I screwed things up so badly. As Ray says, what man doesn't want to have sex with a willing partner? And if he wants to take things slow, why is he driving me crazy? Platonic, I can do. Sex, I can do. What I can't handle is limbo.

At the end of the day, Penny returns from dropping off the mail with a process server in tow. He serves me with Farnsworth's defense to my complaint. The voluminous document is two weeks early, unbelievably vicious, and so detailed he must have had an entire stable of associates working on it night and day. My heart sinks through the floor. But the worst is yet to come.

"Have you seen this?"

Penny holds up the cover letter and points to the signature at the bottom. My jaw joins my heart on the floor.

"Oh. My. God. He has Evil Reid working the case. I'm doomed." I toss the documents on Penny's desk and grab my coat. "I think I'm going to go and play in the traffic."

"I have a better idea." Penny grabs my arm and pulls me back. "It's Friday night. Why don't we go out and have fun?"

"Fun?"

"Yes." She beams. "Fun. You remember what that is?"

I slump against her desk. "We had fun at the Slugs concert the other night. And I'm not really in the mood for fun. I'm tired and hungover. I think I've lost Jake. And now I'm the subject of a vicious ten-million-dollar countersuit from one of the most powerful law firm partners on the West Coast who says I propositioned him and then irreparably damaged his reputation by spreading false rumors."

"All the more reason to go out." Penny slams her desk drawer closed and turns off her computer. "And I'm not taking no for an answer."

Penny flags down a cab since neither of us is up for a seven-block walk in stilettos. Ten minutes later, we pull up in front of Death's Dungeon, a small, divey death metal bar in the Lower Haight. Everyone is appropriately dressed in black, unlike Penny and I in our work wear.

While we wait in line, I strip off my jacket, roll up my sleeves, pull out my ponytail, and undo a few buttons on my blouse. "You could have told me what kind of bar it was. I have a death shroud at the office."

Penny laughs. "If I gave you too much time to think, you wouldn't have come. And look at me." She gestures to her cream blouse, flared pink skirt, and kitten heels. "I'm not worried."

"That's because they seem to know you here," I mutter as the bouncer unclips the velvet VIP rope to let us through.

The smell of vodka, funk, and pot hits me as we walk deeper into the gloom. Shirtless bartenders mix cocktails at the bar and a group of metal heads play beer pong in the corner. Death metal band posters are plastered over the walls and swag litters every surface. The cocktails have names like Slime-Trail, Pound Smash Face, Maggot Brain, and Infested by Evil. I order a shot of sweet and tangy Filthy Girl while Penny sips her Bloodbath.

I so love the cult of death metal.

Seeing me wince as yet another heavily distorted guitar riff blasts through the speakers, Penny assures me that the DJs know their tech house and minimal, and maintain a good vibe between death metal sets.

Filthy Girl in hand, I follow her through the haze to a red velvet booth near the back with a good view of the raised, central dance floor. "Nothing like some death metal music to cheer a person up." I slide into the booth beside her.

"No sulking." Penny pokes me in the side. "First, you knew what would happen if you filed a lawsuit against Farnsworth, and the Amanda I know would relish the challenge. For most people, taking on a powerful partner who intends to crush you like a bug under his heel would be a terrifying, gut-churning experience. For you, it's fun. So enjoy it."

I gulp down my Filthy Girl and wave to the waitress to order another. "What's second?"

"Second is a lesson on the fragility of the alpha-male ego." Penny grabs a handful of Spawn Droppings. "If a man feels the need to throttle some guy who touches your ass, you stand back and enjoy the show. You don't tell him you have the situation under control, even if you do."

My breath catches and I have an "aha" moment about what happened between Jake and I last night. He doesn't just want me to open up, he wants me to need him, too.

"I didn't even think about it. I'm used to looking after myself."

Penny finishes off her Bloodbath and nods her head to the beat—at least I think there's a beat somewhere in the noise. "That's why you need someone strong enough to take control. Now you've found him, your problem is letting go."

"Now who's the man whisperer?"

The DJ finally loses the death metal vibe and spins a hip-hop tune that entices me onto the dance floor. Penny joins me, lamenting the lapse in death metal sets.

As I wiggle to the beat, I decline offers of drugs, sex, blow jobs, and "titty squeezes." I gently break the news to several guys that, in fact, I am not hot for them. And no, I do not wish to get a "visual" on what they are "packing" or host a "face party" between my "tits."

I dance. I drink. I dance some more. So much fun. So much time wasted. How did I forget how much I liked to dance? And why isn't Jake here with me?

Someone pinches Penny's ass. His face makes five new friends, and she doesn't even miss a beat.

After dancing through a few more songs, Penny suddenly squeals and waves at someone coming in the door. I watch her bounce her way through the crowd to a knot of people near the bar, all clustered around Vetch and the band. Vetch smiles when he sees her and pulls her in for a long, wet, tongue-down-the-throat, don't-care-who's-looking kiss.

And…I'm outta here.

Although Penny hadn't expected Vetch and the band to show up after she sent him a text from the office, she's okay with me leaving her alone with the band, especially when she catches the bassist giving me an evil look. A few moments later, I'm in the quiet comfort of a cab, my ears still ringing from the noise.

"Where to?" The cab driver looks over his shoulder after I close the door. With his blue eyes and soft face, he reminds me of Fuzzy's dad. Fuzzy's dad reminds me of Fuzzy, who reminds me of Redemption, where Jake is fighting tonight. I check my watch. Even if traffic is bad, I still have time.

Should I go?

My heart skips a beat. Somewhere deep inside, I know he wants me to be there. And I want to be there too. At the very least to be in his corner, but more than that, I don't want to throw away our second chance. Not yet.

⁓

Over an hour later, I stand in front of the side door to Redemption. The parking lot is empty and only a faint glow shines through the windows. Underground fights are unsanctioned fights and have to be kept on the QT.

The cab driver patiently waits for me to go inside. Even though everyone knows Redemption is a respectable club, at this time of night in Ghost Town, there are not many respectable people around. Last chance to change my mind.

After a few deep breaths, I open the door and cross the threshold. The gym is dimly lit by emergency lights on the perimeter walls and the spotlights hanging over the cage. As I inhale the fresh scent of disinfectant and stale sweat, I spot Blade Saw, Obsidian, and Rampage talking in the corner.

My steps slow as I near the group. Why am I here? How can I even contemplate getting close to yet another person I am sure to disappoint? And yet, in the brief time we've been together again, Jake has been kind, attentive, and caring. I can't stop myself from believing he feels something for me. That his waiting game is not a game at all. That I'm not just a bit of fun. So I close my eyes and let myself believe. And I keep walking.

Rampage sees me first and jogs across the floor to greet me. "'Manda! Haven't seen you at one of these fights for…well forever. Renegade's in the changing room. Does he know you're here?"

His eyebrow lifts when I shake my head, but he doesn't pry. Instead he introduces me to Fists of Fury, the small, wiry Irishman with thick, black hair who took over Jake's class while he fondled me on the mats, and the Minotaur, a massive hunk of muscle with a neck so short and thick he can't fully turn his head.

Blade Saw is first in the cage. He is pitted against a huge boulder of a fighter from the competing club. He wins his fight in thirty seconds. Then he does a crazy dance around the ring. I can't help but laugh.

"Finally, a smile," Rampage says. "Renegade is up next, so that'll give you something to keep smiling about. He's fighting Axe Man. Same weight class but a more experienced fighter and a submission expert."

Jake crosses the mats to the cage. His orange fight shorts hug his perfect ass like a second skin. His pecs ripple as he opens the door to the cage and I breathe out a sigh. I'll never tire of looking at his perfect body.

"Let him know you're here," Rampage says, pushing me forward.

"Maybe I'll wait until after the fight."

"Oh fer…RENEGADE! 'MANDA'S HERE." He shoves me and I stumble toward the cage. My heart thuds wildly in my chest and I force a smile, but Jake's face remains an expressionless mask. When he turns away to talk to the referee, my stomach clenches.

"I should go."

Rampage's gaze flicks from me to Jake and back to me. "I don't think you wanna do that."

"I don't know what I want."

Rampage chuckles and throws an arm around my shoulder. "If you didn't know what you wanted, you wouldn't have come here."

The ref blows the whistle. Jake is quick to start, moving Axe Man back with a flurry of punches. He lands a solid jab and a leg kick that throws Axe Man against the cage, but Axe Man isn't even winded. He comes raging back with a combination of powerful kicks and punches that have Jake staggering across the mat until the fence is at his back. With Jake trapped, Axe Man hooks Jake's head and unloads with some devastating uppercuts. Jake reels back against the fence, but Axe Man continues his assault, firing away with some brutal lefts.

"Oh God." My hand flies to my mouth and Rampage frowns. Quickly swallowing my fear, I shout and cheer instead. My enthusiasm draws Jake's attention. His eyes focus like laser beams on my shoulders and Rampage snatches his arm away with a muttered string of curses.

Axe Man takes advantage of his distraction to deliver some more devastating lefts. Jake sags to a seated position and bile rises in my throat. For the first time ever, I understand Makayla's intolerance for violence.

The referee raises the whistle to his lips, but Jake jumps up and sweeps Axe Man's feet from under him. Within moments, he has Axe Man on the mat in a vicious chokehold. He pummels Axe Man's head and face until blood drips onto the mat. The referee stops the fight and announces Jake the winner by brute force.

Jake descends triumphant from the cage, high-fiving the Redemption fighters clustered around the base of the stairs, but his gaze is firmly fixed on me. A sheen of sweat covers his broad chest and his hard abs ripple with movement as he stalks across the mats toward me. Confident. Sure. Predatory.

So beautiful. Inside and out.

Swallowing my anxiety, I smile when he finally reaches my corner. "Great fight."

"What are you doing here?" His abrupt tone and his level gaze make me tremble, but I hold my ground.

"I came to see you fight and…maybe talk about the other night."

He shrugs. "Not much to talk about. You made it pretty clear backstage at the concert that you don't need me in your life."

Frowning, I glance quickly around to ensure we're alone. "I didn't need to see you getting beat up by eight security guards in a tiny room, then getting arrested and destroying your fight career. That's what I didn't need."

"You didn't trust me." He grasps my chin and tilts my head back. "I had no plans to start a brawl. I just wanted to send a message."

With an annoyed grunt, I wrench my head away. "And you didn't trust me to be able to deal with a guy like him on my own. You think I haven't had my ass squeezed before? Or dealt with inflated egos and potty mouths? If you and Fuzzy hadn't shown up, Shilla the Killa and I would have had them groaning on the floor."

He lifts an eyebrow and a smile ghosts his lips. "I can imagine."

My gaze drops, skimming over the contours of his pecs, and then follows the dusky trail of hair to the waistband of his orange fight shorts. Black dragons curl down the sides, breathing a fire as dark as my despair.

"Look at me."

Without thinking, I snap my gaze back to his. Exhaustion lines his face but his eyes gleam fever bright and the raw hunger in their blue depths makes my nipples harden.

"I get your issue with what happened backstage," he says softly. "But you need to understand mine. You caught me at a moment when I was feeling particularly possessive about your ass, and when I saw that bastard's hand on you, I snapped."

"I do understand. That's why I came here tonight. To say I'm sorry. I care about you. I didn't want to see you get hurt. But I should have let you do what you do best. I like that you're protective. If things had gotten ugly, there's no one else I would have wanted in my corner."

Jake steps forward. Instinctively I step back. Although I know he would never hurt me, he is intimidating just the same, and with blood splatters on his chest, his body still vibrating from the adrenaline of the fight, I react as anyone would react when faced with a predator. Heart pounding, pulse racing, I retreat.

When my back hits the wall, Jake leans one forearm beside my head and touches his forehead to mine. "Say it again."

"I'm sorry?"

His lips quiver with a repressed smile. "That was a good part, but there was a part I liked better."

"I care about you."

"You care about me." His lips brush over my ear, soft as butterfly wings, and he drops one hand to my hip, pulling me close. "You want me."

"More than anything." Tentative at first, and then with firm pressure, I press my hands against his chest, drinking in the feeling of smooth skin over rock hard muscle. His scent of soap and sweat and the essence of male surrounds me, overwhelms me, and I bite back a moan.

"Christ." He draws in a deep breath and pulls away. "Go home, Amanda."

Chapter 13
TIGER. TIGER. TIGER

MY BREATH CATCHES AND my blood chills. "You want me to go home?"

"I want to fuck you." His jaw tightens and he licks his lips. "I want to push you onto the mat, rip off your clothes, and bury myself so deep you can't tell where I end and where you begin. I want to lick your pussy until you scream, flip you over, take you hard, and make you scream again. But that's not going to happen. You're going to go home and climb into your frilly little bed and dream your sweet little dreams. I'm going to step into the cage with Carnage and take out my frustration on him."

My lower half turns liquid, and I slide my hands around his neck, pulling him down to my lips. "What if I don't go?"

He nips my bottom lip, sending a blade of heat straight to my core. "You have to go, baby. I won't be able to control myself. I've wanted you so bad for so long, and after I've been in the cage, I can't think straight. Even now…" He gives a guttural groan and his fist clenches on my hip.

Primitive. Primal. His need speaks to me. I tighten my grip on his neck and rock up to kiss him, gliding my tongue over the seam of his lips before he has a chance to protest. He allows me only that brief moment of control before he takes over. His kiss is hard and demanding. Cupping my jaw, he thrusts his tongue deep, leaving me in no doubt of his possession.

"Mine." His voice is raw, savage, and for the first time, I truly believe he may lose control.

A whistle blast startles us back to reality. The fights are over and it's time for clean up and take down. Jake wrenches himself away and without a backward glance, stalks over to the cage. I take a few deep breaths to calm my pounding heart and then I join Rampage putting away the chairs.

"All sorted then," he murmurs.

"Shut up, Rampage. And by the way, gloating is not a good look on you."

For the next fifteen minutes, I manage to keep my distance from Jake by helping clean up the fight zone. Rampage ushers everyone out and then gives me a wink and a wave as he closes the door. Heart pounding, I head back to the cage where Jake is disinfecting the mat. At first I wonder if he's seen me, but then he looks up and his eyes blaze like coals in the night.

"Have you ever been in an MMA cage?" He returns to his work, scrubbing the mat with an unsettling vigor. But something in his voice catches me off guard. An edge that makes my senses tingle.

"Um…no."

"Come and check it out. You'll have to make a decision sooner or later about whether you want to fight in the cage. Might as well get a taste for it when it's not being used."

My pulse kicks up a notch when he glances up at me, and I catch a wild, almost feral gleam in his eyes. His lithe body burns with energy. His muscles twitch. Violence simmers beneath his skin. Danger whispers around him.

"I'm good. I'll just wait here."

He studies me for the longest moment and then his voice drops to a low rumble. "Come here, baby. I won't bite." He tilts his head to the side and smiles. The familiar gesture eases the tightness in my chest. Taking a deep breath, I walk up the steps to the cage.

Bang. Bang. Bang. My heart thuds a warning against my ribs.

As if he can sense my anxiety, Jake continues to wipe down the already clean mat, his back to me, tight ass perfectly outlined in orange and black satin.

Tiger. Tiger. Tiger. Instinct joins my heart in warning. My skin prickles and I am almost overcome with the urge to flee.

But I am the master of myself. Always in control.

Stiffening my spine, I open the cage door. Jake's head whips around.

A shudder runs through his body. He drops the cloth and sits back on his haunches, watching, assessing.

Tiger. Tiger. Tiger. I freeze midstep and my breath catches in my throat.

"Come." His voice is soft, coaxing. "It's just a fight cage."

Instinct and my rational mind war over what to do. My muscles lock. I force myself to step into the cage. Sweat beads my brow. I wipe it off. Blood pounds through my veins. I release the door and it clangs behind me. Adrenaline surges through my body. My mouth goes dry.

Jake stands and prowls to the opposite side of the cage. His feet pad softly across the mat as he hunts for traces of blood. My breath comes in short pants as he stalks closer and closer to my safe little space beside the cage door.

Tiger. Tiger. Tiger. I reach blindly behind me for the latch.

"What's wrong?" Jake's hand slides over mine and he tugs my fingers off the latch. "You afraid of the cage?"

"You." I swallow hard and force the words through the pounding in my chest. "In the cage, you weren't in control."

"I'm always in control." His hands slide through my hair, cupping my head, pulling me toward him, and the adrenaline rush of fear becomes tinged by lust.

"You…you…aren't in control now."

He brushes his lips over my ear and whispers, "If I wasn't in control, you would be naked, on all fours, in the middle of the cage, and I'd be fucking you so hard you wouldn't remember your name."

My heart slams into overdrive and a heat flush sweeps through my body, searing my skin. I grasp for a way out, knowing even as I say the words that I've made a poor choice. "It's a good thing then that we're just friends."

Jake growls low in his chest. With two steps, he backs me up to the edge of the mat and then slams his hand against the fence beside my head, sending a chill through my veins. "I told you before, I don't want to be your friend."

"Okay." Definitely not in control.

Drawing in a ragged breath, I try to slide away, but his hand curls around my neck and tightens, holding me still. "I want to be your everything." His breath is soft on my cheek. "I want all of you, baby. When I make you mine, really mine, there will be no part of you my lips, my hands, and my cock won't touch, no desire you have that I will not fill. And when I fuck you, there will be no fear, no hesitation, and no regrets. My cock will be so deep inside you that you will know nothing but me. You will be mine; I will be yours and it will be so right we'll feel it in here." He thumps his chest over his heart and something inside me snaps.

So much longing. So much wanting. Fear. Confusion. Frustration. And anger. "Then do it." I shove at his chest with two hands. "I've made it clear that I want you. I've given you all I can give. But still you just tease me and run away. Close but not too close—is that the game?"

Far from making him back down, my anger is fuel to his fire. He grabs my wrists and slams them against the fence over my head. The impact jolts my body, but I feel no pain, only an overwhelming physical and emotional need to slake my lust.

"Do you think it's been easy?" He presses his body against me. "Do you think I didn't want you every minute of every day since I saw you again? But I am NOT fucking this up like I fucked up everything else in my life. I want this to be the one thing that goes right. We were good in bed together, baby, but you never let me close. This time I want to know you inside and out, and I want you to know me, so when we are finally together, it is something more than just a good time. It's something we both know will last. So yes, when I feel like I'm going to lose control, I back away."

"I do know you." I shiver in his grasp. "I haven't stopped thinking about you since the day we broke up. You're generous and thought-ful. Not many people would sacrifice the way you have to help your family. You're an amazing teacher. You can get people to do things they never thought they could do. You're a skilled carpenter and a gifted fighter. I love those things about you. What more do you want?" I struggle against his grip, writhing between the fence and the hard press of his body.

"I want you to want me until you ache." He groans, but still doesn't release me. "I want you to need me with every breath in your body. I want to turn around and know I will always see you in my corner. I want you to want me the way I want you. Body, heart, and soul."

He wants me.

He wants me.

Fuzzed with lust, my brain barely takes in more than those three words. My body aches with need. If he would only step back so I couldn't feel his hard chest against my breasts, inhale his scent of sex and sweat, or hear the deep tremor of his voice that betrays his arousal. Desire wouldn't be curled around my lungs so tight I have to fight to breathe.

"I want you," I whisper. I will do anything, say anything, to get him inside me to have the one thing I understand, the intimacy that tells me his words are real.

With a groan, I move against him, pressing and rubbing, grinding my hips against his. He may be holding my hands but I still have power, and if I've learned one thing over the years, it's how to use it.

"Stop, Amanda." He groans. "Fuck, baby. Don't... I want you so bad. I won't be able to... Stop."

But I can't stop. I am helpless to stop. I need him too much, and I let him know it with every twist of my body, every whimper from my lips. This is how I speak. This is how I communicate the torrent of emotion inside me.

His hand tightens painfully around my wrists. He leans closer, so close I can feel every wire of the fence against my body. I can breathe every breath with him. My skin is his skin. My heart is his heart. My head falls back and I moan and grind against him.

"Fuck." And then he screams it, "Fuck." Still holding my wrists with one hand, he tears open my shirt with one swift, brutal jerk. Buttons patter across the mat in a hailstorm of plastic tears.

I have unleashed the tiger.

With a low growl, he rips open the front closure of my bra. My breasts spill into his palm. There is no gentleness in his touch, no soft caresses. Rough, calloused fingers squeeze soft flesh, pinch and tweak taut nipples. Teeth nip, lips suck, skin bruises. But all his rough ministrations do is inflame me even more until my body is wound so tight, one touch in the right place will set me free.

"Christ. I didn't want it to be like this." Muttering under his breath, he shoves my skirt up to my waist. "I wanted to wait. I wanted it to be perfect. I wanted past the walls you've built up around your heart. But you're too fucking much to resist. Too damn hot. Too damn sexy. I've wanted you so bad for so long. And you pushed me too fucking hard."

A yank. Fabric rents. My panties flutter to the ground like a discarded tissue.

A low carnal snarl escapes his lips and he kicks my legs apart. "Open."

I suck in a sharp breath at his demand and I part my legs as all my dark fantasies come true.

And then his hand is on his waist, untying his shorts. Silk whispers over his skin. He peels off his bike shorts and then his cup and releases one of my hands.

"There's something you need to know."

Before my frantic mind can conjure up all manner of terrible things a woman might need to know two seconds before having sex with the object of her deepest desires, he guides my hand down to his cock and wraps it around the base. Almost giddy with lust, I hold him tight, luxuriating in the feel of him, hot, heavy, and throbbing in my hand.

"Keep going."

I stroke up. Silky smooth skin ripples over a core of steel, the sensation mouthwateringly erotic. But when I reach the tip I stop.

Steel.

For real.

My hand jerks away so hard it flies back and hits the fence.

Jake grasps my hand and forces it back down. He wraps my fingers around the tip of his erection and I run my fingers over a round knob at the top and another at the bottom. Finally, I look down so my mind can process what my fingers feel.

"Oh God, Jake. You're pierced right through."

"It's an apadravya piercing and if you keep touching me like that I won't be able to hold on. You got any condoms?"

"My purse." I point to my black leather handbag, discarded not so long ago beside the cage door.

He pulls away, leaving me bereft, but only for a moment. Within a minute he returns, sheathed, his cock jutting toward me from its golden nest of curls. Then he slams me back against the cage.

"This is not how I wanted you to find out." His deep voice rumbles through me. "I wanted it slow. I wanted it easy. But fuck, baby, you've wound me up so tight, I'm gonna fuck you so hard, you're gonna forget where you start and where I end."

Hand shaking, I trace a finger along his throbbing shaft, hot despite the latex. "Does it hurt?" I whisper. "When you're hard?"

Jake fists my hair and tugs my head back. "The harder I am, the better if feels, and I can tell you, it's never felt so fucking good as it does right now."

He slides his hands under my ass and lifts me against his hips. "Fingers in the fence," he orders. "I want you doing nothing but thinking about how I feel inside you."

Trembling, I reach up and hook my fingers through the wire, palms toward him. My back arches and my breasts brush against his chest.

"Such beautiful breasts." He nuzzles his way down. "Want to play with them all night."

"Please…don't."

He gives me an evil smile and draws one taut nipple into his mouth. So warm. So wet. His tongue circles, his teeth nip, his lips suck. Over and over again, his tongue teases my nipple until my breast is sore, swollen, and I am writhing against him, near mindless with need. When he turns his attention to the other one, I resort to begging.

"I need you inside me, Jake. Please. Now. I can't take any more."

Taking my weight with one hand, he slides his fingers along my wet folds and then up over my swollen clit. My body coils tighter and tighter and when he dips two fingers inside, I suck in a sharp breath and whimper.

"Christ, you're wet." His lips are hot on my ear. "So goddam wet. I was worried you wouldn't be ready, but my baby needs me bad."

"Yesss. God, yes."

His growl of satisfaction inflames me. I wrap my legs around his waist and tighten my thighs, drawing him so close his piercing bumps against my clit and my entire body shudders violently.

"None of that, little minx. You're only getting off with me buried deep inside you." And without warning, he lifts me and then slams me down over his jutting cock.

No easing in. No taking it slow. No giving me a chance to get used to the piercing. Instead he impales me and my breath catches in my throat as sensation floods my brain. So big. So thick. So hard. He is everything I remember…but more.

But it isn't the depth or girth of him that fries my brain. It isn't the violence of his thrust or the slide of his cock through my swollen channel. It's the exquisite, electrifying scrape of his piercing over my most sensitive inner tissue that makes me scream.

I am not one of those women who wonders if G-spots really exist. Or if she has a G-spot. Or even where her G-spot might be. My G-spot and I are intimately familiar. I have a special set of toys for G-spot pleasuring. I can direct a man's fingers or cock—or once even his tongue—to the exact spot for maximum pleasure. I know where, when, why, and how I want my G-spot touched. But nothing can match the feel of cold, hard steel.

He lifts me almost all the way up and then thrusts inside, deeper this time, sending shockwaves of pleasure through my body. Then he pounds into me, hands curled tight on my ass. Every thrust is a new burst of mind-numbing sensation as his piercing drags over my most sensitive area, and although I am coiled tight and ready to explode, I almost don't want the beautiful torture to end.

Almost.

"Ready for me, baby?" He slides his hand between us, fingers brushing over my swollen clit as my body slams against the fence again and again. Even as I am driven to new heights of pleasure, an unfamiliar heaviness curls low in my belly. Deep, dark, and delicious, it almost pulls me out of the moment.

Fingers pinch. My world explodes. A shriek rips from my throat as I am rocked by an earth-shattering orgasm. Pleasure thunders through my body, sending wave after wave of sensation all the way to my fingers and toes. With one last violent thrust, Jake joins me, coming hard in hot, heated jerks. And as he pulses against my swollen tissue, the heaviness deep inside me becomes a second wave of brain-fuzzing, scream-inducing exquisite pleasure.

Jake groans and leans against me, still supporting my weight. I can feel his heart pounding. I can feel the rapid rise and fall of his chest. I can feel liquid trickling down my legs from my G-spot release. Now that was a first.

"Fuck, baby. We were always good together, but never like that."

We hold each other for a few moments and then Jake withdraws and leaves the cage to dispose of the condom. When he returns, he has a first aid blanket with him and, in true fighter form, a water bottle.

"Always good to stay hydrated in the cage." He spreads the blanket on the mat and then pulls me down on top of him so my head is resting on his chest. Emotionally and physically drained, I listen to the steady thud of his heart and the rasp of his breathing. My fingers trail over the soft hair leading down from his chest to the piercing, glinting in the overhead lights.

"Did it hurt?"

He gives a bitter laugh. "Made me a better fighter. After pain like that, I don't feel anything else."

"But…why?"

His jaw tightens, and for once he won't meet my gaze. "After we broke up, it was something I just wanted to do. Maybe it's the rebel in me. Or maybe in some twisted way I wanted to punish myself for losing the best thing that ever happened to my life."

My heart squeezes in my chest. "That wasn't you, Jake. That was me."

"You tried to make it right," he says softly. "I almost fucking lost my mind the night you and Makayla went looking for me and got kidnapped. And the other times you tried to talk to me…I knew you were genuinely sorry. I could have listened. I've just never been good with forgiveness. I don't come from a forgiving family."

I stroke a finger gently over the tip of his cock, toying lightly with his piercing. He comes semierect almost instantly in my hand. "So you do things like this? You really are a renegade. I can't imagine many men who could even conceive of getting pierced. The guys I know take out their frustrations in the gym or sports field or usually the bar—not on themselves."

He draws my hand away and brings my fingers to his lips, kissing each tip with a featherlight brush of his tongue. "Ever since I was a kid, I couldn't follow the rules. I was constantly getting into trouble. My parents blamed me for everything that went wrong, even my father's alcoholism. So I became who they thought I was. A rebel. Hung out with the wrong crowd, got into trouble with the law…the total opposite of Peter."

"I can't imagine what that was like."

"Fucked up. That's what it was like." He rubs his hand up and down my back, warm and soothing.

"I finally decided I had to get out. Moved here because it was warm and I had a friend from high school who offered me a job on his construction crew. He fought at Redemption and invited me along. One night was all it took. Torment helped me get my life back together, showed me how to use fighting to deal with the anger I had inside, and he asked me to teach some classes. I would never have discovered how much I enjoy teaching if not for him. Redemption saved me in more ways than one."

"Me too," I whisper, remembering the shadows of the Redemption fighters descending on the alley outside Hellhole.

Jake chuckles. "Everything was going so well. I thought I had sorted myself out. But when you broke it off…that cut me bad. And then when I came to sort it out and caught you with Drake, that was the end for me. It was like I had failed again. I was still who my parents always thought I was. A fuckup. But this time I couldn't hurt myself with booze or drugs or stupid, petty crime. I had my fight career to think of and my teaching. So I got pierced. Painful but cathartic."

My body stiffens and guilt winds its way up my spine. I try to pull away, but Jake tightens his grip, holding me close. "When I saw you again at your firm, all cool and calm like I was any other client when I was fucking shook up inside, I thought nothing had changed. You were still totally in control of yourself, your life, everything. You'd moved on."

"In control? I dropped my notepad and pen like a total klutz." I snort a laugh. "I could barely breathe. I said stupid and inane things. You were the one who was all cool and calm. You intimidated me."

"Don't remember it that way." He presses a kiss to my forehead. "But I like to hear it."

I shift in his arms, tilting my head up so I can look at him. "So what changed?"

His body tenses and he draws in a ragged breath. "Seeing you in that alley... Fuck. You were covered in blood, and we couldn't wake you. I thought you were gonna die, and I wished to God I could have one more chance."

His arms tighten around me, and I blink back my tears as I remember how desperately I wished I could have one more chance with him too.

"But it wasn't just that," he says softly. "In the hospital, with your parents on your case, so cold and detached, and you so desperate for their approval... I totally understood that. Same thing I struggled with all my life. You looked so defeated. Like you needed someone in your corner. Changed everything for me." His voice cracks, breaks. "I thought maybe you did actually need me in a way I need to be needed. And maybe this time, you would let me in."

Chapter 14
I LIKE THE SOUND OF THAT

"Ray, shoes off the table. Have some respect."

Ray shoots me a curious glance as I storm through the office. His feet don't move.

"And, Penny. Change the screensaver back to the corporate logo. A thirty-inch close-up of Vetch's face is going to scare clients away."

"Awwww." Penny's lips quirk into a smile but I don't acknowledge the joke.

"Seriously, guys. This is a law office, not a social club."

Ray snorts from behind his paper. "Who's being social? I'm reading the news. Pen's working. You're the one yammering on."

Despite the fact he can't see me, I shoot him a searing glance. "New rules. When a client comes in, we'll enact Operation Client protocol. This means Ray will sit up and read a magazine and pretend this is not his living room. No lounging. No swearing. No feet on the table. Penny will type. It doesn't matter if you have anything to type; the sound of fingers hitting keys makes it sound busy. No personal conversations. No calls."

Penny frowns. "Something the matter?"

"Nothing's the matter. Do I look like something's the matter? It's Monday. We have cases to run and new clients could walk in the door at any moment. How will they know we're a law office? I don't have a sign. I don't have a brand. All we have is the monogrammed stationery and the firm colors. I think we should…"

Ray peers over his newspaper and raises a warning eyebrow. "We should what?"

I rethink my decision to remove his comfy Victorian couch and also my new idea to have everyone wear firm colors. I've never seen Ray in anything but commando clothes and commandos don't wear navy blue. "Never mind."

"Thought not."

"What's this all about?" Penny persists. "I thought you were finally chillaxing about the firm. We were having fun, going to dangerous areas of town, taking on more pro bono files. You gave Ray his couch. I thought you were leaving the big law firm behind for a brave new Amanda Westwood & Sons world."

Wincing at her all too accurate assessment, I shake my head. "Fact is, Penny, sometimes the old things are best. There was a method behind the Farnsworth & Tillman madness. I understood it. This half Victorian, half modern firm with you two hanging out chatting all day and me never knowing where the next client is going to come from, or what the hell I'm doing, or where the hell I'm going…is not comfortable. I need stability and certainty. I need to get some control over my life."

"She's running scared," Ray mumbles from behind his newspaper.

"I heard that, Ray. I am not scared of anything."

"Definitely scared."

"Seriously?" Penny glances over at me. "So, spill. What's going on?"

Blood rushes through my ears so fast I can barely hear her words. Damn Ray. But until he said the word, it hadn't occurred to me the unsettling feelings I've had all weekend might be…fear.

But what do I have to be afraid of? After we left Redemption, Jake dropped me home because he had to catch an early morning flight to Portland on business. He texted me from the cab, the plane before takeoff, the cab again, and his hotel. Warm texts. Sweet texts. Sexy texts. I dutifully texted him back, relieved I didn't have to face him. But all the while my stomach roiled and my mind twisted itself in knots. I pushed when I shouldn't have pushed. And now he's going to expect something from me in return.

"Nothing."

Ray snorts from behind his newspaper. "That's what Pen said to me when I asked what the fuck is up with her. She's almost bouncing out of that chair."

For the first time this morning, I take a good look at Penny. Her eyes are sparkling and she is, indeed, bouncing in her chair.

"What's up?"

She taps on her new Vetch screensaver and makes a lewd pumping motion with her fist, then mouths "tonight."

Laughter bursts from my chest, a sudden release of the tension I've carried with me all weekend. For a moment, I can't believe this is the same Penny who wears floaty florals and drinks tea.

"Are you sure?" I whisper. "Is he safe?"

"Seriously." Ray shakes his head. "I'm a fucking PI. You two think I can't figure out what's going on over there? Pen's got a new man. Amanda doesn't like him. Come on, Pen. Let's see him." He motions to the screen with his chin and waggles his finger. "Turn it around. I know he's there."

Swallowing hard, Penny turns the screen.

Silence. And then…

"Jesus Christ, lookit that loser. Gimme a different visual." Penny taps on the keyboard and pulls up a full picture of Vetch and then a couple of the band. Ray's eyes widen. "Hell. You can do better than that, Pen."

"He's the *lead* singer of the Slugs." She gives him an affronted stare. "And he's asked me to come to his hotel tonight for a private dinner."

"Guy like that'll use you and send you packing."

To my great surprise, Penny just shrugs. "That's fine with me. I haven't had a good shag for six months, and afterward, I'll be able to work the street cred of having slept with the lead singer of the Slugs."

"Slug is right. You're not goin'. Final."

Penny frowns. "Sorry?"

"Nothin' to be sorry about. You're not going. Done." Ray drains his cup and slams it on the table then slaps open his newspaper.

Penny gives a thin laugh. "Like you can stop me."

Ray drops his feet to the floor and leans forward, his voice dropping to a low growl. "I will stop you, Pen. Guy like that sees you as a play toy. Shagging you is the last thing he'll do. You're gonna get hurt, sweetheart, and it's not gonna happen on my watch."

Penny sucks in a sharp breath. Ray puts his feet back on the table. I cough and suggest we get to work.

"I can take care of myself," Penny blurts out.

"Girl like you knows nothin' about guys like him. You're all sweet innocence, pearl buttons on your blouse, tight little pencil skirts, and fucking sexy shoes. You're class and he's an ass. You want to get laid that bad, I'll take care of you."

I choke. Penny splutters. Ray casually turns the page.

"You're offering to sleep with me so I don't sleep with Vetch?" Penny's voice rises in pitch.

"Lookin' the way you do, being sweet as you are, it's not a sacrifice, sweetheart."

Penny's cheeks glow red and her fingers drum on her desk.

"I think in a perverse, twisted kind of way, he's trying to be nice," I whisper. "He's worried about you."

Penny's eyes narrow. "Or maybe it's been a while since he had a shag."

"Actually." I raise my voice loud enough for Ray to hear. "I don't allow interpersonal relationships at my firm. Especially when I only have two employees."

Ray shoots me a glance "Not an employee. Independent contractor."

"Well, I'm going." Penny folds her arms and glares.

"You're not." Ray doesn't even bother to lower the newspaper.

Poor Penny. After suffering through years of failed relationships with her, I totally get why she wants this date. And who am I to stand in her way? Maybe we shouldn't judge him by the needle tracks on his arms or the pupil-less, drugged-out eyes. Maybe he's that thin because he has a high metabolism and pale because he's a vampire and can't go out in the sun. Who am I to judge? Maybe, like Sandy, he has a good heart.

The front door opens and closes. A process server walks in, this one bald and burly. He looks around and scratches his head. "Sorry to disturb you folks. I'm looking for a law office. Attorney's name is Amanda Westwood? Don't suppose you know where it might be?"

"Arrrrrgh." I glare at Ray and then at Penny before I smooth my face and hold out my hand for what I already know is going to be another life-destroying package from Farnsworth.

After the process server leaves, Ray swings his feet to the floor. "Unfortunate timing."

"There is no good timing when Farnsworth is involved." I throw myself onto the couch beside Ray. My blood chills as I flip through page after page after page. "I can't believe this. He's making every application in the known universe. It will take me months to address them all, maybe even half a year. Usually attorneys try to drag out a case, but I can see what he's doing. He's coming down hard and fast, hoping to scare me off." I toss the documents on the couch and bury my face in my hands.

"You need help, you just ask." Ray gives my shoulder a squeeze.

"You know I'm happy to work overtime," Penny says.

"Thanks." I choke up before I can tell them it's not just the time; it's the money. And Farnsworth must know I don't have much. Certainly not enough to hire the number of contract attorneys I now know I will need to run this case, and definitely not enough to afford big law fees to hire someone else to run the case. My parents are out of the picture. No way could I borrow more money from Max, and no bank will lend me money with my loan to Max outstanding. What the hell was I thinking? How could I have been so naïve?

Before they can ask any questions, I head toward my office. Once I'm at my desk, I bury my face in my arms, resting my forehead against the cool wood, and take a few deep breaths. My only option is to sell my grandmother's house. It's just a house, and really, it's too big for one person. I'll be able to keep the furniture my grandmother and I bought together and the special ornaments and furnishings. I'll have her memories in my heart. And I can use the money to keep the business going, pay Ray and Penny, rent a new apartment, and best of all, see justice done.

Hands shaking, I pick up the phone and call the real estate agent.

An hour passes. I try out different screensavers and different variations of my initials. Then I comb through the Redemption website and pull up a picture of Jake, triumphant after a victory in the cage. He is covered in sweat, bruised, and battered, but he looks beautiful to me. I imagine calling him up and telling him about my house and how much it hurts to sell it. I imagine he puts his arms around me and hugs the pain away. I imagine it so hard I ache inside.

The phone rings and Jake's name appears on the screen. Speak of the devil.

"Hey, baby." His deep, rich voice chases away some of my sadness, and a fierce longing grips me hard, frightening me with its intensity.

"Hey, yourself." I stifle a sigh and try to sound cheery.

"I had a break between meetings and I had a favor to ask," he says softly. "But...you sound kinda down. Is something wrong?"

My throat seizes, and for a moment I can't breathe. The words sit on the tip of my tongue. But what would be the point of telling him? He can't do anything to help me. With a failing business to manage and a fight career to get off the ground, he has enough on his plate. Why add to his stress or to mine?

"No. Just the usual Farnsworth delivery where he tries to hammer home the point I'm just one lawyer and he has a firm full of minions ready and willing to do his bidding."

"Anything I can do?"

"No, I'm good," I say quickly, maybe too quickly. "I've got it under control."

Jake sighs and his voice tightens, almost imperceptibly. "You always say that even when it's not true. Just like you always say you don't need help when you do."

His words cut so close, my pain bleeds out. "That's because the people I've been close to have let me down. It's because I was left on my own so much I learned how to figure things out for myself. It's easier if I don't rely on anyone. That way, I'm never disappointed."

But this is Jake, and he's not letting me off so easy. "You think you can't open up. You think you can't give yourself. But in the last few minutes you've told me more about yourself than you ever did in our two months together and I'm still here. I'm not going anywhere. Our night in the cage isn't how I imagined our first night back together would be, but I wouldn't trade it for anything. It just makes me want you more, but this time I'll make love to you the way I imagined the first time I saw you again."

Warmth spreads through my body, rippling outward to my fingers and toes. "I like the sound of that. When are you back from Portland?"

Jake chuckles. "Late tomorrow night…which is part of the reason I called to ask for your help. Note how I'm asking for help and I'm still breathing."

"Ha ha. Funny guy. What's up?"

Jake sighs. "I kinda dropped the ball on that case I brought to you at Farnsworth & Tillman and missed the deadline for filing a response. Now Duel Properties has applied to have a default entered against us. There's been so much upheaval in our office that I also missed the fact that the hearing is tomorrow afternoon and I'm stuck in Portland until late tomorrow night."

"You want me to represent you?"

Silence. And then, "Would you…or is there an issue since we…"

I stifle a laugh. "Actually, if you had wanted to retain me before we'd had amazing sex, then yes, it might have been a problem. However, our night of wild monkey sex smoothes the way for me to represent your company if that's what you want."

"Wild monkey sex?" The tension from his voice eases into amusement.

"We were in a cage and I was clinging to the fence."

"Baby?"

"Yeah?

"On second thought, maybe having you involved isn't such a good idea. If I had to sit with you in the meeting room, going over documents and talking legal talk, while trying not to think about how sexy you look in your tight little suit, not much would get done."

"Except me…hopefully."

His voice deepens. "Oh, you would get done. On the table. On the floor. Against the window…"

My cheeks protest the excess laughter. "How about I fax you the documents that will allow me to represent you just for the hearing, and then I'll send you a list of attorneys I know who could take over the case. I can explain it to the judge. I don't think it will be a problem."

"Thanks, baby. I'll see you tomorrow."

"Actually, tomorrow night I'll be at the legal aid center, but the next day…"

"I'm going to see you tomorrow night," he says firmly. "No matter where you are."

———

The next morning I am awakened, not by the dulcet tones of a nightingale or the soft croon of Easy Listening radio, but by a string of cuss words that would made any mother run for a bar of soap, and which end with a shouted question.

"Jesus fucking Christ. Did you sleep in the office?"

Blinking to clear my vision, I struggle to orient myself. Big comfy couch with hideous pattern of birds and flowers, boring blue corporate curtains, dull framed print of blue and gray lines, office reception, me in my work clothes. And Ray fuming above me.

"Morning, Ray. Sorry I'm in your space. I lay down…" I check my watch. "…three hours ago to rest my eyes after going through the tape of the new witness statement Penny and I got last night. Great stuff. And we have more leads to follow up so—"

"Go home and get some sleep." He points to the door as I push myself into a sitting position.

"I believe I'm the boss." I fix him with a sleepy glare. "And I have too much work to do to waste time sleeping."

Lips pressed tight together, he fixes me with his best scowl. Pretty scary stuff. "Is that why you started your own firm? So you could work the way you were working before?"

Holding up my hand as if to ward Ray away, I shake my head. "I don't have a choice. It's me against Farnsworth and until my house sells I have to do it all myself."

I don't realize my slip until Ray's eyes narrow. "You're selling your house?"

My breath catches. "Uh…"

"Dammit, Amanda. Why didn't you tell us you were in trouble?"

The door opens and I jump up as Penny walks in the door. "It isn't that bad. And it's too big for one person anyway."

After freshening up and emailing Jake the contact details of a few attorney friends I know, I do a little prep and then head into the reception room. "I'm going to the courthouse. Back in a few hours."

"Hold up." Ray folds his newspaper and drops his feet to the floor. "I'm coming. Eugene is across the street. Idiot must think I wouldn't recognize his piece of shit Volvo. Don't like you going alone with him on your tail. I'll send him a little warning first, let him know I'm with you. Maybe scare him away."

He opens the front window and leans out over the sill to make a rude pointing motion at a beaten-up red Volvo parked across the street. Then he does the threatening, mafia, "I see you" gesture, stabbing at his chest, touching his eyes, and then pointing again at the vehicle. Seconds later the vehicle roars away.

"Well, that was effective."

"Gotta look after my girls. But he's probably just around the corner, so I'll stay with you." Ray ushers me out to his Jeep parked on the side of the road.

"I'm a woman, not a girl." I wave my hand over my fitted black suit, white button-down shirt, and modestly heeled pumps.

Ray snorts a laugh. "You're the girliest girl I ever met. Girl like you stirs a man's most basic protective instincts. Man like me, more. Protection. Done. Ass. Jeep. Now."

Once we are inside the courthouse, Ray goes commando for real. He literally sweeps people from my path as we walk to the courtroom and insists we only walk down hallways he has pronounced "clear." No other attorney has a commando-cum-PI bodyguard, and we attract a lot of unwanted attention.

When we finally reach the courtroom, I spot Evil Reid in the hallway with an entourage of slaves…er, interns behind him. Oh God. Of all the people I did not want to accidentally meet. I briefly toy with the idea of telling Ray he has a grenade in his briefcase, but I don't want to waste any time.

Ray offers to take my document boxes into the courtroom, and I try to fly under Evil Reid's radar by hiding behind a potted palm on the pretense of looking out the window.

Unfortunately, the eagle-eyed Evil Reid sees through my palm fronds.

"Westwood! What a surprise. Don't tell me you've come looking to settle our case already? Did our little delivery on Friday scare you? That was my idea, by the way. Go big or go home, like you always said. So I went big."

Mouth dry, stomach churning at the thought of years of litigation with both Evil Reid and Farnsworth on the other side, I feign a laugh. "Didn't you have enough work of your own? Did you have to ask Farnsworth to help you make up the billable hours?"

Evil Reid's eyes narrow and he closes the distance between us until my personal space is filled with the foul odor of Drakkar Noir and bacon bits.

"Maybe you don't realize what it means for me to be on the file. It means I now have access to all the documents. And that means I know everything about you, Westwood. *Everything*. And you know what I'm wondering after reading your file? I'm wondering…where's mine?"

I suck in a sharp breath and take an involuntary step back. He's read the blue file. Evil Reid has read the file. But that's not the worst of it. Stiffening my spine, I spit out, "Are you threatening me? Because if you're threatening me, you'd better—"

"Back off, Cravath." Ray steps between us, returning just in the nick of time to save Evil Reid from my new Redemption fight moves.

Evil Reid frowns. "Ray? What are you doing here? I heard you'd quit the firm and…" He cuts himself short and looks from Ray to me and back to Ray. "You're working for her?" His voice rises and his lips curl. "You're fucking working for her now? Talk about a breach of confidentiality. You are so going down. I'll have your ass hauled up—"

Ray growls low in his chest. "I do not break my word. I signed the confidentiality agreement; I abide by the terms. But if you plan on doing what I think you're planning on doing, you will have me breathing down your neck for the rest of your miserable life."

"Call off your dog, Westwood," Evil Reid snarls. "We're in a courthouse. Maybe you've forgotten basic court decorum since you started slumming it in Hippie Land."

My hand curls into a fist. I imagine I am Shilla the Killa and Evil Reid has just landed a hard right to my jaw. *Bam. Bam.* I hit him in the stomach and when he doubles over, I go for a knee to the nose. I imagine a slow motion clip of blood flying across the hallway and splattering on the canvas print of the Golden Gate Bridge as he staggers into his stable of minions. Jake would be proud.

"Not worth it," Ray says quietly, as if he knows what I'm thinking. But then, he's Ray, so I expect he does.

Shaking off the daydream, I turn my back on Evil Reid and walk away.

"You're going down, Westwood," Evil Reid calls after me and then he chuckles and lowers his voice, "and not just in court."

The hearing goes smoothly, and two hours later, I am back in my office and poring through Farnsworth's documents again when Penny interrupts me.

"You're due down at the community legal aid clinic in an hour."

My heart sinks as I look over the pile of paper on my desk. "Ahhh…maybe you should call and cancel."

A pained expression crosses Penny's face and she shakes her head. "Too late. The cab is waiting outside. You missed one session. I won't let you miss another. You love going there and the clients love you. Not only that, they're depending on you. They don't have anyone else. Don't let them down."

I drop my pen and push back my chair. "Penny?"

She grimaces and lifts a questioning eyebrow. "Yeah?"

"Thanks."

At seven p.m., I am at the Bay Area Community Center where I share legal aid duties with five other attorneys. Although I know I should find some paying clients, over the next three hours, I take on five new pro bono cases for people in desperate need of legal assistance. As the clinic winds to a close, the clinic coordinator, a social worker and an old friend, shakes his head and tells me my heart is too soft. I tell him if my heart were soft, I would be at the airport right now, waiting for a hard-bodied, blue-eyed fighter with unkempt blond hair. He tells me I don't have to worry about going to the airport, because my fighter is waiting at my table.

My heart thuds wildly against my ribs and I slowly turn around.

There he is.

Damn, he looks good. The slight sheen of his tailored gray suit subtly reflects the light giving him an almost ethereal glow. His shirt is crisp white, his tie red silk. And yet the civilized veneer cannot hide the strength and power of his muscular body.

"So…what can I do for you this evening?" I take a seat on the other side of the table I use as a desk and fold my hands on my notepad so he doesn't see them tremble.

"Caught an earlier flight 'cause I wanted to see my girl."

"Here she is." Like a love-struck teenager, I can't stop staring at him and smiling a goofy smile. He came back early. For me. And he's here. HE'S HERE!

Jake places a cooler on the table and shoves it toward me. "Since you have a habit of forgetting to eat, I assumed you didn't have dinner, so I brought us a snack."

"Us?"

"Us." He reaches around the cooler and gives my hand a squeeze. "We're having dinner together. You aren't working tonight."

"Um…"

Jake shakes his head. "Not an option."

I vacillate for all of ten seconds. "'kay."

"I made it myself," he says proudly, tapping the top of the cooler. "Whipped it up after I got home from the airport."

Curiosity gets the better of me and I stand and tug off the lid. Inside, I find two large plastic containers, two forks, two napkins, and two protein shakes. "What's in the containers?"

Jake beams. "A gourmet feast. Mac 'n' cheese with hot dogs! Carbs, Amanda. We're having carbs."

Never have I been so torn between laughter and tears. Oh God. So sweet. But seriously, who considers mac 'n' cheese a gourmet feast?

"I'm sure it will be delicious. And protein shakes…you really know how to treat a girl."

Completely missing the irony, Jake nods. "I do. They have twenty-five grams of satiating protein to help maintain lean body mass, no added sugars, and I got chocolate because it's better at masking the taste of whey."

"Mmmmm."

"You done here?" He looks behind him, but the last client is with one of the other attorneys and everyone else is packing up.

"Yeah."

Jake frowns. "Baby?"

I raise my eyebrows.

"Not used to you being so quiet."

"To be honest, I'm feeling a little overwhelmed." I shove my papers into my briefcase and pretend not to see the clinic coordinator watching us with avid interest.

Jake grabs the cooler and leans over to kiss my cheek. "I promise by the end of the night, you'll be feeling something else."

My body heats in an instant. "Jake Donovan, I hope you didn't make dinner just to lure me into your bed, because I might be tempted to skip a meal and move straight to dessert."

He gives me a wicked smile. "You are dessert."

Chapter 15
SLOW AND GENTLE

FUN AND HAPPY TIMES end once we hit the parking lot. Jake has an agenda, and he is adamant that we follow it to the letter.

First, kissing in the parking lot. The minute we clear the front door, he pushes me up against the brick wall and kisses me so long and deep I forget we're outside. In a frenzy of lust, I try to tear off his clothes. Jake gives me an admonishing "tsk tsk" and gently disengages my hands from his shirt. Clothes tearing is further down the agenda. Definitely after we reach my house.

Second, Jake removes Amanda's panties. Also in the parking lot. This is accomplished with him on his knees in front of me while I try not to moan too loudly.

Third, a quick check to see how much Amanda enjoys exhibitionism. Jake's finger glistens under the streetlamp. Apparently Amanda enjoys it a lot.

Fourth, Jake drives Amanda's car since he planned ahead and arrived in a taxi. This allows Amanda to recline the passenger seat while Jake tests his driving-with-one-hand-and-finger-fucking-Amanda-with-the-other skills. He passes with flying colors.

Not on the agenda is the traffic jam of epic proportions on the bridge that prevents a very aroused Amanda and an equally aroused Jake, as evident from the erection straining against his fly, from getting home quickly. The agenda is quickly rearranged. Jake and Amanda dine on lukewarm mac 'n' cheese with hot dogs, washed down with chocolate protein shakes.

Fifth, the agenda once again in place, Amanda and Jake finally arrive at Amanda's house. Time for dessert.

Door closed. Lights off. I press my hands against Jake's chest and back him slowly up against the wall. "No more teasing. I want my sexy times."

"Mmmmm. He nips my ear and tickles kisses along my earlobe. "I love it when you talk dirty."

"Well, you're in luck because I'm a very dirty girl who has spent the last hour and a half having very dirty thoughts." I yank on his belt, freeing it from the buckle before he grabs my hand.

"Slow down, baby."

But I don't want to slow down. First, Farnsworth; then my house, Reid and his threats, Jake showing up unexpectedly. Too much. Too many things spinning out of control. I need to get off the merry-go-round. I need to regain control in just one aspect of my life. And this way I can lose myself, making Jake feel as good as he makes me feel.

Dropping to my knees, I unzip his pants. "You were very sweet to show up with dinner. I want to say thank you, but in an impolite, talking-with-the-mouth-full kind of way."

Jake growls low in his throat and fists my hair, tugging my head back. "There's a reward I'd like better because it involves both of us enjoying it."

My fists clench on his thighs and I meet his gaze. "Please."

He studies me for a long time and a pained expression crosses his face, so fleeting I wonder if I imagined it and then so quickly replaced with raw desire I'm almost sure I did. "I want your mouth on me so fucking bad, baby. I've wanted it since that day we were fixing up the house and you were all cute and mussed, with dirt on your face and those plump lips wet and glistening. Fuck. You were talking and I was wiping your face, all I was thinking about was watching those lips slide down my cock."

My cheeks heat. "I'll take that as a yes."

Jake shrugs off his jacket and loosens his tie. "Hell yes."

I ease his clothing down and his cock springs free, already hard and erect. It bounces gently in my direction and I wrap my hand around the base then slowly glide it toward the piercing, barely visible in the shadows. My stomach cartwheels. God. Oh God. I have fantasized about tasting his piercing since I first touched it in the cage.

Jake's hand drops to the back of my head and for a moment I think he's going to push me away, but instead he pulls me forward and I run my lips along his hot, silky skin.

"Wasn't so hard to twist your arm."

Jake chuckles. "Oh I'm still gonna follow my agenda, baby. But gentleman that I am, I'll let you go first." He hisses in a breath as I lean over and flick my tongue across his head, soft and slick. Then I lick slowly over the piercing and explore the two steel knobs with tentative flicks, the metallic tang deliciously naughty on my tongue. Jake's cock swells and pulses, and I pump my fist along his length in counterpoint to my licks.

"Suck me, baby. Don't tease." Jake fists my hair, holding my head still as he thrusts into my mouth. He fills me, thick and hot, and I close my eyes and lose myself in the sensual scrape of his piercing over my tongue, the scent of his soap, and the musk of his arousal.

"Take it all." He groans and thrusts deeper. "You know how to do it."

My clit throbs and pressure builds fast in my center. I release his cock and slide one hand between my legs. Thank God he took off my panties.

"That's it, baby," Jake whispers. "You get off with me."

Moaning against his cock, I spread my wetness up and over my clit while Jake surges in and out of my mouth, following the slide of my lips. With each thrust, the piercing drives farther into my throat, the sensation both frightening and deliciously arousing.

Suddenly his hand tightens on my neck and he thrusts hard and deep. "Fuck, baby. Oh fuck." A low guttural groan tears from his throat as his cock thickens and swells.

And then he pulls away.

"Jake…what's wrong?"

Jaw tight, body tensed, he takes a deep breath and then another. "Gotta stop. I love your sweet mouth, but something's eating you, and I'm gonna find out what it is. And to do that, I need to love you, not take you. I'm gonna love you until you break and let me in."

Nonononononononono. I don't want loving. I want Jake coming in my mouth. I want hard, fast, furious fucking. I want my body slamming into the wall, his piercing dragging over my G-spot, freezing my brain with exquisite pleasure until I can't take any more.

But Jake has other ideas. Suddenly I'm in his arms and his lips are pressed against mine and he's kissing me the way I imagined he would kiss me every night after we broke up. Lips soft and teasing, teeth nibbling, questing tongues and heavy breathing. My body sags, melts into him. He groans softly, curls his hand around my neck, and draws me in to feast on my lips until I am panting and breathless, ready to offer him anything for another taste of the steel that throbs between us.

"That's it," he whispers. "Slow and gentle. The way we should have done it the first time. The way I wanted to do it the day we met again." He undoes the buttons on my shirt one by one, his fingers lingering on my bare skin as he exposes me ever so slowly to the heat of his gaze. He takes similar care with my skirt, following it over my hips and down my legs with the smooth caress of his fingers until he is kneeling in front of me.

"There is not an inch of your beautiful body I don't want to touch."

He jumps easily to his feet and leads me to my living room, then spreads his suit jacket over the center of the area rug, a soft, thick French Provençal–inspired cottage floral with pastel tones to set off the white shabby-chic covered sofas and faux-chipped light green tables.

"Down you go, baby."

Moments later I am surrounded by Jake, the silky slide of his suit jacket under me, the scent of his cologne around me, and his body, hot and heavy, on top of me. His lips slide down my neck, and he peppers tiny kisses over the crescents of my breasts. I arch my back and he reaches behind me to unclasp my bra, and then flings it on the rapidly growing pile of clothing beside us. Without another word, he proceeds to ravish my breasts like he's never seen them before, kissing and licking, nipping and sucking, until they are sore and swollen and my nipples peak, reaching for the ceiling.

With a quiet moan, I slide my hands through his soft curls and hold him tight against me as my body trembles beneath him.

"Shhhhh. Let it go."

Then his lips are back, skimming over my heated skin, my abdomen, and brushing gently over my mound, but never going where I want them to be. My body throbs and pulses with need, and even the cool, silk lining of his jacket gives me no respite.

"Do you know why I like you bare?" he whispers.

My clit pulses under the heat of his breath and I moan. "Why?"

"Because I can give you more pleasure." His fingertip slides through my folds and, when I least expect it, brushes right over my throbbing clit.

My back arches at the exquisite sensation and a whimper escapes my lips.

"Oh yes. You're gonna give it all up for me. All that fear. All that stress. You're going to let go because that's what you need and that's what I want."

A violent shudder wracks my body and fear twists icy tendrils around my spine. I can't give myself to him. What if he sees me, all of me, and finds me lacking? What if I give myself to him and he lets me down? What if I open up and he walks away? "Jake…"

"Let me take care of you."

My brain fuzzes with lust and I tug on his shirt, trying to pull it off. I want to smooth my hands over his warm skin, feel his muscles ripple under my touch. But more than that, I want to feel him hot and hard and heavy in my hand.

I get nothing.

Jake grasps my wrists and gently lifts my hands up and over my head. Then, balancing on one knee, he loosens his tie and dangles it in front of me. "Are you okay if I restrain you with this?"

Pulse quickens, lungs tighten, skin tingles. Trembling as arousal rockets through my body, I moan, "I thought you were going to love me."

He gives me a half smile. "I am loving you. But you need to think about only my touch and you can't do that if your hands are in the way. Plus, you're so damn sexy, I don't think I could take your hands on me. Not if we're going to take it slow."

My head falls back and I groan. "No slow. Bad slow. Let me up and fuck me hard."

Jake's jaw tightens and he growls, his hands tightening on my wrists. "You got that in the cage. Now we're doing it my way."

Swallowing the ache of desire, I lift an eyebrow. "Your way or the highway?"

Jake chuckles. "My way. Period."

"Okay. Tie away."

He wraps the cool silk around my wrists, tying them firmly together. I test the bond and it gives slightly, enough that I know if I really needed to get free, I could.

Jake watches me experiment and winks. "Didn't want to scare you the first time."

"I'm not scared with you."

He gives a satisfied grunt, and then slides his hand through the planes and valleys of my body, his touch so light, I strain toward him, unable to think of anything but where his hand might go next.

"What do you feel?" His breath is warm and moist in my ear, demanding, insistent.

"Hot."

"You are so fucking hot, lying here, available for my pleasure. I could tease you all evening. Or I could fuck you. Or maybe I'll just bring you close and walk away." With easy grace, he rolls up and kneels between my legs to position my feet, knees bent up and out, heels planted in the soft, thick carpet. Then he traces lazy circles along my inner thighs.

"Legs do not move," he says. "Not an inch."

My sex clenches as his light caresses come closer and closer to my very wet center. Have I ever been so wet from just a touch?

Jake reaches over to the clothing pile and pulls a tissue from the packet in his jacket pocket. With a wicked grin, he brushes the tissue lightly over my clit. Despite the barely there flutter, I am so swollen, so needy, my body jumps as if he had pinched me and moisture floods my sex.

"Oh God."

With a soft laugh, he places the tissue over my mound and sits back, away from my body. The tissue rocks gently in the air current, a whisper of a touch, an exquisite torture. I rock my hips seeking friction from something so light a breath could take it from me at any moment.

Carnal satisfaction flickers through his eyes as he watches me undulate my hips only the barest inch, enough for a touch but not too much that I would lose my only path to release.

"Do you need something, baby?"

"I need to come."

He slides one finger along my folds and then dips into my swollen center. My body stiffens. When he crooks his finger and gently pumps my G-spot, I whimper.

"Yes, you do." He withdraws his finger and flicks the tissue away, leaving me bereft.

"You are so damn wet, baby. Your body is on board. Let the rest go." He leans over and kisses me. Soft, sweet, gentle kisses that make me ache inside. My body is awash with sensation: the erotic ache in my nipples, the exquisite throb of my sex and the smooth silk under my back. The familiar scents of oak and furniture polish mix with the heady scent of Jake's cologne and the musk of his arousal. His face is framed by the soft track lights above us and I taste chocolate on his lips as the bone-melting rumble of his voice coaxes, assures, but above all, demands.

Too much. My senses overload. I squeeze my eyes shut and a groan rips from my throat.

The tear of a foil packet. The snap of a condom. Oh happy sounds! When I open my eyes, Jake is kneeling between my legs. "Open."

Instantly, my legs fall apart.

For a moment I expect him to crawl over me. Lie on top. Missionary style. But this is Jake and in that, he hasn't changed. He is so *not* a missionary man.

He hooks one arm under my thigh at the back of my knee, drawing my leg up and out, opening me wider. And then his cock is at my entrance and I am almost hyperventilating with need.

"This might be intense, baby," he says softly. "The piercing is most effective when you're at the peak of arousal. For some women it's the ultimate pleasure, but for others it's a pleasure that borders on pain. That's why I wanted to get you ready. Tell me if you need me to slow down."

Dark desires awaken inside me with a roar. A deep, long-hidden need claws at my belly. The thought he planned this from the start, with this goal as the ultimate end, sends a rush of molten heat through my body. I close my eyes and give myself over to him with a raw, guttural groan. Utterly and completely.

"There we are," he whispers. And then he breaches my entrance, stretching me, filling me. My body trembles in fearful anticipation.

"Jake…?"

"Shhhh. Hold on. It'll be good. I promise." He thrusts deeper and the metal knob glides over my G-spot.

Pleasure pain sears through my body like white hot lightning, so intense my vision goes white and my body arches high off the ground. My eyes water, my jaw clenches, and a scream of pleasure rips from my gut, rolling through me like a tidal wave. Jake covers my mouth with his own, swallowing my passion, and I am only vaguely aware he is moving, thrusting, sending new jolts of sensation through my sex with every scrape of the piercing. My body coils tight, bones, tendons, muscles fusing into one pulsing ball of need. My womb is heavy and every fiber of my being is centered on my core.

"Fly, baby." Jake slicks a finger over my clit, the barest touch, and then he drives in again. Moisture spurts from my swollen inner tissue, making my sex so slick he glides in and out faster even than before. One pinch of my clit. One thrust of his cock. And I explode into a thousand pieces in the most intense orgasm of my life. Pain. Pleasure. Release. Over and over again. His every thrust drags out my orgasm. Endless waves of pleasure thunder through my body. And I am screaming and he is thrusting and I am lost in the ether, in a world of never-ending exquisite sensation.

"Christ. Fuck." He hammers deep and fast. His cock thickens, becomes impossibly hard, and then he comes with a yell, pulsing against my swollen tissues.

Boneless, spineless, still floating, I am vaguely aware he has released my leg and collapsed on top of me, weight on his elbows, head resting between my breasts. As we come back down, he reaches above me and releases my hands with one tug of the tie. Quick release. And then he rolls onto his back and pulls me across his chest.

"I have you now," he says softly, his hand stroking gently along my spine.

Yes, he has me.

But I've never felt so afraid.

"You okay, baby?"

My mouth opens and closes, but words fail me. I am ripped open, exposed, bared to the world and scrambling around in the dark.

He cups my jaw with his hand, forcing me to look up. His brow is creased and his eyes crinkle with concern. "Talk to me. Tell me what you're feeling. I'm here. I won't let you go."

A tidal wave of emotion floods through my veins too fast, too powerful to stop. I bite through my lip to stop the overflow leaking from the corners of my eyes, and then the words spill out. Crazy words. Untimely words. Words I never thought I'd say. "I have to sell my house."

His brow creases in a frown, but I see the moment understanding dawns. His face softens and he squeezes me tight, chasing away the fear, filling the void. Just like I imagined.

But unlike how I imagined, he doesn't say soothing words and tell me he understands or sympathizes with how I might feel. He is not a fantasy man. He is a real man. And real men feel compelled to solve problems, not throw out meaningless platitudes even when they have torn open a woman's soul and that is what she wants to hear.

Why are you losing the house? Do you need money? Did you talk to Max? Did you go to the bank and ask for a loan? How about hiring another firm? What about your parents? A mortgage? Can I help? I have money saved. What about dropping the case? And on and on.

When he has finally run out of questions, I kiss him softly. "I told you about it. That's a big step for me. Don't push. Just hold me."

I can almost see the physical effort involved in reining in his natural inclination to problem solve. His body tenses, jaw tightens, even his pulse beats more rapidly in his neck. But he manages to overcome the burden nature has thrust upon men, and moments later, I am being hugged and stroked while he whispers that he knows how much that house means to me and he will do anything to help.

Just like I imagined.

Chapter 16
WELL, THAT WAS JUST STUPID

A FEW NIGHTS OF sex and sleep and more sex and less sleep leaves me with a happy buzz that lasts until Friday morning when I walk into my office and find a giant, unwelcome stack of medical reports on my desk beside the humongous pile of Farnsworth-related paperwork.

"What are these?"

Penny hands me a file and grimaces. "Hellhole case. Medical reports documenting the injuries of your friend, Bob, and his bouncer buddy."

"And this?" My voice rises as I stare at the file in my hand.

"Originals of the retainer agreements for the Redemption case. Jake still hasn't signed his. You don't have much time left to get that defense filed. I've put a note in your calendar."

With a sigh, I drop the file on my desk. "We decided it wasn't a good idea for me to represent him on either case. He's going to find someone else. We're too…close."

She finally smiles. "That's a good thing."

Maybe. Maybe not.

"Anything else to ruin my morning?"

Penny gives me a sympathetic smile and points to a stack of files on the credenza beside the microwave. "Your pro bono files need some attention. I've flagged the deadlines coming up. Ray won't be around today. He has a lead on the Hellhole guys, and he's gone to see if he can get a video of them without their casts. I have to leave on time because I have a date with Vetch. And…Jill called to see how the case was progressing and to let you know if you need help, she's still looking for work. I seriously think you should consider hiring her."

"Thanks, Penny, but right now I can't even afford you."

The day passes in a blur as I prepare the defense for the Redemption case and read through the unintelligible medical reports. I research broken bones and street fighting, trying to understand how two men could suffer the exact same injuries. Desperately in need of medical advice, I call Drake to ask a few questions. He offers to bring me some of his old medical school books and, since he'll be in the area on his way home, he can also help me wade through the medical reports. Oh, and since it's dinnertime, he'll bring Chinese.

For a brief moment, I wonder if this is a good idea, given Jake's raging bull tendencies and his antipathy toward Drake. But this is work and I'm on a deadline. Plus, Jake should be happy I've actually asked for help. And we'll be in my office, not my house. So it should all be good.

Two hours later, over chow mein and orange duck washed down with a crisp but unexpected bottle of Chardonnay, Drake and I sift through the medical reports. I take copious notes as he explains all the abbreviations and cryptic messages, and then flags pages in the reference books that discuss how bones are broken, where the force needs to be applied, and the types of breakages one can expect in hand-to-hand combat.

Finally I have had enough. Head spinning from too many gory pictures, I toss my notepad on the couch beside me, kick off my shoes, and put my feet up on the table, Ray style. Drake settles back on the cushions beside me.

"So…do I conclude from Jake's performance the other night, you two are back together?"

"I guess so."

He gives me a quizzical look. "You don't sound convinced."

"It's all kind of intense." I twist my bracelet around my wrist. "I haven't been in a serious relationship since he and I broke up. I think I'm out of practice. I keep thinking he's going to leave or it's not right…"

Drake taps the back of my hand and raises an admonishing eyebrow. "You were in a relationship with me."

My skin prickles and I jerk my hand away. "We weren't in a relationship. We were friends with benefits. There's a big difference."

"You're right." He sighs and pats my knee. "I just never expected to fall for you. It complicated things. At least for me."

Annnnd I'm off the couch. "Drake…" I lean against Penny's desk, hoping I've put enough distance between us. "Why didn't you tell me?"

He twists his lips to the side and shrugs. "I know what you're like. You keep everyone at a distance, always protecting yourself. I didn't want to scare you away."

Nausea roils in my belly. What's wrong with me? Why do I hurt everyone I care about? Why can't I give what everyone wants? "You're a special friend to me, but I don't feel the same way about you. What we had was temporary. I've seen how happy Makayla is with Max, and I want what she has. I want something that will last."

He slumps back against the cushions. "But not with me."

My stomach clenches at the defeated expression on his face. "Not in that way. I enjoy being with you. We have a lot of fun together. But in the morning, we can both walk away. I don't want to be able to walk away. I want to ache at the thought of walking away."

His jaw tightens and he clenches his fist on his knee. "Is that how you feel about him?"

The word comes out before my mind has even sifted through the tangle of emotion twisted around my heart. "Yes."

And it's true. Even now I ache for him, already my fingers are twitching in anticipation of the moment Drake leaves and I can send Jake a text.

Drake gathers up his things in silence and then sighs. "Don't forget: you left him, Amanda. And you had good reasons for it. You should take some time to think about why you pushed him away in the first place and whether it will be worth the heartache when you find yourself in that place again."

A gentle touch on my cheek pulls me out of a dream about Jake and me on Max's kinky desk at Redemption. Every hidden D-ring was in use, his warm hands were on my body, and his deep voice rumbled in my ear.

"Wake up, baby."

My eyes open to the semidarkness of my office reception room and blue eyes glittering in the moonlight beside me.

I bolt awake, shooting up on the couch, heart pounding. Jake puts an arm around me and whispers soothing nonsense in my ear as he threads his fingers through my hair.

"Did I text you?"

He gives me a puzzled look. "No. Were you trying to text me?"

Head still woozy, I lean into his chest. "I was trying to drunk text you. Fortunately, I didn't succeed. But how did you get in?"

Jake strokes his hand up and down my back, and I fight back the urge to purr. "Your landlord has a key. Very useful when he's trying to find you. Saves him from breaking down doors."

I bury my face in his neck, breathing in his fresh, clean scent of soap and the essence of him. "Mmmm. I'd like to see you break down a door. I think it would be hot."

Jake laughs. "You think everything is hot."

"Only when you're involved."

He sits back on the couch and pulls me into his arms. The table in front of us is littered with a sea of takeaway cartons, medical reference books, and diagrams of arms and bones.

"Working late? Please don't tell me you drink and draft."

Relaxed in his arms, floating on a sea of endorphins, my mind still fuzzy from sleep, I murmur, "No. Drake was here. He was teaching me about broken arms."

Jake stiffens. Moments later I am alone on the couch and he is pacing the floor in front of me. "Drake was here?"

"For work stuff, that's all. I needed medical advice for the Redemption case."

He flicks the wine bottle with his thumb and forefinger, and it crashes to the ground. "Do you usually drink while you're working? Or eat, for that matter? Why didn't I know you like Chinese food?"

"Jake." My voice rises in pitch as our moment of intimacy crumbles. "It's over between us. He was just here as a friend to help out." I struggle to my feet, but when I take a step toward Jake, he holds up his hand.

"What's over?"

Damn. Damn. Damn. The last thing I wanted was for him to know my relationship with Drake went beyond that one night he caught us together. And explaining the whole friends with benefits thing…there's just no way he's going to understand. I take a deep, calming breath and choose my next words carefully.

"You know Drake and I…were together. And that's over."

"When?"

Oh God. I can't tell him I cleared up any misconceptions Drake might have had tonight. "That's hard…um…we haven't been together for a long time. Months. Four or five at least."

"Did you fuck him tonight?" His eyes glitter in the shadows and I wince at his harsh words, anger edging into my fear.

"No. Of course not. You're totally overreacting."

His hands clench and unclench, and his biceps quiver beneath the sleeves of his T-shirt. For the longest time he just stares at me, jaw clenched, chest heaving. "But you were drinking with him. Alone. Here."

My stomach twists in knots, and unwanted images flood my mind. Farnsworth's blue file. My father's words in the hospital. Jake's face when he walked in on Drake and me two years ago. But what have I done wrong? Certainly nothing to warrant his accusatory tone. Or his lack of trust. And definitely nothing that would explain the guilt worming a hole through my heart. All that stands between us is a past we cannot shake.

"Maybe you should go, Jake. We can talk about it tomorrow when you're calm and I've got a clear head."

He startles at my words. I don't know if he expected tears or anger or excuses, but he's getting none of them from me. He's judged me and found me wanting. Even more than when I judge myself.

Without a word, he grabs his backpack and walks out the door.

<hr>

"Well, that was just stupid," Makayla snaps when I call her in Fiji to tell her it's over. Although I don't like to disturb her on vacation, the most desolate moments in a person's life must be shared with best friends when and as they happen.

"Which part?" I push off my comforter and let the cool breeze blow over my skin, imagining I'm lying on an exotic beach beside her, but it does nothing to ease my discomfort. I ache all over and nothing will make the pain go away.

"All of it. First, inviting Drake over in the evening. Second, drinking alone with Drake. You know what's he's like. You saw him with me. He gloms on to you and then he won't let go until someone hits him over the head with a fire extinguisher. Third, telling Jake he was there."

"It was pretty obvious. There were two wineglasses and enough food for an army."

Makayla gives a derisory sniff. "Fourth and worst, you sent him away. I can't believe you did that. How could you send him away?"

My hand clenches around the phone. "He didn't trust me. And one day he's going to find out about the file and realize he was right. I am the person he thinks I am."

Silence.

"Makayla?" I sit up in the bed. "Makayla?"

"Did you sleep with Drake?"

"No, of course not."

She sighs. "Then you're not the person you think he thinks you are. You're the person who is letting the past define her. You're letting Farnsworth and his damn file define you. No one cares what happened before. No one cares if you slept with ten guys or fifty. Do you think your friends wouldn't be your friends if they read that file? Do you think I would love you any less? Do you really think it matters to Jake?"

My throat tightens until I can barely breathe. "But…"

She draws in a ragged breath. "What matters to him is now. He wants to know you're with him and only him now. He cares about you, Amanda. He cares enough to show up at your office late at night. He cares enough to be upset that you were drinking with your ex and not just an ex, the ex you left him for. He respects you enough to leave when you asked him to go."

Sick remorse floods my veins. "I should never have asked him to go."

"Oh, honey. The real issue is that you let him in and now you're scared." Her voice softens. "I get that. I felt that with Max. But you have the benefit of knowing what happens if you push him away. You know how it feels and you know this time there will be no second chances. He wants you, Amanda. All of you. The good and the bad. Don't be afraid this time. Give yourself to him. You know he would never hurt you."

Chapter 17
You've never been spanked?

Lucky for me, Makayla has no qualms about searching Max's phone for Jake's new address, and I have no trouble finding his new apartment in the SOMA district. After following a couple through the security doors, I take the elevator up to the penthouse—a big change from when we were first going out and Jake shared a house with five other guys, assorted pizza boxes, and a cockroach named Fred.

My heart pounds faster and faster, and by the time the elevator doors slide open, my pulse is racing so wildly I can barely breathe. What the hell am I doing? It's midnight. He doesn't know I'm here. I could easily turn around and be home in less than an hour, saving myself further heartache. But by the time my mind has decided to leave, my feet are already moving, and suddenly I'm in a long, spacious, red-carpeted hallway, and the elevator door is closing behind me.

The walk to the sole door at the end of the corridor takes forever. I count the trendy spotlights in the ceiling, and admire the abstract red and blue prints on the stark white walls. My steps follow the rhythm of my pounding heart. Tap. Bang. Tap. Bang. By the time I reach Jake's door, I'm out of breath, shivering like the potted palm in the corner. Mustering what little courage I have left, I knock softly on the door.

Silence.

Maybe I should go.

But before I can turn away, the door swings open.

Chest heaving, fight shorts clinging to his narrow hips, bare torso glistening with sweat, Jake studies me, his face an expressionless mask.

Go big or go home.

"I'm sorry," I blurt out. "I just keep messing everything up."

Without a word, he lifts me in his arms, spins me around into his apartment, and kicks the door shut.

Afraid to look at his face, I lean my forehead against his chest and squeeze my eyes closed. "I called Drake to ask some questions about broken bones. He showed up with his medical books and dinner. We're good friends, Jake, but I've never felt anything more than that for him. I told him I wanted to be with you and he left. Nothing happened."

He cups my face between his hands, and I look into eyes, as deep and blue as the ocean, as warm as the summer sand.

"You came to me. Nothing else matters." He kisses me slowly, sweetly, maneuvering me until I hit the door. Then he deepens the kiss. Greedy, hard, and hungry, his tongue works past my lips to rasp over the inside of my mouth, each stroke sending tiny shock waves down to my core.

"Jake...I need to explain..."

"Shhhh, baby. You. Here. Tells me everything I need to know." He trails butterfly kisses along my jaw and then up to the sensitive spot behind my ear. I tilt my head to give him better access and he growls his approval.

"I want you so much, it scares me," I whisper. "I thought for a second at my office you didn't want me, so I tried to push you away."

"I want you too, baby. I fucking ache with wanting you. Been working out all evening trying to make that feeling go away, but all I keep thinking about is how soft and sexy you looked in my arms last night, and how lucky I am to have found a smart, sweet, attorney with a big heart, a whole lot of determination, and a bent for kinky sex."

A warm, melty feeling pools in my belly. He's been thinking about me. "I like this look." I glide my hands over his chest, still damp from his workout, then follow the trail of soft curls to the waistband of his shorts. "You're all pumped and sweaty, and you look like you want to pound on someone. But you have to rein it in sometimes. Talk instead of fight. Tonight...the way you reacted...it almost scared me away."

A pained expression crosses his face. "That bastard sets me off like no one else. He knows we're together. I've made sure of it. And yet he pulls a stunt like he did today. I just want to beat the crap out of him."

"He's my friend, Jake. I can't stop seeing my friends because you don't like them." I run my finger along the inside edge of his fight shorts and tug him gently toward me. "But I should have thought about how it might look to you. Next time I plan on meeting up with him, I'll invite you along."

A low growl erupts from his throat. "Friendship is the last thing on his mind. Trust me on this one. I know."

"So you're still going to pound on him?"

Jake chuckles and covers my hand with his own, sliding my palm over the steel of his erection straining against his fight shorts. "I want to pound in someone— my girl. I wanna love her and make her feel so good. But first, I'm gonna spank her ass for making me think I lost her."

"Oh God." My heart skips a beat, then slams against my ribs.

Jake's voice drops to a rough, husky growl. "Then I'll keep you on edge until you're dripping with arousal and begging me to let you come."

I breathe out a soft "oh," and he gives me a wicked grin.

"It's gonna be a long night."

He gives me no time to mull over the sweet sentiment or ponder whether his words mean he forgives me, because I am suddenly whisked away from the door and bent over his dining table, my cheek and breasts pressed tight against the cool, polished wood surface.

"What happened to loving me and making me feel good?" I strain to check out Jake's new place from my bent-over-the-table vantage point.

"You're too fucking sexy. I'll spank you first, then I'll make it better." He grunts his annoyance when I push myself up to my elbows and then slaps my ass. The sharp sting makes me gasp, and I am suddenly very grateful I am still wearing my clothes.

"Don't move. Gotta get a box of condoms." He crosses the room in front of me and heads toward the raised platform where his massive low-rise bed is situated. Big and comfy-looking. Much comfier than a table.

"A box? Not just one or even five?"

He looks back over his shoulder and his eyebrow lifts. "You walk around in your tight little suit, we need five. You make me think it's over and then you appear at my door in the middle of the night with your eyes all big and soft, your heart open, and your hair looking like you just got out of bed, we need a box."

"I see we're not wasting any time with foreplay." I rest my chin in my hands and mentally drool as he bends over the night table, giving me an unobstructed view of his ass outlined to perfection by the thin fabric of his fight shorts. "Your girl shows up at your door, you bend her over the table, take her hard and fast, maybe order a pizza, grab a beer, and watch some TV. I'll bet it's every man's dream."

The warning look he gives me, cold and calculating, sends a shiver down my spine. I always seem to take it that one step too far.

"Jeans, panties, and shirt off."

I suck in a sharp breath and heat flushes my cheeks. What is it about his voice that makes everything inside me melt? Or maybe it isn't just his voice, but his tone. Confident. Commanding. Unyielding.

When he disappears down the hallway beside the bed, I shrug off my clothes and quickly check out the vast open-plan space, at least five times as big as my old apartment, and dominated by floor-to-ceiling windows covering two walls. Cross-training and weight equipment take up a corner of the room along with a spread of mats and a giant punching bag. A sitting area in front of a sleek sandstone fireplace looks both masculine and comfortable with a big, gray, overstuffed couch and matching chair, curved glass tables, and blue accent pillows. His pristine kitchen, all black granite and stainless steel appliances, looks like it has never been used. And of course, beneath me, a delightfully cold, polished, hardwood table. Very Jake.

"You have a great place here," I say when he reappears with the box of condoms in one hand.

"Back in position."

A thrill of excitement floods my veins as I bend over the table. This is clearly Jake's show.

Minutes pass and then his warm hand caresses my ass, smoothing over my cheeks. "Fuck," he murmurs. "You've got the sweetest ass. I could look at it all day."

"I love it when you whisper sweet nothings in my ear."

"Only thing I'm putting in your ear, baby, is my tongue, and that's after I've licked every part of your body, including your pussy."

My gasp goes unheard as his feet thud across the marble floor to a credenza beneath the flat-screen TV. My heart pounds against the table, and I push myself partway up.

"I've…never allowed anyone to spank me before, Jake." My voice drops to a low whisper. "I don't know if I'll like it."

He holds up a coil of soft rope and a pair of nylon cuffs. "You've never been spanked? With that smart mouth?"

Affronted, I frown. "This mouth is usually busy doing things that warrant the opposite of a spanking, and I've never had any complaints."

Jake freezes midstep. "Baby. Do NOT, and I repeat do NOT put images into my head of you and other men. There is no past. There is only *now* and *soon*, and you're going to get spanked in both of them. And knowing what I know about you and seein' the way you're nibbling on your lip and watching your cheeks burn, I know it's gonna make you fucking hot."

He squats in front of the table and tilts my head up with a gentle finger under my chin. I push myself up on my elbows to meet his gaze.

"You okay if I restrain your arms? It will give you something to brace against and knowing you can't interfere…it heightens the sensation."

I look from Jake to the cuffs and back to Jake. "In the past, which I know exists only in the hypothetical universe, and aside from the tie episode at my house, which was escapable, I only ever allowed restraints I could release myself."

"Then you weren't really restrained," he murmurs. "You won't be able to let go if you're in control. Trust me, baby. You don't like anything we're doing, you say the word and I'll stop."

"I trust you."

Jake wraps the padded Velcro straps around my wrists and then threads the rope through the attached rings to the legs of the table, spreading my arms wide.

"These cuffs are handy," I mumble through my trepidation. "I guess you never know when you might need padded Velcro cuffs with rings attached. Maybe when you need to hang from your arms or if you have a lot of shopping to carry home. I should get a pair."

Jake chuckles and looks away. "If you don't stop talking and making me laugh, I'm gonna gag you too, or maybe I'll fill that lush mouth with my cock and give it something else to do." He makes me pull against the restraints until he is certain they won't hurt me and I am certain I won't be able to get free. My first taste of real restraint is a heady experience. By the time Jake walks behind me, I am struggling through both intense fear and intense arousal.

"I can't do this," I rasp. "Let me up."

Jake smoothes his hand down my back and then over my ass. "Give it a minute, baby. Let your mind and body adjust."

He kicks my legs apart and strokes a rough finger through my folds, then trails my wetness along my inner thigh. "I'm thinking you're already there."

Oh yes. Hot, wet, and desperate to be touched. Arching my back, I look over my shoulder, just as Jake leans over me, pressing his bare, slick chest against my back, covering me with his body. His erection presses against the cleft of my ass and I moan.

Jake brushes a kiss over my cheek, trailing his lips down my neck to the sensitive spot between my neck and my shoulder. "Need to mark you." The deep rumble of his voice vibrates through my body. "Let everyone know you're mine."

"Okay."

He bites gently at first and then sucks hard until my eyes slit closed at the pleasure pain and my breath comes in short, hard pants. He licks over the wound and then kisses the bruised skin.

"Mine."

"Yours," I agree. "In the most primal sense of the word."

He licks again over the wound. "Wish I could make it permanent."

"Like a tattoo on my forehead that says 'Renegade's girl. Don't fucking touch or I'll break your arms'?"

Chuckling, he brushes my hair to the side and then nuzzles my neck. "That would be a good start."

A shiver of pleasure runs down my spine as his five o'clock shadow rasps over my sensitive skin. I gasp and arch under him, pushing back against his hardened length. His obvious arousal sends a wave of need through my body, and I whimper and wiggle my ass, hoping he might forget the spanking and skip to the good stuff.

"Naughty girl," he warns. "Punishment first, then pleasure." He pulls away, leaving me cold and bereft, then his hand smacks my ass with a loud, terrifying crack.

My breath leaves me in a rush, as does my brain's ability to register the sensation. Stunned, I don't move until suddenly fire streaks across my left cheek. I suck in air and release it with a gasp as he murmurs in a calm, perversely soothing voice.

"Next time you feel scared or overwhelmed, you talk to me. I'll listen. I'll be there for you. You don't guess what I'm thinking and you don't push me away."

Smack. He hits my other cheek, harder this time and pain radiates down my thighs. Then he alternates side to side, never striking the same place twice. The sound of his sharp, hard slaps on my skin fills the room, a curiously erotic sound that makes my sex tingle despite the burn.

Instinctively, I tug against the restraints and instantly understand the appeal. Without them, I might have turned around and given back what he gave me: a few slaps on the chest, maybe a punch to the jaw. With them, I am totally at his mercy, but I'm not afraid. Deep inside, I know Jake would never hurt me. Relieved of the burden of having to decide how much of myself to give, I let go and the burn turns into gut-churning arousal.

Jake rubs his hand lightly over my heated skin. "Beautiful." His fingers slip between my thighs and glide along my dripping folds.

"You like being spanked." He gives a satisfied grunt and then eases two fingers inside me. "So hot, baby. So wet."

With a whimper, I rock up on my toes, riding his fingers as hard as I dare. "Can't take any more."

He presses his hand against my lower back, pinning my hips to the table. "I decide how much you can take, and I know you can take a lot more."

I brace myself for more smacks, but instead, he eases a third finger inside me and pushes in deep. My body tenses up so tight I can barely breathe. But with his hand on my lower back, I can't move, can't rock, can't even squirm or writhe or wriggle. I am helpless, spread open, impaled by the relentless thrust of his fingers, and I am hotter and wetter than I have ever been in my life.

My need escapes in a low, guttural groan and sweat sheets my body.

"I'll take care of you, baby, but I need you ready. You have me wound up so tight, I'm gonna be rough when I slide between those sweet thighs, but when I come, I want you coming with me." He angles his fingers inside me and rubs over my sensitive tissue. Heaviness curls low in my belly and I ease my legs farther apart to give him better access.

"Good girl. Now relax for me."

Relax? Not with every muscle in my body tense and aching, my need coiled tight and ready to spring. Not with my calves burning and my thighs shaking and my nipples rock hard and pressed painfully against the table. I am primed and ready to detonate, not relax. "I...can't."

"Wrong answer." He pulses his fingers against my G-spot and the heaviness in my womb increases in intensity until moisture gushes from my body and I am engulfed in a tidal wave of sensation, deep, fierce, and unrelenting—a low roll of thunder instead of the sharp crack of lightning. My G-spot orgasm pounds through my body overwhelming every nerve, every fiber, every tissue of my being, and when I am finally able to suck in a breath, it rips a scream out of me that doesn't end until I am limp on the table.

"Christ." Jake's voice in my ear is thick with desire, and only then am I aware he is leaning over me, covering me with his body, holding me through the last waves and tremors of my climax.

"You still with me, baby?"

Unable to speak or move and barely able to think, I whimper, resting my cheek against the cool surface of the table.

Jake eases away, and I hear the crinkle of a condom wrapper and the whisper of latex.

"Need you now." His voice drops to a low, husky growl. "Never seen anything so fucking hot in my life." His hand cups the curve of my sex and he circles my throbbing clit with his finger. Almost instantly I am shot back to the peak of arousal, and I draw in a ragged breath.

"I can't, Jake. Not again."

"You can."

He grips my hips, and with one hard thrust, he is inside me, his piercing scraping over my swollen, overly sensitive tissue. I let out a long, low wail, and then he drives in farther, filling me until my inner muscles clench around him.

"You got me running so fucking wild." He groans, twists his hand through my hair, and yanks my head back as he rocks hard inside me, and my whimpers melt into a deep, guttural moan.

"Oh God, Jake. Fuck me."

My words set him off. He pulls out and drives forward, his piercing tearing a sob from my throat as it slides over my swollen, oversensitized G-spot. With his free hand, he grips my hip and moves faster, harder, deeper, riding me until my breaths come in short, choked pants, and I am slick with sweat and need and poised on the edge of a cliff so high I am afraid to jump.

"Now, baby." He slides his hand over the curve of my hip to my throbbing clit and gives it a merciless pinch.

I come. Screaming. Falling. Splintering into a million pieces as a tidal wave of pleasure rushes through me, pounding in time to the frantic beating of my heart.

And Jake is with me, shouting his release as he comes with one last hard thrust, his cock pulsing against my swollen inner tissue. Then he collapses on top of me and for a long moment we don't move.

"My baby's so fucking hot." He presses a soft kiss to my cheek. "So damn beautiful it hurts."

Finally, he releases the restraints and carries me to the bed then disappears to dispose of his condom. My heart pounds violently in my chest, and I am caught in a maelstrom of emotions so thick I can barely breathe. Every time we're together, he pushes me further. What if he doesn't stop? He's a fighter, and fighters fight until the opponent breaks. Anxiety surges through me like a tidal wave, and I push myself up to sitting just when Jake climbs up beside me and gently strokes my cheek.

"Breathe."

"Jake…"

"Shhh. You're safe. Let me hold you."

So I bite my tongue and snuggle into his arms, and I pray he can keep the fear at bay.

We lie in blissful silence for all of three minutes, and then…

"Fuck."

Hovering on the verge of sleep, I murmur into his chest, "You swear too much."

"Baby." He pulls me up so I am lying flat on top of him, his unbelievably ever-hard erection pressing against the juncture of my thighs. "When a man feels strongly about something, he doesn't waste time choosing words."

I rest my chin on my hands, cupped together over his chest, and look up at him through my lashes. "What are you feeling strongly about now, when the only thing you should be feeling is relaxed and sleepy like me?"

He strokes a gentle hand over my cheek. "When you told me about having to sell your house, that meant a lot to me. More than you could possibly know. And when you showed up at my door…" He chokes on his words. "I love you, Amanda. I love you so much I don't know what to fucking do when things go wrong. I want you with me all the time so I can make sure nothing bad happens to you and no one hurts you and nothing makes you sad. I want to wrap you in a blanket and keep you in my arms, safe and protected and mine. You had a hard time growing up, and I know you're having a hard time now. I just want to make the world beautiful for you again."

My body stiffens. Oh God. *Nononononononono*. Not that word. I don't want to hear that word. My breath leaves me in a rush and I look up and study him—his golden hair curling at his temples, lightly tanned skin, chiseled jaw, the faint shadow on his jaw, his blue eyes curious, silently questioning.

My chest constricts and my stomach clenches. Closing my eyes against his penetrating stare, I fight off the waves of panic, wrestling the urge to push him away and run. When did things stop being just sexy and fun? When did it suddenly get so serious?

Emotion wells up in my chest, a fierce, unsettling, rush of

affection, deeper and more powerful than anything I've felt before. But ultimately where can it go? I am fundamentally flawed in both the happiness giving and receiving departments. He's shown me how to let go in the bedroom, but in the real world, I'll never be able to give myself completely to him. Not in the way he needs. Not in the way love demands.

"You just had to throw a *fuck* in there, didn't you?" I say, gently teasing, hoping he won't notice that I haven't said it back.

He gives me a beautiful, sleepy smile and pulls me up for a kiss. "Fuck, yeah."

⸻

I am warm. Safe. Secure.

I drift. Content.

And then I am not so warm. Awake. Displeased.

"Wake up, baby. Time to play." Jake gives me only a second to focus before he whips the covers off me and pounces like an overeager puppy. First stop: my breasts.

"Beast. Get off." I slap his head as he draws my nipple into his mouth, shifting his position so he straddles my hips.

"I feel like I just fell asleep a minute ago." I look over at the clock on his bedside table. "Ohmigod. I've only been sleeping for an hour."

"And I've been ready for you since you drifted off. I couldn't wait any longer."

From the rock-hard erection poking into my thigh, I believe him. "You couldn't wait an hour?"

He gives my nipple a sharp nip and then turns his attention to the other one. "You've actually been sleeping for twelve hours, so don't be grumpy. It's late afternoon."

"It doesn't count as twelve hours of sleep since you woke me up ten times to satisfy your insatiable sexual appetite." Then my sleep-fuzzed brain kicks into gear and I shoot up to sitting, dislodging him from my breast. "TWELVE hours. Omigod. I'm supposed to be at work."

Jake slides a thick thigh between my legs and gently presses me back down. "Couldn't bring myself to let you go, especially when you were naked in my bed. Decided not to tell you. It's Saturday, after all. Time for a day off."

"I'll make sure to buy some pajamas next time I stay over," I say, "so as not to entice you."

Jake nuzzles my neck, sending a delicious shiver down my spine. "There's nothing you can wear that wouldn't entice me because I know what's underneath."

"Don't I get a chance to wake up?" I moan as little bursts of pleasure zing straight to my core.

"No. You get this." He sits back and hands me a tiny butterfly-shaped vibrator from the bedside table. The elastic straps dangle between my fingers.

"You bought me a butterfly?"

Jake holds up a tiny remote control and presses a button. The vibrator buzzes in my hand. "Special, deluxe butterfly. Controllable only by me. I can turn it on or off and control the intensity." He pushes a button and the butterfly almost takes flight. "Have you ever used one?"

"Um…no." Anything with a remote control that would give someone else control over my orgasms has never had a place in my sex toy pie cupboard.

With a wicked smile, he takes the vibrator from my hand. "The top two straps fasten around your waist. The other straps wrap around your thighs. And the butterfly"—he makes it buzz again—"rests against your clit."

My body heats in an instant as all sorts of naughty scenarios play through my head. But no way. Not unless I'm holding the remote control. "Thank you. But…"

He slides his hand around my waist and pulls me hard against him as his lips brush over my ear. "You're wearing it tonight at Redemption. I have a class to teach and I want you to watch."

I look at him aghast. "I am not."

"You are."

"You want me to hang out with a bunch of fighters with a vibrator buzzing inside my panties?"

He licks his lips. "God, yes. I'm going to keep you on edge all evening, so when I fuck you at the end of the night, you'll come so hard you'll pass out."

My lips quiver with a repressed smile. "Coming so hard I pass out isn't really one of my lifetime goals. I didn't even know it was possible." I push myself higher on the pillows, away from him. I shouldn't be tempted. Not at all. But the whole idea is so deliciously naughty and so deeply erotic, I can't stop the beat of desire pulsing between my thighs.

"It is possible."

"And you know this, how?" I don't really want to know, but I do. Has he really made a woman come so hard she passed out?

The look he gives me is oh-so smug. "I read about it."

I snort a laugh. "Nice. I'm glad to know you spend your time in worthwhile pursuits. Those are fantasies. Not real."

He takes the butterfly from my hand and glides it down my body, skimming between my breasts, over my belly, and then he rests it on my mound and makes it buzz, a little tease before he snatches it away. "Let's find out. Even if you don't pass out, I'll bet it will still be freaking amazing."

"You have a lot of faith in your abilities." I tremble as he dangles it above me.

"I have a lot of faith in what will happen when I take control away from someone who doesn't like to give it up." Kneeling between my legs, Jake leans forward and presses a soft kiss to my mound. Oh God, yes. I hiss in a breath and part my legs by way of encouragement.

"You want my mouth, baby?"

My breath comes in short pants and I nod. Jake flicks his tongue over my clit and then sinks lower, slipping through my slick folds and then back up to torture and tease.

"Such a pretty pussy," he croons. "So goddam wet. I'm tempted to keep going, but…" He pushes himself to his knees. "I have a class to teach."

A violent shudder racks my body, a protest at desire unfulfilled. "No. Don't stop. You can't stop now. Maybe you should warm me up."

"I can stop, and I will." He slides the elastic straps over my feet and up my legs, tightening them one at a time around each thigh before he fastens the elastic around my waist. As the soft plastic vibrator comes in contact with my throbbing clit, I let out a whimper and my body arches. I'm so close, if he turns it on now…

"None of that." He slaps my thigh hard, diverting my attention from the ache in my soaking wet sex to the sting on my skin.

"Three rules for tonight after we make a quick stop at your place." He adjusts the position of the butterfly as I take long, deep breaths, trying to control the beat of my arousal.

"First, once you commit, there is no going back. If you leave your house wearing the butterfly, it doesn't come off until I take it off." He raises a questioning eyebrow and I nod my assent.

"Second, you can't make yourself come. You come when I say you come." I bite my lip and look away so he can't see my face when I agree. That one might not be so easy.

"Third." He strokes a finger down my cheek. "No begging."

Affronted, I glare. "I don't beg for sex, Jake."

The look of pure unadulterated lust in his eyes sends a shiver down my spine.

"You will."

Chapter 18
BUZZ. BUZZ. BUZZ.

REDEMPTION IS HOPPING WHEN we arrive. Every piece of equipment is in use, every training ring booked, and Shayla has had to commandeer Sandy to help her manage all the waiting lists. The regulars wave when we walk in, but my attention is focused on Jake's hand, casually tucked into the pocket of his jeans where he has secreted the remote control.

"Gotta get changed, baby."

"I'll go wait for you in the studio."

He gives me a soft kiss. "Wait for me here."

"Okay."

Buzz. The butterfly vibrates gently against my clit. I suck in a sharp breath and glare over my shoulder.

"Seriously?"

Jake lifts an eyebrow. "Reward for good behavior. I like it when you do what I say."

"Lucky me to find myself a rough, gritty fighter who is into kinky sex. My parents wanted me to go out with a doctor or lawyer. But no. I had to have you." I press a kiss to the side of his neck, and he rumbles a warning low in his throat.

"Behave. I know what you're up to."

"Mmmmm." I nuzzle his neck, inhaling his delicious scent of sex and soap and me. "What am I up to?"

"Level 2."

The vibrator jumps to life, more intense than before and my hands tighten around his neck as I try to breathe through my desperate need to come.

"Not funny," I pant, resting my forehead against his chest.

He strokes his hand down my hair. "Maybe not funny, but very amusing and so damned fucking hot I don't know how I'll get through my class."

Jake leaves the vibrator on its lowest setting for the duration of his jiu-jitsu class, and I am forced to endure not only the maddeningly gentle buzz, but also sitting on the floor watching Jake teach in his gi. I try not to think about how hot he looks when the gi opens as he demonstrates a move or how kind and patient he is with his students. I also try not to think about orgasms and how good they feel and how many seconds are in each minute until the class is done.

But why wait?

Suddenly seized with the desire to send him over the edge, I throw my jacket over my lap and lean against the wall. The class is facing Jake, their backs to me, so I am free to slide my hand under the jacket and engage in some naughty rule-breaking behavior to relieve the ache in my clit. Pressing my palm over the butterfly produces miraculous results. The vibrations intensify, carrying me closer and closer to the edge.

My skin prickles and I look up. Jake is staring at me. He does not look pleased. But ha ha. He had to leave the remote on the side ledge and he has twenty students waiting for his instructions.

Gaze locked on mine, his jaw tightens and he pulls a student from the front row and tosses him on the mat. I press harder on the butterfly and lick my lips as my body heats. *Slam.* Another student joins the first. *Slam.* And then another. A few students glance my way, but I am not concerned. All they see is a woman with her jacket casually thrown over her lap and overly flushed cheeks.

Jake, however, sees something else. Something that seems to make him quite agitated. He leaps on a student and shouts as he brings the poor fellow down to the mat and locks him in some kind of pretzel twist head and arm lock. *Mmmmm.* I'd like him to twist me that way.

I cross my legs, ensuring my naughty hand is still hidden. This is much better. Easier access, and my entire hand can get in on the action as I curve it over my sex. I rock my palm over the butterfly on my clit. *God. So good.* My back arches and I bite my lip to stifle a groan.

Jake stills and his eyes widen. He clenches his jaw and barks a few commands. The students pair off and tussle on the mats. Uh-oh. Now they don't require his attention. But apparently, I do. Jake stalks through the grunting, rolling students toward me, murder in his eyes. Well…maybe not murder. More like lust.

Closer and closer he comes. Higher and higher I climb. My body heats. Muscles tighten. Clit throbs. Panties dampen. Danger and desire are an explosive combination and just as he reaches my corner, I hit the peak. The forbidden orgasm seizes me, forcing a sharp breath from my lungs, throwing my head against the wall, squeezing my eyes closed and rocking my world.

When I open my eyes, Jake's jaw is locked tight, his eyes hard, pulse throbbing in his temple. A man on the edge. A man about to lose control. He turns and barks an order and a portly, bald black belt runs to the front of the class. Without another word, Jake grabs my hand, pulls me up, snatches the remote from the ledge, and drags me out of the studio.

"Am I in trouble?" I try to keep up with his long, furious strides, my body still tingling from my climax.

Buzz. Buzz. The butterfly suddenly comes to life, vibrating on my now overly sensitive clit. Jake grabs my arm, half leading and half dragging me down the hallway until we reach a storage closet. After a quick look around to ensure we are alone, he opens the door and pulls me inside.

The dark, dusty space, filled with brooms and mops, reminds me of the anniversary of our first date, but this is clearly not the time to reminisce. Jake's body is taut, trembling, his forehead glistening with a fine sheen of sweat, hands curled into fists. My skin prickles and my heart gives a warning thump.

"Jake? Are you okay? It's just a game…right?"

"Driving me out of my fucking mind is not a game, baby." He swallows hard and takes a step toward me. "Watching you make yourself come with all those other guys around you, knowing I couldn't touch you or stop you, knowing they might see something only I should see…it was the hottest thing I've ever seen."

My tension eases until he slams his hands on either side of my head, sending a frisson of fear down my spine.

"But I can't handle not being in control."

"Okay," I whisper.

He cups my face with his hands and leans down. "I'm barely in control now."

With deep, sensuous strokes, he kisses me with a hunger matched only by my need. His hands roam my body, cupping my ass, brushing over the curve of my breast, sifting through my hair and, although only moments ago I was desperate to take the butterfly off, I can't stop myself from pressing up against him and grinding my butterfly clad clit against his thigh.

Oh God. I'm building, building, so close. "Turn it up." I rasp out the command, staring pointedly at his pocket. "Make me come."

Jake growls deep in his throat. "Oh no. You're going to pay for breaking the rules. I'm gonna edge you. I'm gonna take everything from you until you lose control and beg me to let you come, just like you told me you would never do."

In response to my puzzled frown, a slow, devilish smile spreads across his face. "Poor baby. You never edged before?"

My lips part, but no sound comes out. All my energy is focused on taking deep, calming breaths. I manage a head shake but nothing more.

He presses his lips to my ear. "Edging is where I bring you up and take you down but never let you come. I'm gonna let you climb so high you can see over the other side, and then I'll take it away. And when I finally give it to you, baby, you'll want it so bad, you'll take everything I give you and you'll beg for more, and you'll never disobey me again."

The butterfly comes to life and a groan rips from my throat. Jake gives me a soft kiss and then he steps back and folds his arms over his chest.

"Strip."

This time I understand his need to be in control. This time I don't argue. His dark, sensual promises inflame me; his commands arouse me; and his hard, muscular body, clad in that mouthwatering gi, make it easy to strip off my clothes and toss them in a pile on the dusty floor.

Naked, vulnerable, and needy, I reach to remove the butterfly but

Jake shakes his head. "Sorry, baby. It's gonna be tough, but that has to stay on."

Moments later, I understand his apology. He flicks the remote and the butterfly increases in intensity until it is buzzing so hard I can barely breathe. My body tightens until I am on the edge, and then the buzzing fades away.

"No." I gasp.

Jake wraps his arms around me and murmurs soothing words in my ear. "I'm afraid it doesn't get easier." And then the butterfly is buzzing again, taking me up faster this time, so fast that when the buzzing stops, the drop is a painful, beautiful ache, spreading from my clit through my core.

"Jake…" I cling to him through the next wave and the next as his hands caress my breasts, my ass, my stomach, hips, and my thighs. His touch is at once soothing and arousing, but never enough to take me where I want to go.

I have no idea how many minutes pass or how many times he brings me up and down. I only know my body is slick with sweat, my brain fuzzed with lust, my core aching with a pleasure pain that drives the breath from my body, and every fiber of my being is focused on the overwhelmingly painful need to come.

Finally, he slips his hand between my legs and spreads his fingers, forcing my thighs apart. "Open for me."

With a moan, I part my legs and he slicks his fingers up the wetness trickling down my inner thigh and then along my dripping folds.

"Christ." He thrusts one finger into my swollen center. "Thought you'd be wet, baby, but not like this."

My sex tightens around the exquisite intrusion, and I clutch his shoulders, pulling him closer. "Please."

"That's what I like to hear." His deep voice rumbles as he adds a second finger, and then a third, angling them to hit my sensitive inner tissue. My body turns liquid and I lean against the wall for support as the vibrator buzzes and his fingers thrust and my muscles tighten. My breath becomes a whine, my knees tremble, and my vision blurs, and in that moment I would do absolutely anything to come.

"Fuck. You won't be able to take much more." Chest heaving, eyes burning with sensual promise, he withdraws his fingers. Through the haze of intense arousal, I am vaguely aware of him rummaging through my purse. I hear the slide of clothing over skin, the crinkle of a condom wrapper, and the snap of latex.

And then his hands are cupping my ass and he is lifting me against him. No ceremony. No warning. My back hits the wall and a bottle falls off the shelf, crashing to the floor.

With a low groan, he sucks my nipple, licking it until I whimper. And then his mouth is gone and his fingers are gliding through my folds, testing my wetness. I gasp a shocked breath.

"My baby needs me bad."

"Yes. God, yes." I writhe against him, out of control, legs quivering, hips rocking, back arching, trying to entice him to dip more than his fingers inside or turn off the damn vibrator.

"Open wider for me, baby."

I tighten my grip on his neck, pulling myself closer to him, easing my thighs around his hips.

"Good girl. I like to feel your wet pussy sliding over my cock."

His words break down the last of my walls, and I lose myself to sensation. My body is no longer my own. I don't recognize the low guttural groan that escapes through my lips. I don't know the dirty words I whisper in his ear. Catapulted into a world of pure carnal desire, I barely register his voice when he murmurs, "There we are."

And then he's inside me. His forceful intrusion scatters my thoughts. So big. So hard. Sensually savage. He fills me the way I have been desperate to be filled all evening. Painfully. Completely.

"That's it baby," he croons as he stills, giving my muscles a chance to accommodate him. "Take it deeper." But the second I start to relax, he drives in until he is tight up against me.

Finally he begins to move. But it isn't hard and fast as I imagined. Instead he thrusts with a slow, tortuous rhythm clearly designed to drive me out of my mind.

"Aaaaaaaaah…"

Despite my protestations, he continues his slow, steady strokes, his piercing sparking against my G-spot over and over until my sex is clenched tight around him and I am fisting his gi, whimpering and begging to come.

Just like he said I would.

He adjusts his angle and then he is pounding inside me. Moisture trickles from my sex. The vibrator buzzes. His piercing sears across my sensitive tissue. I feel at once filled and violated. Dirty and cherished. Totally and utterly out of control. Scared and so goddamn close to climax, I don't care. Every muscle, every joint, every fiber of my being is coiled tight and coherent thought is a distant memory.

"Don't stop. Don't stop. Don't stop."

"Come for me," he demands with a guttural rasp, and he kicks up the butterfly one last notch.

And I do. I explode. Shatter. My orgasm overtakes me with frightening power, a lightning sheet ripping through my body. Pulsing, throbbing, wet, my sex grips his cock as the waves ride me hard and I am overwhelmed by an all-consuming, terrifying pleasure. Jake hammers into me until his cock stiffens and swells and then he follows me into oblivion with a shout of his own.

"Are you with me, baby?" He clicks off the vibrator and braces me against the wall, freeing his hands, then he gently turns my head to study my face. "You okay?"

"I didn't pass out."

Jake chuckles. "You sound disappointed. You wanna have another go?"

"No." I draw in a ragged breath, struggling against my natural inclination to cover up my real feelings with humor or diversion. "Being out of control like that scared me."

His face softens and he smoothes the hair away from my face. "But it made you hot, didn't it? It turned you on. You gave yourself to me, and I took care of you."

"Yes."

"And I didn't let you down."

I give him a reluctant smile but my heart sinks. He doesn't understand. He doesn't see that he has bared me, body and soul, and without my armor I am lost in the world.

He releases me and we straighten our clothes, then Jake wraps his arms around me and gives me a hug. "Are you sure you're okay?"

"Yeah, I'm good," I lie. Disconcerted, trembling, unbearably exposed, I desperately want to go home.

Monday morning, after a weekend of work interrupted by nightly sexathons that leave me physically sated and emotionally wrecked, I stumble into the office. Almost immediately, my pulse kicks up a notch and my stomach clenches. What was I thinking, taking Saturday and Sunday night off? How will I ever make up that time? How many applications have Farnsworth's minions prepared over the weekend? Will I be able to keep a grip on the emotional turmoil that has been threatening to rip me apart all weekend? I gave up my control and it scared me, and although part of me wanted to run, another part couldn't stay away.

"How was the weekend?" Ray looks up from his newspaper and my cheeks heat in an instant.

"Good."

"Looks like."

I stiffen and frown. "What's that supposed to mean?"

"Nothin'."

I give Penny a smile and pour myself a coffee. "How was your weekend?"

She shrugs. "Fine."

Coffee in hand, I join Ray on the couch. Then I put my feet up on the table. Quite comfy. As I sip the hot, bitter liquid, I look around the office. The dark drapes and navy blue pillows make for a somber atmosphere. Maybe we should change them out for something light. Cream. Or a soft toffee color. Maybe some pale pink accents. Lighter furniture. And that monogram has to go. Everywhere I look, the office pities me. AW. AW. AW.

Or maybe not. Maybe the tried-and-true corporate style is best. None of this halfway nonsense. The couch has to go.

Or should it?

Ray shoots me a knowing look. "Thinking of redecorating?"

Gritting my teeth, I snatch the newspaper from his hands. "Can you read my mind? Seriously. How do always know what I'm thinking?"

"You're very easy to read. Right now, you're confused. Don't know what to do."

Worried I might be too transparent about the weekend too, I tighten my voice and switch to work mode. "Penny, could you please pull the Redemption file? I have some new surveillance ideas I want to run past Ray."

"Sure." She pushes herself out of her seat and shuffles across the room.

Ray frowns. "You okay, Pen?"

Penny's cheeks brighten and she nods. "Yeah good. Just stiff...fell down the stairs this weekend. Woke up at night to get a glass of water and didn't turn on the light."

Ray gives Penny a considered look. "You didn't go out with that fucking loser again did you?"

"If I did, Ray, it wouldn't be any of your business."

His jaw tightens and his voice drops to a warning growl. "If he laid a hand on you, Pen, I would damn well make it my business."

A pained expression crosses her face and she yanks open the filing cabinet then winces. "Not that I'm saying I went out with him, but we don't all have a choice like both of you. We don't all have so many people so desperate for our attention that we can play with them and toss them away when they get too close."

I look at Penny aghast. "Is that what you think?"

"I think you never see what's staring you in the face," she says bitterly. "I think you're so afraid to let people get close, you can't even see when you've found the very thing you've been looking for. The thing everyone else is looking for and few of us ever find. And Ray's the same. He's a love 'em and leave 'em type of guy."

"You don't know anything about me, Pen," Ray says quietly. "Don't presume."

Penny pulls a file from the cabinet and tosses it on the desk. "Fine then."

My mouth drops open. "Is something wrong, Penny? Did I do something to upset you? Did Ray?"

Tears glitter in her eyes. "Nope. I'm good. Everything is good."

Over the next few days, I try to get Penny to tell me what's going on, but for the first time since I've known her, she refuses to talk. Instead, she throws herself into work alongside me.

Fortunately, Jake is also busy with work, but when he does find time in his schedule, I invent meetings to keep us apart. Disconcerted by the three words he whispered while we lay on his bed, and confused by my body's heated response to his relentless pushing in the bedroom, I need some distance, and work is a good place to hide.

Or maybe it's not.

Chapter 19

POUND, POUND, POUND GOES MY HEART

FRIDAY AFTERNOON, THE REAL estate agent calls. We've had an offer from a development company. They plan to knock down my grandmother's house and build condos. When I suggest to the agent maybe we should leave it on the market a little longer for a family or even a young couple starting out, she almost hyperventilates. Full asking price. Cash. Quick sale. Almost unheard of in this market. I'll never get a comparable offer, and even if I do, it might not be for up to a year. So I say yes even though my heart says no.

After staring at my computer screen for an hour and billing no time, I grab my gym bag and head to Redemption. Although I had planned to work through my new fight class, I'm getting nothing done. Might as well make sure I'm in top physical condition for the work marathon ahead. And as an added incentive, Jake texts that he has a meeting tonight. I won't have to face him after successfully avoiding him all week. Coward that I am.

When I present myself at the training ring for Fight or Flight, Shayla introduces me to a new instructor, Razzor, a tall, Nordic blond with iceberg eyes. Razzor informs me his name is spelled with two Zs because there is already a Razor with one Z on the cards. He says we are to say his name with an extra hiss so everyone knows we are talking about Razzor with two Zs and not one. He does not smile when he says this, so we know he is serious.

Blade Saw stops by and invites us to the Redemption prefight barbecue at his place two weeks from Saturday. He says the Redemption fighters always have a big party before they move into a serious regimen of dieting and training before a big event, and this time it's his turn to host. Shayla accepts for both of us. After Blade Saw leaves, she tells me she needs a wingman at the party, and I'm it. Refusal is not an option.

Razzor informs me Shayla will be my sparring partner. I whimper. He tells me to breathe deep, swallow my fear, and focus on the fight. Shayla gives me an evil smile and cracks her knuckles, then her neck, then my ribs. Still, I learn some new punching techniques, a few fight moves, and how a head to the solar plexus can drive all the air from your lungs.

"Sorry." Shayla massages my ribs as I wheeze and gasp on the mat. "Been having a rough week and needed to blow off some steam."

"Me too." My words come out as a low whistle. Those are the last words I say for the next twenty minutes. When the class finally ends, I lie on the mat and vow never to step into a ring with Shayla again.

Curiously, the painful hour in the gym restores my energy, and I return to my office to put in a few more hours of work. On impulse, I stop along the way and buy a bottle of wine. One glass to cheer me up. It is a Friday night, after all, and I should be celebrating the sale of my house.

Back in the office, I check my phone messages. Lots from clients. None from Jake. Three days and no contact, and Shayla said between punches that he'd never missed a practice until tonight.

My heart sinks. All this time I thought I've been avoiding Jake, but maybe he's avoiding me. I never said anything after he told me he loved me. Not at Redemption. Not over the weekend during our sexathon. And not in any of our very brief conversations at the beginning of the week. How would I feel if he did that to me? Maybe the same way I felt when no one showed up at my piano recitals, soccer games, or Christmas concerts, or when my birthdays passed by unnoticed.

Nausea roils in my gut at the thought I might have hurt him. What the hell have I been doing? Maybe Penny is right. The torrent of tender emotions I feel when I'm with Jake. The thrill that sets my heart pounding when he walks into a room. The freedom to let go, trusting he won't let me fall. This deep tugging on my heart. Maybe this is what I've been looking for. Not lust or infatuation. Not friendship. But love. The kind of love that means commitment.

I need to speak to him. Now.

A rattle at the front door startles me before I can pick up my phone and I freeze. My heart seizes in my chest. Jake? It has to be. Who else would come here so late at night? Hope blossoms in my chest and I race out into the reception room just in time to hear the shatter of glass and the crunch of shoes in the hallway.

My mouth opens to call out Jake's name when a warning tingle makes me think again. Jake wouldn't break the window. He has a key. As do Penny and Ray.

A chill of fear runs through my veins. The only light on in the building is in my office, not visible from the street. Does the intruder know I'm here? If I take a step, will he hear me?

Back into my office. Turn off the lights. Quietly close and lock the door. *Phone. Need phone. Move feet move.* But my feet won't listen, or maybe they can't hear over the frantic pounding of my heart.

Footsteps circle the reception room, once then twice, ringing out loudly against the hardwood floor. Doors open and close. Penny's chair rolls. Then I hear the hum of her computer. Sweat trickles down my back. What does he want? Not drugs or money. The computer? Files?

Finally, I force myself into action, tiptoeing cautiously across the floor. But the boards creak with every step and by the time I reach my desk, I am sure he has heard me. Hands shaking, I call 911, whispering the information into the phone. Then I text Fuzzy in case they don't come. Or in case they come too late.

Over to the window. Tug and pull. Pull and tug. Damn window won't budge. Sweat trickles between my breasts and my fingers claw uselessly at the catch. I'll have to break it.

The roll of chair castors. The thud of footsteps. Then the doorknob rattles. "Someone in there?" I don't recognize the thin, reedy voice.

Violent shudders wrack my body, almost as bad as when I first stepped into the ring. So I follow Razzor's advice. I breathe deep. I swallow the fear. I focus on the fight. And right now, my fight is with a goddamn window that won't open.

The doorknob rattles again. Adrenaline surges through my body and my heart pounds so hard I fear I will break a rib. I curse the Redemption fighters for not fixing the window, and Jake for owning a house with windows that don't open, and carpenters who install windows that get stuck, and old houses for warping and twisting frames, and me for not having the foresight to have something in my office that I can use to break the window. Pens, books, and paper won't cut it. No statues or paperweights in my office. I need something big and heavy. My eyes fall on the microwave.

Something thuds against the door and the wall shakes. Oh God. Is he trying to break the door down? I pull the plug on the microwave and stagger with it across the floor. Even as I heave it at the window, I know my plan won't work. Too heavy and not enough force. The microwave bounces off the glass and crashes to the ground. Apparently I didn't pass the Get Fit part of Get Fit or Die.

Despite all my weeks at Redemption and my determination to become a fighter, terror escapes me in a loud piercing scream.

"Fuck." The intruder's voice is harsh and angry, and now I wish I'd kept quiet. He didn't know I was here after all.

Pound, pound, pound goes my heart.

Crunch, crunch, crunch go shoes over broken glass.

Oh God. Did he bring a friend?

The man gasps. His feet thud across the floor, down the hallway, and fade into the kitchen. Then the back door crashes open. And he is gone.

"Amanda, open up. It's Fuzz."

Recognizing the voice, I race to the door. A few moments later, Fuzzy is in my office dressed in jeans and a T-shirt, a gun in his hand. I throw my arms around him and hold on tight.

"Shhhh." He rubs a soothing hand down my back. "I was in the neighborhood when you sent your text. Are you okay? Is he still here?" He places a gentle hand on my shoulder as sirens fill the air.

"Out the back. He went out the back."

Fuzzy races out of my office and disappears around the corner. Shouts. Yells. Police swarm into the building in a thunder of boots and a clatter of weapons. A female police officer takes my statement while I sit on Ray's couch. For the first time ever, I wish I had a cup of tea.

No, I didn't see him. No, I have no idea who it could be. Possibly it could do with one of my cases. Thirteen cases. Only one paying client. Yes, that's right. Only one. The rest I'm doing pro bono. I agree. Not really an economically viable way to run a business, but I like to help people. No, not something I got from my parents. More like in spite of my parents. No, nothing was missing. Yes, I felt threatened and scared hence the microwave tossing.

"Do you have a boyfriend or a husband, maybe an ex?" Her voice drops from cold and abrupt to soft and gentle. "Maybe you had a fight and he was angry. Maybe he came here to scare you or hurt you. When emotions run high, things like that happen."

"I have a boyfriend," I say quietly. "But everything is fine between us."

Boyfriend. I called him my boyfriend. A big step for a commitment-phobe like me, and one I'm sure she doesn't appreciate. But is it the truth? Is he my boyfriend and is everything fine?

Shouts from the hallway. Yells. A thud. Then Fuzzy calls, "Let him through." Feet pound across the floor, and then Jake appears in the doorway.

Seeing him there, his chest heaving, eyes wild, his face etched with concern, something inside me breaks, and all the terror of the night leaks through, trickling over my cheeks in hot, wet tears.

"See. Here he is," I whisper. "He came." And I didn't even call.

Without a word, Jake sweeps me into his arms and holds me until my tears dry.

An hour later, statements given, glass and wood swept away, police disbursed, Fuzzy, Jake, and I convene in the reception room. Jake sits on one end of the couch. I sit on the other. Fuzzy sits on my poor, abused coffee table and asks me questions about my cases and potential culprits.

As he takes notes, I glance over at Jake. Why is he sitting over there? Is he angry that Fuzzy called him? Was he trying to avoid me and felt obliged to come? Why hasn't he spoken to me since he arrived? Or looked at me even once since he released me from his arms? I twist my bracelet around my wrist and then knot my fingers in my lap. What's going on?

Finally, Fuzzy rubs his hand over his fuzzy head and sighs. "You got a friend you can stay with tonight, Amanda, or another place to go? After something like this, it's best not to be alone."

"Um…" I glance over at Jake, but he's gazing out the window. Why would Fuzzy think I wouldn't be staying with Jake? Did he say something? My heart sinks as I wrack my brain trying to think who would be the best person to call since Makayla is away. One of my law firm colleagues? Penny? Ray? Drake?

"Why don't you just call up the guy you were waiting for?" Jake's tone is so cool it chills my blood. "The guy you were drinking with." He points to the open bottle of wine on the table. "Who was it this time?"

Shock freezes my tongue, and for a long moment, all I can do is stare. Finally, I peel my tongue off the roof of my mouth. "My house sold today. I was upset. I thought I'd have a beat-the-blues away drink before I dove back into my work. You'll notice there are no glasses on the table. And the only glass you'll find with wine in it is the water glass on my desk."

A pained expression crosses Jake's face. "Why didn't you call me if you were that upset?"

My voice trembles. "I didn't need you. I should really have been celebrating, but I got a bit emotional. I would have been fine after an hour if someone hadn't broken into the office. "

"You didn't need me?" Jake's incredulous look sends a shiver down my spine.

"I knew you were busy at work—so busy you missed your session at Redemption. I didn't want to bother you with a pity party I knew would be over as soon as I got my head buried in my paperwork."

His face smoothes to an expressionless mask, and I sense he knows I'm not giving him the whole truth.

"And when you were in danger, you called Fuzzy, not me?"

The skin on the back of my neck prickles at his tone, so cold and detached, but I don't heed the warning. "I…uh…he's a police officer. I thought…in case the police didn't get here in time…he would know what to do."

"And I wouldn't?"

This is worse than being cross-examined. Every question he asks slices through my heart. Every answer I give sends me even deeper into the sinkhole I seem to have created.

"He has...a gun."

Fuzzy shifts uneasily on the table and then pushes himself to his feet and holds out a hand to me. "You can stay with my family. My parents have lots of room."

Jake shoots to his feet. "I'll take her to my place."

I am tempted to tell Fuzzy I'll just go to a hotel. But the thought of being alone makes my stomach clench. And I don't want to be with a friend. I want to be with Jake, even if he doesn't want to be with me. I need to explain everything. I need to get my foot out of my goddamn mouth.

We make the trip to his place in silence. Silence in the Jeep. Silence as we walk up to his building. Silence in the elevator. Silence after we step inside and he closes the door. Silence until I can't stand the silence any more.

"We need to talk."

He scrubs his hands over his face and sighs. "There's nothing to talk about. I thought maybe this time you would let me in and for a while you did. You needed me. At the hospital, Redemption, even your office. You accepted my help. You shared yourself with me. You gave yourself to me. I thought that would be enough. That's what we didn't have before."

I wrap my arms around my stomach, hold on tight, and brace myself for the train wreck of my life.

"But I need more than that," he says quietly. "I need to matter. And I need to know you're in my corner. Not halfway. Not with one foot out the door, ready to run in case it all goes wrong. After the weekend, you made it clear you needed some space. So I gave it to you. But you didn't come back. You didn't get in touch. When you were hurting, you didn't want me. When you were in danger, you didn't call me. I know you're still sitting on the fence. Just like before, you gave me your body, but you won't give me your heart. And until you're ready to give me everything, we don't belong together."

His words hit me like a punch in the gut, and for the first time in my life I have nothing to say. I've lost him, and this time I didn't do anything. I lost him just because of who I am.

Jake makes up the couch and points me to the bed. But for the longest time I can't move. I sit at the counter while he brushes his teeth and changes. I stare into space as he stretches out on the couch. At some point, I make it to the bed. I curl up, still wearing my work clothes, and wrap myself in his duvet so I am surrounded in him. I breathe in deep, inhaling his scent, and try to make a memory that will last a lifetime.

I drift. In and out of nightmares. Breaking glass. Harsh laughter. Thin, reedy voices. Pounding on doors. My cries awaken me. And then I drift again.

In the haze of sleep, I imagine the bed dips. An arm wraps around me, holding me tight. A warm body spoons me, keeping me safe and warm. The deep rumble of a voice soothes me. A hand strokes my hair and brushes the tears from my cheeks. I cling to the dream. I try to remember the feel of the body pressed tight against mine, the rise and fall of a solid chest, the pounding of a heart in time with mine. I imagine I curl my fingers into his and hold his hand tight against my cheek as I am pulled under again. But this time I don't dream.

When I awake, I am alone. The bed is cold, empty. The couch is bare. Jake is gone.

Chapter 20
THOUGHT YOU WERE A FIGHTER

"GOT BAD NEWS FOR you, Amanda."

Monday morning, ten days after Jake and I broke up, still an emotional mess, I raise an eyebrow as Ray drops into the chair across from my desk.

"Is this in retaliation for me swapping out your Victorian monstrosity for my nice blue corporate couches over the weekend?" I lean back in my chair and give him a resigned look. "I already explained it to Penny, I need paying clients, and they'll be expecting a professional firm with a corporate image. I've been too relaxed about everything. Letting things slide. I'll never be successful if I don't treat this like the serious business it is."

"Old Amanda's back."

"Exactly. At least *you* understand. Penny gave me a hard time when I told her I wouldn't be doing any more off-site witness interviews or lunches during work hours. You do your job. Penny can do her job. And hopefully, we'll see some justice done and make enough money to pay the bills."

"What about your pro bono cases?"

My eyes flick to the pile of cases on my credenza beside the empty space where Jake's microwave used to sit, and I swallow past the lump in my throat. "I'll have to transfer some of them to one of the other attorneys in the community legal aid clinic. I need to free up some time for paying clients. Maybe after I show everyone I can make a success of the firm and we're in the black, I can pick them up again."

For a while, we sit in silence and then he says softly, "You miss him."

And suddenly days of battening down the hatches and shoring up my heart are blown away in an unexpected and unwanted gust of sympathy from the one person who is supposed to be as hard as me.

Gritting my teeth, I stare down at my desk and blink the tears away. "Ray…" My voice cracks, breaks. I take a sip of coffee and follow it with a long, deep breath. "You said you had bad news. Let's discuss that.".

"Right." He tosses a disk on my desk and leans forward. "You asked me to find out why the women on the witness list you put together from the names you got from Jill Jackson suddenly started canceling their interviews and stopped returning your calls this week. I visited everyone on that list. No one will talk. And I mean no one. It's like Farnsworth knew exactly who you were going to contact and got to them first. Some of them were definitely scared."

"So, you're saying he had the list? Maybe that's what the intruder took when he broke in. The witnesses didn't start clamming up until after Jake and I…" My throat tightens. "After the break-in."

Ray leans back and crosses his ankle over his knee, brushing his thumb over his lower lip. "Could be. Or maybe someone hacked into your computer system. I'll call a guy I know and get him to sweep the place for surveillance."

"Sounds exciting for my humble little office."

"Sounds fucking suspicious." Ray leans forward in his chair. "You should be more worried."

Swallowing hard, I shrug. "I would be, but to be honest, I'm thinking of giving up on Farnsworth…and my new firm. The things he's done so far are only the start. Every day he files a new motion or makes a new request, or comes up with another way to make my life hell. I can't keep up, and as we get closer to trial, it's only going to get worse. Max's in-house attorney has been helpful but I can't call him every day. Farnsworth has all the resources of Farnsworth & Tillman, LLP behind him. I have me. Even if I hired someone to do the work, either contract lawyers or even a firm, the fees would kill me."

Ray's mouth tightens into a thin line. "You have Penny and me. You have friends and family. You have colleagues that left the firm. After everything that's happened, all the work you've done, you're going to let him win because you still can't bring yourself to ask for help?"

Sweat trickles down my back. He makes it sound like it was an easy decision, but it has kept me up night after night. I've thought through all the options and possibilities but, in the end, although I may have a case, I am an unarmed, impoverished David to the Goliath that is Farnsworth & Tillman.

"No one could help me, Ray. Even if I asked." With a sigh, I slide a check across the desk. "I settled Sandy's case for her last week. There was just enough to cover office rent and expenses, your contract fee, and Penny's salary. I don't have the money from the house sale yet. I can't take out any loans with Max's loan outstanding. And, except for a few small cases I'm doing for a couple of the Redemption fighters, I have no more paying clients. The big case I'm doing for them, I'm doing for free 'cause they're like family and they wouldn't have been in that alley if it wasn't for me."

Ray frowns and leans back in his chair. "Thought you were a fighter too."

My brow creases. Who is Ray to judge me? He doesn't understand what I'm dealing with. He isn't drowning under a sea of Farnsworth & Tillman embossed paper. He isn't alone.

"I'm no fighter. I went through all that training. I suffered through Get Fit or Die. And for what? An intruder showed up at my office and what did I do? Did I rush into reception and knock him over with a double-leg takedown? Did I wrap him in a gogoplata? Did I hit him with a right hook? No. I locked myself in my office, screamed, and busted my microwave. There was a message in there for me. I'm an attorney. I should do what attorneys do, and really the best place for me to do that is in a big firm where I can work hard, bill high, and maybe one day make my parents proud."

Ray studies me for a long, uncomfortable moment. "And Redemption?"

"I'm cleaning out my locker today. Even if I wanted to stay, it's Jake's gym. He trains there. He teaches there. Those guys are all his friends. They won't want me around now."

His response, a disdainful sniff, sets my teeth on edge.

"So that's it. You give up. What about justice? What about the pro bono clients who think the world of you and who have nowhere else to turn? What about Pen? Did you know she left Farnsworth & Tillman on bad terms after storming up to Farnsworth's office to give him a piece of her mind? How will she get another job without a reference? What about the next woman Farnsworth blackmails, and the next? Whether you like it or not, you created something here. Something you believed in. And you made others believe in it too. You can't just walk away."

He pushes himself out of the chair and stalks across the room. Just before he opens the door, he hesitates and then turns.

"Although you're hell-bent on pushing people away, you are not alone."

Saturday afternoon, after another hellish week fighting Farnsworth, fielding visits from the police about the break-in, managing workers sent by Jake to fix the door and install a security system, and dithering over whether to close up shop forever, I am awakened by my phone vibrating on the night table.

I pull the pillow over my head to block out the sound. *No.* This is the one day I need to catch up on my sleep if I'm to keep up the pace of long days and longer nights. I need a break. A big break. A quiet break.

But there is no respite from the noise just as there is no respite from the torrent of emotion raging through me. Even after two weeks, I can barely make it five minutes without thinking about Jake and what I did wrong.

Buzz. Buzz. Buzz. Over and over and over again. If I had a flyswatter, I would get rid of the damn phone once and for all. Since I don't have a flyswatter, I answer it.

Shayla barks my name into the phone and follows it with an angry string of questions. *"Where are you? What are you doing? Why haven't you picked me up? Did you forget we are going to the Redemption prefight barbecue this afternoon at Blade Saw's house?"*

Oh God. The barbecue. Last thing I want is to spend the evening with the Redemption fighters. Especially since Jake will likely be there. I give her my regrets.

She calls me a few choice names. I compliment her on her foul mouth. She tells me that's nothing. If I don't show, I'll be getting a personal tour of her foul mouth because she's gonna eat me alive. Even when I tell her I'm an emotional wreck because Jake and I broke up, she doesn't relent. She tells me she'll get me so drunk I won't even remember his name. Oblivion. Alcohol style. Oh, and by the way, Jake is outta town on business.

Two hours later, we are drinking champagne on the terrace of Blade Saw's mansion, secreted away at the edge of a lake, the grounds lush with acres of flower gardens and beautifully manicured lawn.

"Can't fucking believe it," Shayla says for the hundredth time since we arrived. "Lookit this place. You see Blade Saw wandering around in his old clothes at Redemption, all quiet and unassuming until he gets in the ring, and you would never think he runs the biggest distillery in the U.S."

On Sandy's advice, she has purchased an actual dress, a straight navy sheath with a thin white belt. On anyone else it might look plain, but Shayla is super fit and has an amazing figure. The belt highlights her tiny waist and the short, tight skirt showcases her long, lean legs. Low-rise pumps, straightened hair, and the faintest brush of makeup make her look almost girly. Too bad her discomfort is so evident. She constantly shifts from foot to foot and smoothes down the dress, although we haven't once sat down. I silently dare Fuzzy to thump her on the back, but he hasn't shown up yet.

"So you really did need a wingman?" I wave vaguely over her dress and she nods.

"Not good with the girly stuff. But I figure if I can't get Fuzzy's attention being me, I need to try something more drastic. You're so girly it makes my teeth ache, so I thought you'd be able to help me out. Plus, Sandy's easily distracted when there are guys around."

"Maybe he's just not the right guy for you." I take a long sip of champagne and let the bubbles dance across my tongue. At least one part of me is enjoying the party. "Maybe you need a guy who likes you for who you are."

Glass in hand, Shayla beckons to one of the waiters carrying a tray of what appear to be mini éclairs. Hurrah! As I reach for a little bundle of heaven, my thighs rub together in warning. I take only two. When the waiter raises an eyebrow, I take two more. Then I take six.

"I'm depressed," I tell him. "Nothing is better for depression than high-calorie, cream-filled, chocolate-covered snacks."

Another waiter refills my glass. I sip and sip and sip. I eat and eat and eat. My dress starts to feel tight and I wish I'd worn my sweats, always good in times of depressive episodes and extreme self-indulgence.

Cheers and laughter from the doorway draw our attention, along with calls of "Fuzz" and "Renegade." Shayla's smile fades and she pats her hair. My heart sinks and I pat my new belly.

"You said he was out of town."

Shayla shrugs. "I lied. Don't know what's going on with you two, but whatever it is won't be solved by staying away from each other. You can thank me later."

My heart hammers in my chest as the cheers get louder. I twist the gold rope belt on my white layered chiffon dress and wish I were actually an angel so I could fly away.

"Hey, Shilla." Fuzzy pushes his way through the crowd and then pulls up short in front of us. His gaze rakes over her and then he frowns. "How are you going to fight in that getup? Blade Saw is setting up a ring out back and everyone's gonna have a go at taking Rampage down."

"Well, damn." Shayla deposits her glass on a nearby table and holds her hand out to me. "I've got my fight clothes in a bag in your car. I'll go get changed."

"I'll come with you." I pull my keys from my bag. "I need to get going."

Fuzzy frowns. "You can't leave now. The party's just getting started. You gotta have at least one drink with me and then have a go at Rampage in the ring." He and Shayla share a glance and then he snatches the keys from my hand and tosses them to her. Before I even finish my "hey" of protest, she is pushing her way through the crowd.

"That wasn't nice."

His face softens. "Not nice, but necessary."

Catching his drift, I quickly change the topic. "So, did you notice anything different about her?"

He shrugs. "Yeah. She's wearing a dress. Totally impractical for fighting."

Clueless. Poor Shayla. Definitely not the guy for her. And maybe Jake isn't the guy for me.

Before I can make a quick escape after Shayla, the crowd parts and I catch sight of Jake, breathtakingly gorgeous in his snug, ripped jeans and hand-tooled leather belt. His thick, gold hair curls just above his collar, broad shoulders straining against his linen button-down shirt.

And there is Sia. A dark sprite with wide green eyes, high cheek-bones, and a full, generous mouth. She is gazing up at him and her heart is in her eyes.

And there is Jake's arm around her shoulders, holding her tight against his side.

And here is my heart, squeezing in my chest so hard I can barely breathe. He didn't waste any time.

Five minutes pass and then ten. Fighters join Fuzzy and me on the terrace. I make small talk but barely follow the conversations. Sweat trickles down my back. My head aches from too much champagne and too much tension and the effort of conversing when really all I want is to escape. Belatedly, I realize it doesn't matter when Shayla brings the keys. I am in no condition to drive home.

When Fuzzy is called away to help set up the makeshift fight ring, I slip away from the party and wander through the mansion in search of Shayla. As I turn down yet another marble hallway, someone calls my name.

Jake.

Hope dies a second death today.

Within seconds he is in front of me, sweat beading his brow, his chest heaving as if he was just running. His face is a curious mix of puzzled alarm and irritated anxiety, but still so painfully beautiful to me, my heart squeezes and longing grips me so hard I can barely breathe.

"Where are you going?" Cold. Abrupt. To the point.

"Home. I'm trying to find Shayla. She's got my keys."

Jake studies me for all of three seconds and then frowns. "You are in no condition to drive."

"I'm well aware of that. I'm going to call a cab, but I need my keys first; otherwise I won't be able to pick up my car tomorrow."

He scrapes his hand through his hair. "I'll take you home."

"I'd rather take a cab."

"Still can't accept help?" His jaw tightens and suddenly we're back to the question game that so devastated me two weeks ago.

"This is who I am," I say with a quiet voice that belies the turmoil inside. "I've been this way for as long as I can remember. I learned to be independent and self-reliant by necessity. I learned to trust only myself because inevitably people let me down. You want me to give that up. You want both of my feet over the line. You want me to give myself completely to you. I tried, and it terrified me. Clearly, that's just not something I can do."

"People change."

Shayla races past us wearing fight shorts and a spandex bra top. Her hair is scraped back into a ponytail and all traces of her makeup are gone. She tosses the keys to me and then yells "Rampage, you're going down," as she hits the patio, fist pumping in the air.

"Maybe on the outside they change," I say to Jake as I tuck the keys into my purse and pull out my phone. "But at heart, they are always the same. We just have to find the person who will love us for who we are."

"You think I let you down?" He looks at me aghast. "You think I gave up on you?"

"No. True to form, I did it all by myself."

―〰―

"'Manda! Where you been? You missed a lot of classes. Fuzzy is foaming at the mouth." Rampage drops his duffel bag and gives me a big hug as I step through the doors of Redemption a few days after Blade Saw's party. He is freshly showered and looking very unlike his fighter self in a pair of designer jeans and a fresh white shirt.

"Busy at work."

"Poor 'manda." He pats my head and the gentle gesture almost tips the bubbling cauldron of emotions I am so desperately trying to hide.

"Um…I just came to empty my locker and get you and the other guys involved in the Hellhole case to sign some documents. Are they around?" My heart pounds in fearful anticipation of encountering Jake. Although Shayla assured me he wasn't going to be in tonight, I still can't stop myself from shooting covert glances down the hallway and toward the locker room.

Rampage shakes his head. "Everyone's gone to the Protein Palace. I'm heading there now if you want to join us."

"Protein Palace?"

He throws an arm over my shoulders and leads me back to the door. "New establishment. Run by a coupla retired MMA fighters. Protein is their specialty—protein shakes, grilled meat, eggs, and every supplement you could want. Very popular, especially before big events since everyone is dieting and trying to make weight. They've decorated the place to look like a '50s-style diner. You're gonna love it."

I look up at a grinning Rampage. "Sounds…healthy."

An hour later, I am squeezed into a tiny red vinyl booth between Rampage and Blade Saw. Clearly the owners of the Protein Palace forgot to take into consideration the size of their prospective patrons. The booth would comfortably fit Rampage alone, but with the place absolutely heaving, it's three to a seat, or two, after I'm squished to death. But Rampage was right. The place looks like a '50s diner with its shiny, red vinyl stools and booths, glistening chrome, and sparkly tiles. The waitresses wear mini dresses and scoot around on roller skates. But the music is decidedly modern and consists solely of fight songs blasted at a high decibel level through tinny speakers.

"Oh. My. God." I grab Rampage's arm. "Is that Pierre Peterson?" I point out the number one ranked heavyweight UFC fighter in California. "And is that…Tommy the Terminator?"

Starstruck, I momentarily forget my mission as Homicide Hank, sitting across from us, points out some other famous fighters standing around the old-fashioned jukebox.

"Does the press know about this place?" My eyes widen when two more big name fighters walk past, brushing up against the wheatgrass planters in the glass brick wall beside us. The diner smells of grass, grass, and more grass. If I close my eyes, I can imagine I'm on a picnic, but with bad food.

"Yeah, but they usually show up closer to the big events when the hype starts to build. You can't get in without having a California State Athletic Commission card or as a guest."

A huge, muscle-bound giant bumps shoulders with an even bigger, more muscle-bound giant beside our table. They stop and growl at each other. Knuckles crack. Biceps flex. I huddle down in my seat.

"Isn't it dangerous?" I whisper, as the giants glare at each other. "I mean, all this testosterone in a small, enclosed space…"

"Big risk if they get in a fight," Homicide says. "They could lose their license or get seriously injured and have to drop out of an event. There are a lot of close calls, but in the end, the risk isn't worth it."

As if on cue, the giants step down and go on their way. I release the breath I didn't realize I was holding.

"So what are you having?" Blade Saw hands me a menu and I peruse the selections:

Tin of tuna, side of steamed mixed veg

Boiled egg whites, side of steamed mixed veg

Steamed chicken, side of steamed mixed veg

Whey protein shakes, all flavors, with your choice of: waxy vol, wheatgrass, omega-3 capsules, flaxseed oil capsules, L-glutamine, cod liver oil.

"Maybe just a plate of grass." I point to the wheatgrass display slash decoration on the wall beside us and repress the urge to moo. "And…I wonder if they have any steamed mixed veg." Why, oh why didn't I eat before I went to Redemption? I am craving a thick, juicy burger covered in cheese and a plate of greasy fries. Maybe even a milkshake. Nothing like food to beat the blues away.

Rampage, so not getting the joke, frowns. "It doesn't taste good on its own. Better to have it in a protein shake. It will help build up those scrawny arms." He circles my upper arm between his thumb and forefinger. Point taken. I order a chocolate whey shake with a helping of grass and a scoop of waxy vol simply because I have no idea what it is. I am daring tonight.

And sort of happy. The fighters don't seem to care that Jake and I have split up. They treat me the way they have always treated me. My hair is ruffled numerous times. My shoulder is slapped. I am poked and teased and included in every conversation.

Soon, I am sipping on my grass and waxy vol shake and trying not to gag as I celebrity spot with Homicide. Ten points for pros. Five points for amateurs. Minus five points for mistaken identity. I score ten points for spotting Don "the Man" Smith over by the protein shake bar chatting with Drake and Shayla. Drake catches my eye and gives me a wink. My lips twitch with a smile. My world might be off kilter, but Drake hasn't changed.

Fuzzy joins us and leans against the wall of wheatgrass. He growls at me for missing Get Fit or Die and tells me I'm going to suffer next week. When I dare to tell him I cleaned out my locker and I'm leaving the gym, I am lambasted with a ferocity that makes even Rampage cringe. By the time Fuzzy is finished, I have promised to attend every class offered at Redemption, train for the amateurs, volunteer at the registration desk, and hand over my firstborn child. Fuzzy gives me a warm smile and pats my head. Everyone at the table cheers, and I buy the next round of waxy vol shakes.

More Redemption fighters gather around our booth. A discussion about the benefits of the Paleo diet ensues. Basically it involves eating only meat. I tell them they should have no problem since they all behave like cavemen. Rampage throws up his arms to beat his chest and whacks me in the head with his elbow. Stunned, I slide down on the seat and stars flash in my eyes. A worried Fuzzy brings Drake over. Drake diagnoses a minor concussion and says I need a shot of Busta Bicep. He extracts me from my cozy nest of sweat and muscle, and escorts me to the protein bar.

"I don't have a concussion," I say as I sit on the wooden barstool.

Drake laughs. "True. But I wanted to get you away to apologize. I was out of line the other day at your office. It's just hard seeing you with Renegade when I know he didn't make you happy before." He commandeers a bag of ice from the "bartender," a pumped-up version of Hulk Hogan who can blend a mean wheatgrass shake while tossing scoops of waxy vol like there's no tomorrow.

Brushing my hand away, he holds the ice pack against my head and gives me shot of a noxious-looking green and brown slime-like liquid.

"Spinach, whey, and acai," he says. "Delicious and full of vitamins."

"I'd rather have a beer. Maybe two or three."

He holds the drink to my lips. "Try it. Visually it lacks appeal, but it has a good nose and a rich bouquet of flavor."

With a sigh, I take a sip and shudder. "It tastes as disgusting as it looks."

"Try again. It's better the second time around," he says softly. He holds the glass up again and I take a second sip. This time my nose wrinkles and I gag. "Definitely worse on the second taste."

I glance up. Drake is watching me with a searing intensity that reminds me of our intimate history. Fun and laughter and hot, kinky sex. Easy. Relaxed. No demands. No commitments. We never had one fight because in the end we both knew the score. So why am I not with Drake instead of lusting after a mercurial fighter who isn't satisfied with just my body, but who wants my heart and soul as well?

Drake strokes a finger over my cheek. "Miss you."

"Miss you too." And I do. I miss him for the fact that he was easy to be with. There were no emotional swings. No confusion. No fear. He was safe, familiar. Undemanding. He wanted nothing from me I couldn't give. And he made me feel good.

He lifts the ice pack and runs his hand over the injured part of my head, now pleasantly numb, then strokes his hand gently through my hair. The tender, caring gesture makes my heart squeeze, but not in a good way. I want Jake's hand in my hair. I want Jake's finger on my cheek. I want Jake holding the ice pack and making sure I'm okay.

"Five more minutes and then we'll break for fifteen and do it again. That way you won't be going to work with a bruise on that beautiful head."

As I study Drake, all blue eyes and fine, chiseled charm, his mouth tips up at the corners and he traces a pattern over my knuckles with his fingertip. "If you keep looking at me like that I might need to give you some personal medical attention."

My cheeks flush and I drag my eyes away. "This isn't such a good time. Jake and I just broke up."

"I heard."

A disturbance by the door distracts me from our conversation. God, what if it's Jake and he sees me talking to Drake? Or would he care? I try to look through the sea of fighters, half hoping it is Jake come to find me. Or to save me from temptation. But when the crowds part, I see only the door closing and a new arrival waving to his friends. A pang of longing washes through me. I just want to go home.

Ten minutes later, I say good-bye to the Redemption team, now thick around Rampage's table. Drake insists on walking me to my car. He throws a casual arm over my shoulders as he tells me about the time he brought squeamish Makayla to a private club where they only served meat rare. My laughter dies away when he grips my shoulder hard and tips his chin in the direction of my car.

"Renegade is here."

I suck in a sharp breath and then smile when I see Jake leaning against my vehicle. "Hi."

His eyes narrow. "I should have known you'd be with him. You never waste any time."

My smile fades. "He was just walking me to my car."

"He was doing more than that inside."

I look at him aghast. "You were there? Why didn't you come over?"

His eyes flick to me, but there is no warmth in his gaze. "Didn't want to interrupt your intimate moment."

"Jake…"

Ignoring me, he stalks over to Drake. "I warned you before. You don't seem to get the message."

Far from being afraid, Drake laughs and holds his ground. "Last I heard you weren't together. Which means there is no message I need to get."

My breath leaves me in a rush. What the hell is Drake doing? Does he have a death wish? He might as well slap Jake in the face and challenge him to pistols at dawn.

"What the fuck?"

"You don't get her," Drake says, his arm tightening around my shoulder. "She can't handle emotional intimacy. That's why she pushed you away. You wanted more than she could give. I didn't push. I accepted her for who she was. And in the end, it looks like I made the right decision. She's with me right now, not with you."

"Drake." I wrench myself away and glare. "What the hell are you talking about? We're friends. Nothing more."

Wham. Jake lands a punch to Drake's jaw before my brain has even registered he has moved. He strikes hard and he strikes fast, letting loose an uppercut that has Drake reeling backward into the cars. Desperate to stop the fight, I lunge forward, grab Jake around the waist, and try to pull him away.

"Stop. Stop. Don't hit him."

"My fight." Jake rips my hands off his waist and pushes me to the side, then throws himself at Drake. Oh God. This is worse than anything I could imagine.

But Drake is now as much into the fight as Jake, throwing Jake against a car and pummeling him with his fists. The car bounces and shakes and then Jake twists and frees himself, knocking Drake to the ground. Drake hits the cement hard and then Jake is on top of him, and they are rolling on the ground. My stomach clenches and bile rises in my throat. This isn't MMA fighting, with its rules and moves and procedures. This is street fighting, and if anyone reports Jake, it will be the end of his dream.

Fists fly. Blood spatters. Even at the cage fight, I have never seen Jake like this. He is violence with a capital V. Pure, uncontrolled, seething rage.

Terrified to leave them alone, I text Fuzzy. Almost instantly the door flies open and Fuzzy races across the parking lot with Obsidian, Homicide, Rampage, and Blade Saw following close on his heels.

"Fuck." He rakes his hand over his fuzzy head when he spots Jake and Drake now on their feet, bruised and bleeding but not slowing down in the least. "Rampage! Get her out of here."

"No." I shake my head. "I'm not leaving."

"'Manda. Please go," Rampage says quietly. "It will be easier for everyone."

"What do you mean easier?" I spit out. "I'm not part of this equation. Drake knows where he stands with me, and Jake...he said I don't belong with him."

Rampage frowns and scratches his head. "Doesn't matter what he says. What matters is what he does. And what he's doing right now is saying you're his."

His?

He ruffles my hair and gives me a half smile. "Looks like you're the last one to figure that out…again."

Chapter 21
RUN, TEAM, RUN

PICK UP THE PHONE. Put it down. Pick it up. Dial Jake's number. Put it down.

He doesn't need me to call and check up on him. I have Rampage's text telling me the two miscreants were bruised and battered but neither of them needed a hospital visit. Still, after Rampage's comment in the parking lot, I want to call.

I pick up the phone. Dial. Hit SEND.

My heart pounds. His phone rings. And rings. And rings. Then it goes to voice mail. I hang up. A fitting end to a horrible day.

Twenty minutes later, I'm changed and cozy in my bed. Head on the pillow. Covers tucked up to the chin. A soft breeze blows the curtains in the window, caressing my cheek like the touch of Jake's lips. I close my eyes and imagine his kiss at Redemption, the taste of his lips, the scent of his soap, the rough fabric of his gi. My breasts swell and my panties dampen. Need coils tight in my belly. I slide my hand down my body, between the valley of my breasts and over my abdomen. And suddenly it is Jake's hand resting on my mound, his fingers sliding over my aching clit, his voice in my ear.

The phone rings. Half asleep, my body soft and heavy in the darkness, caught up in my fantasy, I answer it, knowing in the back of my mind it has to be him.

"Amanda."

"Jake." My voice is a breathy whisper of need. "I just…called to see if you were okay."

His voice drops to a low, husky growl. "Gimme a sec. I'm just gonna close the office door."

A thump. A slam. Another thump. A squeak. The rustle of clothes. My heart drums against my ribs. One last chance to hang up the phone. One last chance.

"Why are you at the office so late?"

His deep voice is a delicious murmur in my ear. "I was just about to leave. We had an emergency board meeting about another offer for the company. This one with a deadline. Usually I just tell them where to go with the offers because that's what my dad wanted me to do, but tonight…" He sighs. "What I did in the parking lot was just stupid. Made me think about what you'd said about not treating every confrontation like I'm in the ring. I decided to listen to the board about the offer this time so I could discuss it with my father and maybe convince him selling is actually the best thing for everyone. "

My hand slides into my panties as he talks in his delicious, deep voice, telling me about the board and how relieved they were that he'd finally decided to hear them out—girly panties, sexy panties. Jake loved my panties. He would love these.

The ache in my center becomes an ache in my heart. Emptiness claws at my chest, a dark void needing to be filled. As familiar as the scars on my knees from the day I tried to teach myself to ride a bicycle. I have spent a lifetime trying to fill it, poured in caresses and kisses and fumbles in the dark, sweaty hands on my body, cocks and toys and kinks and perversions. But it hungers still.

I know only one way to make the ache go away. Throwing back the covers, I lie back and with a soft gasp, I sink two fingers into my wet, swollen center. Alone in the dark, I imagine Jake is here, touching me, caressing me, and then deep inside me, showing me he cares with actions I understand, not words that confuse me.

A soft moan escapes my lips. Immediately, I slam my lips shut, but I'm not fast enough.

"God, baby. I know that sound. Talk to me." Thick with desire, his voice alone almost sets me off.

Mortification at being caught gives way to longing and desire, hope, and the fact I have nothing left to lose. My back arches as my finger spreads my wetness up and around my sweet spot, close but never touching, drawing out the pleasure. I breathe into the phone, short, panting breaths of need. "Panties, pink, silk, ruffles on the edges. Soft. Wet."

"Take them off."

My body flames as if his words lit a spark inside me. I furrow my brow. Dampen the heat. My game. My rules. My pace.

"Not yet."

"Now."

I suck in a sharp breath, my body quivering at the unyielding tone in his voice. Maybe this is why I called.

Betraying fingers drop to my hips, easing inside the elastic. I tell myself I am taking off my panties because I want to do it. And I want it now.

"Okay."

"And the covers."

"They're already on the floor."

"You were hot for me already, weren't you, baby?" My heart squeezes in my chest. Was Rampage right after all?

Goose bumps scatter across my body as the cool air dances over my heated skin, bringing with it the lush, heady scent of honeysuckle from the garden. "Yes," I whisper.

"Were you touching yourself when I was talking to you?"

My body trembles in horrified anticipation. For all the crazy things I've done, my own private pleasure has always been that...private.

"Amanda..."

Breath catching at his warning tone, I whisper, "Yes."

He groans softly and then his chair squeaks. Feet thump. I hear the click of a lock and then the rustle of clothing. Flesh slides over flesh and his breathing changes from smooth and controlled to rough and uneven. "Touch yourself now."

Oh God. My blood rushes downward, filling tissues, flaring nerve endings, until my sex throbs and my core aches. I slick my fingers through my folds and then up and around my clit, then down to dip into my core, the sensation so exquisite I moan.

"I need..."

"I know what you need." His breath catches in his throat. "But you started without me and now you have to wait for me to catch up.

I promise it won't take long. Hands on your breasts, cup and squeeze. Tell me, how do they feel?"

My hands are already sliding over my body before he finishes his words. "Soft, hot, silky, swollen."

Another groan. I imagine him in his office in his suit, pants undone, and his cock hot and heavy in his hand. My sex clenches and I writhe on the bed.

"Now your nipples, pinch them, roll them between your thumb and forefinger until they peak, ready for me."

Already hard, the tingle in my nipples becomes a deep ache as I imagine Jake's mouth sucking and nipping until I am frenzied with lust. A whine escapes my lips, so soft I don't think he can hear.

But he does.

"Good girl. Are you wet for me?"

"So wet."

"Are you hot for me?"

"So hot."

"I'm so hard, baby, so damn hard for you. When you go off, I'm coming with you."

"Now?" I tremble with need.

"Now. Two fingers in your pussy. Tell me how you feel."

I exhale a relieved breath, and my fingers slide through the wetness between my thighs. I dip two fingers deep inside my throbbing center. "Wet, slick, tight."

A growl tears from his throat and his breathing becomes raw, ragged. "Thumb over your clit. Slick that wetness around. Pump your fingers." His voice cracks, breaks. "Tell me when."

My body tightens as I ease my thumb around my swollen clit. Need coils tighter and tighter until I am only one touch away.

"When," I whisper. I slide my thumb over my clit as my orgasm rips through me like a firestorm. Back arching, core pulsing, desire unwinding, I scream my release into the phone.

"Christ. Fuck. Oh God, baby." Jake chokes back his own release, as my orgasm washes through me, rippling down to my fingers and toes.

Sated, wrung out, limp, and desperately lonely, I press the phone to my ear. "Jake?"

Silence.

"Jake?" My voice wavers this time, and a sliver of fear works its way through my chest.

"Someone's at the door. I gotta go. Fuck. We shouldn't have...I don't want...you're just... Fuck."

A bruise of sadness forms in my chest, and I steel myself to pretend nonchalance. "Hey, it's not like only one of us was involved. It was...fun. After a stressful night, we both needed to blow off some steam."

More silence. And then he says, "I don't want you to think my feelings have changed."

My breath leaves me in a rush as he drives the sword home and it takes me a minute to get myself together. "Sure."

We say good-bye.

In the end, I did have something left to lose: the chance to tell him how I really feel. I love him.

I know that now. Too late.

"Ah, there's the quitter now, draggin' her sorry ass into the office ten minutes late." Ray rattles his newspaper as I walk past Penny's desk and over to the coffee pot.

"If you're going to insult me, Ray, do it to my face. I had a bad weekend. Normal people do. And when they have a bad weekend, sometimes they're late for work. Normal people don't get up at four am, run a marathon, eat a healthy breakfast, then work out for two hours, do all their work, and then swan into the office to laze around reading the paper."

His eyes flash with amusement. "Mornin', quitter."

I pour my coffee and then settle myself on the blue couch across from him, inhaling the rich, buttery aroma of Ray's favorite Columbian roast. "That's nice. Just what I need when the world is dumping on me and I'm facing Evil Reid in court this afternoon. I've been trying to dig up some dirt on Farnsworth with discovery requests for HR and personnel files, and they've blocked me at every turn, so today I'm taking my requests to a judge. How about giving me your unequivocal support? Rah, rah. Go, team, go."

"More like 'Run, team, run,'" he says evenly. "Isn't that what quitters do?"

The blue couch, now returned to its rightful place front and center in my corporate office, is damned uncomfortable. Hard as nails. How the hell does he sit on it for so long? I shift on my seat and then put my feet up on the coffee table to distribute my weight just as Penny shuffles into the office.

"Another one late." Ray huffs through his nose. "No wonder you're throwing in the towel. Can't run a viable business when no one gets here on time."

I glance over at Penny, but she's already sitting down and hidden behind her giant computer screen.

"How was your weekend, Penny?"

"Fine."

Curious at her unusually quiet tone of voice, I round her desk. "You don't sound like it was really fine. Last week when you said 'fine' it was in a completely different tone of voice."

She turns to look at me, her face hidden behind an enormous pair of sunglasses. "Really. It was fine."

A chill races through my veins and I drop my voice to a whisper. "Why the sunglasses?"

"Screen's too bright."

I gently tug the sunglasses off her face, knowing before they slide into my hand what I will see. My stomach clenches at the sight of her eye, bruised and swollen. Gently, I tug at the scarf around her neck only to gasp at the sight of finger-shaped bruises around her throat. My vision turns red. But because Ray is across the room, I keep my voice low. "Who did this to you?"

She shakes her head and snatches the sunglasses away. "Walked into a door."

Glancing over my shoulder at Ray, directly behind me, I whisper, "You know the community legal center is partnered with the battered women's shelter. I've seen bruises like this before. You've assisted on those files. So you know that excuse doesn't cut it with me. Was it Vetch?"

Penny's shoulders sag and her eyes glitter with tears. "He's different when he's not around the band. He's really sweet and kind, and we have a good laugh together. It's just when he's with the band, he has to keep up appearances and things get a bit crazy. But he's always sorry, and this time he was appalled when he saw my eye. He promised it would never happen again. He even bought me a…"

"Ray will go crazy." I interrupt her with a warning shake of my head. "You know he's got a protective streak a mile wide."

But I'm too late. The couch creaks and I spin around, perching on the side of Penny's desk to keep her completely hidden from view.

"Why you sittin' there staring at me?" he says from behind his paper as if he has X-ray vision.

"Nothing better to do."

He lowers his paper and glares. "Don't give me that lame-ass excuse. Never once saw you with nothing to do. What are you hiding?"

Penny gives a squeak of fear and I slide off the desk. "Nothing. I just need Penny in my office for a minute." I cover for her as she slips out of her chair and heads to my office.

"Stop right there, Penelope Ann McDonald," Ray barks.

But Penny doesn't stop. She runs into my office and slams the door.

Ray's eyes slide over to me. "What's going on? A man can't get any peace at your office. A man likes peace first thing in the morning. Man like me, more."

"It's a woman issue."

Ray snorts a laugh. "Amanda, you can't lie for fuck."

"Watch your language," I snap. "This is a law firm, not…"

He cuts me off. "Was a law firm."

My lips tighten. "It's not closed yet. I have to finish the Redemption case, make my court appearance today, and deal with the pro bono files. I can't just wave a magic wand and shut everything down. I also have all the legalities to deal with."

"Humph." His eyes flick to my office door and back to me, and then his voice softens. "He hurt her, didn't he?"

I open my mouth to cover for her, but the planned lie doesn't come out. Instead, a wave of anger washes over me. Poor Penny. I may have spent a lifetime looking for love, but I never once thought I was unworthy of it.

Ray pushes himself off the couch and grabs his leather jacket from the coat stand. "Got someplace I need to be. Something I need to do."

"Ray…" I follow him out the door. "Can I come with you?"

His eyebrows lift. "Thought you weren't a fighter."

"Maybe I was wrong."

A smile spreads across his face. "Good to hear, but I can't let you—"

"There's more than one way to fight. You do what you do outside, and I'll do what I do inside. I need to go to the courthouse and then to the police station and then the community law center. Talk to a few people. Collect a few documents. Then I'll sit down with Penny and see if she wants to go ahead with civil or criminal prosecution."

Ray scratches his head. "Guess I should leave him alive then."

"Yeah, Ray. I guess you should."

"Westwood. Good to see you. Ready for a beating? I thought for sure after you got all those applications you would run away with your tail between your legs."

Evil Reid smirks beside the courtroom door, a vision of overly tanned, vicious elegance in an Armani suit, crisp white shirt, silver cuffs, and red silk tie.

"You thought wrong. I'm a fighter, and I'm fighting this all the way."

"Well, this is one fight you're going to lose." He folds his arms over his chest. "Farnsworth golfs with Judge Vickers every Friday. He knows how the judge thinks, and he says there's no way the judge is going to make us respond to your interrogatories or produce all the documents you requested."

I check my watch and motion toward the door. Regardless of who golfs with whom, neither of us can afford to be late. Evil Reid pulls open the door to the courtroom and holds it, gesturing for me to precede him.

"There's no way he *can't* refuse my request." I glance over my shoulder at Evil Reid and sigh loudly when his gaze does not lift from my ass as he follows me down the aisle. "You just slapped the same boilerplate objection on every request I've made. Everything can't be covered by privilege. And I know you did it to buy time because there are documents Farnsworth doesn't want me to see. I've been there, Reid. I've played the game. But this time I'm on the other side."

Evil Reid's lips curl into a snarl. "You're forgetting I have something you want. I can make this all go away. I can get Farnsworth to settle. But you know the price."

"What price?" I spin around to face him, and for the first time, I am unnerved by his cold, dark gaze and the determined set to his jaw.

He steps into my personal space, his face only inches from mine. "I get what I should have gotten the first day we met. I get what you promised with every brush of your hand on my arm, every surreptitious touch, every giggle and smile and tease. I get what you gave everyone else but me."

Every instinct screams for me to retreat, but I stand my ground. "I never promised you anything, Reid. I never led you on, and if you think I did, or if I said or did anything to make you think I saw you as anything other than a professional colleague, then I apologize."

We take our seats and the judge arrives. After listening to our arguments, he peppers Reid with questions about the documents I've requested and Farnsworth's reasons for refusing to produce them. After an interminable silence, the judge says he will have a decision for us next week. Court dismissed.

Reid immediately whips out his phone, no doubt to call Farnsworth and report a possible defeat. Apparently, Farnsworth didn't know the judge's mind quite so well, or maybe it was the other way around and the judge knew him. Either way, Farnsworth will be worried. If those files contain complaints of harassment from staff and associates, as I think they do, he'll definitely not want them to fall into my hands.

Humming a happy tune, I pack up my stuff and join Ray at the elevator. But before I can tell him the reason for my good mood, Evil Reid catches up to us, his hair slightly mussed and his tie askew, as if he'd been running. "I need to talk to you." He slicks his hand over his hair, smoothing everything into place. "I just got off the phone with Farnsworth. Although he has nothing to hide, and he is not at all concerned about the outcome of the hearing today, he wants to make an offer to make this lawsuit go away."

My breath catches in my throat, and for a moment I can't believe my ears. Farnsworth never settles. *Never*. He litigates everything to the death. Why break the tradition for me?

"He's afraid of what's in those files, isn't he?" I try and fail to repress a smile. "Farnsworth & Tillman would certainly get some bad press if the managing partner was found to have engaged in sexual harassment and blackmail. And it would be especially bad if I found some witnesses who would testify against him."

Reid snorts his derision. "He's an upstanding member of the legal community. You won't find anyone willing to drag his name through the mud. Guaranteed."

His conviction and the emphasis he puts on the word *guaranteed* niggle at my brain. Maybe Farnsworth or Reid were somehow involved with the break-in at my office. A quick glance at an unusually silent Ray confirms my suspicions. He's thinking the same thing, too.

"What's the offer?"

Evil Reid shifts from one foot to the other and then sighs. "It's not that simple. There's a catch."

"Of course there's a catch. We're talking about Farnsworth. What is it?"

"Timing. He's flying to Kuala Lumpur later tonight and he wants it wrapped up by then. Quick and dirty."

So tempting. Settle with Farnsworth. Make the stress go away. Vindication. Revenge. "I might be interested if I saw the terms."

Evil Reid glances over his shoulder and then turns his gaze to me. "His secretary is typing something up now and will fax it to your office. I can meet you there and we can go over it and, if you're happy, we can draft up a settlement agreement I can take to Farnsworth at the airport."

Anticipation ratchets through me, but I hold it at bay. Something about this doesn't feel right. It can't be this easy. If Farnsworth really wanted to keep the documents out of my hands, he would find a way to destroy them. Nothing stops the Barracuda. Nothing gets in his way. Especially not a former junior associate with no money and only one trick up her sleeve.

Still, it can't hurt to take a little peek. "Think you can handle slumming it in Hippie Land?"

Reid's eyes darken, taking on an almost feral gleam. "Actually, I'm looking forward to it."

Chapter 22
THIS IS NOT ME

"I DON'T LIKE IT." Ray paces across the reception room. "Cravath can't be trusted. Not only that, my contact at the police department thinks they have a match on the prints from the break-in. He's pretty sure it's Farnsworth's PI, Eugene. He's got a criminal record, so his prints came up in the database search. I would stay, but I've got an urgent meeting after I drop Penny off."

"I'll be fine." I give his shoulder a reassuring pat. "I'll work at Penny's computer so we're out in the open. And I'm a fighter. If he tries anything funny, I'll twist him up in a quick triangle."

"I'm sorry I can't stay either," Penny says. "My mum jumped on the first plane from London when I told her what happened, and I'm picking her up at the airport this evening."

Almost giddy at the thought of settling the case, I give them a reassuring smile. "You guys go and do what you have to do, and hopefully tomorrow we'll be celebrating the end of Farnsworth and the start of a whole new law firm."

Ray gripes for another ten seconds and then shouts something unintelligible at me before following Penny down the hallway. I pull out my files and then fire up Penny's computer. Although I'm not worried about being alone with Evil Reid, I wouldn't want him in my office. Too personal and too far from the front door, as I learned the other night.

Reid arrives five minutes later with his briefcase in his hand and a grimace on his face. "Ready to do business?"

"I haven't received anything from Farnsworth. Do you have the terms of the offer?" My hands hover over the keyboard, shaking slightly with nervous anticipation.

"One hundred grand."

My shoulders slump. "That's it? What about an apology? Or stepping down from his position? It's not about the money. It's about the principle. Sexual harassment. Blackmail. He has to be stopped. And I know he's been spreading rumors. That has to be addressed as well. My reputation is worth something to me."

Reid reaches into his briefcase and pulls out the blue file. "According to this, you have quite the reputation, but not the kind that can be saved."

My blood chills and the hair on the back of my neck stands on end. "Where did you get that?"

"I'm on the case. I have access to all the documents." He perches on the desk and drums his fingers over the file.

"What's this all about, Reid?" I push my chair away from the desk, away from him. "Is there a settlement offer, or are you here to blackmail me just like he did? Because if you are, the answer is still no. I don't do blackmail. I also have nothing to lose. I have no job. No employer. No reputation. Soon I will have no house. And my friends wouldn't give a damn."

"But your parents would," he says softly. "Farnsworth told me about them. And what about your fighter boyfriend? What would he think if he found out what kind of person you really are? I don't know any man who would be too happy to know his girlfriend was intimately familiar with most of the eligible males in the Bay Area. Makes her hard to trust, don't you think? The kind of girl who would be with him one minute and someone else the next? The kind of girl who can't commit." He shoves the file across the desk toward me, and I push myself to my feet and back up to the wall.

"I'm not ashamed of anything in that file, Reid. In fact, all the time I spent looking for love made me realize what love really is. Plus, Jake and I broke up. So if that's why you're here, then it's time for you to leave. But if there really is an offer, then it's time for us to work."

Reid closes the distance between us and leans his forearm against the wall beside my head. "There's an offer from me. One time. You and me. Down and dirty. Right here. On the chair. On the desk. On the fucking floor. I don't care. But I want you out of my system and that's what it's going to take to do it."

My hands clench into fists, my nails biting into my palms. "Are you crazy? You came here on false pretenses. You're trying to blackmail me. You and Farnsworth have had someone following me, and I think your PI is responsible for the break-in at my office. In fact, I'm pretty damn sure he is. Not the kind of behavior one engages in if they want to get a woman into bed."

His eyes darken to black, narrowing at the corners. "Yeah, I arranged to have you followed. But this case is all about reputation, so you should have seen that coming. And since you broke up with your boyfriend, what's the big deal? He may not want you, but I do, and it's driving me fucking crazy."

My hands find my hips and I clench my fists to contain my fury. "You want to fuck me in my office? Is that what I'm hearing?"

Evil Reid sighs. "You don't want to do it here, we can go someplace else. But at the very least give me a kiss. We've known each other for almost three years. It's not like we're strangers. Just a kiss and, as a show of good faith, I'll give you the file."

We don't belong together.

We shouldn't have.

I don't want you to think my feelings have changed.

Jake's words echo in my mind. Evil Reid is right about one thing. Jake doesn't want me. Evil Reid does, and he wants to show me in a way I understand. And…oh God…to get rid of that file…

"Just a kiss and that's the end of it. You give me the file. You leave and you never harass me again."

His eyes shine triumphant, but his face softens. "There's been a spark between us since the day we met, but you never gave it a chance." He brushes my hair behind my ear with a gentleness I would never have expected from him. "We have that chance now."

Evil Reid bends down and brushes his lips over mine, engulfing me in the scent of nicotine and cloying cologne. And then I'm kissing him. I'm kissing Evil Reid, trying to soothe the ache in my heart with the knowledge someone wants me, even if only for a heartbeat.

This is not me.

Soft, wet, milky kiss. I try to pull away and Evil Reid's arm snakes around my waist, holding me tight as his thick, rubbery tongue tries to push its way through the barrier of my teeth. When he paws at my breast, I slap his hand away. Evil Reid is going down.

"Get off me." I shove Evil Reid away with one of Razzor's signature moves. He stumbles back, catching himself on the corner of the desk. Only then do I see Jake and Ray in the doorway.

For a long moment nobody moves. Then Jake turns and walks away.

My heart plunges to the floor. I shove past Evil Reid and grab the file off the desk. Then I fly past Ray and out the door.

"Jake." I am running, running, down the steps and along the sidewalk, so fast the world is a blur except for the tall, blond fighter walking away from me. "Wait. Please." Breathless, panting, I catch him just as he reaches his Jeep. I hold out the file.

"You want the real me?" My voice trembles. "The part I was holding back? The reason I always had one foot out the door? Why I could never give myself completely to you? Here it is. This is part of who I am. I pushed you away not just because I was afraid to get close, but also because I couldn't accept who I was and I was afraid you wouldn't either."

Jake's eyes flick to the file and back to me, but he makes no move to take it.

Tears prickle the backs of my eyes. "Fine. If you won't look at it, I'll tell you what it says and what it would say if it started from the beginning. It would say Amanda slept around since Cory Rissoli touched her behind the garden shed when she was fourteen, and for fifteen minutes she actually felt someone cared. And when Peter Long took her virginity when she was sixteen, she felt loved and wanted in a way she never had before. And she's been chasing that feeling ever since."

I pause for a breath and still Jake doesn't move. So I keep talking about looking for love with men who wanted anything but, and I can only hope I will say something that will change his mind about walking away.

"But nothing ever lasted because sex isn't love and love doesn't happen if you don't let people in. And it's hard to let people in when your whole life the people you love have let you down. You stop believing you are worth being loved or even that you have love to give."

"You were wrong," he says quietly.

For a long moment we stare at each other. Finally, I hold out the file. "Take it."

Jake shakes his head and pulls open the door to his Jeep. "I don't care what's in the file. What kills me is that you ever thought I would."

Strung out and emotionally drained, I sit in my office and stare at my computer for hours, watching AW AW AW bounce across my screen. I bill no time, do no work, and shuffle no papers. Somewhere in the back of my mind, my body registers hunger. But of course, my microwave is broken and I don't know how to fix it. When I finally pack up my stuff and leave my desk, I am totally unprepared to find Ray stretched out on the reception couch in the dark. "Ray. It's two a.m. Why are you still here?"

"Waiting for you."

My chest tightens. God, what does he think of me? All the time I spent slagging off Evil Reid only to be caught in a lip-lock with him. "What you saw…it was a mistake to start with and then things got out of hand."

"Don't need an explanation. I know Cravath and I know you." He swings his legs down and pats the seat beside him. With a sigh, I join him, thankful for the dark shadows that hide my tear-stained face.

"You don't know me as well as you think."

He snorts a laugh. "I know you're judging yourself and finding yourself lacking. I know you're putting a value judgment on something that was out of your control. And I know you're hurting because Jake took off."

"What was he doing here…with you?"

He cuts me off with a grimace. "Stuff I know about Cravath meant I couldn't in good conscience leave you alone with him. I dropped Penny off, made a few calls, and told the people I was supposed to meet I had an emergency and to fucking screw themselves if they didn't change the date. Jake was just getting out of his vehicle when I arrived. Said he'd come here to talk to you."

I don't know what to say, so I stay quiet. Instead, I feign interest in the patterns on the couch, gray in the moonlight filtering through the window.

"I know what Cravath was doing here," he says quietly. "I know he came to blackmail you with the file. And I know what's in that file."

My eyes snap to his. "How could you know?"

A pained expression crosses his face and he sucks in his lips and swallows hard before answering. "Because I put it together. Farnsworth hired me to watch you."

"Oh God." My stomach clenches so tight I can't breathe. I scoot along the couch, away from Ray and look at him aghast.

"*You* followed me? *You* wrote those reports?" My voice rises with my distress and I push myself off the couch and cross the room, hugging myself tight. "How could you, Ray? I thought we were friends. I hired you for all my work because I thought you were…honorable and trustworthy and…the best." Realization hits me hard. "That's why he hired you, isn't it? Because you're the best."

Ray gives me a curt nod. "I didn't want the case. Damned worst case I've ever had. I've done things in my life that would make normal men weep. Things I'll never be able to tell a single soul. But I could always get out of bed in the morning and look at myself in the mirror because I was hunting criminals—not just criminals, but the worst dregs of humanity. And I knew my actions would make a difference. I served my country and I was proud to do it. But this…" His voice breaks and he shakes head.

A sob rips out of my throat. Losing Jake was unbearable, but now I'm losing Ray too.

"You're a good person, Amanda," he says quietly. "I watched you helping your friend through her troubles with that fighter, Torment. I followed you to the battered women's shelter and the community legal aid center and saw how much you gave of yourself to help people. I was there when you showed up at all your parents' award ceremonies to support them even when they never once were there for you."

"Stop, Ray." I hold up my hands. "I don't want to hear it. I know who I am, what you must think of me. Please…just leave."

"I'm not leaving you like this. You're gonna hear what I have to say and then I'll go."

Emotionally numb, I stare up at the ceiling and shrug. I have nothing left. No fight. No will. Nothing. I can't feel any worse than I do now.

"The firm was mandated to investigate potential partners," he continues. "You know that. But Farnsworth took the investigations further than the mandate. And this I can tell you because the work I did for him was outside the contract I had with the firm. He wanted the dirt. He wanted leverage. He has a file on every partner that came after him. It's how he always gets his way. He's destroyed a lot of people. Good people. Like you. But always with a secret to hide."

Ray is silent for a moment and then leans forward. "That's why I took your case. I knew the day we met that you were a good person. Instinct. Trust it. Kept me alive countless times. It was on the tip of my tongue to turn it down when I realized it would be better for me to control that investigation than anyone else. So I accepted it even though it made my fucking skin crawl."

"Ray…please."

He scrubs his hand over his face. "Yeah, you dated a lot of guys, sweetheart. But I've dated a lot of girls—a lot. And yeah, there's a double standard… But regardless of whether you slept with them or not, it doesn't make you a bad person. Who you are is in here." He taps his chest lightly.

I shake my head and open my mouth to cut him off, but the usually taciturn Ray is on a roll, and he just keeps talking.

"You have a good heart. You're a kind, giving, thoughtful, and generous person. Look how you're helping the guys from Redemption. And Penny. And all your pro bono clients. I mean, fuck, you had to sell your house to stay afloat and still you wrote a check to pay me." He opens my clenched fist and puts a pile of torn paper in it. "Which, by the way, I don't accept."

"But…"

"Do. Not. Accept."

I bite my lip against the emotion welling up in my chest.

"The day you left Farnsworth & Tillman was the day I canceled my contract. Because I know what kind of person you are. The best kind. The kind that will swap out a brand-new couch for a Victorian monstrosity to make someone happy. Jake knows that or he wouldn't be beating people up or driving out here to fix things between you. Someone cares about you that much, the file won't change the way he feels. But he's the kind of guy who needs a message hammered home."

"The couch isn't that bad."

"It looks like shit, sweetheart, but it's the most comfortable couch I ever sat on." He sighs and his face softens. "For what it's worth, I'm sorry. But better me than anyone else. There is a lot in that file, but there is also a lot missing. Most times, I reported I couldn't get a good camera angle to assess what went on behind closed doors, or I reported that I lost sight of you during surveillance. Sometimes, one entry was as good as three."

Swallowing past the lump in my throat, I say, "Thank you for that."

Ray gives me a curt nod and pulls his jacket off the coat rack. "Seeing as you're heading home, I'll be going now."

I wait until he's through the doorway before I call out, "Ray?"

He looks back over his shoulder.

"See you tomorrow."

Chapter 23

EVERYONE CHEERS

THE NEXT DAY IS a flurry of activity. Couriers arrive with packages of documents courtesy of an irate Farnsworth. The settlement offer was genuine. Reid told him I turned it down. Partly true. I would never have accepted his first offer. But I suspect he didn't tell Farnsworth we didn't conduct any further negotiations.

Farnsworth doesn't like to be turned down. If I thought he was playing hardball before, it is nothing compared to the sea of paperwork on my desk. He must have had a dozen associates working all night long, and there is just no possible way I can deal with everything he is throwing at me before the deadlines. Not without help.

Penny organizes, catalogs, and diarizes like there is no tomorrow. But by the end of the day, even she knows we are underwater.

"We can't do it." She sighs and bangs her forehead gently on her desk. "We would need to hire at least six contract lawyers."

"That's the power of a big firm. That's why people pay the big money. They can make the irritating cases go away simply by overwhelming the opposition with paper."

When the sixth courier arrives, I send Penny home. Then I draft up the settlement agreement for the amount Farnsworth offered and type Farnsworth & Westwood at the bottom. I stare at it for the longest time. All it would take is a signature, and I can move on with my life. No more Farnsworth and his sea of paper. No more fruitless attempts to interview witnesses who have been blackmailed to keep quiet. Farnsworth will continue his reign of terror and I will be able to start again. But this time without Jake.

What would he do in my situation?

What do fighters do? They fight. Jake would never give up, no matter how dire the circumstances. He would find a way to break the hold, even if he was locked in submission.

A soft knock on the door startles me. I glance up and there, silhouetted in the setting sun, is my mom.

She is impeccably dressed, as usual, in beige pants, a soft pink blouse, and a long cream trench coat. Her shoes and handbag would put Sandy to shame. Her neat bob swings gently around her face as she walks into my office.

As usual, she doesn't waste time with pleasantries. "Someone couriered this to your father and I at work." She slides a disk across my desk and my heart sinks. I don't need to take it from her to know what it is. Evil Reid made good on his threat. And, of course, he didn't just have a hard copy of his file.

"I'm sorry."

"No, I'm sorry." She takes a seat across from my desk and drums her fingers on the armrest. "If we had given you the love and attention you needed as a child, you wouldn't have had to look for it elsewhere."

My heart squeezes in my chest. "You can't take the blame for my choices."

"You made those choices because you had to." She sucks in her lips and sighs. "You were so competent, even as a child. So independent. You never asked for our help, never seemed to need us. You made it too easy to let you deal with things on your own. But I often wondered if it was the chicken or the egg. If you had been a different person, would we have treated you the same?"

"I don't know," I say honestly. "I don't remember being any other way."

We sit in silence for a long moment, and then Mom leaves her seat and wanders around the office, trailing her fingers over the polished bookshelves and the ornate moldings around the windows.

"Believe it or not, we are very proud of you. Starting up your own firm, obtaining the financing, finding clients. I've been following your case against Farnsworth through the court documents. I never believed his defense. Although I wasn't there for you, I know my daughter. And

I know Farnsworth. I believed you at the hospital when you said he propositioned you."

She believes me. Afraid of embarrassing myself with the kind of emotional outburst frowned upon in my family, I just nod.

"Your lawsuit was very brave, but also naïve," Mom continues. "As a junior associate, you're only starting to learn the ropes. But you had to know he would use every resource at his disposal to make you drop the case."

"I didn't think it would get this bad." I point to the pile of papers on my desk. "He just sent those today. And he always seems to be one step ahead of me."

Sympathy fills her eyes. "That's just the start."

I look down at the settlement offer on my desk and then I tear it in half. "Mom…" I draw in a ragged breath. "I need help."

"I know," she says softly. "That's why I came."

The next week passes in a blur. Mom lends me the money to cover the cost of hiring contract lawyers to help with the paperwork until the sale of my grandmother's house goes through. She finds the time to stop by every day to help me with strategy and tactics. Ray charms the pants off her in under five minutes, and she never once asks him to take his feet off the coffee table, nor does she ask why he lives on our client couch. She brings him coffee, buys his paper for him, and smiles every time he calls her *ma'am*. She does suggest the blue corporate couches would look better than Ray's comfy Victorian, but I tell her that couch is special and even if Ray finds a new place to hang his hat, I'm keeping it.

But even with Mom's help, Farnsworth predicts my every move. Except for the two witnesses who gave evidence early in the case, everyone else is too scared to talk. Ray drags his surveillance friend in to check things out, and they discover our computers have been hacked. Not only that, they trace the hack to Farnsworth & Tillman.

Ray explodes and stomps around the office cursing and muttering to himself about how only Farnsworth and Reid would have the nerve to pull this off. Mom tells him to watch his language. He tells her he's been in places so bad the words he's saying would be considered a lullaby. Mom says that may be true, but she's over twenty years older than him and she expects a certain propriety in her presence. She suggests he curse outside. He says, "Yes, ma'am," and storms out the door.

As soon as he steps outside, Mom starts laughing. She laughs until her eyes water. I've never seen my mother laugh like that before. She says although she still doesn't fully approve of my choice of friends, Ray's not too bad. My eyes water too.

***

With the Farnsworth file under semicontrol, Ray plans a surveillance mission, trailing Bob and Clive around the city. He got a tip that they frequent a boxing gym, and he's pretty sure they'll have to take off their casts to fight. Although Ray wants to go alone, I insist on tagging along. After reading his reports for so many years, I want a taste of the action. The new Amanda isn't tied to her office. Sometimes she likes a little bit of fun, and what is more fun than going on a stakeout with Ray?

We trail Bob and Clive around the city in Ray's Jeep until they pull up in front of an all-night boxing gym. Ray finds a side door, and we slip inside and hide behind a wall of lockers. A pang of nostalgia fills me when I see the makeshift boxing ring in the center. I miss Redemption. But more than that, I miss Jake with an ache that reaches into my soul.

Why the hell have I been staying away from two of the most important things in my life? If I want to embrace the Amanda who asks for help, associates with unsavory characters, runs a law firm with mostly pro bono files, and goes on stakeouts in the middle of the night, I need to embrace that part of myself too. I can't give up. I've dishonored myself by staying away. And that has to change.

A cough from Ray wakes me up, and I turn my attention back to the ring. A middle-aged redhead with curves to die for throws her arms around Bob and greets him with a big smooch. Ray snorts under his breath, and I jab my elbow in his ribs to keep him quiet.

"Silence. Name of the game," I whisper.

I am treated with the scowl to end all scowls. I stifle a laugh.

Bob climbs into the ring and peels off his shirt. Then he peels off his casts and tosses them to the floor. Over in the far corner, Clive does the same. My heart leaps in my throat and I film the action on my phone while Ray takes pictures of them punching and grappling, unbroken arms flying in the air. The redhead slips into Bob's corner and cheers him on.

And suddenly, I know how to get Jake back. I will be in his corner. Every day. Every way. I will be in his corner.

In my excitement, I drop my phone. When I step into the hallway to pick it up, Bob turns in my direction. His eyes widen and he shouts for Clive. Ray grabs my hand and yanks me up the stairs.

"Discretion. Name of the game."

Bob and Clive chase us with a speed and agility belied by their supposedly broken arms. Ray and I race for the door and hit the pavement running. We throw ourselves into the vehicle and Ray peels away from the curb, burning rubber like he's been doing it all his life.

"My God." My heart pounds in my chest. "Look what I've missed out on all those years at Farnsworth and Tillman. This sure beats an afternoon of drafting documents."

"Fuck, yeah." Ray squeezes my shoulder, the extent of his excitement.

The next day, Ray prepares a report setting out the details of the castless fight. Penny and I put together a photo slideshow and edit my video clip. We spend more time laughing than working. I send a copy of Ray's report to Simmons & Clarkson, the attorneys hired by Bob and Clive. Frank Simmons calls ten minutes later to set up a settlement meeting.

High fives all around.

—⁓—

A few days later, I pack all my documents into my bag and drive out to the settlement meeting at Simmons & Clarkson. I have arranged through Shayla for the Redemption fighters to meet me there. Jake's attorney has given me authority to represent him and Jake at the meeting.

Anxiety ratchets through me as I drive. I haven't seen anyone from Redemption since Jake saw me with Evil Reid at my office. I imagine he told them what happened, and I imagine their derisory faces when we meet. By the time I get to the office, I am so nauseous I can't get out of the car. With my forehead resting on the steering wheel, I struggle to calm myself with slow, deep breaths. What will I say to everyone? How should I act?

A knock on the window startles me and my head jerks up. Rampage. He's smiling a goofy Rampage smile. "'Manda!'" he shouts. Then he waves a giant arm in the air. "Guys, 'manda's here!" He opens the car door and pulls me out and into a huge bear hug. I hug him back. Suddenly I am swarmed by fighters. My hair is ruffled. I am squeezed. My back is thumped. Someone cops a feel of my ass. Tears leak from my eyes. They don't hate me. I'm still part of the family. Everything's going to be okay.

After Bob and Clive arrive, we all squeeze into Frank Simmons's boardroom. I set up the projection equipment, and he pulls down the screen. Rampage asks for popcorn. I tell him he isn't allowed any carbs until after the big fight event coming up, but if he's good, he can have an extra scoop of waxy vol in his protein shake. He thinks I'm being serious and thanks me.

The movie starts. Everyone claps and cheers when Bob and Clive make an appearance in the ring. Someone whistles when Bob's girlfriend gives him a kiss, and Bob growls.

"Wait for it," I whisper. "Wait for it…"

Then my favorite movie scene ever. Bob and Clive strip off the fake casts in preparation for the fight. The room erupts into chaos. I have to pause the video so everyone can high-five everyone else. When I turn the video back on, the now cheerful audience jeers and catcalls at the poor fight techniques and the shoddy state of the ring. The video ends with a montage of photos of Bob and Clive, castless and free, which Penny and I have set to "So Long and Good-bye" by Deception. Blade Saw wipes a tear from his eye and tells me it was a beautiful film. Obsidian is disappointed I didn't ask him to narrate.

Bob and Clive make a hasty exit with their attorney. A few minutes later, the attorney returns with an offer to withdraw the lawsuit and pay our costs. There is a unanimous acceptance of the offer, a frenzy of feet pounding down the stairs, and then a riot in the street as the fighters go crazy. I am hoisted in the air and tossed around like a grapple dummy. Rampage squeezes me so hard, my ribs crack.

"'Manda, 'manda, 'manda." He gets everyone to chant. Fuzzy suggests we keep it down or someone might call the police. Obsidian yells "Fuzzy," and Homicide Hank collapses in hysterics.

We retire to the Protein Palace for a celebration. I order a big plate of grass with a side of steamed veg. I drink shot after shot of slime and waxy vol. It doesn't taste so bad.

The only thing missing from this perfect moment is Jake.

The next night, I return to Redemption.

"'Manda." Rampage ruffles my hair. "We missed you. Good to see you back. I told Fuzzy you were coming. He was really pleased. He rubbed his hands together and smiled like this." He gives me the most evil, terrifying smile I have ever seen.

With a gasp of horror, I step back toward the door. But I am too late to run.

"WESTWOOD," Fuzzy bellows from the gym. "I can see you. Don't you even *think* of running away. You get your sorry ass in here now. That's an order."

"Sir. Yes, sir."

"Don't worry, 'manda." Rampage pats me on the back. "We're family here. We won't let him hurt you." He pauses and grins. "Much."

After I change, I sneak into the back of Get Fit or Die and pray Fuzzy doesn't notice me until well after class.

"Westwood. Front and center."

Stomach clenched, I jog up to the front of the class. Fuzzy throws a deceptively friendly arm around my shoulders. "Westwood here missed almost a month of classes. What do we think of that?"

"Sir. Unacceptable, sir," the sycophantic class yells, no doubt grateful to be spared Fuzzy's evil attentions.

"Who thinks she should get down on the mat and give us fifty to prove she's still fit enough to attend this class?"

Everyone cheers. Even me. Because *ha ha* Fuzzy, I might not have been coming to Redemption, but every night I did my push-ups.

I position myself on the mat, take a deep breath, and go for it. By the time I hit thirty-five, my muscles are feeling the burn. At forty, I'm starting to tremble. Forty-five and sweat drips off my forehead. But I force myself to keep going. The class cheers me on. Unbelievably, Fuzzy squats down beside me and, in a low voice, says I'm doing great and he's proud of me.

When I get to forty-nine, I catch a glimpse of Jake in the crowd— or is it Jake? Blond hair. White gi. Black belt. I blink to clear my vision, but when I look up again, he's gone. My body seizes, and my arms shake. But I'm a fighter, just like him. So I pretend it is Jake. And he's cheering me on. I go down, and then inch by inch, I force myself up.

Success! I jump up and raise my arms in a victory salute.

The crowd cheers. Fuzzy thumps me on the back. I don't see Jake in the crowd, but he is with me just the same.

The rest of the class is as miserable as I could have ever imagined. Fuzzy rides my ass something fierce. He is constantly breathing down my neck, cursing my ineptness, threatening to make me take the class again. I smile at every curse. Laugh at every insult. And the more pleasant I am, the meaner he gets. Then he pulls out all the stops. Circuits, weights, sprints, and an endless number of starfish jumps. By the end of the class, I never want to see the ocean again.

But the class was not the only reason I came to Redemption tonight. And when Shayla waves me over to the practice ring, my stomach ties itself in a knot.

By the time I reach the ring, Razzor is already in his corner, air boxing his immense shadow. With a force of will I never realized I had, I stand outside the opposite corner. Jake's corner. And there he is, his gi draped over his muscular body, hair damp and curling at his temples. So handsome. Breathtaking. I drink him in with a never-ending thirst.

His eyes flicker over me, but he doesn't acknowledge my presence. Instead, he climbs into the ring and prepares for his fight.

I stay in his corner until Razzor is moaning on the mat. Then I slip away.

Over the next week, I dash out of the office whenever Shayla calls to tell me Jake has booked the practice ring for the evening. He never acknowledges my presence, and I never push. But I am always there. Every fight. Every night. I hammer my message home, just like Ray told me to do. I am in his corner. And I tell Shayla I will be there until the week before the big fight event, when the fighters cloister themselves to physically and mentally prepare for the fight.

When the house sale finally goes through, I donate my navy and gray furniture and furnishings to the community legal aid clinic, and Makayla, happy and relaxed after what she calls a "sexcation," takes me on a shopping spree in antique stores and country chic emporiums. Ray's couch remains the focal point of the reception room. Penny now recovered and determined to see Vetch pay for what he did to her, replaces her screensaver with a picture of Ray on the couch. Ray is not amused.

Alone at night, I flip through the pictures on my phone. Me and Jake renovating the house. At Redemption after his fight. A photo of us with Penny, Fuzzy, and Shayla at the Slugs concert. My heart squeezes in my chest, an ache I carry with me all day. And then I put the phone away and think about tomorrow and the hope it brings.

~~~

The day before the big fight event, I return to Farnsworth & Tillman, LLP.

Farnsworth has agreed to meet me after being hit with my one-two punch of a court order from his golfing buddy judge to deliver up his personnel and HR files, followed by a hint that I might have evidence of inappropriate advances toward other associates and a computer hack traceable to his firm. Mom offers to come with me or to hire someone to represent me. I tell her this is one fight I have to fight alone.

Mom says the sentiment is nice but the reality is that I'm a junior associate going up against a seasoned partner with a ruthless, cutthroat reputation. As a result, she spends two days coaching me, ensuring I am prepared for anything and everything Farnsworth could throw my way. By the time she's finished, I am more than ready to step into the ring.

Taking a deep breath, I pull open the immense glass door leading to the lobby. The firm is built around a central atrium, and above me, associates beaver away at their desks. The murmur of voices and the occasional bark of laughter echo through the vast space. I inhale the familiar scents of lemon polish, leather, and money as I walk toward the reception desk, my heels clacking on the marble tiles. How many times did I walk through this lobby on my way to my office? Why did I never notice the austerity, or the cold, corporate colors, the garish, gold F&T logo in metallic mosaic tile on the wall, or the grim faces around me?

As I walk toward the security desk, my hands tremble and sweat trickles down my back. My steps slow. Maybe Farnsworth has already found a way to refute the new evidence. Maybe he's waiting with a team of associates and boxes of documents and a smirk on his smarmy face.

Heart pounding, I grind to a halt. Maybe this is all part of the game.

Footsteps ring out behind me. A firm hand on my shoulder freezes me in place. Soft lips brush over my ear and an arm snakes around my waist holding me tight. "You'll do great, baby. I know you will."

I don't need to turn around. I know that voice. I hear it on every street corner and in every café. I hear it as I drift to sleep every night. I hear it in my dreams.

"Jake."

I close my eyes and lean my temple against his cheek, soaking in his warmth. Although I desperately want to turn around, I know I'll cry if I do, and I can't let Farnsworth see I am anything other than cool, calm, and collected.

"I'm fighting tomorrow." His breath is warm in my ear.

"I'll be there."

His hand finds mine and he slips something into my palm. And then he's gone.

For a long moment, I remain motionless, remembering the feel of his arm around me, his heat, the softness of his cheek, the steady beat of his heart.

Finally, I raise my hand. He's given me a picture. Me. In Redemption. My arms raised after my fifty push-up triumph. And on it, he has written, "In Your Corner."

—◊—

The meeting takes place in room thirteen. My lucky room.

Farnsworth postures and swaggers. He threatens to bring to light every sordid detail of my past, every sexual encounter I've ever had, every man I ever propositioned. I tell him I never had to proposition men. They came to me. Just like he did. But he was one of the few I turned down. His face turns an interesting shade of red, almost purple.

Undaunted, he stalks around the meeting room. He says he will ensure I am humiliated and embarrassed, my reputation in tatters, and my bank account empty when he's done with me. He says I'll have nothing left. Not even self-respect.

I tell him I will live on love, but of course he doesn't understand.

Then I check my watch. I tell him I have a full schedule this afternoon, which involves kicking Reid's ass in court again, and if he has no more stories to tell, perhaps we can get on with the settlement meeting.

He tells me Evil Reid is no longer with the firm. Given the complaint Mom filed with the California State Bar, I am not surprised.

My mouth waters when I shove a thick, blue—I told Penny it had to be blue—file folder across the table. "Take a look."

Farnsworth takes a look. He pales when he sees the evidence I have collected about his penchant for propositioning vulnerable associates and the evidence Ray has collected tracing the hack on my computer to his firm, and the police report matching the fingerprints of his PI, Eugene Clements, to the fingerprints the police took from the break-in.

He pales even further when I give him my settlement terms: the equivalent of five years' salary donated to the community legal aid clinic and the local battered women's shelter and a public apology.

Farnsworth offers more money instead of the public apology. He also offers to retire early. This is not a big sacrifice on his part, since my mom told me had been talking about it for the last year. In the end, I accept his offer on the condition that the money is used to set up a self-defense program for women at the firm. I tell him I know a good teacher with an expertise in kickboxing.

That night, Mom invites me home for a celebratory dinner. The lights are on when I arrive. My parents are both there. The rich, tangy scent of spaghetti sauce fills the air. These are not normal things in Amanda's world, but I don't complain.

Mom gives me an awkward hug, and I thank her for all her help. She tells me she's expecting me to call whenever I need her and she'll always be there for me. My father and I stare at each other. After a long, heavy silence, he says I have, in a way, actually upheld the family tradition and done one better. Albeit my firm isn't a big law firm, I made partner before I turned thirty-two. Not only that, it's a damn good firm. They aren't the exact words I wanted to hear, but they're good enough for me.

Chapter 24
BAM. BAM.

"I CAN'T BELIEVE I'M going to a real MMA fight."

An excited Penny bounces around the reception area as I rush to finalize the settlement agreement. Farnsworth is going out of the country tomorrow, and I need everything signed before he leaves. Ray stretches out on the old Victorian couch, folds up his newspaper, and sighs.

"You better keep your ass in the seat at the fight, or I'll tie you to the fucking bench. I heard about you at the Slugs concert. There'll be none of that on my watch." He taps his chest, then points at his eyes, then points at Penny. Maybe he *was* in the mafia.

Penny freezes mid-bounce and her eyes narrow. "If I want to dance around the cage, that's my business."

Ray swings his feet down and glares. "You just *try* to dance around the cage, Pen. I'll be all over your ass. We gotta find you a man who will look after you. A good man. Someone who'll treat you right."

"I had a man." She folds her arms and glares.

"You had a worm." He tosses the newspaper on the table, folded at the entertainment page. The headline catches my eye.

Slugs Front Man, Vetch Retch, Discharged from Hospital.

From a quick skim of the article, it appears Vetch was attacked in an alley outside a concert venue a few weeks ago. He suffered broken limbs, cracked ribs, a broken nose, and a concussion. He appears in the picture in a wheelchair, his arms and legs in casts, and his face a mass of bandages.

I look at Ray. Ray looks at me. I don't ask. He doesn't tell.

"I wasn't talking about Vetch," Penny snorts. "I had a life in

England before I came out here. A different life with a decent man. And I had to leave it all behind."

Penny has never talked about her past before, and I'm filled with curiosity. But before I can ask, she shakes an admonishing finger at Ray.

"You shouldn't be offering dating advice. You don't even have a girlfriend. In fact, in the time I've known you, except for Sandy, I don't think you've ever had a date."

Ray sips his coffee and his gaze flicks to me. "Private things should stay private. Always believed that. Always will. And I didn't have a date with Sandy. Not my type."

Curiosity piqued, Penny assails him with questions about what exactly he might be keeping private, why he didn't go out with Sandy, and what was his type, none of which he answers. And I know he never will.

"You coming?" He taps his watch and looks at me. "We're gonna be late. I thought you wanted to be there to watch your man fight."

"All signed and ready to go. Penny's going to take it down to the courier while I change. Shouldn't be more than ten minutes."

"Five," Penny says, picking up the envelope. "I'm actually going to run. No way am I going to be late."

Ray pushes himself off the couch. "I'll go with you and pick up a coupla coffees for the road."

After they've gone, I race into my office and slam the door. Moments later I've stripped off my suit and pulled on studded jeans and a T-shirt. Fight events are dress down, but I can't resist throwing on a pair of heels. Jake loves heels. Clackity clack. Clackity clack. I race to the washroom to put on my "Amanda" face. A slap of blush, a slip of lipstick, a stroke of mascara, and I'm ready to go. I pull out my ponytail and fluff my hair as anticipation ratchets through me. I'm going to see Jake.

My heels click down the hallway to the rhythm of the Slugs's latest single, "Danger Lies Ahead." Damn. Penny forgot to turn off her radio. I race back to reception at top speed. After only a few sessions of Get Fit or Die, my top speed is pretty damn fast, and I am at her desk in a heartbeat.

Wham. Someone shoves me against the wall from behind. My purse flies out of my hand and hits the floor with a soft thud.

"I've been waiting for you."

Who's been waiting for me? I don't recognize the voice and my inquiring mind wants to know. I look back over my shoulder. Oh. It's Evil Reid. Just hanging around my reception room as evil doers do. The skin on my neck prickles and I fight for calm.

"Reid. Hi. I'm in a hurry. I have to go. Something I can do for you?"

Reid spins me around to face him and his cruel smile cannot hide the darkness in his eyes.

"There's a lot you can do for me. You fucking owe me, Westwood. Farnsworth kicked me out of the firm. He said I didn't meet the moral standards for the partnership. Can you believe the irony? And not only did you humiliate me, you did this." He pulls a sheet of pink paper from his pocket and waves it in front of me.

Heart thumping, I try to focus on the blur of black letters. "What is it?"

"Your complaint to the State Bar. I'm going to lose my practice license. Because of you."

One less attorney in California. And an unstable one at that. Well, it's a start.

"I didn't report you to the Bar." I try and fail to keep my voice from wavering. "You decided to send a copy of that file to my parents. They reported you."

"I have no doubt you put them up to it."

Breathe. In. Out. Slow. Deep. Swallow the fear. Focus on the fight. "What do you want, Reid?" I try to keep the conversation going as I take stock of the room. Why don't we have emergency psychopath attack supplies alongside the fire extinguisher and flashlight? Maybe a knife or a bat or even a frying pan?

"You're gonna pay for ruining my life." He grabs my shoulders and shoves me against the wall.

"Get your hands off me, Reid. I'm warning you."

He snorts a laugh. "You're warning me? You think you're tough because you hang out at an MMA gym?" His eyes slither over my body as he twists his hand through my hair and grips the top of my head. "You're so tiny I could break you in two."

Not this time. No one is taking me down.

Holding my hair, I spin out of his hair-grab using a technique Makayla's stepdad taught me long ago. But Evil Reid is quick; he lunges for me, and in that split second, I smile. Poor Evil Reid is in for a whole world of pain.

Bam. Bam. I punch Evil Reid in the solar plexus just like Razzor taught me how to do. Then I follow it with an uppercut to the jaw. Evil Reid staggers back and he gasps for breath. This time I don't need to imagine I'm Shilla the Killa because Amanda Westwood has her own moves.

Taking advantage of Evil Reid's momentary weakness, I rush in with a Shilla-style head butt. When Evil Reid doubles over, I sweep his legs. Success! Evil Reid goes down.

Now what? Should I follow him down and lock him in submission? Hmmm. That would involve lying on top of him, and if I don't do it right he might get the wrong idea. Also, I haven't learned any submissions from a dominant position. How damn irritating is that?

My moment of hesitation is my undoing. Evil Reid jumps up with preternatural speed. He grabs me and shoves me into the corner. And suddenly I'm in Get Fit or Die, and Fuzzy is making us jog on the spot with our knees as high as they can go.

Someone's got you in the corner. What do you do, Westwood? Do you stand around with your mouth hanging open? No, you loser. Use your knees. Knees! Knees! Knees! Get those knees up or you'll have me all over your sorry ass.

I don't want Fuzzy all over my sorry ass. Nor do I want to face his wrath. I knee Reid in the sternum, and when he doubles over, I knee him in the chin. Then I hit him in the jaw with a left hook followed by a right cross, just like Jake did in the cage. Evil Reid stumbles backward, and I kick him between the legs.

"You want me to keep going?" I scream. "I survived Get Fit or Die. I can go all damn night."

But Evil Reid is down for the count. Winded, gasping for breath, he drops to his knees, and I kick him while he's down. Illegal move, I know. But who's around to see?

Clap. Clap. Clap.

"Sounds like that was some class you took," a bemused Ray says as he peels a sniveling Evil Reid off the floor. Penny watches in stunned silence, a tray of coffees in her hand.

"It was a nightmare."

"Might have to look into it." He shoves Reid against the wall and pulls a pair of handcuffs from his pocket.

Penny's eyes widen. "Um…those are handcuffs."

"Yup." Ray snaps the handcuffs around Evil Reid's wrists and then reads him his Miranda rights from a card in his pocket.

"You're reading him his rights," Penny astutely points out.

"Yup."

"I thought you were a private investigator."

"I wear many hats."

Still stunned, Penny says, "I've never seen you wear a hat."

"And you never will, sweetheart." He glances over at me and taps his watch. "Don't you have someplace to be?"

"Oh. My. God. I'm going to miss him."

I can't be late.

By the time we reach the Kezar Pavilion, the event has started. There are fifteen fights on the card, but lucky for me, Jake is near the end.

Team Redemption, easily identifiable by the huge banner strung over the seats and the sea of shaved heads, has blocked off a section near the ring. Blade Saw and Homicide Hank wave us over. Penny is beside herself with excitement as two lightweights battle it out in the huge cage at the center of the pavilion, brightly lit with a circle of floodlights.

"There must be a thousand people here," she gasps, looking over the sea of seats around us.

But I'm not interested in the cheering crowd, the excitement in the air, or the rattle of bodies against the cage.

"I need to see Renegade," I whisper to Blade Saw as we slide into our seats.

He shakes his head. "He's in the changing room and warm-up area. This promotion is following CAMO rules, so the top fighters have a shot at the Amateur State Championships. No one except licensed seconds, media, or officials are allowed out back. Better for the fighters that way because they need to focus."

My stomach clenches. "But how will he know I'm here?"

Homicide pats me on the back. "He'll walk through our section. Gives the fighters a boost to have their team cheering them on before they step into the cage. Just make sure you're standing where he can see you and make a lot of noise."

We sit through several fights before Ray makes an appearance. He edges in front of us to the seat Penny has saved for him. "Never been to an MMA event. Quite the atmosphere in here."

I introduce him to Blade Saw and Homicide and then to Razzor, Minotaur, and Master Mayhem sitting behind us. Then I point out a few of the other fighters I know. So many. They are the brothers I never had.

Ray leans over and squeezes my hand. "You okay? Bastard's been taken down to the police station. I gave them your details and said you'd give a statement after the event."

"I'm good. And now that I'm here and I didn't miss him, more than good."

I am treated to a rare Ray smile. "That's my girl."

Team Redemption surges to their feet as Shilla the Killa walks in with Sandy as her second. She is looking incredibly toned and fit, having shed a few pounds to make weight. She's wearing a sports bra and a pair of fight shorts with the "Team Redemption" logo stamped across her ass.

We stomp and cheer and clap as she climbs the steps into the cage. She is joined by a heavily muscled blond covered in tattoos.

"That's Sergeant." Blade Saw takes his seat beside me. "She's a former Marine. Four tours of duty in Afghanistan and the Middle East. She's won eight of her ten last fights in the Amateur Open and hoping to go pro after this fight."

"She looks…formidable."

Blade Saw nods. "Shilla's the only one who would take her on."

The whistle blows. Almost immediately, Shilla is on the attack. Using a move I haven't learned yet, she throws Sergeant to the ground and locks her arm around Sergeant's neck.

"Bulldog choke from side control." The Minotaur gives an appreciative nod. "Unique variation of that choke. Hard to break."

Sergeant tries to roll to escape the hold, but she can't break Shilla's grip. The clock ticks. The crowd cheers. Sergeant taps out. The referee lifts Shilla's arm and Team Redemption explodes around us. Even Ray is on his feet.

"Christ. That's some woman. Lookit her. Fucking amazing fighter. It was almost like she was dancing in the ring."

I sit through fight after fight, my heart drumming against my chest. Why do the fights take so long? Why are there so many? Who scheduled Jake near the end?

Rampage gets his turn against Corn Dog, a giant of a superheavyweight with a tattoo of a corn dog on his back. Rampage avoids two takedown attempts from Corn Dog, who throws kicks to Rampage's leg and abdomen. Rampage growls and drops Corn Dog to his knees with a solid right punch. Then he dives in with more punches. Corn Dog is unable to get up and turtles on the ground. Rampage is declared the winner at sixty-five seconds. I have never seen a bigger smile in my life.

Finally, Jake is on the card. I squeeze Penny's hand in nervous anticipation and edge along the row of seats so I can see.

The team cheers as he walks down the aisle, Fuzzy by his side. My God, he takes my breath away. With the weight he's lost to make his weight class, his muscles are sharper and more defined, rippling as he high-fives his friends. His fight shorts, emblazoned with the Team Redemption logo, cling to his tight ass, and his tattoos shimmer under the light.

But nothing draws my attention as much as his shaved head.

For a moment I lament the loss of his thick, wavy hair. But he looks like a serious fighter now, and without his hair, his jaw seems more chiseled, his eyes more piercing, and his lips more full. Sensuous. Breathtaking.

Emotion wells up in my chest and my throat tightens as he approaches my aisle. I've wanted this moment so badly, dreamed about it, longed for it…and I freeze.

And then he walks by.

And he's gone.

"RENEGADE!" Penny shoves me into the aisle and jumps on the chair just vacated by Hammer Fist. She jumps. She screams. She waves her hands in the air. She draws the attention of everyone nearby. Jake pauses. Turns. Then he sees me.

He sees me.

His eyes meet mine, dark and full of emotion. For a long moment, he holds my gaze. I try to tell him without words that I love him. I have loved him since the day we met. And I will always be in his corner.

A smile ghosts his lips and he nods.

He knows.

My heart fills and tears trickle down my cheeks as he climbs into the ring.

We're going to be okay.

"So that's The Man?"

Blade Saw rubs his finger over his bottom lip and checks out Jake's opponent, a bald, tattooed bruiser who keeps moving his head from side to side as if he's listening to his own personal hip-hop beat.

Homicide nods. "Vastly more experienced than Renegade. He's 9–3–1 and held the amateur light heavyweight title a few years ago. He was stripped of his title when they found out he'd been taking banned substances and was thrown off the circuit. He's only just come back, so they've been pairing him up with the newbies. He's never been through a fight without at least one foul. Still, it's a big step for Renegade. He's only 2–0 with two submission victories."

"Fucking stupid ring name." Blade Saw shakes his head. "The Man."

Round one starts with Jake stalking The Man from the center of the cage, cutting him off every time he tries to move away from the fence. Even I can see his strategy effectively nullifies the advantage The

Man would have from his longer reach. Jake closes in on his opponent with power shots, and The Man tries to tie him up in a clinch. But Jake easily shrugs him off and continues to hammer with powerful punches, eventually backing his opponent to the cage. Suddenly The Man rears back and smashes his head into Jake's forehead. Jake staggers back and drops to his knees. With a roar, Team Redemption surges to their feet shouting foul.

"No fucking way," yells Homicide. "Deliberate head butting."

The referee calls a break, and Fuzzy and the ring doctor race into the cage. Jake shakes his head and Fuzzy goes to speak to the referee. Jake is taking the maximum five minutes allowed to recover from a foul. My heart seizes in my chest. Now I know it's bad. No one is allowed near the cage, and I have to suffer through watching Fuzzy ice Jake's head while he argues with the ring doctor.

"If the ring doctor says he's not fit to fight, that's it." Blade Saw glares at The Man's corner. "The match will then be decided on points."

When the five minutes are over, Jake pushes himself to his feet and nods that he's ready to go on. The ring doctor gives the thumbs-up. The Man smirks when Jake staggers to the center of the ring and my lungs tighten. I pray Jake is still my renegade fighter, feigning injury, playing the game.

Although slightly unsteady on his feet, Jake dives in with a huge, overhand right followed by a left that misses The Man by at least six inches. The Man roars with laughter. I grab Blade Saw's hand and squeeze it so hard he gasps. "Don't worry," I whisper. "He's faking it. I've seen him do it before."

Blade Saw chuckles and extricates his hand from my vice-like grip. "Now I know you're really one of us."

Brimming with overconfidence, The Man goes all out with a big right hand. But Jake is ready. He slips inside The Man's guard and batters his opponent with a flurry of fierce, powerful blows that leave The Man groaning on the mat. Seconds later, The Man taps out.

The ever-bloodthirsty Penny is on her feet right away, punching her fist in the air and screaming. "Whooo. Renegade. Whooo."

I join her. But without the "whooo."

The wait outside the changing room is the longest of my life. What's he doing in there? Why has almost every other fighter managed to shower and change? It's not like he even has hair to wash. I tap my foot, drum my fingers on the wall, and pace up and down the corridor.

"Impatient, aren't you?" The surly bouncer chuckles.

"Very impatient. It's one of my defining characteristics. Total lack of patience, especially for men who take too long in the shower."

"Boyfriend, brother, or husband?"

I hesitate. I don't really know. Maybe he forgives me but just wants to be friends. Or less. Or more. Uncertainty worms its way into my heart.

Fuzzy appears in the doorway and motions me over. "The ring doctor wants him to go to the hospital to have his head checked out, but he refuses to go. Maybe you can convince him."

After a quick word with the bouncer, he leads me into the warm-up room, a large, windowless space covered with thick practice mats. Jake is sitting on a bench in the corner, leaning against the wall. He has showered and changed into jeans and a T-shirt, but he looks pale, haggard. His head is tilted back and his eyes are closed. The ring doctor looks up when I approach and shakes her head.

"If he doesn't go to the hospital, he'll need someone to stay with him for the next twenty-four hours in case of concussion."

"I'll stay with him."

Jake's eyes open, and he gives me a warm smile. "You sure, baby? I can be a difficult patient."

"I think I can handle you."

He raises one eyebrow and the look he gives me sends warm flutters through my belly. But before he can say something that would turn my cheeks into a raging inferno, the ring doctor pushes herself to her feet.

"I'll be back in a minute with the paperwork."

Fuzzy follows her out and I make a quick visual assessment of my Renegade, looking for injuries other than the obvious lump on his head. "Do you need anything? Ice, water…"

"You."

Delicious warmth spreads over my body, like I've just dived into a warm vat of chocolate. Naked.

"Here I am," I whisper.

Jake holds out his arms. "Here you are."

I fly across the room and throw myself against his chest. He squeezes me tight, burying his nose in my hair, and we hold each other for the longest time.

"I'm sorry." I murmur against his chest. "I was afraid if you saw that file you wouldn't want to be with me. And Reid…I wouldn't have…I was pushing him away…I didn't…"

"Shhhh." Jake presses a soft kiss to my hair. "I don't care about your past except that it made you who you are. And who you are is who I love. Everything. The good, the bad, the past, the present. I love you."

He loves me. Emotion overwhelms me. Weeks of hoping and dreaming, hours of self-chastisement and self-loathing, the stress and anxiety I've been carrying around…everything disappears in a rush, leaving a vacuum that can only be filled with tears.

"Not quite the response I had expected." He strokes his hand down my back. "I was hoping for a smile."

"Cry now. Smile later."

"I'm sorry it took me so long to get myself together." He sighs and brushes my hair behind my shoulder. "I had to seriously think about what made me happy. You, first of all. Any way I can get you. Whether you give yourself fully to me or not. My life is better with you in it."

"You have me," I whisper. "All of me."

He holds my face in his hands and catches me with his gaze, then kisses me softly, and smiles. "Yeah, baby, I think I do."

"What else makes you happy?"

Jake sighs and releases me. "Fighting. Teaching. Not the company. Not living in the past. And I was risking it all to make my Dad proud when I should have seen nothing I did would be enough. It was never enough when I was a kid and nothing has changed. But I convinced him of the benefits of selling the company and now my life is my own to live.

I watched you do that, baby. You found a way to practice law the way you wanted to practice. How could I do any less?"

"I'm happy for you." I press my cheek against his chest and listen to the steady drum of his heart.

"It all worked out for the best. My dad realized the money meant he had the freedom to do what he wanted. All his life he was tied to that company; even when I took it over, he wanted to stay involved. Now he has time to enjoy life. He and my mom booked a cruise; he took up golfing…not only that, the accountant who handled the books for the sale showed him it was Peter who had run the company down, and I had saved it."

I lean up and kiss his cheek. "For all it's worth, I'm proud of you."

He smiles. "So was he. I'd waited a lifetime to hear it from him, but coming from you, it means more than you can imagine."

Gently, I trace his smile with the pad of my thumb. With a low growl, he pulls me close and seals my lips with a kiss I feel clear to my toes. Want and need become one. I melt against him and he tightens his arm, deepening the kiss, burning me from the inside out.

"Jake…" I try to look over my shoulder at the door, worried we'll be interrupted by Fuzzy or the ring doctor, but Jake doesn't seem to care. His head dips down and he kisses the side of my face, his soft lips trailing down my cheek and chin to the pulse at the base of my neck.

"I can feel your heart here."

"I can feel it too. You set my heart free."

He pulls back and studies me, his eyes the deep azure blue of the warmest, deepest ocean.

"I love you. I should have told you a long time ago."

Chapter 25

YOU'RE MY EVERYTHING

I AM WARM. COZY. Safe. Drifting.

Freezing.

"What the…" I open my eyes to the sight of a naked and fully erect Jake kneeling between my legs with the bed covers in his hand.

"Time to play, baby."

"I was sleeping. And you should be too. The doctor was worried you might have a concussion."

He traces lazy circles along the insides of my thighs. "Too much sleeping. Not enough playing."

My core tightens as his thumbs glide closer and closer to my center. I'm already wet and it's been what? Thirty minutes? "How can you possibly get it up again? And I thought we ran out of condoms."

"Went to the store and bought some while you were asleep. Then I stroked your sweet pussy and listened to you moan." He slicks a finger along my folds and trails my wetness along my inner thigh. "You liked it."

My cheeks burn with the fire of one hundred suns. "I was asleep."

"And dreaming of me." He bends down and nibbles a trail from my belly button to my mound. I rub my hand over his head easing him down to where I want him to go.

"I miss your hair," I say softly. "It was handy for giving directions."

The look he gives me is carnal, intent. "Where do you want me to go, baby?"

Swallowing hard, I point to the dresser. "How about over there to get my purse and you can have your present."

Jake sits back on his heels. "You bought me a present?"

"Fetch."

His eyes narrow. Two seconds later, I am over his lap at the end of his bed, my ass in the air.

Smack. His hand lands on my cheek with a sharp crack.

I shriek and try to wiggle away as fire explodes across my backside, but Jake just tightens his grip and smacks again.

"Very disrespectful." *Smack.* "Just so you understand, in the time we've been apart, nothing has changed." *Smack. Smack.* "In the bedroom, I am in control." *Smack.*

Shrieking and writhing on his lap, I look back over my shoulder and scowl. "You can be in control without smacking my ass."

He drives two fingers deep inside me and curls them to stroke against my sensitive spot. "But then you wouldn't get this wet, baby. And I like you this wet. I want you this wet all the time."

"I do have a life beyond sexing it up with you." My betraying body heats and I grind against his fingers, desperate for more.

Jake laughs and smacks me again. "Not anymore. I'm gonna sex it up with you every chance I get. Now, go get my present."

He releases me and my burning ass and lies back on the bed, hands behind his head, legs spread, fully erect, and awaiting my pleasure. My very own pinup.

Gingerly, I walk across the floor and grab my purse from the dresser.

"Drop it." His bark of warning startles me and I drop the purse.

"What? What is it? Spider? Bee? Bomb?"

Jake licks his lips. "Bend down and pick it up. Nice and slow. Show me that beautiful pink ass."

"Seriously? You almost gave me a heart attack so you could watch me bend over."

"Seriously, baby. You have got the finest ass I've ever seen. And now that it's all pink and marked with my hand prints, it's a work of art."

With a snort, I bend over and pick up my purse. Fast. But I do give him a wiggle.

When I return to the bed, I fish around for the tiny package the courier delivered yesterday afternoon. With a flourish, I hand it to Jake.

He opens the little box and pulls out a small silver ring, open on one end, with two knobs on the edges. A smile curls his lips and he laughs. "This is a present for you."

"According to the woman at the body jewelry shop, it's a present for both of us." I brush my finger over the head of his cock and my cheeks heat. "Can I put it in?"

Jake shakes his head. "If I have to sit here while you touch my cock with those soft hands, it will never happen."

I touch him.

It doesn't happen.

At least, not that night.

Heaven.

This is heaven. I look around my office and smile. The workmen finally finished the renovations on the extra rooms last week. Good-bye paint cans, dust, and plastic. Hello country-chic decor, bright windows, polished chandeliers, and reclaimed antique furniture.

Yes, I have a country chic law firm, from the mint green pie cupboard holding my files, to the chipped oak desk. Pastel prints of small French towns decorate the walls, and my white credenza holds a brand-new microwave, courtesy of Jake, and several framed pictures. Me and Jake on a boat ride across the Bay, the wind whipping my hair into a frenzy. The two of us with Max and Makayla at the racetrack. Penny, Ray, and I after one of Fuzzy's classes. And even one with my parents and me on the official opening day of my new law firm, since I never really had one.

Claire, our new receptionist since Penny was promoted to PA, buzzes to let me know my new client has arrived for his five o'clock appointment and is waiting in the meeting room.

When I walk into the reception area, Ray looks over his newspaper and nods. After much hemming and hawing, he finally agreed to let me recover the Victorian couch but insisted on choosing the fabric. He looks very comfortable on the almost-identical beige print of leaves and flowers, and, for a moment, I am tempted to join him. My clients are used to him by now. They know not to sit in his seat or touch his coffee table.

"How was Get Fit or Die last night?"

Ray snorts a laugh. "Fuzz thought he could break me. End of the night, he was the one doing push-ups. Next week, I'm in that ring. Man joins an MMA gym to fight. Man like me, more. I'm not there to jump around, waving my hands in the air."

Penny joins us from her office. "If you wanted to get out of Get Fit or Die, you should have done what I did: rip the head off Grapple Man and toss it at Fuzzy's feet. Made him laugh so hard he was helpless to refuse my request to take Grunt 'n' Grapple. I was on that mat faster than you can say psychopath. Got a good beating for it from Shayla."

She holds up her makeup kit and gives me a wink. "Little touch-up before your meeting? Client is in his early to mid-thirties, well-dressed, hot, and has a housing issue."

"Hmmm. Sounds like someone I know with a newly fuzzy head, but his housing issue is that he wants us to live together since I spend all my time at his place anyway."

Claire and Penny share a glance. Then Penny whips open the makeup kit and places it on Claire's desk. "Just a tiny bit under the eyes. You're looking a little tired."

"That's because Jake and Max had it out in the practice ring yesterday and Jake won. He was…" I hesitate and my cheeks burn. "Very pleased."

Ray snorts a laugh. Penny gives me a touch-up. Claire fluffs my hair. Ray muses about why people make a big production out of simple things. I wonder what the hell is going on.

Finally, I grab a notepad and pen and walk down the corridor to the newly appointed meeting room. Along the way, I check out the two rooms that will become offices for the new associates I hired: Jill, to help with the paying clients, and a friend from the community legal aid clinic to manage the pro bono side of the firm. We are busy at Amanda Westwood, LLP. And I hope it stays that way.

The door to the meeting room, a normal-height slab of beige wood, stands ajar. Taking a moment to compose myself, I step into the room, ready to meet my newest client.

Light floods across the thick, cream carpet through floor-to-ceiling windows. Dust motes dance in the sunbeams. A small, polished oak table with four comfy, cream leather chairs takes up the center space. I inhale the scents of leather and furniture polish and a whiff of something else, sharp and clean like an ocean breeze.

Familiar.

Across the room, the client is pouring himself a glass of water from the tray on the credenza. From the back, he takes my breath away. A tight, white T-shirt stretches across his broad shoulders and follows the frame of his body down to a narrow waist and a deliciously sexy pair of worn, ripped jeans that hug his perfect, tight ass. No more suits and ties for my carpenter and licensed amateur fighter who has dreams of going pro. He is back where he wants to be, doing what he loves to do, and looking damn fine as he does it.

I close the door. As the latch clicks, he turns to face me.

My heart squeezes as it always does when I see him. I place my legal pad on the table and close the distance between us. "What a nice surprise," I whisper, brushing my lips over his. "You look beyond hot in those jeans. Did you come to sex me up?"

"Mmmm." He nibbles my ear. "I need an attorney."

"Mmmm. You have one." I run my tongue over the seam of his lips until he opens for me, and then I slip inside to taste him. Two seconds later, he hauls me against his body, hand fisting my hair, as he devours my mouth.

"Down, girl," he mumbles against my lips, although now he's the one in charge. "Seriously, I need an attorney."

"Why didn't you just talk to me about it last night?" I stroke my hand over the Team Redemption logo on his shirt, and then lower, toward his belt.

Jake grasps my hand and pulls it away. "This is why. You're too distracting."

"Um…who came home all pumped from his big fight, stripped off my clothes, and carried me into the shower with him?"

"Only after you decided to check if I was wearing your present." He backs away and perches on the edge of the table.

With a soft harrumph of disappointment, I fold my arms. "What's the problem?"

He pulls a file folder from his briefcase and holds it out to me. "I've got this property, a heritage property. It's empty and I need someone to live in it, or the neighbors might deem it abandoned and call for it to be torn down."

My head falls back and I groan. "Not another one. You and your vacant heritage homes. Well, I've helped you out once already at an incredible sacrifice to myself. Really, I should be working from a sterile, characterless prefab office overlooking the Bay."

Jake's eyes sparkle and he motions to the folder. "Just check it out."

"Fine." I open the file. It contains a key and a bundle of real estate documents.

I give Jake a questioning look and he taps the top paper. "Read."

So I read. And a sob wells up in my throat.

"This company...?" I tap the page.

"Belongs to me."

"You bought my grandmother's house?" My words are barely a whisper.

"Yeah, baby, I did."

I grab a tissue and dab at my eyes. "But we weren't even together when the sale went through."

"You're mine, baby. Always were. I needed some time to clear my head, but I never stopped loving you."

"I can't tell you—"

He cuts me off and pulls a shopping bag off the chair. "Bought you another present."

"I don't need another present. This is the best present I ever got."

"This one's better." He shoves the plastic bag toward me.

Smiling through my tears, I reach inside and pull out a pair of fight gloves. My smile becomes a grin. "Does this mean I passed Pulverize or Perish?"

"Try them on," he urges. "The fit is critical. Once you find the perfect fit, you'll never want anything else."

I slide my hand into the glove and my finger hits cold metal. "There's something inside this one."

"Pull it out."

So I do.

A diamond ring glitters in my palm. Eyes wide, I meet Jake's warm gaze.

"You can't live in that big house alone," he says softly. Taking the ring from my hand, he slips it over my finger. "Perfect fit."

"Yes, you are."

He kisses me softly, sweetly, tenderly. And then he eases me back on the boardroom table. "I've never done it in a boardroom."

"Me neither."

"So I'm your first?"

"You're my first, my last, my everything."

ACKNOWLEDGMENTS

Many thanks to my editor, Cat Clyne, for loving Redemption and giving it sparkle, and to my agent, Laura Bradford, for her infinite patience and wisdom. To CaRWA for their continual support and friendship, and to Bev Katz Rosenbaum, whose wicked pen helped mend my wicked ways. And always thanks to my family for their endless patience and growing tolerance of burned dinners.